Echoes
from the
Dead

Echoes *from the* Dead

JOHAN THEORIN

Translated by
Marlaine Delargy

DELTA TRADE PAPERBACKS

ECHOES FROM THE DEAD
A Delta Trade Paperback / December 2008

Published by Bantam Dell
A Division of Random House, Inc.
New York, New York

Book design by Catherine Leonardo

Delta is a registered trademark of Random House, Inc.,
and the colophon is a trademark of Random House, Inc.

Library of Congress Cataloging-in-Publication Data

Theorin, Johan, 1963–
[Skumtimmen. English]
Echoes from the dead / Johan Theorin.
    p.   cm.
ISBN 978-0-385-34221-6
1. Öland (Sweden)–Fiction. I. Title.
PT9877.3.H46S5813 2008
839.73'8–dc22
2008006631

Printed in the United States of America
Published simultaneously in Canada

www.bantamdell.com

10 9 8 7 6 5 4 3 2 1
BVG

To the Gerlofsson family, Öland

ÖLAND, SEPTEMBER 1972

The wall was built of big, rounded stones covered in grayish white lichen, and it was the same height as the boy. He could only see over it if he stood on tiptoe in his sandals. Everything was gray and misty on the other side. The boy could have been standing at the end of the world, but he knew it was just the opposite—the world began on the other side of the wall. The big wide world, the world outside his grandparents' garden. The thought of exploring the world on the other side of the wall had tempted the boy all summer long.

Twice he tried to climb over the wall. Both times he lost his grip on the rough stones and fell backwards, into the damp grass.

The boy didn't give up, and the third time he succeeded.

He took a deep breath and heaved himself up, held on tight to the cold stones, and managed to get on top of the wall.

It was a victory for him—he was almost six years old, and for the first time in his life he was on his way over a wall. He sat there on the top for a little while, like a king on his throne.

The world on the other side of the wall was huge, with no boundaries, but it was also gray and blurred. The fog that had drifted in over the island this afternoon prevented the boy from seeing much of what lay outside the garden, but at the bottom of the wall he could see the yellow-brown grass of a small meadow. Further away he could just make out low, gnarled juniper bushes and moss-covered stones, sticking up out of the earth. The ground was just as flat as in the garden behind him, but everything looked much wilder on the other side; strange, enticing.

The boy put his right foot on a big stone that was half buried in the ground, and climbed down into the meadow on the other side of the wall. He was outside the garden all on his own for the first time ever, and nobody knew where he was. His mother had gone off somewhere today, left the island. His grandfather had gone down to the shore a little while ago, and when the boy put on his sandals and crept out of the house, his grandmother had been fast asleep.

He could do whatever he wanted. He was having an adventure.

He let go of the stones in the wall and took a step out into the wild grass. It was sparse, easy to get through. He took a few more steps, and the world in front of him slowly became a little clearer. He could see the juniper bushes taking shape beyond the grass, and walked toward them.

The ground was soft and any sound was muted; his footsteps were nothing more than a faint rustling in the grass. Even when he tried jumping with both feet together, or stamping his feet really hard, all that could be heard was a slight thud, and when he lifted his feet the grass sprang up and all trace of his footsteps quickly disappeared.

He covered several yards like this: *Hop, thud. Hop, thud.*

When the boy left the meadow and reached the tall juniper bushes, he stopped jumping with both feet together. He breathed out, inhaled the cool air, and looked around.

While he had been hopping across the grass, the fog that had been drifting ahead of him had crept silently around, and was now behind him. The stone wall on the other side of the meadow had become indistinct, and the dark brown cottage had completely disappeared.

For a moment the boy considered turning around, walking back across the meadow, and climbing over the wall again. He had no watch and precise times meant nothing to him, but the sky above his head was dark gray now, and the air around him had grown much colder. He knew the day was drawing to a close, and the night would soon come.

He'd just go a little bit further over the soft ground. After all, he knew where he was; the cottage where his grandmother lay sleeping was behind him, even if he couldn't see it anymore. He kept walking toward the hazy wall of fog which could be seen but not touched, and which slid just a little bit further away from him all the time, in a magical way, as if it were playing with him.

The boy stopped. He was holding his breath.

Everything was silent and nothing was moving, but suddenly the boy had the feeling that he wasn't alone.

Had he heard a noise in the fog?

He turned around. Now he could no longer see the wall or the meadow; he could see only grass and juniper bushes behind him. The bushes were all around him, motionless, and he knew they weren't alive—not alive in the way that he was—but he still couldn't help thinking about how big they were. They were black, silent figures surrounding him, perhaps moving closer to him when he wasn't looking.

He turned again, and saw more juniper bushes. Juniper bushes and fog.

He no longer knew in which direction the cottage lay, but fear and loneliness made him keep moving forward. He clenched his fists and ran across the grass; he wanted to find the stone wall and the garden behind it, but all he could see was grass and bushes. In the end he couldn't even see that much; the world was blurred by his tears.

The boy stopped, took a deep breath, and the tears stopped flowing. He could see more juniper bushes in the fog, but one of them had two thick trunks—and suddenly the boy realized it was moving.

It was a person.

A man.

The man came forward out of the gray fog and stopped just a few short steps away. He was tall and broad-shouldered; he was dressed in dark clothes, and he had seen the boy. He stood there in the grass, heavy boots on his feet, looking down at the boy. His black cap was pulled down over his forehead and he looked old, but not as old as the boy's grandfather.

The boy stood still. He didn't know the man, and you had

to be careful of strangers, his mummy had said. But at least he wasn't alone in the fog with the juniper bushes anymore. He could always turn around and run if the man wasn't nice.

"Hello there," said the man in a deep voice. He was breathing heavily, as if he'd just walked a long way in the fog, or as if he'd been running fast.

The boy didn't reply.

The man turned his head quickly and looked around. Then he looked at the boy again, without smiling, and asked quietly:

"Are you on your own?"

The boy nodded silently.

"Are you lost?"

"I think so," said the boy.

"It's all right . . . I can find my way anywhere out here on the alvar." The man took a step closer. "What's your name?"

"Jens," said the boy.

"Jens what?"

"Jens Davidsson."

"Good," said the man. He hesitated, then added, "My name's Nils."

"Nils what?" asked Jens.

It was a bit like a game. The man gave a short laugh.

"My name is Nils Kant," he said, taking another step forward.

Jens stood still, but he'd stopped looking around. There was nothing but grass and stones and bushes in the fog. And this strange man, Nils Kant, who had begun to smile at him as if they were already friends.

The fog closed in around them, not a sound was to be heard. Not even birdsong.

"It's all right," said Nils Kant, stretching out his hand.

They were standing quite close to each other by now.

Jens thought that Nils Kant had the biggest hands he'd ever seen, and he realized it was too late to run away.

I

When her father, Gerlof, rang one Monday evening in October, for the first time in almost a year, he made Julia think of bones, washed up onto a stony shore.

Bones, white as mother-of-pearl, polished by the waves, almost luminous among the gray pebbles at the water's edge.

Fragments of bone.

Julia didn't know if they were actually there on the shore, but she had waited to see them for over twenty years.

Earlier that same day, Julia had had a long conversation with the social security office, and it had gone just as badly as everything else this autumn, this year.

As usual she had put off getting in touch with them for as long as possible in order to avoid hearing their sighs, and when she had finally called she was answered by a robotic machine asking for her personal ID number. When she had keyed in all the numbers, she was put through to the next step in the telephone network labyrinth, which was exactly the same as being put through to total emptiness. She had to stand there in the kitchen, looking out of the window and listening to a faint noise on the other end of the line, an almost inaudible rushing like the sound of distant running water.

If Julia held her breath and pressed the receiver against her ear, she could sometimes hear spirit voices echoing in the distance. Sometimes they sounded muted, whispering; sometimes they were shrill and despairing. She was trapped in the ghostly world of the telephone lines, trapped among those pleading voices she sometimes heard from the kitchen fan when she was smoking. They echoed and mumbled through the building's ventilation system—she could hardly ever make out a single word, but she would still listen with great concentration. Just once she'd heard a woman's voice say with absolute clarity, *It really is time now.*

She stood there by the kitchen window, listening to the rushing noise and looking out onto the street. It was cold and windy outside. Autumn-yellow birch leaves tore themselves away from the rain-soaked surface of the road and tried to escape from the wind. Along the sidewalk's edge lay a dark gray sludge of leaves, crushed to a pulp by car tires, which would never leave the ground again.

She wondered if anybody she knew would pass by out there. Jens might come strolling around the corner at the end of the terrace, wearing a suit and tie like a real attorney, carrying his briefcase, his hair newly cut. Striding out, his gaze confident. He would see her at the window, stop in surprise on the sidewalk, then raise his arm, waving and smiling at her . . .

The rushing noise suddenly disappeared, and a stressed-out voice filled her ear:

"Social security. Inga."

This wasn't the new person who was supposed to be dealing with Julia's case; her name was Magdalena. Or was it Madeleine? They'd never met.

She took a deep breath.

"My name is Julia Davidsson, and I wanted to ask if you could—"

"What's your personal ID number?"

"It's . . . I've already entered the number on the telephone keypad."

"It hasn't come up on my screen. Can you give me the number again?"

Julia repeated the number, and there was silence at the other end of the line. She could hardly even hear the rushing noise anymore. Had they cut her off on purpose?

"Julia Davidsson?" said the voice, as if she hadn't heard Julia introduce herself. "How can I help?"

"I wanted to extend it."

"Extend what?"

"My sick leave."

"Where do you work?"

"At the hospital, Östersjukhuset, the orthopedic department," said Julia. "I'm a nurse."

Was she still a nurse? She'd had so much time off in recent years that she probably wasn't even missed in orthopedics anymore. And she certainly didn't miss the patients, constantly moaning about their ridiculous little problems when they didn't have a clue about real unhappiness.

"Have you got a note from your doctor?" asked the voice.

"Yes."

"Have you seen your doctor today?"

"No, last Wednesday. My psychiatrist."

"So why didn't you call earlier?"

"Well, I haven't been feeling very well since then . . ." said Julia, thinking, *Nor before then, either.* A constant ache of longing in her breast.

"You should have phoned us the same day . . ."

Julia heard a distinct breath, perhaps even a sigh.

"Okay, this is what I'm going to have to do," said the voice. "I'm going to have to go into the computer and make an exception for you. Just this time."

"That's very kind of you," said Julia.

"One moment . . ."

Julia stayed where she was by the window, looking out onto the street. Nothing was moving.

But then someone came walking along the sidewalk from the busier road that cut across; it was a man. Julia could feel ice-cold fingers clutching at her stomach, before she realized that this man was too old, he was bald and in his fifties and dressed in paint-spattered dungarees.

"Hello?"

She saw the man stop at a building on the opposite side of the street, key in a security code, and open the door. He went in.

Not Jens. Just an ordinary, middle-aged man.

"Hello? Julia?"

It was the voice again.

"Yes? I'm still here."

"Right, I've made a note on the computer to say that your doctor's note is on the way to us."

"Good. I . . ." Julia fell silent.

She looked out onto the street again.

"Was there anything else?"

"I think . . ." Julia gripped the receiver. "I think it's going to be cold tomorrow."

"Right," said the voice, as if everything were perfectly normal. "Have you changed your account details, or are they the same as before?"

Julia didn't reply. She was trying to find something ordinary and normal to say.

"I talk to my son sometimes," she said in the end.

There was a brief silence, then the voice could be heard again:

"As I said, I've made a note . . ."

Julia hung up quickly.

She remained standing in the kitchen, staring out of the window and thinking that the leaves out on the street were forming a pattern, a message she couldn't understand however long she gazed at it, and she longed desperately for Jens to come home from school.

No, it would have to be from work. Jens should have left school many years ago.

What did you become in the end, Jens? A firefighter? An attorney? A teacher?

Later that day she was sitting on her bed in front of the television in the narrow living room of her one-room apartment, watching an educational program about adders; then she changed channels and watched a cooking program where a man and a woman were frying meat. When that finished, she went back into the kitchen to see if the wineglasses in the cupboards needed polishing. Oh yes, if you held them up to the light, you could see tiny white particles of dust on the surface, so she took the glasses out one by one and polished them. Julia had twenty-four wineglasses, and used them all in rotation. She drank two glasses of red wine each evening, sometimes three.

That evening, when she was lying on her bed beside the TV, wearing the only clean blouse left in her closet, the telephone in the kitchen began to ring.

Julia blinked when it first rang, but didn't move. No, she wasn't going to obey it. She wasn't obliged to answer.

The telephone rang again. She decided she wasn't at home, she was out doing something important.

She could see out of the window without raising her head, even if all she could see were the rooftops along the street, the unlit streetlamps, and the tops of the trees stretching above them. The sun had gone down beyond the city, and the sky was slowly growing darker.

The telephone rang for the third time.

It was dusk. The twilight hour.

The telephone rang for the fourth time.

Julia didn't get up to answer it.

It rang one last time, then there was silence. Outside, the streetlamps were starting to flicker, beginning to spread their glow over the tarmac.

It had been quite a good day.

No. There weren't any good days, actually. But some days passed more quickly than others.

Julia was always alone.

Another child might have helped. Michael had wanted them to try for a brother or sister for Jens, but Julia had said no. She had never felt sure enough, and in the end Michael had stopped asking.

Often when Julia didn't answer the telephone, she got a recorded message as a reward, and when it had stopped ringing this evening, she got up from the bed and picked up the receiver, but all she could hear was the rushing noise.

She put the phone down and opened the cupboard above the refrigerator. The bottle of the day was standing there, and as usual the bottle of the day was a bottle of red wine.

To be perfectly accurate, it was the second bottle of red wine of the day, because at lunchtime she'd finished off a bottle she'd started the previous evening.

The cork came out with a soft popping sound as she opened the wine. She poured a glass and knocked it back quickly. She poured a fresh glass.

The warmth of the wine spread through her body, and now she could turn and look out through the window. It had grown dark out there, the streetlamps illuminating only a few round patches of tarmac. Nothing was moving in the glow of the lamps. But what was hiding in the shadows? It was impossible to see.

Julia turned away from the window and emptied her second glass. She was calmer now. She had been feeling tense since the conversation with the benefits office, but now she was calm. She deserved a third glass of wine, but she could drink that more slowly, in front of the TV. She might put on some music soon, Satie perhaps, take a pill, and get to sleep before midnight.

Later the telephone rang again.

On the third ring she sat up in bed, her head bowed. On the fifth she got up, and by the seventh she was finally standing in the kitchen.

Before the telephone rang for the ninth time, she picked up the receiver. She whispered:

"Julia Davidsson."

The reply was not a rushing noise, but a quiet, clear voice: "Julia?"

And she knew who it was.

"Gerlof?" she said quietly.

She no longer called him Dad.

"Yes . . . it's me."

There was silence once more, and she had to press the receiver closer to her ear to hear.

"I think . . . I know a bit more about how it happened."

"What?" Julia stared at the wall. "How what happened?"

"Well, how it all . . . with Jens."

Julia swallowed.

"Is he dead?" she asked.

It was like walking around with a numbered ticket in your

hand. One day your number was called, and then you were allowed to go up and collect the information. And Julia thought of white fragments of bone, washed up on the shore down in Stenvik, despite the fact that Jens had been afraid of the water.

"Julia, he must be–"

"But have they found him?" she interrupted him.

"No, but . . ."

She blinked. "Then why are you calling?"

"Nobody's found him. But I've–"

"In that case, don't call me!" she screamed, and slammed the phone down.

She closed her eyes and stayed where she was, beside the telephone.

A numbered ticket, a place in the queue. But this wasn't the right day, Julia didn't want this to be the day when Jens was found.

She sat down at the table, turning her gaze to the darkness outside the window, thinking nothing, then looked at the telephone again. She got up, walked over to it, and waited, but it remained silent.

I'm doing this for you, Jens.

Julia picked up the receiver, looked at the scrap of paper which had been stuck to the white kitchen tile above the bread bin for several years, and dialed the number.

Her father answered after the first ring.

"Gerlof Davidsson."

"It's me," she said.

"Julia. Yes."

Silence. Julia gathered her courage.

"I shouldn't have slammed the phone down."

"Oh, it's . . ."

"It doesn't help."

"No, well," said her father. "It's just one of those things."

"What's the weather like on Öland?"

"Cold and gray," said Gerlof. "I haven't been out today."

There was silence once more and Julia took a deep breath.

"Why did you call?" she said. "Something must have happened."

He hesitated before replying.

"Yes . . . a few things have happened here," he said, then added, "But I don't know anything. No more than before."

No more than I do, thought Julia. *I'm sorry, Jens.*

"I thought there was something new."

"But I've been doing some thinking," said Gerlof. "And I think there are things that can be done."

"Done? What for?"

"So that we can move on," said Gerlof, then quickly went on: "Can you come over here?"

"When?"

"Soon. I think it would be a good idea."

"I can't just take off," she said. But it wasn't that impossible–she was signed off work long-term. She went on: "You have to tell me . . . tell me what it's about. Can't you tell me that?"

Her father was silent.

"Do you remember what he was wearing that day?" he asked eventually.

That day.

"Yes." She'd helped Jens to get dressed herself that morning, and afterward she'd realized he was dressed for summer, despite the fact that it was autumn. "He was wearing yellow shorts and a red cotton shirt," she said. "With the Phantom on it. It had been his cousin's, it was one of those transfers you could do yourself, with the iron, made of thin plastic . . ."

"Do you remember what kind of shoes he had on?" asked Gerlof.

"Sandals," said Julia. "Brown leather sandals with black rubber soles. One of the straps across the toe of the right one had come loose, and several straps on the left one were about to come loose too . . . They always did that at the end of the summer, but I'd stitched it back on . . ."

"With white thread?"

"Yes," said Julia quickly. Then she thought about it. "Yes, I think it was white. Why?"

There was silence for a few seconds. Then Gerlof replied:

"An old sandal is lying here on my desk. It's been mended with white thread. It looks as if it would fit a five-year-old . . . I'm sitting here looking at it now."

Julia swayed and leaned against the countertop.

Gerlof said something else, but she broke the connection and there was silence once again.

The numbered ticket—this was the number she had been given, and soon her name would be called.

She was calm now. After ten minutes she lifted her hand from the receiver rest and keyed in Gerlof's number. Her father answered after the first ring, as if he'd been waiting for her.

"Where did you find it?" she asked. "Where? Gerlof?"

"It's complicated," said Gerlof. "You know how I . . . you know it's not so easy for me to get about, Julia. It's just getting more and more difficult. And that's why I'd really like you to come here."

"I don't know . . ." Julia closed her eyes, hearing only the rushing noise on the telephone. "I don't know if I can." She could see herself on the shore, see herself walking around among the pebbles, carefully collecting all the tiny parts of the skeleton she could find, pressing them close to her breast. "Maybe."

"What do you remember?" asked Gerlof.

"What do you mean?"

"About that day? Do you remember anything in particular?" he asked. "I'd really like you to think about it."

"I remember that Jens disappeared . . . He . . ."

"I'm not thinking of Jens at the moment," said Gerlof. "What else do you remember?"

"What do you mean? I don't understand . . ."

"Do you remember the fog lying over Stenvik?"

Julia didn't speak.

"Yes," she said softly. "The fog . . ."

"Think about it," said Gerlof. "Try to remember the fog."

The fog . . . The fog was a part of every memory of Öland.

Julia remembered the fog. Thick fog in northern Öland wasn't usual, but sometimes in the autumn it drifted in from the sound. Cold and damp.

But what had happened in the fog that day?

What happened, Jens?

The man who is to spread so much sorrow and fear throughout Öland later in life is a ten-year-old boy in the middle of the 1930s. He owns a stony shore and a large expanse of water.

The boy is called Nils Kant; he is sunburned and is dressed in shorts in the summer heat, and he is sitting on a big round stone in the sunshine, down below the houses and the boathouses in Stenvik. He is thinking:

All this is mine.

And it's true, because Nils's family owns the shore. They own large tracts of land in northern Öland; the Kant family has owned this land for centuries, and ever since his father died three years ago, Nils has felt that it is his responsibility to take care of it. Nils doesn't miss his father, he remembers him only as a tall, silent, strict man who could be violent sometimes, and Nils thinks it's a good thing that only his mother, Vera, is waiting for him in the wooden house above the shore.

He doesn't need anyone else. He doesn't need friends; he knows that there are children of all ages living in the villages along the coast, and older boys where he lives who are already working in the quarry—but this particular stretch of shore belongs only to him. The millers in the mill up above and the fishermen who use the boathouses up on the ridge are no threat.

Nils gets ready to jump down from the stone; he's going to have another swim, one last swim before he goes home.

"Nils!" shouts a high, boyish voice.

Nils doesn't turn his head, but he can hear the gravel and the pebbles on the slope up above the shore loosening and trickling down, then rapid footsteps approaching.

"Nils! I got toffees from Mum too! Lots of tòffees!"

It's his brother. Axel, three years younger than Nils and full of life. He's carrying a knotted gray cloth in his hand.

"Look!"

Axel hurries over and stands beside the big stone, looking excitedly up at Nils, and he undoes the bundle and spreads the contents out on the piece of cloth.

There's a little pocketknife in there and toffees, dark, shiny butter toffees.

Nils counts eight toffees. He only got five from his mother before he came out this morning, but he's eaten them all by now, and his heart races in a sudden spurt of rage.

Axel picks up one of his toffees, looks at it, shoves it in his mouth, and gazes out over the sparkling water. He chews slowly and with satisfaction, as if not only the toffees belong to him but also the shore and the water and the sky up above them.

Nils looks away.

"I'm going for a swim," he says, facing the water. He jumps down and pulls off his shorts and places them on the stone.

He turns his back on Axel and begins to walk out into the waves, balancing his feet on the stones, shiny with algae. Little tendrils of brown seaweed get stuck between his toes.

The water has been warmed by the sun, and foams out to the sides as Nils throws himself in a dozen or so steps from land. This summer he has learned to swim underwater. He takes a deep breath, dives beneath the surface, wriggles his way down toward the stony seabed, turns, and comes hurtling up into the sunshine again.

Axel is standing on the shoreline.

Nils glides around in the water, splashing it all around him, turning somersaults, the bubbles sparkling around his head. He swims a few yards further out, so far that he can no longer touch the bottom with his feet.

Out here there's a big boulder, a block of stone lying just beneath the surface like a slumbering sea monster. Nils clambers up onto its back, stands with his feet just below the surface of the water, then dives in. He can't touch the bottom here. He floats, treading water, and sees Axel still standing by the water's edge.

"Can't you swim yet?" he yells.

He knows Axel can't.

Axel doesn't reply, but he drops his eyes, his expression darkening with both shame and rage beneath his bangs. He tugs off his shorts and sets them on the stone beside the toffees.

Nils swims calmly around the boulder, first on his stomach, then on his back, just to show how easy it is when you can do it. A kick with his legs, and he's back on top of the boulder again.

"I'll help you!" he calls to Axel, and for a moment he considers actually doing it, being a big brother and teaching Axel to swim today. But it would take too long.

He just waves.

"Come on!"

Axel takes a wobbly step into the water, feeling his way across the pebbles with his feet, his arms waving about, as if he were balancing on the edge of an abyss. Nils watches his little brother's unsteady progress from the shore in silence.

After four paces Axel is standing there with the water up above his thighs, looking at Nils, his face rigid.

"Are you brave enough?"

A joke, he's just having a little joke with his brother.

Axel shakes his head. Nils quickly dives off the boulder and swims toward the shore.

"It's quite safe," he calls. "You can touch the bottom almost all the way out."

Axel reaches for him, leaning forward. Nils moves backwards, and his little brother takes an involuntary step forward.

"Good," says Nils. The water is up to their waists now. "One more step."

Axel does as he says, takes one more step, then looks up at Nils with a nervous smile. Nils smiles back and nods, and Axel takes another step.

Nils leans over, falling slowly backwards with outstretched arms, just to show how soft the water is.

"Everybody can swim, Axel," he says. "I taught myself."

He kicks his legs and swims slowly out toward the boulder. Axel follows him, keeping his feet on the bottom. The water is up to his chest.

Nils jumps up onto the boulder again.

"Three more steps!" he says.

Although that isn't quite true, it's more like seven or eight. But Axel takes one step, two steps, three steps, has to stretch his neck upward to keep his mouth above the surface, and there are still three yards to go before he reaches the boulder.

"You have to breathe," says Nils.

Axel takes a short, panting breath. Nils sits down on the boulder and holds his hands out calmly to Axel.

And his little brother throws himself forward. But it's as if he quickly regrets it, because he takes a big breath and his mouth and throat are filled with cold water, he's flailing around with his arms and staring at Nils. The boulder is just out of reach.

Nils watches Axel struggling in the water for a second or two, then quickly leans over and pulls his brother up onto the safety of the boulder.

Axel holds on tight, coughing and taking short, jerky breaths. Nils gets to his feet beside him and says what has been in his mind the whole time:

"The shore is mine."

Then he throws himself off the boulder, diving straight as an arrow, and comes up several yards away, swimming with long, sure strokes until his hands touch the pebbles by the shore and his joke is complete. Now he can enjoy it. He shakes his head to make his ears pop and goes over to the stone where Axel unwrapped his bundle.

The little shorts Axel took off are there too. Nils picks them up, imagines he can see a flea crawling along a seam, and throws them away on the shore.

Then he bends over the bundle. The butter toffees are lying there in a pile, shining in the sun, and Nils picks one up and places it slowly in his mouth.

He hears an infuriated roar across the water, from the boulder, but takes no notice. He chews carefully, swallows, picks up another toffee.

The sound of splashing reaches him from out there. Nils looks up; his little brother has finally thrown himself off the boulder and into the water.

Nils is already beginning to dry off in the sun, and overcomes his first impulse, which is to go out to Axel. He picks up a third toffee from the cloth on the stone instead.

The splashing continues, and Nils watches. Axel can't touch the bottom with his feet, of course, and he's desperately trying to get back onto the boulder. But his hands keep slipping off.

Nils chews on the toffee. You have to get some speed up to get onto the boulder.

Axel has no speed, and turns to make his way back to the shore. He's flapping his arms wildly, the water foaming all around him, but he isn't moving forward. He's looking at Nils with wide, terrified eyes.

Nils looks back at him, swallows the toffee, and picks up another one.

The splashing quickly grows fainter. His brother yells something, but Nils can't hear what it is. Then the waves close over Axel's head.

Now Nils takes a step toward the water.

Axel's head pops up, but not as far out of the water as before. All Nils can actually see is wet hair. Then he sinks beneath the surface again. Air bubbles come up, but a little wave sweeps them away.

Nils is in a hurry now, he jumps into the water. His legs kick up foam and he's fighting with his arms, his eyes fixed on the boulder. But there's no sign of Axel.

Nils makes his way quickly to the boulder, and when he's almost there he dives, but he's not very good at keeping his eyes open underwater. He closes his eyes, feeling his way in the cold darkness, touches nothing with his hands, and comes up into the sunlight again. He grabs the boulder with his hands, coughs, and pulls himself up.

Nothing but water all around him, wherever he looks. The sunlight sparkling on the waves hides everything that exists beneath the surface.

Axel is gone.

Nils waits and waits in the wind, but nothing happens, and in the end, when he starts to feel cold, he dives in and swims slowly back to the shore. There's nothing else he can do. He gets out of the water, breathes out, and leans on the big stone.

Nils stands there in the sun for a long time. He's waiting for the sound of splashing, a familiar shout from Axel, but he hears nothing.

Everything is quiet.

There are four toffees left on Axel's cloth, and Nils looks at them.

He thinks about the questions that will be waiting for him, from his mother and others, and thinks about what he's going to say. Then he thinks about when his father died and how gloomy everything had been during the long drawn-out funeral up in Marnäs church. Everybody had been dressed in black, singing hymns about death.

Nils tries a sob. That sounds good. He'll go up to his mother and sob and tell her Axel is still down on the shore. Axel wanted to stay, but Nils wanted to go home. And when everybody starts looking for Axel, he can think about the sad organ music at his father's funeral and cry along with his mother.

Nils will go up to the house soon; he knows what he's going to say and what he's not going to say when he gets there.

But first of all he finishes off Axel's toffees.

2

Gerlof Davidsson was sitting in his room at the residential home for senior citizens in Marnäs, watching the sun go down outside the window. The kitchen bell had just fallen silent after ringing for the first time, and it would soon be time for dinner. He would get up and walk to the dining room. His life wasn't over.

If he'd still been living in the fishing village he came from, Stenvik, he could have sat by the shore watching the sun sink slowly into Kalmar Sound. But Marnäs was on the east coast, which meant that each evening he watched the sun disappear behind a grove of birch trees, between the residential home and Marnäs church in the west. At this time of year, in October, the branches of the birch trees were almost completely bare, and looked like slender arms reaching out toward the orange disc of the sinking sun.

The twilight hour had arrived—the time for bloodcurdling stories.

When he had been a child in Stenvik, this had been the time when the work in the fields and around the boathouses was over for the day. Everyone would gather in the cottages as the evening drew in, but the paraffin lamps wouldn't be lit just yet. The older people would sit there in the twilight hour, discussing what had been achieved during the day and what had happened elsewhere in the village. And from time to time they would tell the children a story.

Gerlof always thought the scariest stories were the best. Tales of ghosts, dire warnings, trolls, and evil deeds in the Öland wilderness. Or tales of how ships were driven toward the shore along the stony coastline and smashed to pieces against the rocks.

The kitchen bell rang for the second time.

A boat captain who had been caught up in the storm and drifted too close to the shore would sooner or later hear the rocks on the seabed scraping against his keel, louder and louder, and that was the beginning of the end. Sometimes he might be skillful enough and fortunate enough to drop an anchor and slowly haul himself against the wind back into clear water again, but most boats couldn't move once they'd gone aground. Usually the captains had to abandon their vessels quickly in order to save themselves and their crews, trying to make their way onto dry land through the crashing waves; then they would stand there on the shore, soaking wet and frozen to the marrow, watching the storm drive their boats harder and harder aground until the waves began to smash them to pieces.

A small cargo boat that had run aground was like a battered coffin.

The kitchen bell rang for the last time, and Gerlof grabbed the edge of the wooden desk and pulled himself up. He could feel Sjögren coming to life in his limbs. He could feel it, and it was painful. He considered the wheelchair standing at the foot of his bed, but he had never used it indoors, and he had no intention of doing so now. But he picked up his cane in his right hand, gripping it tightly as he made his way toward the hallway, where his outdoor clothes hung on their hangers and his shoes were neatly arranged. He stopped, leaned on the cane, then opened the door to the corridor. He went out and looked around.

He could hear shuffling steps along the corridor, and saw them coming along one after the other: his fellow residents. They came slowly, with the help of canes or walkers. The residents of the Marnäs senior center gathering to eat.

Some of them greeted each other quietly; others kept their eyes fixed on the floor the whole time.

So much knowledge moving along this corridor, thought Gerlof as he joined the tired stream on its way into the dining room.

"Good evening, lovely to see you all!" said Boel, who was in charge of their section, smiling among the food trolleys outside the kitchen.

Everybody sat down carefully in their usual places around the tables.

So much knowledge. Around Gerlof sat a shoemaker, a churchwarden, and a farmer, all with experience and knowledge that nobody was interested in anymore. And then there was Gerlof himself; he could still tie a bowline knot with his eyes closed in just a few seconds, to no purpose whatsoever.

"Could be a frost tonight, Gerlof," said Maja Nyman.

"Yes, the wind's coming from the north," agreed Gerlof.

Maja was sitting next to him, tiny and wrinkled and skinny, but brighter than anyone else in there. She smiled at Gerlof, and he smiled back. She was one of the few who could pronounce his name correctly, *Yairloff.*

Maja came from Stenvik but had married a farmer and gone to live northeast of Marnäs in the 1950s; Gerlof himself had moved to Borgholm when he became a boat captain. Before he and Maja met up again in the residential home, they hadn't seen each other for almost forty years.

Gerlof picked up a piece of crispbread and began to eat, and as usual he was grateful that he could still chew. No hair, poor eyesight, no strength, and aching muscles—but at least he still had his own teeth.

The aroma of cabbage was spreading from the kitchen. There was cabbage soup on the menu today, and Gerlof picked up his spoon as he waited for the food trolleys to arrive.

After dinner most of the residents would settle down to watch TV for the rest of the evening.

These were different times. All the stranded ships had disappeared from Öland's shores, and no one told stories in the twilight hour any longer.

Dinner was over. Gerlof was back in his room.

He placed his cane beside the bookshelf and sat down at the desk again. It was evening now outside the window. If he leaned over the desk and pressed his nose right up against the glass, he would just be able to catch a glimpse of the fields north of Marnäs and beyond them the shore and the dark sea. The Baltic, his former workplace. But he couldn't manage such gymnastic contortions any longer, and had to content himself with looking out across the birch trees behind the old people's home.

It wasn't called an "old people's home" by those who decided these things any longer, but of course that's what it was. They were always trying to come up with new words that would sound better, but it was still a collection of old folk bundled together, far too many of whom simply sat around waiting for death.

A black notebook lay beside a pile of newspapers on the desk, and he reached out and picked it up. After sitting at his desk just staring out of the window for the whole of his first week at the home, Gerlof had pulled himself together and gone into the village to buy the notebook in the little grocery store. Then he'd begun to write.

The notebook consisted of both thoughts and reminders. He wrote down things that had to be done, and crossed them out when they'd been accomplished, except for the reminder SHAVE! which was written at the top of the first page and was never crossed out, as it was a daily task. Shaving was necessary, and was something he'd remembered to do earlier today.

This was the first thought in the book:

PATIENCE IS WORTH MORE THAN VALOR; BETTER A DISCIPLINED HEART THAN A STORMED CITY.

This was a worthwhile quotation from Proverbs, chapter sixteen. Gerlof had started to read the Bible at the age of twelve, and had never stopped.

At the back of the book were three lines that hadn't been crossed out. They read:

PAY THIS MONTH'S BILLS.

JULIA COMING WEDNESDAY EVENING.

TALK TO ERNST.

He didn't need to pay the bills for the telephone, newspapers, the upkeep of his wife Ella's grave over in the churchyard, and his monthly fees for staying at the home until next week.

And Julia was on her way, she'd finally promised to come. He mustn't forget about that. He hoped Julia would stay on Öland for a while. After all these years she was still full of sorrow, and he wanted to take her away from that.

The last reminder was just as important, and also had to do with Julia. Ernst was a stonemason in Stenvik, one of the few people who lived there all year round these days. He and Gerlof and their mutual friend John spoke on the telephone every week. Sometimes they even sat there in the twilight hour telling each other old stories, something Gerlof really appreciated, even though he'd usually heard them already.

But one evening a few months earlier, Ernst had come to Marnäs with a new story: the one about the murder of Gerlof's grandchild, Jens.

Gerlof wasn't at all ready to hear the story—he didn't really want to think about little Jens—but Ernst had sat over there on the bed and insisted on telling his tale.

"I've been giving some thought to how it happened," said Ernst quietly.

"Oh yes," said Gerlof, sitting at the desk.

"I just don't believe your grandchild went down to the sea and drowned," Ernst had said. "I think perhaps he went out onto the alvar in the fog. And I think he met a murderer out there."

"A murderer?" said Gerlof.

Ernst had fallen silent, his callused hands folded on his knee.

"But who?" Gerlof had asked.

"Nils Kant," said Ernst. "I believe it was Nils Kant he met in the fog."

Gerlof had just stared at him, but Ernst's gaze had been serious.

"I really believe that's what happened," he said. "I believe Nils Kant came home from the sea, from wherever he'd been, and caused even more misery."

He hadn't really said any more on that occasion. A short story in the twilight hour, but Gerlof hadn't been able to forget it. He hoped Ernst would soon come back and tell him more.

Gerlof kept flicking through his notebook. There were far fewer thoughts noted down than reminders, and soon he'd got to the end.

He closed the book. He couldn't do much more at the desk, but remained there anyway, watching the swaying birch trees in the darkness. They reminded him a little of sails in a stiff breeze, and from that thought it wasn't far to the memory of himself standing on deck in autumn winds like these, watching the coast of Öland slipping slowly by, either at close quarters with its rocks and cottages, or as just a dark strip along the horizon—and just as he was picturing the scene, the telephone on the desk suddenly rang.

The sound was shrill and loud in the silent room. Gerlof let it ring once more. He could often sense in advance who was calling; this time he wasn't sure.

He lifted the receiver after the third ring.

"Davidsson."

No one answered.

The line was open, and he could hear the steady hiss of electrons or whatever it was that whirled around the telephone cables, but the person holding the receiver didn't say a word.

Gerlof thought he knew what the person wanted anyway.

"This is Gerlof," he said, "and I received it. If it's the sandal you're calling about."

He thought he could hear the sound of quiet breathing on the other end.

"It came in the mail a few days ago," he said.

Silence.

"I think it was you who sent it," said Gerlof. "Why did you do that?"

Only silence.

"Where did you find it?"

The only thing he could hear was the hissing noise. When Gerlof had been pressing the receiver to his ear for long enough, it began to feel as if he were sitting there all alone in the entire universe, listening to the silence of black outer space. Or to the sea.

After thirty seconds, someone gave a deep cough.

Then there was a click. The receiver at the other end had been put down.

3

Julia's older sister, Lena Lundqvist, was clutching the keys firmly and looking nervously at the car. She glanced briefly at Julia, then looked back at their shared car.

It was a small red Ford. Not new, but still with shiny paint-work and good summer tires. It was parked on the street, next to the driveway of Lena and her husband Richard's tall brick house in Torslanda; they had a big garden, and although there was no sea view, they were so close to the sea that Julia thought she could smell the tang of the salt water in the air. She heard the sound of shrill laughter from one of the open windows, and realized all the children were home.

"We're really not keen on lending it out . . . When did you last drive?" asked Lena.

She was still holding the car keys in one hand, her arms firmly crossed over her chest.

"Last summer," said Julia, adding a quick reminder: "But it is *my* car . . . at least, half of it is."

A cold, damp wind swept along the street from the sea. Lena was wearing only a thin cardigan and skirt, but she didn't ask Julia to come inside where it was warm so they could discuss things fur-ther—and even if she had, Julia would never have agreed. Richard was bound to be inside, and she had no desire to see either him or their teenage children.

Richard was some kind of big boss at Volvo. He had his own

company car, of course, as did Lena, who was head of a primary school in Hisingen. They were very fortunate.

"You don't need it," added Julia, her voice steady. "You've only had it while . . . while I haven't wanted to drive."

Lena looked at the car again. "Well, yes, but Richard's daughter is here every other weekend, and she wants—"

"I shall pay for all the gas," Julia interrupted her.

She wasn't afraid of her older sister, she never had been, and she had made the decision to drive to Öland.

"Yes, I know you will, it isn't that," said Lena. "But it doesn't feel right, somehow. And then there's the insurance. Richard says—"

"I'm only going to drive to Öland in it," said Julia. "And then back to Gothenburg again."

Lena looked up at the house; there were lights behind the curtains in almost every room.

"Gerlof wants me to go," Julia went on. "I spoke to him yesterday."

"But why *now*?" said Lena, then went on without waiting for an answer. "And where are you going to stay? I mean, you can't stay with him at the home—there aren't any guest rooms there, as far as I know. And down in Stenvik we've closed up the cottage and the boathouse for the season . . ."

"I'll sort something out," said Julia quickly, then realized that she didn't actually know where she was going to stay. She hadn't even thought about it. "But I can take the car, then?"

She could sense that her sister was on the point of giving in, and wanted a quick answer before Richard came out to help his wife put off lending her the car.

"Well . . ." said Lena. "All right, you can borrow it then. I just need to get a few things."

She went over to the car, opened the door, and took out some papers, a pair of sunglasses, and half a bar of Marabou chocolate.

She walked back to Julia, held out her hand, and let go of the keys. Julia caught them, then Lena handed her something else.

"Take this too," she said. "So we can get hold of you. I just got a new one through work."

It was a cell phone, a black one. Perhaps not the smallest model, but small enough.

"I don't know how to use these," said Julia.

"It's easy. There's a code that you key in first . . . here." Lena wrote it down, along with the telephone number, on a piece of paper. "When you make a call, you just key in the whole number, with the area code, and press this green button. There's a bit of credit left on it; when that's gone you'll have to pay yourself."

"Okay." Julia took the phone. "Thanks."

"Right . . . Drive carefully," said Lena. "Love to Dad."

Julia nodded and walked over to the car. She got in, smelled the fragrance of her sister's perfume, started the engine, and drove off.

It was already dusk. And as she drove through Hisingen, at twenty kilometers below the speed limit, she thought about why she and Lena could never look at each other for more than a few seconds at a time. They'd been close in the past—after all, Lena was the reason why Julia had moved to Gothenburg once upon a time—but now it was just the opposite. And things had been this bad since that Friday several years earlier when Julia had been inside Lena and Richard's house for the last time, at a small dinner party without the children, which had ended with Richard putting his wineglass down, getting up from the table, and asking:

"Do we have to sit here constantly going over this tedious nonsense about things that happened twenty years ago? I'm just wondering. Do we have to?"

He was angry and slightly drunk and his voice was rough—despite the fact that Julia had merely mentioned Jens's disappearance in passing, simply as the reason why she was feeling the way she was.

Lena's voice was calm as she looked at Julia, then made the comment that had made Julia refuse to accompany her sister to Öland two years later, to help Gerlof move from the cottage in Stenvik to the residential home in Marnäs:

"He's never coming back," Lena had said. "I mean, everybody knows that . . . Jens is dead, Julia. Even you must realize that?"

Standing up and screaming hysterically at her sister across the dinner table hadn't helped at all, but Julia had done it anyway.

Julia got home, parked the car on the street, and went inside to pack. When she had packed clothes for a ten-day stay, a few toiletries, and some books (and two bottles of red wine and some pills), she ate a sandwich and drank some water instead of wine. Then it was time to go to bed.

But once in bed she lay staring up into the darkness, unable to sleep. She got up and went into the bathroom, took a prescription pill, and went back to bed.

A little boy's shoe. A sandal.

When she closed her eyes, she could see herself as a young mother, putting on Jens's sandals, and that memory brought with it a black weight that settled on her breast, a heavy uncertainty that made Julia shiver under the covers.

Jens's little shoe, after more than twenty years without a single trace of him. After all that searching on Öland, all that brooding through those sleepless nights.

The sleeping pill slowly began to work.

No more darkness now, she thought, half asleep. *Help us to find him.*

It was a long time before morning came, and it was still dark outside when Julia awoke. She had breakfast, then she washed up, locked the flat, and got into the car. She started the engine, switched on the windshield wipers to clear the leaves, then she was finally on her way out of the street where she lived, on her way out of the city in the sunrise and the morning traffic. The last traffic light turned to green, and she turned eastward onto the freeway, away from Gothenburg and out into the country.

She drove for the first few kilometers with the window down, letting the cold morning air blow away all trace of her sister's perfume from the car.

Jens, I'm coming, she thought. *I'm really coming, and no one can stop me now.*

She knew she shouldn't talk to him, not even silently to herself. It was unbalanced, but she'd been doing it on and off ever since Jens disappeared.

After Borås, the freeway came to an end and the houses grew smaller and more sparse. The dense fir forests of Småland crowded the road. She could have turned off and headed for an unknown destination, but the tracks into the forest looked so desolate. She drove on, heading across the country toward the east coast, and trying to take pleasure in the fact that she was undertaking a longer journey by herself than she had done for many years.

She pulled in at a service station a few kilometers from the coast to fill up with gas and to eat a few mouthfuls of a stew that was chewy and sticky and not worth the money, and then she set off again.

Toward the Öland Bridge. North of Kalmar, the bridge led to the island; it had been built over twenty years earlier, completed and opened the autumn that . . . That day.

She wouldn't think about it anymore, not until she arrived.

The Öland Bridge stood tall and firm, spanning the sound, resting on broad concrete pillars, completely unaffected by the sharp gusts of wind that tore at the car. It was wide and completely straight, apart from an arched section close to the mainland, which allowed taller ships to pass beneath the road. The arch was a viewing point, and she could see the flat shape of the island. It extended along the horizon, from north to south.

She could see the alvar, the grassy plain that covered large parts of Öland. Dark, low clouds drifted by, like long airships above the landscape.

Both tourists and residents loved to go walking and bird-watching out there, but Julia didn't like the alvar. It was too big— and there was nowhere to take shelter if the vast sky above came tumbling down.

After the bridge she drove north, toward Borgholm. The road was almost dead straight for several kilometers along the west coast, and she met few cars now that the tourist season was over. Julia kept her eyes fixed firmly on the road ahead in order to avoid looking out across the desolate alvar and the great expanse of water on the other side, and she tried not to think about a little sandal with a mended strap.

It didn't mean anything, it didn't have to mean anything.

The journey up to Borgholm from the bridge took almost half an hour. When she arrived, there was just one crossroads with a set of traffic lights, and she decided to turn left, down to the little town by the water.

She stopped at a cake shop at the edge of Storgatan, thus avoiding the harbor, the square, and the church; the church behind which she and her parents had lived when Gerlof had his own cargo boat and wanted to live near the harbor. Her childhood was in Borgholm. Julia had no desire to see herself running along the streets around the square like a pale ghost, a nine-year-old girl with her whole life ahead of her. She didn't want to meet any young men, striding toward her along the street and making her think of Jens. She had enough reminders of that kind in Gothenburg.

The bell above the cake shop door tinkled.

"Afternoon."

The girl behind the counter was blonde and pretty, and looked extremely bored. She listened to Julia with a vacant expression as she asked for two cinnamon pastries and a couple of strawberry cream cakes for herself and Gerlof.

This girl could have been her thirty years earlier, but of course Julia had moved away from the island when she was just eighteen, and had lived and worked in both Kalmar and Gothenburg before the age of twenty-two. In Gothenburg she had met Michael and gotten pregnant with Jens after just a few weeks, and much of her restlessness had disappeared then and never returned—not even after their separation.

"There aren't many people here now," she remarked as the girl lifted the cakes out of the glass display counter. "In the autumn, I mean."

"No," said the girl, without smiling.

"Do you like living here?" asked Julia.

The girl shook her head briefly. "Sometimes. But there's nothing to do. Borgholm only comes to life in the summer."

"Who says that?"

"Everybody," said the girl. "People from Stockholm, anyway." She fastened the box of cakes and handed it over. "I'm moving to Kalmar soon," she said. "Will that be all?"

Julia nodded. She could have said that she too had worked in Borgholm as a teenager, in a café down by the harbor, and that she too had been bored, waiting for life to begin. Then all of a sudden she wanted to talk about Jens, about her sorrow and the hope that had made her come back. A little sandal in an envelope.

She said nothing. A fan was humming away; otherwise the cake shop was silent.

"Are you a tourist?" the girl asked.

"Yes . . . no," said Julia. "I'm going up to Stenvik for a few days. My family has a cottage there."

"It's like Norrland up there now," said the girl as she handed Julia her change. "Practically all the houses are empty. You never see a soul up there."

It was half past three in the afternoon by the time Julia emerged from the cake shop and looked along the street. Borgholm was virtually deserted. There were a dozen or so people around, one or two cars, not much else. The huge ruined castle looked down from the hill above the town, its windows dark, empty holes.

A cold wind was sweeping along the streets as Julia walked back to the car. It was almost eerily silent.

She passed a big notice board covered in a patchwork of posters, all stuck on top of one other: American action films at the cinema in Borgholm, rock concerts in the ruined castle, and various evening classes. The posters had faded in the sun, and their corners had been chewed to pieces by the wind.

This was the first time Julia had visited the island as an adult so late in the year. During the low season, when Öland slowed down. She walked back to the car.

I'm coming now, Jens.

North of the town the dry, grassy plain of the alvar continued on both sides of the road. The road headed slowly inland from the coast, pointing straight into the flat landscape, where round, lichen-covered gray stones had been lifted from the fields and used to build long, low walls. The walls formed a gigantic pattern right across the alvar.

Julia had a slight feeling of agoraphobia out here beneath the vast sky, and longed for a glass of red wine—a longing which grew stronger as she got closer to Stenvik. At home she was trying to stop drinking every day, and she never drank when she was driving, but out here in this desolate place the bottles of wine in her bag seemed like the only interesting company she had. She wanted to lock herself in somewhere and devote all her attention to them until they were empty.

On the way north she met only two vehicles, a bus and a

tractor. She drove past yellow signs bearing the names of small villages along the road, names she remembered from all those earlier journeys. She could recite them by heart, like a nursery rhyme. They were places she had only driven past for years. For her mother and father there had been only Stenvik every summer, and the holiday cottage they had built there at the end of the 1940s—many years before the tourists had discovered the village. Autumn, winter, and spring in Borgholm, but the summer had always been Stenvik for Julia. Before she went up to Marnäs to see Gerlof, she wanted to see the village again. There were bad memories up there, but many good ones too. The memory of long, hot summer days.

She saw the yellow sign from some distance away: *Stenvik 1,* and beneath it the word CAMPSITE crossed out with black tape. She braked and turned onto the village road, away from the alvar and down toward the sound.

After five hundred yards the first little cluster of summer cottages appeared; they were all closed up, with white blinds pulled down at the windows. Then the kiosk, where the villagers gathered in summer. Its front had been cleared of notices and adverts and pennants, and there were shutters at its windows. Next to the kiosk was a sign pointing south toward the campsite and a minigolf course. The campsite was run by a friend of Gerlof's, she remembered.

The road led toward the water, curved to the right along the rocky ridge above the shore, and led northward, where more closed-up cottages lined the eastern side of the road. On the other side was the shore, covered in stones and pebbles; small waves ruffled the surface of the water out in the sound.

Julia drove slowly past the old windmill, standing up above the water on its sturdy wooden base. The mill had stood there abandoned for as long as Julia could remember, but now it had turned gray and lost almost all of its red color, and all that remained of its sails was a cross of cracked wooden slats.

About a hundred yards past the windmill lay the Davidsson family's boathouse. It looked well cared for, with red wooden walls, white windows, and tar-black roof. Someone had painted it recently. Lena and Richard?

Julia had a picture in her memory of Gerlof, sitting there mending his long nets on a stool in front of the boathouse in the summer, while she and Lena and their cousins ran about on the shore down below, the sharp smell of tar in their nostrils.

But Gerlof had been down at the boathouse cleaning his flounder nets. That day.

Now there was no one at the boathouse. Dry grass quivered in the wind. A wooden skiff, painted green, lay on its side in the grass beside the house—it was Gerlof's old boat, and its hull was so dried out that Julia could see strips of daylight between the upper planks.

She switched off the engine, but didn't get out of the car. Neither her shoes nor her clothes were suitable for the Öland autumn wind; besides, she could see an iron bar with a large padlock across the boathouse door. The blinds were pulled right down inside the small windows, as they were in the cottages in the rest of the village.

Stenvik was empty. Scenery, it was all just scenery for a summer theater. A gloomy play, at least as far as Julia was concerned.

Okay. She would go and look at Gerlof's house, the holiday cottage. Gerlof had built it himself on land the family had owned for years. She started the car and drove along the village road, which forked up ahead. She took the right-hand road, inland. There were groves of low-growing trees here, protecting the few houses that were occupied over the winter, but all the trees were leaning slightly away from the shore, bowed by the constant wind.

In a large garden stood a tall, yellow wooden house which looked as if it were about to fall to pieces behind the tall bushes. The paint was flaking off the walls, and the roof tiles were cracked and covered in moss. Julia couldn't remember who it had belonged to, but had no recollection of the place ever having looked smart and well cared for.

Among the trees a narrow track led off the road, a strip of knee-high yellow grass growing down the middle. Julia pulled in and switched off the engine. Then she put on her coat and got out into the chilly air.

The wind was soughing in the dry leaves on the trees, and behind that was the more muted sound of the waves on the shore.

But apart from that, there was no sound: no birds, no voices, no traffic.

The girl in the cake shop had been right: this was just like the mountains of Norrland.

The track leading to Gerlof's cottage ended at a low iron gate set in a stone wall. Julia opened the gate and it gave a faint squeak. She went into the garden.

I'm here now, Jens.

The little house, painted brown with white eaves, didn't look quite so closed up as many of the other cottages in Stenvik. But if Gerlof had still been here, he would never have let the grass grow so tall, or allowed yellow pine needles and leaves to litter the garden.

They had been a hardworking couple, Gerlof and Julia's mother. Ella, who had remained a housewife all her life, had sometimes seemed like a visitor from the nineteenth century, from an age of poverty when there was neither the time nor the energy for laughter and dreams on the island, and every scrap of kitchen paper had to be dried and used several times. Ella had been small and silent and had a dogged determination about her; the kitchen was her empire. Julia and Lena had had a pat on the cheek from their mother occasionally, but never a hug. And of course Gerlof had been away at sea most of the time while she was growing up.

Nothing was moving in the garden. When Julia was little, there had been a water pump in the middle of the lawn, a yard high, painted green, with a big spout and a pretty curved handle, but it was gone now. All there was in its place was a concrete cover over the well.

To the east of the cottage was a stone wall, and beyond it the grassy alvar began. It ran all the way to the horizon in the east. If the trees hadn't been in the way, Julia would have been able to see Marnäs church sticking up like a black arrow over there; she had been christened in that church when she was just a few months old.

Julia turned her back on the alvar and walked toward the cottage. She went around a trellis covered in vines that had grown wild, and climbed up the pink limestone steps that had seemed so enormous when she was a child. The steps led up to a little veranda with a closed wooden door.

Julia pushed down the handle, but the door was locked. As expected.

This was both the beginning and the end of her journey.

It was remarkable that the cottage was still here, thought Julia, because so much had happened out in the world since Jens had disappeared. New countries had come into being, others had ceased to exist. In Stenvik, the village was now virtually empty of visitors for most of the year—but the house that Jens had left that day was still there.

Julia sat down on the steps and let out a sigh.

I'm tired, Jens.

She looked at a little collection of stones that Gerlof had piled in front of the house. On the top lay an uneven, grayish black stone that he maintained had fallen from the sky as a burning lump and had made a crater over in the quarry sometime toward the end of the nineteenth century, when Gerlof's own father and grandfather were working there. This ancient visitor from outer space was spattered with bird dirt.

Jens had walked past the stone from space that day. He'd put on his little sandals, left the house where his grandmother lay sleeping, gone down these steps and out into the garden. That was the only thing that was absolutely definite. Where he had gone after that, and why, nobody knew.

When she got home from the mainland that evening, she'd expected Jens to come racing out of the house. Instead, two policemen were waiting for her, along with a weeping Ella and a stony-faced Gerlof.

Julia wanted to get out a bottle of red wine right now. To sit there on the steps drinking steadily, losing herself in dreams until darkness came—but she quashed the impulse.

Scenery. This empty garden felt just as much like a stage set as the rest of the village, but the play had ended many years ago, everyone had gone home, and Julia felt a crippling sense of loneliness.

She remained there on the steps for several minutes, sitting perfectly still, until a new sound combined with the rushing of the sea. An engine.

It was a car, a tired old car, chugging slowly along the village road.

The sound didn't go away. It continued, grew closer, and then the engine was switched off very close to the garden.

Julia got up, leaned forward, and glimpsed a round, dumpy car through the trees. An old Volvo PV.

The gate by the road squeaked as someone opened it. Julia straightened her coat, ran her fingers automatically through her pale hair, and waited.

The footsteps approaching through the dead leaves were short and heavy.

The old man who appeared without saying a word, standing at the bottom of the steps and looking sternly up at Julia, was also short and heavy. He reminded her of her father, but she couldn't say why; perhaps it was the cap, the baggy trousers, and the ivory-colored woolen sweater that made him look like a real boat captain. But he was shorter than Gerlof and the cane he was leaning on suggested that he hadn't sailed for a long time. His hands were heavily marked with old and new abrasions.

Julia vaguely remembered meeting this man many years earlier. He was one of Stenvik's permanent residents. How many were left?

"Hello there," she said, forcing her lips into a smile.

"Good day to you."

The man nodded back at her. He took off his cap and Julia could see the strands of gray hair combed in thin lines across his bald head.

"I just called to have a look at the place," she said.

"Yes . . . It needs somebody to keep an eye on it from time to time," he said in the strongest Öland accent Julia had ever heard, a harsh, low dialect. "That's what he wants."

Julia nodded. "It looks really good."

Silence.

"I'm Julia," she said, adding quickly with a nod toward the cottage, "Gerlof Davidsson's daughter. From Gothenburg."

The old man nodded, as if it were obvious.

"Of course," he said. "My name is Ernst Adolfsson. I live over there." He pointed behind him, diagonally toward the north. "Gerlof and I know each other. We have a chat from time to time."

Then Julia remembered. This was Ernst, the stonemason. He'd been walking around the village rather like some kind of museum exhibit even when she was young.

"Is the quarry open now?" she asked.

Ernst lowered his eyes and shook his head.

"No. No, there's no work there now. People come and fetch the reject stone sometimes . . . but nothing new is quarried anymore."

"But you work there?" asked Julia.

"I do craft work in stone," said Ernst. "You're welcome to come and have a look, see if you want to buy anything . . . I've got a visitor this evening, but tomorrow is fine."

"Okay. I might do that," said Julia.

She probably couldn't afford to buy anything, but she could always go and have a look.

Ernst nodded and turned away slowly with small, unsteady steps. Julia didn't realize the conversation was over until he'd completely turned his back on her. But she hadn't finished, so she took a deep breath:

"Ernst," she said, "you must have lived in Stenvik twenty years ago?"

The man stopped and turned back toward her, but only halfway.

"I've lived here for fifty years," he said.

"I was just thinking . . ."

Julia stopped speaking; she hadn't been thinking at all. She wanted to ask a question, but didn't know which one to choose.

"My child disappeared at that time," she went on with an enormous effort, as if she were ashamed of her grief. "My son Jens . . . do you remember that?"

"Of course." Ernst nodded briefly, without emotion. "And we're working on it. Gerlof and I, we're working on it."

"But . . ."

"If you see your father, tell him something from me," said Ernst.

"What?"

"Tell him it's the thumb that's most important," said Ernst. "Not just the hand."

Julia stared at him, bewildered, but Ernst went on:

"This will be solved. It's an old story, it goes right back to the war . . . But it will be solved."

Then he turned away again, with short unsteady steps.

"The war?" said Julia behind him. "Which war?"

But Ernst Adolfsson left without replying.

ÖLAND, JUNE 1940

When the horse-drawn cart has been unloaded for the last time down on the shore, it is hauled back up to the quarry and the men can begin to load the newly cut and polished limestone onto the boats. This is the heaviest work, and for the past six months it has been done by hand, since the two trucks belonging to the quarry have been requisitioned by the state and are being used as military vehicles.

There's a world war on, but on Öland the everyday work must continue as usual. The stone has to be quarried and taken to the cargo ships.

"Load up!" yells Lass-Jan Augustsson, the foreman of the stevedores.

He is directing the work from the deck of the cargo ship *Wind,* gesturing to the men loading her with his broad hands, dry and cracked from the rough blocks of stone. Beside him the stevedores are waiting to take the stone on board.

Wind is lying at anchor a hundred yards or so out in the water, at a safe distance from the shore in case a storm should suddenly blow up along the Öland coast. In Stenvik there is no pier in the harbor behind which a ship can shelter, and close to the shore the shallow, rocky seabed is waiting to smash any boat if it gets the opportunity.

The blocks being loaded on board are ferried out in two open rowboats. In one of them the starboard oar is manned by boatman

Johan Almqvist, who is seventeen and has been working as a quarryman and oarsman for a couple of years.

The oar on the port side is manned by Nils Kant, who is new to the job. He's fifteen now, almost fully grown.

His mother gave Nils a job at the family quarry after he failed his examinations at school. Vera Kant has decided that he is to be a boatman despite his tender age, and Nils knows that he will gradually take over the responsibility for the whole quarry from his uncle. He knows he will one day set his mark deep in the hillside. He would like to excavate the whole of Stenvik.

Sometimes Nils dreams of sinking down through black water at night, but during the day he rarely thinks of his drowning brother Axel. It wasn't murder, whatever the gossips in the village say. It was an accident. Axel's body has never been found; it was dragged down to the bottom of the sound, as is the case with so many who drown, and it never came up again. An accident.

The only memory of Axel is a framed picture of him on his mother's desk. Vera and Nils have grown much closer to each other since Axel drowned. Vera often says Nils is all she has left, which makes Nils realize how important he is.

The rowboats are lying waiting for their load beside a temporary wooden jetty extending a dozen or so yards out into the sea; the carts arrive on the shore, piled high, and the stones are then carried out onto the jetty in an endless cycle—youngsters, women, older men, and those few men in their prime who have not yet been called up for military service. Girls too; Nils can see Maja Nyman walking around in a red-checked dress out there on the jetty. He knows that she knows he watches her sometimes.

The war hangs like a shadow over Öland. Norway and Denmark were invaded by the Germans a month or so earlier without presenting any particular difficulty. There are extra news bulletins on the radio every day. Is Sweden really equipped to repel an attack? Foreign warships have been spotted out in the sound, and several times it has been rumored in Stenvik that southern Öland has been invaded.

If the Germans do come, the islanders know they will have to fend for themselves, because help has never come in time from the mainland when enemy forces have landed on Öland in centuries gone by. Never.

People say the army intends to put parts of northern Öland underwater in order to prevent an invasion of the island, which would be a bitter irony now that the serious spring floods out on the alvar have finally begun to evaporate in the sun.

When the sound of a distant engine was heard across the water earlier that morning, the unloading of the stones stopped, and everyone gazed anxiously at the overcast skies. Everyone except Nils, who wonders what a real bombardment by a plane looks like. Are there whistling bombs that turn into balls of fire and smoke and tears and screams and chaos?

But no plane appeared over the island, and the work resumed.

Nils hates rowing. Hauling stones might not be much better, but the tedious process of rowing gives him a headache right from the start. He can't think when he has to steer the heavily laden boat with his oar, and he's being watched the whole time. Lass-Jan follows the progress of the boats with his peaked cap pulled right down to his eyebrows, directing the work with his voice.

"Let's have some effort, Kant!" he roars across the water once the last stone has been loaded at the jetty.

"Slow down, Kant, look out for the jetty!" he yells as soon as Nils pulls on the oar too hard once the boat has been unloaded and is easy to row back.

"Get a move on, Kant!" Lass-Jan shouts.

Nils glares at him all the way out to the cargo ship. Nils owns the quarry. Or to be more accurate, his mother and uncle own it, but even so Lass-Jan has treated him like a slave right from the start.

"Load up!" yells Lass-Jan.

In the morning people chatted and laughed with each other when they began unloading, there was almost a party atmosphere, but the stone has mercilessly subdued them with its silent weight and its hard edges. Now people are carrying it doggedly, with their backs bent, their footsteps dragging, and their clothes powdered with white limestone dust.

Nils has nothing against the silence; he never speaks to anyone anyway unless he has to. But from time to time he looks over at Maja Nyman on the jetty.

"She's full!" shouts Lass-Jan when the blocks of stone are piled a yard high in the boat Nils is sitting in, and the seawater is almost lapping at the gunwale.

Two loaders climb down and sit on the piles of stone, looking down on a little nine-year-old boy who's there to bail out. The boy sneaks a terrified glance at Nils before he picks up his wooden pail and begins to scoop the water from the bottom of the boat, which is not watertight.

Nils pushes hard with his feet and heaves on the oar. The boat glides slowly off toward the cargo ship, where the other rowboat has just been emptied.

Back and forth with the oar, back and forth without a break. Nils's hands ache, and the muscles in his arms and back are screaming in pain. He longs to hear the roar of German bombers right now.

The boat finally hits the hull of the ship with a dull thud. Both loaders move quickly to the stern, bend down, take hold, and begin lifting the stone blocks over *Wind*'s gunwale.

"Let's put our backs into it!" yells Lass-Jan from the deck, standing there in his stained shirt with his fat belly sticking out.

The stones are lifted over the gunwale and carried over to the open hatch, then they slide down into the hold along a broad plank.

Nils is supposed to help with the unloading. He lifts a few slabs up to the ship, then hesitates just a fraction too long with a thick block on the edge, and drops it back into the boat. It lands on the toes of his left foot, and it bloody hurts.

In a fit of blind rage he picks the block up again and heaves it over the gunwale without even looking where it lands.

"Bugger this!" he mutters to the sea and the sky, sitting down at his oar.

He undoes his shoe, feels his aching toes, and rubs them gently with his fingers. They might be broken.

Around him the last of the blocks are unloaded from the boat, and the loaders jump over the gunwale to finish sorting them out down in the hold.

Johan Almqvist follows them. Nils stays in the boat with the little boy who was bailing.

"Kant!" Lass-Jan is up above him, leaning over the gunwale. "Get up here and give us a hand!"

"I'm injured," says Nils, surprised at how calm he sounds, when in fact an entire squadron of bombers is screaming into action like furious bees inside his head. Equally calmly, he places his hand on his oar. "I've broken my toes."

"Get up."

Nils gets up. It doesn't actually hurt all that much, and Lass-Jan shakes his head at him.

"Get up here and start loading, Kant."

Nils shakes his head again, his hand closing around the oar. The bombs are falling now, whistling through the air inside him.

He undoes the oarlock and lifts the oar a fraction.

He swings it slowly backwards.

"Broken his toes . . ." Another of the loaders, a stubby broad-shouldered lad whose name Nils can't remember, is leaning over the gunwale next to Lass-Jan. "Better run off home to Mummy, then!" he says scornfully.

"I'll take care of this," says the foreman, turning his head toward the loader.

This is a mistake. Lass-Jan never sees Nils's oar come swinging through the air.

The broad blade of the oar hits the back of his head. Lass-Jan utters a long, drawn-out "Hooooh," and his knees give way.

"I own you!" yells Nils.

He balances with one foot on the side of the boat, and swings the oar again. This time he hits the foreman across the back, and watches him fall over the gunwale like a sack of flour.

"Bloody hell!" shouts someone on board the cargo ship, then there's a loud splash as Lass-Jan falls backwards into the water between the rowboat and the hull of the cargo ship.

Shouts echo from the shore, but Nils takes no notice of them. He's going to kill Lass-Jan! He raises the oar, smashes it down into the water, and hits Lass-Jan's outstretched hands. The fingers shatter with a dry crack, his head jerks backwards, and he disappears beneath the surface of the water.

Nils brings the oar down again. Lass-Jan's body sinks in an eddy of swirling white bubbles. Nils raises the oar with the intention of continuing to hit him.

Something whizzes past Nils's ear and hits his left hand; the fingers crunch even before the pain almost numbs his hand. Nils wobbles and is no longer able to hold the oar; he drops it into the boat.

He closes his eyes tightly, then looks up. The loader who was making fun of him is standing up by the gunwale with a long boathook in his hand. His eyes are fixed on Nils, terrified but resolute.

The loader draws the boathook back toward him and lifts it again, but by this time Nils has managed to push off from the hull of the ship with his oar, and is on his way back to the shore. He leaves the loaders on the ship and Lass-Jan on his way to the bottom of the sea, and fixes the portside oar back in the oarlock.

Then he rows straight for the shore, the broken fingers of his left hand throbbing and aching. The little boy who does the bailing is crouching in the prow like a trembling figurehead.

"Get him out of there!" someone shouts behind him.

He hears the sound of splashing and shouting from the cargo ship across the water as Lass-Jan's limp body is hauled over *Wind*'s gunwale. The foreman is lifted to safety, the water is forced out of his body, and he is shaken back to life. He's been lucky—he can't swim. Nils is one of the few in the village who can.

Nils has his gaze fixed much further away, on the straight line of the horizon. The sun has found gaps in the cloud cover over there, and is shining down on the water, making it gleam like a floor made of silver.

Everything feels fine now, despite the pain in his left hand. Nils has shown everybody who owns Stenvik. Soon he will own the whole of northern Öland, and will defend it with his life if the Germans come.

The bottom of the boat scrapes against the rocks, and Nils picks up the oar and jumps out. He's ready, but no one attacks him.

The loaders are standing over on the jetty as if they've been turned to stone, women and men and children. They gaze at him mutely with terrified eyes. Maja Nyman looks as if she's about to burst into tears.

"Go to hell!" Nils Kant roars at the lot of them, and flings the oar down in front of him on the pebbles.

Then he turns to run back to the village, home to his mother Vera in the big yellow house.

But neither she nor anyone else knows what Nils knows: he is meant for greater things, greater than Stenvik, as great as the war. One day he will be known and talked about all over Öland. He can feel it.

4

Gerlof Davidsson was waiting for his daughter in his room at the residential home for senior citizens.

Today's edition of the local newspaper, *Ölands-Posten,* lay in front of him on the desk, and he was reading about an eighty-one-year-old man suffering from senile dementia who had vanished outside Kastlösa in southern Öland. The man had simply left his little cottage the day before and disappeared without a trace; the police and volunteers were now searching for him out on the alvar—they'd even had a helicopter out looking for him. But it had been a cold night, and it wasn't at all certain he'd be found alive.

Senile dementia and eighty-one years old. Gerlof was only a year or so younger; his eightieth birthday was coming up. Eighty was not as old as some thought, but of course it was easier to understand when an old person disappeared without a trace than when it happened to a child. He closed the paper and looked at the clock. Quarter past three.

"I'm glad you've come," he said to himself. He paused, coughed, and went on: "You're just as beautiful as I remember, Julia. Now you're here on Öland, there are certain things we must do. There are things you'll need to take care of yourself, too. And we can talk . . . I know I wasn't always a good father to you when you were growing up, I was away a lot and you and your sister were alone with Ella in Borgholm when I was at sea. It was my job, being a captain and transporting cargoes across the Baltic, far away from my family . . . But I'm here now, and I'm not going anywhere anymore."

He fell silent and stared down at the desk. He'd written his speech to Julia down in his notebook. Ever since she'd told him which day she was coming to the island, he'd been trying to learn it—and it *sounded* that way. He had to get it to sound like a father talking to his child in a perfectly ordinary way.

"I'm glad you've come," said Gerlof, again. "You're just as beautiful as I remember."

Or pretty? Pretty, that was probably a better description of a much-missed daughter.

At last, when it was almost four o'clock and there was only an hour left before dinner, he heard a knock on the door of his room.

"Come in," he said, and the door opened.

Boel stuck her head in.

"Yes, he's here," she said quietly to someone behind her, then in a louder voice: "You've got a visitor, Gerlof."

"Thank you," he said, and Boel smiled as she stepped back.

Another woman came forward; she took several steps into the hallway, and Gerlof took a deep breath so that he could start his speech:

"I'm glad you've come . . ." he began, then fell silent.

He saw a middle-aged woman in a crumpled coat looking at him from the hallway; her eyes were tired, her forehead furrowed. After only a couple of seconds her gaze slid away from him, and she wrapped her arms around her brown shoulder bag as if it were some kind of protective shield as she took a few more steps into the room.

Gerlof gradually recognized his daughter in the woman's furrowed, serious face, but Julia looked much more weary than he'd expected. More weary and much thinner. She made him think about bitterness and self-pity.

His daughter had grown old. So how old did that make him?

"Hello, Gerlof," said Julia, then she didn't speak for a few seconds. "Well, here I am again."

Gerlof nodded and noted the fact that she still had no intention of calling him Dad, not even face-to-face. She said *Gerlof,* in a tone that suggested she might be talking to a distant relative.

"How was your journey?" he asked.

"Fine."

She unbuttoned her coat, hung it on a hook in the hall, and placed her bag on the floor. It seemed to Gerlof that she was moving slowly, without any energy. He wanted to ask how she was feeling, but perhaps it was too soon.

"Right." Silence again. "It's been a long time," he said.

"Four years, I think," said Julia. "More than four years."

"Yes. But we've kept in touch by phone."

"Yes. I meant to come and help when you moved here from Stenvik, but it wasn't . . ."

Julia stopped speaking, and Gerlof nodded.

"The move went very well anyway," he said. "I had a lot of help."

"Good," said Julia. She'd come halfway into the room. She sat on the bed.

Gerlof suddenly remembered the little speech he'd been practicing.

"Now you're here," he said, "there are certain things we need to–"

But Julia interrupted him.

"Where is it?"

"What?"

"You know," said Julia. "The sandal."

"It's here. In the desk." Gerlof looked at her. "But first I thought we could–"

"Can I see it?" Julia broke in. "I'd really like to see it."

"You might be disappointed. "It's just a shoe. It has no . . . no real answers."

"I want to see it, Gerlof."

Julia got up. She hadn't even smiled so far, and now she was staring so intensely at Gerlof that he was beginning to think the whole thing was a mistake. Perhaps he shouldn't have called her. But something had already been set in motion, and he couldn't stop it now.

Still, he tried to delay things as long as possible.

"You didn't bring anybody else with you?" he asked.

"Like who?"

"Jens's father, perhaps," said Gerlof. "Mats . . . was that his name?"

"Michael," said Julia. "No, he lives in Malmö. We hardly keep in touch anymore."

"I see," said Gerlof.

Silence again. Julia took another step forward, but Gerlof thought of something else:

"Did you do what I said on the telephone?" he asked.

"What?"

"Did you think about how thick the fog was that day?"

"Yes . . . maybe." Julia gave a distracted nod. "What's all this about the fog?"

"I don't think . . ." Gerlof chose his words carefully. "I don't think anything could have happened . . . that things could have gone so badly if it hadn't been for the fog. And how often do we get fog on Öland?"

"Not very often," said Julia.

"No. Three or four times a year, maybe. As thick as it was that day, anyway. And lots of people knew it was coming; it had been mentioned in the weather forecast."

"How do you know?"

"I rang the weather bureau," said Gerlof. "They keep the forecasts."

"Was the fog so important?" said Julia.

"I think . . . somebody was making the most of the fog," said Gerlof. "Somebody who didn't want to be spotted in the area."

"Didn't want to be spotted on that particular day, you mean?"

"Didn't want to be spotted at all," said Gerlof.

"So somebody was using the fog to . . . take Jens away?" said Julia.

"I don't know," said Gerlof. "But I do wonder if that was the aim. Who knew he was going to go outside that day? Nobody. Isn't that right? Jens didn't even know himself, he just . . . took the chance when it arose." Gerlof could see that Julia had begun to press her lips together as they started to talk about her son's disappearance, and he went on quickly: "But the fog that came that day . . . That was predicted."

Julia said nothing. She was just staring at the desk now.

"We should think about that," Gerlof insisted. "We need to think about who would have had the most to gain from the fog that day."

"Can I see it now?" said Julia.

Gerlof knew he couldn't put it off any longer. He nodded, and spun his chair around to face the desk.

"It's here," he said.

He pulled out the top drawer, reached in, and carefully lifted out a small object. It didn't seem to weigh any more than a few ounces, and it was wrapped in white tissue paper.

5

Julia walked over to Gerlof as he unwrapped the little package on the desk. She looked at his hands, where his age was visible in the wrinkled skin, the brown liver spots, and the thickened veins. His fingers were shaking, fumbling with the tissue paper. It seemed to Julia that the rustling as he opened the package was deafening.

"Do you need any help?" she asked.

"No, it's fine."

It took him several minutes to open the package—or perhaps it just seemed that way. At last he folded back the final layer of paper and Julia could see what it had been concealing. The shoe lay in a clear plastic bag—she couldn't take her eyes off it.

I'm not going to cry, she thought, *it's only a shoe.* Then she felt her eyes filling with an intense heat, and she had to blink away the tears in order to be able to see. She saw the black rubber sole and the brown leather straps, dry and cracked with age.

A sandal, a little boy's worn sandal.

"I don't know if it's the right shoe," said Gerlof. "As I remember it, it did look like this, but it could be a—"

"It's Jens's sandal," Julia interrupted him, her voice thick.

"We can't be sure of that," said Gerlof. "It's not good to be too certain. Is it?"

Julia didn't reply. She knew. She wiped the tears from her cheeks with her hand, then carefully picked up the plastic bag.

"I put it in the bag as soon as I got it," explained Gerlof. "There might be fingerprints . . ."

"I know," said Julia.

It was so light, so light. When a mother was going to put a sandal like this on her little son's foot, she picked it up off the floor by the outside door without even thinking about what it might weigh. Then she stood beside him and bent her back, feeling the warmth of his body and taking hold of his foot as he steadied himself by holding on to her sweater, standing there quietly or saying something, all the childish chatter that she only half listened to because she was thinking about other things. About bills that needed paying. About buying food. About men who weren't around.

"I taught Jens to put on his own sandals," said Julia. "It took all summer, but when I started college in the autumn he could do it." She was still holding on to the little shoe. "And that was why he was able to go out alone that day, to sneak out . . . He'd put on his own sandals. If I hadn't taught him he wouldn't have . . ."

"Don't think like that."

"What I mean is . . . I only taught him to save a bit of time," said Julia. "For myself."

"Don't blame yourself, Julia," said Gerlof.

"Thanks for the advice," she said, without looking at him. "But I've been blaming myself for twenty years."

They fell silent, and Julia realized suddenly the picture in her memory was no longer fragments of bone on the shore in Stenvik. She could see her son alive, bending down with enormous concentration to put on his own sandals, finding it difficult to make his small fingers do what he wanted them to do.

"Who found it?" she asked.

"I don't know. It came in the mail."

"Who from?"

"There was no sender's name. It was just a brown envelope, with an indistinct postmark. But I think it came from Öland."

"No letter?"

"Nothing," said Gerlof.

"And you don't know who sent it?"

"No," said Gerlof, but he was no longer looking Julia in the eye; he was looking down at the desk, and she got no more answers. Perhaps he suspected more than he wanted to tell her.

No answers. Julia sighed.

"But there are other things we can do," Gerlof went on quickly. Then he stopped.

"Like what?" said Julia.

"Well . . ."

Gerlof blinked without replying, looking at her as if he'd already forgotten why he'd asked her to come.

But Julia had no idea either what they should do next, and didn't say anything. She suddenly realized she hadn't looked at her father's room properly; she had been completely fixated on looking at the sandal, holding it in her hand.

She took a look around. As a nurse she quickly noticed the emergency call buttons along the walls, and as a daughter she discovered that Gerlof had brought his memories of the sea with him from the cottage in Stenvik. The three nameplates in lacquered wood from his cargo ships *Wavebreaker, Wind,* and *Nore* were hanging above framed black-and-white photographs of the ships. On another wall hung framed ship's registration certificates with stamps and seals. On the bookshelf beside the desk stood Gerlof's leather-bound logbooks in a row, next to a couple of tiny model ships that had sailed straight into their own glass bottles.

Everything was just as neatly arranged as in a maritime museum, clean and shining, and Julia realized she envied her father; he could stay in his room with his memories, he didn't have to go out into the real world, where you had to make things happen and pretend to be young and sharp and try to prove your worth all the time.

On the table next to Gerlof's bed lay a black Bible and half a dozen pill bottles. Julia looked over toward the desk again.

"You haven't asked me how I am, Gerlof," she said quietly.

Gerlof nodded. "And you haven't called me Dad," he said.

Silence.

"So how are you?" he asked.

"Fine," said Julia tersely.

"Are you still working at the hospital?"

"Oh yes," she said, without mentioning the fact that she'd

taken an extended leave of absence. Instead she said, "I drove through Stenvik before I came here. I had a look at the cottage."

"Good. How are things looking down there?"

"Just the same. It was all closed up."

"No broken windows?"

"No," said Julia. "But there was a man there. Or rather, he turned up while I was there."

"I expect it was John," said Gerlof. "Or Ernst."

"His name was Ernst Adolfsson. I presume you know each other?"

Gerlof nodded. "He's a sculptor. An old stonemason. He's from Småland originally, but . . ."

"But he's all right in spite of that, you mean?" said Julia quickly.

"He's lived here for a long time," said Gerlof.

"Yes, I vaguely remember him from when I was little . . . He said something odd before he left, something about a story from the war. Was he talking about the Second World War?"

"He keeps an eye on the cottage," said Gerlof. "Ernst lives over by the quarry, and he picks up the leftover reject stone sometimes. Fifty men used to work there in the old days, but now there's just Ernst . . . He's been helping me a bit with working all this out."

"All this? You mean what happened to Jens?"

"Yes. We've talked about it, speculated a bit," Gerlof said, then asked, "How long are you staying?"

"I . . ." Julia wasn't prepared for the question. "I don't know."

"Stay for a couple of weeks. That would be good."

"That's too long," said Julia quickly. "I have to get home."

"Do you?" said Gerlof, as if it came as a surprise to him.

He glanced at the sandal on the desktop, and Julia followed his gaze.

"I'll stay for a while," she said. "I'll help you."

"With what?"

"With . . . whatever we need to do. To move forward."

"Good," said Gerlof.

"So what are we going to do, then?" she asked.

"We're going to talk to people . . . listen to their stories. Like in the old days."

"You mean . . . several people?" said Julia. "Did several people do it, then?"

Gerlof looked at the sandal.

"There are certain people here on Öland I want to talk to," he told her. "I believe they know things."

Once again he hadn't given Julia a straight answer. She was beginning to grow tired of it, and really just wanted to leave, but she was here now—and she'd brought cakes.

I'll stay, Jens, she thought. *For a few days. For your sake.*

"Is it possible to get some coffee around here?" she asked.

"It usually is," said Gerlof.

"Then we can have coffee and cakes," said Julia, and despite the fact that she thought she sounded unpleasantly like her older sister, always planning ahead, she asked, "Where am I going to stay tonight? Any suggestions?"

Gerlof reached slowly toward the desk. He pulled out a little drawer and felt around inside. There was a rattling sound, and he took out a bunch of keys.

"Here," he said, handing them to her. "Sleep in the boathouse tonight . . . There's electricity in there now."

"But I can't . . ."

Julia stood by the bed looking at Gerlof. He seemed to have planned everything that was happening.

"Isn't it full of fishing nets and that sort of thing?" she asked. "Floats and stones and tins of tar?"

"All gone, I don't fish anymore," answered Gerlof. "Nobody fishes in Stenvik."

Julia took the keys. "You could hardly get in there before, there was so much stuff," she said. "I remember . . ."

"It's all been cleaned up," said Gerlof. "Your sister's made it really nice in there."

"Am I supposed to sleep in Stenvik?" she said. "All on my own?"

"The village isn't empty. It just seems that way."

Half an hour after taking her leave of Gerlof, Julia was back in Stenvik, standing down by the dark water. The sky was just as cloudy as it had been in the morning, and full of shadows. It was almost twilight, and Julia longed for a glass of red wine—and another one to follow it. Wine, or a pill.

It was the waves' fault. The waves were washing peacefully over the pebbles along the shoreline this evening, but when there was a storm they could be six feet high, hurtling in toward the shore with a long drawn-out thunderous roar. They could carry anything with them from the bottom of the sound—wreckage, dead fish, or fragments of bone.

Julia didn't want to look too closely at what might be lying there among the pebbles on the shore. She had never gone swimming in Stenvik again after that day.

She turned around and looked at the little boathouse. It looked small and lonely, up above the shore.

So close to you, Jens.

Julia didn't know why she'd accepted the keys from her father and gone along with the idea of sleeping there, but it would probably be all right for one night. She'd never been particularly afraid of the dark, and she was used to being alone. One or maybe two days, that would be okay. Then she'd go back home.

A final blast of cold air swept in from the sound and pushed her into the darkness as she undid the padlock on the white door of the boathouse.

When the door closed behind her, the howling of the autumn wind was abruptly cut off. Everything was silent within the boathouse.

She put on the main overhead light and stood there just inside the door.

Gerlof had been right. The boathouse wasn't the way she remembered it at all.

This was no longer a fisherman's working environment, full of stinking nets and broken floats and yellowing copies of *Ölands-Posten* piled up on the floor. Since Julia had last seen it, her sister had completely renovated the boathouse and decorated it as a little holiday cottage, with polished wooden panels on the walls and a varnished pine floor. There was a small refrigerator, an electric heater, and a hotplate by the window facing the shore. On a table beneath the window facing inland stood a big ship's compass made of bronze and polished brass; another of Gerlof's mementos of his years at sea.

The air inside the boathouse was dry. There was only a faint scent of tar, and it would smell even fresher once Julia had pulled up the blinds and opened the small windows. She would be able to live down here without any problems, except for the total isolation.

Presumably Ernst Adolfsson over by the quarry was her nearest neighbor. Ernst had been driving an old Volvo PV and she would have been happy to see it coming along the village road right now, but when she peered out through the window above the compass, nothing was moving out there, only the sparse grass on the ridge in the wind. Even the gulls had disappeared.

There were two narrow beds in the boathouse. She unpacked her bags on one of them: clothes, her toiletry bag, spare shoes, and the bundle of romantic paperback novels she had pushed into the bottom of her bag; she read them in secret. She placed the books on the bedside table.

On the wall by the door hung a little mirror with a varnished wooden frame, and Julia studied her face in it. She looked wrinkled and tired, but her skin wasn't quite as gray as it seemed in Gothenburg. The stiff breeze on the island had actually put a little color in her cheeks.

What should she do now? She'd bought a hot dog that tasted of nothing from a little kiosk next to the old people's home after visiting Gerlof, so she wasn't hungry.

Read? No.

Drink the wine she'd brought with her? No, not yet.

She decided to do some exploring.

Julia left the boathouse and walked slowly back down to the shore and then southward along by the water. It became easier and easier to walk across the pebbles as she began to regain some of the innate sense of balance she'd had as a little schoolgirl in Stenvik, when she'd spent entire days jumping about down by the sea without even stumbling.

Diagonally below the boathouse, Gray-eye was still there, but it had slowly been drawn closer to the sea by the waves and the winter ice. Gray-eye was a narrow, yard-long boulder that resembled a horse's back. Julia had made it her very own stone once upon a time, and now she patted it briefly as she walked past. It seemed to have sunk down into the ground over the years.

The mill also seemed smaller. It was the tallest building in

Stenvik, the old windmill standing on the edge of the ridge a couple of hundred yards south of the boathouse. But when Julia got there, the rocks were too steep for her to be able to clamber up to it.

South of the windmill there were several more boathouses, in the inner part of the inlet where Stenvik's long swimming jetty was placed during the summer. There wasn't a living soul in sight.

Julia went up onto the road, northward, past Gerlof's boathouse. She stopped and gazed out over the water, toward the mainland. Småland was just a narrow gray stripe along the horizon. There were no ships to be seen.

She turned so that she could take in the whole of the surrounding area, as if the coastal landscape were a riddle she could solve if she could just find the right clues.

If what everyone feared had actually happened, if Jens had managed to make his way down to the water that day, then he would have walked along here in the fog that evening. She could search for traces of him now, but of course that had already been done. She'd searched, the police had searched, everyone in Stenvik had searched.

She started walking again, and after a few hundred yards she reached the quarry.

It was closed, of course. Nobody quarried limestone any longer. The letters STEN IK STONE LTD could just be made out on a wooden sign by the coast road, its paint flaking and peeling off. There was a side track leading toward the alvar, but both the track and the yellow-brown landscape ended abruptly, disappearing into a broad pit in the ground. Julia stepped closer to the edge of the cliff, which plunged straight down to the bottom at a ninety-degree angle.

The quarry was no more than four or five yards deep at most, but it was bigger than several football pitches. The inhabitants of Öland had been quarrying there for centuries, working their way down into the rock, but to Julia it looked as if everybody had suddenly thrown down their tools one day and gone home forever. Finished blocks of stone still lay down there on the gravel, neatly lined up.

On the opposite side of the quarry, tall, pale figures were lined up on the alvar; it was too dark and they were too far away for her

to be able to make out any details, but after a moment Julia realized they were stone statues. They looked like a series of artworks
made of stone, all different sizes. Right on the edge of the quarry
stood a block of stone some six feet tall; the top came to a point,
and it looked like a medieval church tower. A replica of Marnäs
church, perhaps.

Julia realized she was looking at Ernst Adolfsson's work.

Behind the stone statues stood a wooden house, a dark red
rectangle out on the alvar among the low-growing trees and the
juniper bushes, and beside the house stood Ernst's bulky, rounded
Volvo. Lights showed in several windows of the house.

She decided to take a closer look at Ernst Adolfsson's artwork
the following morning, before leaving Stenvik.

From here she could also make out Blå Jungfrun, a small
blue-gray mound on the horizon. Blåkulla was another name for
the island, where according to legend the witches would go to
celebrate with Satan. No one lived there, the whole island was a
national park, but you could go there on a day trip by boat. Julia
had gone there as a little girl one sunny day, along with Lena and
Gerlof and Ella.

There had been lots of round, pretty pebbles on the shores
there, but Gerlof had warned her against taking any of them away
with her. It would bring misfortune, he'd told her, so she hadn't
done it. But of course she'd had misfortune in her life anyway.

Julia turned her back on the witches' island and turned back
toward the boathouse.

Twenty minutes later she was sitting on the bed in the boathouse,
listening to the wind and not feeling tired in the slightest. At around
ten o'clock she tried to start reading one of the love stories she had
with her, entitled *The Secret of the Manor,* but it was slow going. She
closed the book and stared at the old compass on the table by the
door.

She could have been in Gothenburg now, sitting at the kitchen
table with a glass of wine and looking out at the streetlamps illuminating the empty road.

In Stenvik it was pitch dark. She had gone out for a pee, stumbling about on the stones and almost losing her bearings in the
darkness just a few yards from the boathouse. She could no longer

see the water down below her; she could only hear the sighing of the waves and the rattle of the pebbles as they reached the shore. Above her dense rain clouds scudded across the sky over the island like evil spirits.

As she squatted out there in the darkness, her bare bottom exposed to the wind, Julia's thoughts turned involuntarily to the ghost who had turned up here on the shore one night at the beginning of the 1900s.

She remembered one of her grandmother Sara's tales in the twilight hour: about how her husband and his brother had gone down one stormy night to haul their little fishing boats up to safety, away from the crashing waves.

As they stood there by the foaming water, hauling and dragging at their wooden gigs, a figure suddenly emerged from the darkness, a man wearing heavy oilskins, who began to tug one of the boats in the opposite direction, out to sea. Grandfather had yelled at him, and the figure had yelled back in very broken Swedish, repeating one word over and over again:

"Ösel!" he'd screamed. "Ösel!"

The fishermen had held on tight to their boat and the figure had suddenly turned and dashed out into the heaving waves. He had disappeared into the storm without a trace.

Julia quickly finished peeing beside the path outside the boathouse, then hurried back into the warmth and locked the door behind her. Then she remembered there was no running water down here; she'd have to go up to the cottage to fetch some.

Three days after the terrible storm, there came news from the northern tip of Öland: a ship had run aground at Böda and had been smashed to pieces by the waves three days earlier. The vessel had come from the Estonian island of Ösel. All those on board had perished in the storm, so the seaman that the fishermen in Stenvik had met and spoken to had been dead by that time. Dead and drowned.

Grandmother had nodded at Julia in the twilight.

A ghost of the shore.

Julia believed the story; it was a good tale, and she believed all the old stories she'd heard in the twilight. Somewhere along the coast the drowned seaman was surely still wandering, lost and alone.

Julia had no desire to go out again. She had no intention of fetching water; she'd just have to do without brushing her teeth tonight.

There were thick red candles in the windows of the boathouse. She lit one with her cigarette lighter before she went to bed, and left it burning for a while.

A candle for Jens. It was burning for his mother too.

In the glow of the flame she made a decision: no glass of wine and no sleeping pills tonight. She would fight against her grief. It was everywhere anyway, not only in Stenvik. Every time she met a young boy on the street, she could still be overcome by a sudden surge of grief.

When she saw her little address book lying on the bed beside Lena's old cell phone, she picked up both of them on an impulse, flicked through the address book to find a number, and dialed it.

The phone worked. Two rings, three, four.

Then a muffled male voice answered. "Hello?"

It was already ten-thirty on a normal weekday evening. Julia had rung too late, but she had to continue now.

"Michael?"

"Yes?"

"It's Julia."

"Right . . . Hi, Julia."

He sounded more tired than surprised. She tried to remember what Michael looked like, but couldn't get a picture in her head.

"I'm on Öland. In Stenvik."

"Right . . . Well, I'm in Copenhagen, as usual. I was asleep."

"I know it's late," she said. "I just wanted to tell you a new clue has turned up."

"A clue?"

"To our son's disappearance," she explained. "Jens."

"Right," he said.

"So I've come here . . . I thought you'd want to know. It probably isn't an important clue, but it might . . ."

"How are you, Julia?"

"Fine . . . I can give you a call if anything else happens."

"You do that," he said. "You still seem to have my number. But if you could call a little earlier next time, that would be good."

"Okay," she said quickly.

"Bye, then."

Michael hung up, and the telephone was silent.

Julia sat there with the cell phone in her hand. Okay. So she'd tested it out and found that it worked, but she knew she'd chosen the wrong person to call.

Michael had moved on long ago, even before they separated. From the beginning he'd been certain that Jens had gone down to the water and drowned. Sometimes she'd hated him for that conviction, sometimes she'd just been crippled by envy.

A few minutes later, when Julia had turned out the light and got into bed, still wearing her pants and sweater, down came the torrential rain that had been hanging in the air all evening.

It started very suddenly, hammering rapidly and frantically on the tin roof of the boathouse. Julia lay there in the darkness, listening to small streams beginning to babble along down the slope outside. She knew the boathouse was safe; it had survived every violent storm up to now, and she closed her eyes and fell asleep.

She didn't hear the rain stop half an hour later. She didn't hear any footsteps over by the quarry in the darkness; she didn't hear a thing.

Nils has owned the shore, he has owned Stenvik, and now he owns the whole of the alvar surrounding the village. When his mother doesn't need his help in the house or the yard, he roams across it every day, taking long strides. In the yellow sunlight he walks over the Öland steppes with a rucksack slung over his shoulder and his shotgun in his hands.

The hares usually sit frozen, huddled right down to the earth, until they think they have been discovered; then they hurtle away across the ground, and you have to raise the gun to your shoulder very quickly. Nils is always ready to shoot when he's out hunting.

His home and the alvar have been his whole world ever since his mother told him he wouldn't be able to work at the quarry anymore after the fight with Lass-Jan some years earlier. None of the other quarry workers wanted him there. Not that it matters to Nils; he refused to go back there anyway, refused to apologize, and the only annoying thing is that his mother had to pay Lass-Jan's wages for the weeks the stevedore couldn't work, while his broken fingers were healing.

Shit. The whole thing was Lass-Jan's fault, after all!

Nils also carries the memory of the fight: two broken fingers on his left hand. He refused to go to the doctor in Marnäs despite the pain, and his fingers have mended badly, curving inward and becoming more difficult to bend. But it doesn't matter, he's right-handed and he can still hold his gun.

People in the village avoid Nils these days, but that doesn't matter either. Maja Nyman has been on the village road a few times when he's gone out onto the alvar, but she just looks at him in silence, like all the rest. Maja has big blue eyes, but Nils can get by perfectly well without her.

His mother has given Nils the double-barreled Husqvarna shotgun to keep him company. And he gives her all the hares he shoots with it, so she doesn't have to pay for expensive meat from the tightfisted farmers in the village.

The white tower of Marnäs church is visible on the horizon to the east, but Nils doesn't need any landmarks. He has learned to find his way around the alvar's labyrinth of long stone walls, boulders, bushes, and endless grassy plains.

Up ahead of him is the memorial cairn: the low pile of stones marking the place where some crazy servant killed a priest or a bishop, several hundred years before Nils was born. People walking by still set small stones there sometimes. Nils never does, but it's a good spot for him to sit and eat his lunch.

He stops, considers, and notices a faint pang of hunger down in his stomach. He goes over to the cairn, takes off a couple of uneven stones, then settles down with the shotgun close beside him and the rucksack on his knee.

He opens it and discovers two cheese sandwiches and two sausage sandwiches wrapped in greaseproof paper, and a small bottle of milk. His mother packed all this; without asking her, Nils himself has filled his slim copper hip flask with the cognac she keeps on the floor of the larder.

He starts his lunch break by opening the flask and taking a long swig, which spreads a feeling of steady warmth down through his throat, then he opens up his packet of sandwiches. He eats and drinks with his eyes closed, letting his thoughts wander.

Nils thinks about hunting. He hasn't got a hare yet today, but he's got the whole afternoon to shoot one.

Then he thinks about the war, which is still filling every news program whenever you switch on the radio.

Sweden hasn't been attacked, although three German destroyers did stray into the minefield just off southern Öland in the summer of 1941, and were blown to pieces. Over a hundred of Hitler's men ended up in the water, and either drowned or died in the burning oil slick. And many inhabitants of Öland thought the war had definitely arrived the following summer, when for some reason a German plane dropped eight bombs in the forest below the ruined castle at Borgholm.

The explosions had been heard all the way up to Stenvik. Nils had been woken by the dull thuds, and stared out of the dark window with his heart pounding; he could have sworn he heard the plane's engines as it flew away from the island. A Messerschmitt, perhaps. He'd listened and longed for more explosions, bombs raining down all around Stenvik.

But there had been no German invasion, and now it's too late for Hitler to do anything. Nils has read the newspaper reports about the big surrender in Stalingrad earlier in the year, during the bitterly cold winter. Hitler seems to be on the losing side.

Nils hears a horse neigh behind him.

He opens his eyes and turns his head. There are several horses behind him. Four young animals, brown and white, have come up to the cairn, and now the animals trot in front of him in a curving line, their heads bowed, the dust whirling around their legs. Their hooves make almost no sound as they move across the grass.

Horses. They roam at will across the alvar in herds. On a few occasions when Nils has been looking for hares rather than at the ground in front of him, his boots have sunk deep into the piles of shit they leave everywhere, like small brown memorial cairns.

This little herd seems to be on the way to a definite goal, but when Nils gives a short whistle and pushes his left hand down into his rucksack, the leading horse slows and turns its head toward him.

All the horses come to a halt and look at Nils. One lowers its head to nuzzle the yellow grass of the alvar, but doesn't begin to graze. They are waiting for something tastier.

Nils keeps his hand in the rucksack, rustling the empty grease-proof paper, while he places his right hand quietly beside him on the stones.

The horses hesitate, sniffing the air and pawing the ground with their hooves. Nils rustles the paper again, and the dark brown lead horse takes a cautious sideways step toward him. The others follow slowly, their nostrils twitching slightly.

The lead horse stops again, five yards away.

"Come on, then, feeding time," says Nils, smiling with anticipation.

You can't get hares to come to you like this, only horses.

The lead horse shakes its big head and gives a low, snorting
neigh.

Then he takes a couple of steps forward, and Nils swiftly lifts
his right hand and throws the first stone.

Good shot! The rough piece of limestone hits the animal just
above its muzzle and it jerks backwards as if it's had an electric
shock. It backs away in terror, bumping into the horse behind,
and spins in a blind panic as Nils stands up quickly and throws the
second stone. This one is flatter and sharper and flies through the
air like the blade of a saw.

It hits the lead horse on the rump. He gives a high-pitched,
terrified neigh, and now all the horses grasp the danger. They turn
and gallop away across the alvar at full speed, their hooves drumming on the ground. They disappear among the bushes.

Nils panics slightly, and his third stone goes too far over to
the left. That's bad. He bends down again quickly, but the fourth
throw is too short.

The last he sees of the lead horse is a bloodred, glittering
stripe along its right flank. The wound is deep, and probably won't
heal for several days. Nils will try to find the stone that cut the
horse before he goes home, to see if there's any blood on it.

The noise of the horses' mad flight dies away. Silence returns
to the alvar. Nils breathes out and sits down again on the cairn,
smiling as he thinks about the stupid, bewildered expression on
the horse's face when the first stone hit him.

Fucking horses.

Nils has shown them who rules the alvar around Stenvik. He
is still smiling to himself as he picks up the rucksack again. Has his
mother put any butter toffees at the bottom?

6

It was evening at the residential home for senior citizens in
Marnäs. Gerlof was sitting at his desk, his notebook open in front
of him. He was holding a ballpoint pen, but hadn't written anything.

When Gerlof sat there at his desk, he could easily convince
himself that he wasn't as old as he thought, and had plenty of
strength left; in a minute or two he would stand up on his strong
legs, stretch, and off he would go.

Out. Down to the shore at Stenvik, push the skiff out, and row
over to the ship that was waiting in deeper water. Weigh anchor,
set sail, and off out into the world.

It had always fascinated Gerlof that a sea captain from the waters of Öland could reach any coast he wanted. With a little bit of
luck, a great deal of skill, the right equipment, and plenty of sup-
plies on board he could sail from Öland to any port in the world,
then come back home again. Fantastic. Such freedom.

A couple of minutes later the bell rang for dinner and Gerlof
was back in his feeble body. His legs were stiff, his arms would
never again manage to hoist a sail.

They had passed quickly, those years at sea. And there hadn't
really been that many. Gerlof had gone out as first mate with his
father on his ketch *Ingrid Maria* at the end of the twenties, and
five years later, when his father came ashore to become a ship's
broker, he'd taken over the vessel, renamed her *Wind,* and carried

cargoes of timber and wooden goods from Småland to Öland. He'd been a captain at the age of twenty-two.

During the Second World War he'd worked as a pilot off Öland, and on two occasions he'd had to watch ships go down with all their crews on board, when their skippers had thought they knew a safer route through the minefields than the pilot boat.

Gerlof had lived in constant fear of mines during those years. In one nightmare, which still woke him in a cold sweat some nights, he was standing by the gunwale of the pilot boat up above the shining sea at sunset, looking down—and suddenly he saw a big black mine just beneath the surface of the water. Old and rusty and covered in rippling seaweed, but its spikes would hit the boat just a few seconds later and detonate the mine.

He couldn't stop the boat, it was slipping silently closer and closer to the spikes ... and just before the hull hit the mine Gerlof would always wake up.

After the war he'd bought his second small cargo boat, *Wavebreaker,* and had begun to sail between two ports, Borgholm and Stockholm, via the Södertälje Canal. His cargo was Öland marble, red limestone for the building work going on in the capital, and on the return journey he often carried fuel or lime to the farmers' cooperative in Borgholm. In the harbors along his route there were always boats he knew, and anyone who needed help could always be sure of getting it from their fellow seamen.

There was no rivalry at that time, and Gerlof had received a great deal of help that December night in 1951 when flames gobbled at *Wavebreaker* as she lay at anchor in Ängsö. His cargo of linseed oil had caught fire, and Gerlof and his first mate, John Hagman, had only just made it onto the deck before the blaze swept through the whole ship. Neither of them could swim, but another cargo boat from Oskarshamn was lying alongside and the two men made it on board. They got all the support they needed, but all they could do for *Wavebreaker* was to sever the anchor and allow her to drift away into the night.

For Gerlof the burning, sinking cargo boat in the winter night was an apt symbol for Öland's shipping industry, even if he couldn't see it at the time. He could have given up when he was acquitted after an investigation, but out of pure stubbornness he had used the insurance money to buy a new cargo boat with an engine, and had continued as a skipper for another nine years. *Nore* had been his last boat, and the prettiest; slender, with a beautiful stern and a wonderful, chugging compression-ignition engine. He could still hear her engine chugging inside his head sometimes, in the moments just before he fell asleep.

In 1960 he'd sold *Nore* and come ashore to work in the council offices in Borgholm, and his sedentary desk-life had begun. The advantage was, of course, that he could go home to Ella every night. He had missed a great deal of his daughters' childhood, but at least now he could watch them growing up as teenagers. And when his youngest daughter, Julia, had become pregnant at the end of the sixties, Gerlof hadn't cared whether she was married or not—he had loved that little boy. His grandchild.

Jens Gerlof Davidsson.

And then came that day.

It was autumn, but Julia had been studying part-time to be a nurse, and had been able to stay in Stenvik with Jens longer than usual. Jens's father, Michael, had stayed behind on the mainland. And Julia had left her son with Ella and Gerlof after lunch and gone across to Kalmar over the new bridge. And after they'd had coffee, Gerlof had left his wife and Jens, with no hesitation, with no premonition that something bad might happen, and gone to disentangle some fishing nets he was intending to put out the following morning.

Down by the boathouse he had watched the fog rise up from Kalmar Sound, the densest fog he'd seen since his years at sea. When it drifted in across the shore, he'd felt it on his skin, and he'd shivered as if he were standing in the cold on a ship's deck. A few moments later the whole world around him was a white mist, where nothing could be seen.

He should have gone home then, to Ella and Jens. And he'd thought about it. But he'd stayed at the boathouse working on the nets for another hour or so.

That's the way it was. But because he'd stayed by the boathouse and his hearing was good, he knew one thing for certain that he'd never managed to convince anybody else of, apart from Julia, perhaps: Jens hadn't gone down to the sea that day. Gerlof would have heard him. Sounds were slightly muted in the fog, but they could be heard. Jens hadn't drowned, as the police believed, and his body hadn't been sucked out to sea and sunk to the bottom of Kalmar Sound.

Jens had gone somewhere else, not down to the water.

Gerlof bent over the table and wrote a single sentence:

THE ALVAR IS LIKE A SEA.

Yes. Anything at all could happen out there, and no one would be any the wiser.

He put his pen down on the desk and closed the notebook, and when he opened the drawer he saw once again the sandal wrapped in its tissue paper, and beside it a slim book that had been published earlier in the year.

It was a memoir, only sixty pages, with the title *Malm Freight–40 Years* on the cover. There was a picture of a ship beneath the title.

Ernst had lent him this book when he last visited Gerlof two weeks ago.

"This might be something," he'd said. "Have a look at page 18."

Gerlof opened the book and leafed through to page 18. Right at the bottom, below the text, was a small black-and-white picture that he'd studied many times before.

The picture was old. It showed a stone jetty in a small harbor, and a pile of long wooden planks lay on the jetty. The black stern of a small sailing ship was visible at an angle behind the wood; the ship was similar to the one Gerlof had sailed, and beside the pile of wood a group of men in black work clothes and peaked caps were lined up. Two men were standing in front of the others, one with his hand on the other's shoulder in a friendly gesture.

Gerlof stared at the men and they stared back.

There was a knock at the door.

"Coffee time, Gerlof," said Boel's voice.

"Coming," said Gerlof, pushing his chair back.

He got up from the desk with some difficulty.

But he found it difficult to take his eyes off the men in the photograph in the book.

Neither of the men was smiling, and Gerlof wasn't smiling at them either, because after his last conversation with Ernst he was more or less certain that one of the men in the old photograph had caused the death of his grandson Jens, then hidden the boy's body forever.

He just didn't know which of them had done it.

With a small sigh he closed the book and pushed it back into the drawer. Then he picked up his cane and slowly made his way to the lounge for coffee.

7

On Öland the dawn comes along the straight line of the horizon like a silent, dazzling light, but Julia slept right through the sunrise this October morning.

There were small roller blinds at each of the three windows in Gerlof's boathouse; once upon a time they had been dark red, but over the years they had been faded by the sun to a pale pink. Just before half past eight the blind next to Julia's bed suddenly flew up, rolling itself up with a bang that sounded like a thunderclap in the silence.

Julia opened her eyes. It wasn't the bang that had woken her but the sunshine suddenly pouring in through the east-facing window. She blinked and raised her head from the warm pillow. She could see autumn-yellow grass swaying in the wind outside the window, and remembered where she was. Strong wind and bright air.

Stenvik, she thought.

She blinked again and tried to keep her head up, but quickly sank back into the hollow in the pillow. She was always slow in the mornings, she had been all her life, and for the past twenty years the oblivion of sleep had often been very tempting. Her bouts of depression after that day had led her to sleep away far more of her adult life than she should have. But getting up in the morning was hard when there didn't seem to be any particular reason to do so.

Getting up in Stenvik was also made more difficult by the fact that there was no nice warm bathroom to stagger to. All there was below the boathouse was a stony shore and ice-cold water.

Julia had a vague memory of heavy rain rattling on the roof during the night, but all she could hear now was the sound of the waves below the boathouse. The rhythmic rushing made her think about jumping out of bed, throwing off her clothes, and dashing down to leap into the sea, but the thought passed.

She stayed in the narrow bed for a few more minutes, then got up.

The air was damp and chilly, and it was still windy outside, but the Stenvik she saw when she had put on her jacket and finally opened the boathouse door wasn't the same ghostly landscape she'd seen the night before.

The heavy overnight rain seemed to have washed away all the grayness; the sun was shining again, and the rocky Öland coast was clean and austere and beautiful. The inlet that had given the village its name wasn't deep, curving out on either side of the boathouse, carved out of the glittering waters of the sound. A few hundred yards from the shore, gulls were bobbing on top of the waves, their wings outstretched, screaming or laughing shrilly at each other through the wind.

Within the sunlight there was a sense of sorrow that not everything was as beautiful as it seemed to be, but Julia tried to suppress it. She just wanted to feel good. She didn't want to think about fragments of bone or talk to the memory of Jens this morning.

She heard a cheerful bark. When she turned her head, she saw a white-haired woman in a red padded jacket walking from the coast road with a little light brown dog; it wasn't on a lead, and it was running backwards and forward, snuffling at the road. With their backs toward Julia they turned off and walked quickly into one of the houses on the other side of the road.

Ernst wasn't the only person living in Stenvik, Julia realized.

Her drowsiness disappeared, and she was filled with energy. She picked up a plastic container and walked quickly up to Gerlof's house to fill it with drinking water from the tap in the garden. In the sunshine the cottage looked really welcoming, despite the overgrown grass surrounding it, but Gerlof hadn't given her a key, so she couldn't go in to look at her own childhood bedroom.

As she was running the water she realized she could actually stay on Öland for longer than just one day. If there was anything useful to be done—if Gerlof could pull himself together and come up with some suggestions as to what she should do, or look for— she could stay for another two days, or three.

Then she looked around the empty garden and decided. *No.* She would go home to Gothenburg today, but not until later.

On the way back to the boathouse, holding the water container tightly, she stopped to look at the yellow house behind the hawthorn hedge below the cottage. It was surrounded by tall, spreading ash trees and was barely visible behind the hedge, but what could be seen wasn't attractive. The house wasn't just empty, it was completely abandoned. Virginia creeper had spread all over the walls and begun to cover the cracked windows.

Julia had a vague memory of an old woman living there, a woman who never went out or mixed with anyone else in the village.

It was strange that the house had been left to decay; it was a fine house beneath all the cracks. Somebody ought to do up the whole place.

Julia hurried back down to the boathouse to make a cup of tea and some breakfast.

Forty-five minutes later she locked the door of the boathouse, one bag over her shoulder and the other in her hand. Inside, the bed had been made, the electricity switched off, and the blinds pulled down. The boathouse was empty again.

Julia walked across the ridge to the car, looked around without seeing a single person along the coast, and got in. She started the engine and took one last look at the boathouse. She looked at the ridge, the decaying windmill, and all the glittering water below her, and felt the sorrow return.

She quickly turned the car toward the main road.

She drove past the farm that was now a summer cottage, past the deserted yellow house, and past the gate to Gerlof's cottage. Goodbye, goodbye.

Goodbye, Jens.

To the left of the village road was another road leading to another group of summer cottages, and there was also a rectangular piece of limestone embedded in the ground with the words

CRAFT WORK IN STONE 1 KM painted on it in white. On an iron post above it was a sign showing the symbol indicating that there was no through road.

Julia saw the sign and remembered what she'd been thinking of doing this morning before she went to say goodbye to Gerlof: stopping off at the old quarry to have a look at Ernst Adolfsson's sculptures.

She didn't really have any money to buy that sort of thing, but she thought she would like to see his work. And perhaps she might try and ask some more questions about Jens, if Ernst remembered his disappearance and if he might be willing to tell her where he himself had been that day. It couldn't do any harm.

She turned off onto the narrow track, and the little Ford immediately began to bounce and list from one side to the other. It was the worst road Julia had driven on so far on Öland, largely because of the cloudburst. The rainwater was still lying in the wheel tracks in long narrow pools; she slowed and crept forward in first gear, but the car still slipped and slid in the muddy hollows.

She left the summer cottages behind and drove along the edge of the alvar. The track curved slowly off toward the quarry along the coast road, then straightened as it approached Ernst Adolfsson's low cottage. It stopped in front of the house at a circular turning area, where Ernst's old white Volvo was still parked.

There was no sign of life, but another flat, polished stone with black lettering had been erected in the middle of the turning area: CRAFT WORK IN STONE—WELCOME.

Julia pulled in behind the Volvo and turned off the engine. She got out of the car and took her thin wallet out of her purse.

The wind was sighing in the long grass, and the landscape was almost completely bare of trees. On one side of the garden was the enormous wound in the hillside that was the quarry, on the other side there was only grass and isolated juniper bushes as far as the eye could see. The alvar.

She turned and looked at the house.

It was closed up and silent.

"Hello?" she called.

The wind muted her cry, and no one replied.

A broad path made of crushed limestone led to the door at the side of the house, where there was a bell.

Julia went over and rang it.

Still no reply. But the car was here, so where was Ernst?

She rang again, keeping her finger pressed on the bell. Nothing happened.

An impulse made her try the door. It was unlocked and swung open, like an invitation.

She poked her head in.

"Hello?"

No one replied. The light was off and the hallway was dark. She listened for the sounds of heavy footsteps and a cane tapping along the floor, but there was only silence.

He's not at home—go and see Gerlof, urged her inner voice. But she was too curious. Didn't people on Öland lock their doors when they went out? Did they still trust each other so much?

WELCOME, it said on a green plastic mat by the door. Julia wiped her feet a couple of times and walked in.

"Hello?" she said. "Ernst? It's Julia. Gerlof's daughter . . ."

From the ceiling in the hallway hung a mobile of small wooden ships, sailing around in the draft. To the right lay a kitchen; it was clean and tidy, with a small table and two wooden chairs. To the left was a bedroom with a narrow bed, which was made.

The hallway led into a living room with a sofa, a television, and a big picture window overlooking the quarry and the blue sound beyond. There were piles of newspapers and books on the table, but the living room was empty too. On one wall was a hexagonal clock made of polished limestone, with the hands made of slate.

The only remarkable thing about the house was the fact that the clock appeared to be the only thing made of stone. Did Ernst get enough of it when he was outdoors?

She moved back into the hallway and looked around a couple of times, as if some unknown attacker might leap out of a crack in the walls. She went back outside and closed the door carefully.

Julia stood there motionless in the sunshine, unsure of what to do next. Ernst Adolfsson was bound to be around somewhere out here: he had merely forgotten to lock his door.

She looked over toward the stone sculptures on the quarry's edge. Beside them was a small shed painted red and surrounded by birch trees; in a pile outside the shed lay several blocks of stone and rocks of different sizes. Some bore the signs of having been worked on, but looked incomplete. Some resembled misshapen human beings, Julia thought. She could see deformed faces and black eye sockets in the stone, and it made her think of trolls who stole away human children and took them inside the mountain forever. Gerlof had told her that when the quarry workers' tools went missing in times gone by, they always blamed the troll. It was unthinkable that any of their fellow workers might have stolen them.

She tore her gaze away from the stones and again looked over toward the completed, polished works of art by the sheer cliff edge above the quarry. Small lighthouses, round well lids, tall sundials, and a couple of broad gravestones. The nameplates on the gravestones were still empty.

Something was missing. There was a wide space in the long row of sculptures, and Julia moved closer. She had seen something from the other side of the quarry the previous evening: the tall church tower that resembled the one up in Marnäs was gone. A small shallow depression gaped in the gravel by the cliff edge above the quarry.

Julia slowly walked forward between the polished stones, and the quarry opened up in front of her like an enormous empty pool.

The quarry wasn't deep here, just a few yards, but the drop was sheer. She stood by the edge, looking silently out across the barren, stony landscape, and suddenly caught sight of the tall church tower immediately below her. It had fallen from the edge, straight down into the quarry, and landed on its side. The top of the tower was pointing westward, toward the water.

The church tower hadn't smashed to pieces.

But beneath the oblong stone sculpture, Ernst Adolfsson lay outstretched. He was staring up at the sky from the bottom of the quarry, his mouth bleeding and his body shattered.

Everything has changed. Big things are going to happen, both out in the world and in Nils Kant's life. He can feel it in the wind.

The sun above the alvar is stronger than ever, the Öland winds are fresher, the air clearer, and the flowers are in full bloom. The grass is green, not yet burned by the sun of high summer. Vague, flickering little marks in the sky grow into swallows, swooping down like black arrows over the flat ground for a few moments, then gathering speed as they soar upward again, and suddenly there they are, high in the sky once more.

Spring has come to Öland with a vengeance, and Nils Kant can sense changes in the air. He is almost twenty years old now, finally grown up and completely free. Life lies ahead of him, and big things are going to happen. He can feel it in the whole of his body.

Nils is getting too old to be wandering around out here in the silence, hunting hares. He has other plans. He's going to go off out into the world when the war is over, anywhere he wants to. He would like to take Maja Nyman with him, the girl who lives in a cottage down by the ridge in Stenvik. He remembers what she looks like, and thinks of her quite often. But they have never really spoken, just said hello when they've met, if nobody else was with her. If he doesn't get the opportunity to talk to her properly soon, he'll travel alone.

On this particular day he is further away from Stenvik than

usual, almost over on the eastern side of the island. Before he crossed the main road he shot two hares; he's left them under some bushes so that he can pick them up on the way home. He's intending to shoot one or two more before he goes home to his mother, and perhaps a few swallows on the way back, just for fun.

The water from the melted snows of winter is still lying in big pools all over the alvar; it's a bit like walking in a boggy landscape, full of small lakes. The water is drying up quickly in the sun. Nils is wearing big, sturdy boots, and can wade straight through if he wants to. He is completely free and he owns the whole world.

Adolf Hitler tried to own the world. He's dead now; he shot himself in Berlin a week or so ago. That was the end for Germany. Nobody there had the will or the strength to fight the Russians and the Americans any longer.

Nils splashes up out of a pool of water and pushes through a clump of juniper bushes. He remembers that he liked Hitler when he was younger; he had great respect for Hitler's strength of will, at any rate.

He used to listen reverently to fragments of Hitler's thundering speeches from Germany when his mother had the radio on in the living room, and for several years he waited for the German bombers to sweep in across Öland, for the war to come at last, but now Hitler is gone and the might of Germany has been smashed to pieces by the English bombers.

Germany doesn't seem particularly interesting any longer. England, on the other hand, is tempting. And America seems huge and full of promise, but too many people from Öland have already gone there and never returned; thousands disappeared without a trace in the nineteenth century. Nils wants to travel the world and then return to Stenvik like an emperor.

Nils hears something, a low but solid sound, and he stops.

There is no sign of a hare, and yet Nils feels as if . . .

He isn't alone.

Someone is there.

He has heard something in the wind, a brief sound which is neither birdsong nor the humming of insects nor the neighing of horses. He has been walking around on the alvar for years; he knows when things are as they should be, and when they are not. Right now there's something that definitely isn't right. He can feel prickles of unease running down the back of his neck and his spine.

This is no hare, this is something else.

Wolves? Nils's grandmother, long dead now, used to tell stories about wolves on the alvar. There used to be wolves there. But not now.

People?

Somebody creeping up on him?

Nils slowly unhooks the Husqvarna shotgun from his shoulder, raises it in both hands, ready to shoot, and releases the safety catch with his thumb. Two cartridges from Gyttorp cartridge factory are ready to fly down the barrel.

He looks around: there are juniper bushes almost everywhere here, most of them twisted and bent by the wind and no more than a yard high, but they are still dense and impossible to see through. If Nils stands up, he can look over them and see a long, long way, and nobody can creep up on him, but when he crouches down the bushes seem to grow and loom over him.

He can't hear a sound now—if he ever did hear anything. Perhaps it was just inside his head; it's happened before when he's been out here alone.

Nils stands there in the grass in silence, absolutely motionless, waiting. He is breathing calmly, and has all the time in the world. The hares always come out when he waits, their nerve always goes in the end and they hurtle out of their hiding places and rush blindly away from the huntsman with their hopping gait. Then all he has to do is raise the gun calmly to his shoulder, aim at the brown shape, and press the trigger. Then walk over and pick up the faintly twitching body.

Nils is holding his breath. He's listening.

He can't hear anything now, but there's a sudden breeze, and he catches the distinct aroma of stale sweat and oily fabric in his nostrils. The acrid smell of a human body, or several bodies, is carried toward him on the breeze.

There are people, very close by.

Nils swings round to the right, his finger on the trigger.

Terrified eyes are staring out of a juniper bush, only a yard or so away.

The eyes of another human being, meeting his own.

A man's face takes shape in the darkness beneath the thick junipers, a man's face gray with dirt and overshadowed with tousled hair. Behind the head is a body pressing itself into the ground, dressed in bulky green clothes. A uniform, Nils realizes.

The man is a soldier. A foreign soldier, with neither a helmet nor a gun.

Nils is holding the shotgun in front of him; he can feel his heart pounding, right to the tips of his fingers. He raises the barrel an inch or two.

"Come out," he says loudly.

The soldier opens his mouth and says something. It isn't Swedish, at least no Swedish that Nils has ever heard. It's a foreign language. It sounds like German.

"What?" Nils says quickly. "What are you saying?"

The soldier slowly raises his hands—he has dirty, cracked hands—and at that moment Nils realizes he is not alone in his hiding place. Behind him beneath the juniper bushes, another staring man in a dirty uniform is pressing himself down into the grass. They both have a hunted look, as if they were running away from terrible memories.

"Bitte nicht schiessen," whispers the soldier closest to Nils.

8

Julia had called Gerlof on Ernst Adolfsson's phone and told him what had happened—that she'd found Ernst, where he'd been lying, and that he was dead.

Gerlof had understood what she was telling him, but had tried not to think or feel too much, but to concentrate almost entirely on listening to her voice. It sounded tense, of course, but not shaky. Julia was in control.

"So Ernst is dead," said Gerlof. "Are you sure?"

"I'm a nurse," said Julia.

"Have you called the police?"

"I rang the emergency number. They're sending somebody. But they won't need an ambulance for Ernst . . . It's too late." She stopped. "But the police are bound to come as well, even if it is an accident. He's . . ."

"I'll come down to you," said Gerlof. He made the decision at the same moment as he spoke the words. "The police are sure to be there soon, but I'm coming, too. Sit down on Ernst's sofa and wait for them."

"Okay, I'll wait," said Julia. "I'll wait for you."

She still sounded calm.

They hung up, and Gerlof stayed where he was at his desk for a minute or two, gathering his strength.

Ernst. Ernst was dead. Gerlof allowed this fact to sink in. Up to now he'd had two close friends remaining in his life, John and Ernst. Now he had only one.

He picked up his cane and got up. He was utterly resolute, despite the fact that his rheumatism and his grief made it more difficult than ever to move. He went out into the corridor, heard laughter coming from the kitchen, and made his way there.

Boel was standing there with some new young girl who was clearly being instructed in how to use the dishwasher. They caught sight of Gerlof and Boel smiled at him, then she saw his face and her expression instantly became serious.

"Boel, I have to go to Stenvik. There's been an accident. My best friend has died," said Gerlof firmly. "Somebody will have to take me."

He didn't look away, and in the end Boel nodded. She didn't like alterations to the routine, but this time she didn't say anything about it.

"Wait two minutes and I'll drive you," she told him.

When they reached the northern turnoff for Stenvik leading down to the quarry, Gerlof raised his hand and pointed straight ahead.

"We'll take the southern road," he said.

"Whatever for?" said Boel. "You said you wanted to go to–"

"I have two friends in Stenvik," said Gerlof. "One was Ernst. The other needs to be told what's happened."

She drove on; the southern turnoff soon appeared, with the CAMPSITE sign taped over to indicate that Stenvik's campsite was closed for the season. It was John Hagman who had done that, despite the fact that there wasn't much risk of anybody turning up with a tent or trailer in October.

The closed kiosk appeared, then the mini-golf course, where a middle-aged man in a green tracksuit was sweeping the track; he glanced shyly at their car as they drove past. It was Anders Hagman, John's only son. Anders was a bachelor and very quiet, and Gerlof had hardly ever seen him wearing anything other than that scruffy tracksuit–perhaps he had several.

The track leading onto the campsite appeared.

"Here," Gerlof told Boel. "It's that house over there."

He pointed to a small house beside the track, a low building with narrow windows that looked like some kind of guardhouse. A rusty old green VW Passat was parked outside the door, which meant John was at home.

Boel braked and stopped the car. Gerlof opened the door and climbed out, using his cane, and almost at the same moment the door of the small house opened. A short man in dark blue dungarees, his gray hair swept back and caught in a little knot at the back of his neck, came out onto the wooden steps in his stocking feet. It was John Hagman, who was always quick to come out and see who was visiting.

John and Anders Hagman ran the campsite together in the summer months. Anders mostly lived in Borgholm during the winter.

John stayed in Stenvik all year, and had to take care of the daily maintenance of the campsite when Anders wasn't around. It was hard work for an old man—Gerlof would have helped him, if he hadn't been even older than John.

Gerlof nodded to John, who nodded back, then pushed his feet into a pair of black Wellington boots standing on the steps.

"Gerlof?" said John as Gerlof walked over. "This is unexpected."

"Yes. There's been an accident," said Gerlof.

"Where?"

"At the quarry."

"Ernst?" said John quietly.

Gerlof nodded.

"Is he hurt?"

"Yes. It's bad," said Gerlof. "Very bad."

John had known him for almost fifty years; they had kept in touch after their years together at sea. He seemed to understand exactly how bad it was from Gerlof's expression alone.

"Is there someone with him?" he asked.

"There should be by now," said Gerlof. "My daughter Julia was going to phone them. She's there now. She came over from Gothenburg yesterday."

"Right." John stepped back into the house, and when he came out again he was holding a padded jacket and a bunch of keys. "We can take my car," he said. "I'll just go and have a word."

Gerlof nodded, that would be good. Boel was bound to want to get back to the senior home, and it would be easier to talk to John if they were alone.

John went over to Anders, stopped in front of him, then pointed at the golf course and said something quietly. Anders shook his head. John pointed at him, and Gerlof could hear his raised voice. The Hagman father and son had a somewhat strained relationship, Gerlof knew that—they were too dependent on each other.

In the end Anders nodded, and John shook his head and turned his back on his son. They'd finished arguing.

As John was unlocking his own car, Gerlof made his way slowly over to Boel to thank her for the lift.

"So Ernst is dead, then," said John behind the wheel.

"That's what Julia thought," said Gerlof beside him, looking out at the shore and the glittering water down below the coast road.

"A stone fell on him," said John.

"A big stone. That's what Julia said," explained Gerlof.

There hadn't been a serious accident for over sixty years in the quarry, he realized—but now that it was closed, Ernst had ended up underneath a stone.

"I brought the spare key," said John. "In case they've taken him away."

"Did he give you a key?" said Gerlof, who had never been entrusted with one by Ernst. On the other hand, he'd never given Ernst a spare key to his cottage either. Perhaps they hadn't really trusted one another.

"Ernst knew I wouldn't go snooping around," said John.

"Maybe we should take a look around in there now, though," said Gerlof. "I don't really know what we're supposed to be looking for. But we ought to look."

"Yes," said John. "It's different now."

Gerlof didn't say anything else, just gazed ahead through the windshield, because there was an ambulance coming toward them along the coast road. Gerlof had never seen an ambulance in Stenvik before.

It was coming slowly along from the track to the quarry, and the dark blue lights on the roof were not flashing. This wasn't a good sign, but it was what they'd expected. John slowed as the ambulance passed them, then they turned off onto the northern road into the village.

"His work sold really well last summer," said John after a while. "We joked about it a bit, the fact that Ernst had more customers than I had fish in my nets."

Gerlof merely nodded; there was nothing more to say right now. Ernst's death still felt like a great weight resting on his shoulders.

John turned onto the narrow track leading to the plateau above the quarry, and Gerlof could see the tracks of several vehicles in the mud. Ernst's and Julia's cars were up ahead, and behind them two police cars and another private car, a shiny blue Volvo. Beside it stood a man wearing a cap, his camera resting on his stomach.

"Bengt Nyberg's bought another new car," said Gerlof.

"I suppose newspaper editors earn good money," said John.

"Do they?" said Gerlof as John pulled up level with the sign CRAFT WORK IN STONE—WELCOME and switched off the engine.

Gerlof got out of the car with some difficulty; his limbs were stiff as usual, protesting at the unfamiliar movements. He balanced himself using his cane, straightened his back, and nodded at the local editor of *Ölands-Posten* for northern Öland, who was ambling toward them with his hand resting on his camera.

"The ambulance has taken him away," said Nyberg.

"We know," said Gerlof.

"I missed him too. I've taken a few pictures of the police and the big mark down there, but I don't think we'll be able to print them. The Borgholm office will decide, of course."

It sounded as if he were talking about pictures of a car that had driven into a ditch, or a broken window. Bengt had always been insensitive, thought Gerlof.

"Best not to use them," said Gerlof.

"Do you know who found him?" said Nyberg, pressing a button on the camera.

There was a whirring sound as the film rewound.

"No," said Gerlof.

He began to walk slowly toward the edge of the quarry. Where was Julia?

"Go home and write your article, Bengt," said John behind Gerlof.

"I'll do that," said Nyberg. "You'll be able to read all about it tomorrow."

He went over to his new car, got in, and started it up.

Gerlof kept walking past the house and the shed toward the quarry. When he was a few yards from the edge, a uniformed police officer came scrambling up from the quarry. He managed to get one leg up onto the edge, heaved himself up, then bent down to help another officer up, a younger colleague. Then he breathed out heavily and looked at Gerlof, who didn't recognize either of them. The policemen must be from Borgholm, or from the mainland.

"Are you relatives?" asked the older officer.

"Old friends," replied Gerlof. "His relatives live in Småland."

The police officer nodded. "There isn't much to see," he said.

"Was it an accident?"

"A work-related accident," said the police officer.

"He was moving a sculpture at the edge here," said the younger officer, pointing at the cliff edge, where there was a small hollow in the gravel. "So he was standing here, and he must have grabbed hold of it. And then . . ."

"He slipped or stumbled and fell down, and it landed on top of him," said the older one.

"It would have been very quick," said the younger officer.

Gerlof took another step forward, leaning on his cane. He could see it now.

The church tower, Ernst's biggest sculpture, was lying down in the quarry. You could clearly see where it had landed when it fell. There was a deep gash in the gravel down below.

A trace of Ernst. Gerlof looked quickly away, out over the quarry, but when he thought about how many gravestones and tombstones had been hacked out of this hillside over the years, he let his eyes gaze even further away, toward the shore and the water, and then he finally felt a little better.

Then he looked to the right along the edge of the cliff, where the other stone sculptures were lined up. Ernst had arranged them a few yards apart, but there was a wider space over there . . . Gerlof walked across.

Another sculpture had fallen down, a smaller one. He could see it down at the bottom of the quarry, a long oval shape that might have been some kind of egg or the head of a troll. Unlike the church tower, this sculpture had split into two pieces.

Gerlof turned away, slowly so that he wouldn't lose his balance on the uneven gravel, and began to make his way to the house.

"Is Julia Davidsson still here?" he asked the police officers. They had stopped to look in Ernst's shed, where hammers, wheelbarrows, and an old stone plane were jammed together with yet more sculptures of different sizes.

"She's in there with Henriksson," answered the older officer, pointing toward the house.

"Thank you."

The door of the house was ajar, so John must have gone in. Gerlof made his way laboriously up the low wooden steps. He wiped his feet on the doormat. Then he pushed open the door.

Several pairs of outdoor shoes were in his way; Gerlof had to push them aside with his cane in order to get past. There was no question of bending down and taking off his own shoes; he kept them on and continued along the narrow hallway. Framed pictures of old quarrymen with picks and spades in their hands hung along the walls.

He could hear low voices up ahead.

John was standing by the window in the big room, looking out. Julia and another uniformed police officer were sitting on the sofa; he was an older man who had politely removed his cap.

Gerlof nodded to him. "Hello, Lennart."

Lennart Henriksson had been a policeman for almost thirty-five years; he worked all over northern Öland, but lived in a house north of Marnäs, and had a local office by the harbor. His hair was gray, and he was slowly heading toward his pension. Normally his expression was rather listless and his broad shoulders were slumped in his uniform, but at the moment he was sitting up very straight next to Julia.

"Hello there, skipper," Henriksson said to Gerlof.

"Hi, Dad," said Julia quietly.

It was the first time in many years she'd used that word to him, so Gerlof knew she was unsettled. He slowly walked over and stood by the table.

"Would you like to sit down?" said Lennart.

"I'm fine, Lennart. I need a bit of exercise from time to time."

"You're looking well, Gerlof."

"Thank you."

There was a silence. Behind them John turned and left the room without a word.

"Julia was just telling me she's your daughter," said Lennart.

Gerlof nodded, and there was silence once again.

"Has the ambulance gone?" said Julia, looking at Gerlof.

"Yes . . . John and I passed it on the road."

Julia nodded. "So he's gone, then."

"Yes." He looked at Henriksson. "Was there a doctor?" he asked.

"Yes. A young one from Borgholm . . . I haven't met him before. He just confirmed what had happened."

"He said it was an accident?" said Gerlof.

"Yes. Then he left."

"But he'd been lying out in the rain overnight," said Gerlof.

"Yes," said Lennart. "It must have happened yesterday evening."

"So there wasn't any blood," said Gerlof. "I suppose all the traces had disappeared in the rain?"

He didn't really know himself why he was asking these questions or where they might lead, but he presumed he wanted to make himself look important. The need to be important is perhaps the last thing that leaves us, he thought.

"He had blood on his face," said Julia. "A little bit of blood."

Gerlof nodded. Footsteps came clomping along the hallway, and the younger of the two police officers looked into the room.

"We're done now, Lennart," he said. "We're off."

"Fine. I think I'll stay a little bit longer."

"You're the boss."

There was something respectful in the younger officer's voice, thought Gerlof. Perhaps the respect came from Lennart's many years in service, or the fact that his father had been a policeman too, and had been killed in the course of his duty.

"Drive carefully," said Henriksson; his colleague nodded and disappeared.

John was standing behind him holding a large brown leather wallet. He held it up to Gerlof and Julia and Henriksson.

"Three thousand two hundred and fifty-eight kronor, from

selling the sculptures," he said. "It was in the bottom drawer in the kitchen, underneath the plastic bags."

"You look after it, John," said Henriksson. "It would be stupid to leave that amount of money lying around here."

"I can take it, until the family divide everything up," said Gerlof, holding out his hand.

John seemed relieved to hand it over.

The room fell silent again.

"Right," said Henriksson eventually. He leaned forward and got up from the sofa with some difficulty. "I suppose I'd better make a move too."

"Thanks for . . ." Julia was still sitting on the sofa, searching for the right words. ". . . for taking the time."

"No problem." Henriksson studied her. "It isn't easy, being first on the scene of a fatal accident. It's happened to me a few times over the years, of course. You feel quite . . . lonely. Powerless."

Julia nodded. "But I feel better now."

"Good." Henriksson put his cap on. "I've got an office in Marnäs. You're welcome to call if anything comes up." He looked at John and Gerlof. "You too, of course. It's open house, just pop in. Will you lock up here?"

"We will," said Gerlof.

Lennart Henriksson nodded his goodbyes and left.

They heard a car engine start, then slowly fade into the distance.

"We'll be on our way soon too," said Gerlof to Julia. He pushed Ernst's wallet into his pocket, then looked at John. "Can we go out for a minute?" he asked. "I just wanted to show you something . . . Something I noticed outside."

"Shall I come with you?" said Julia.

"No need."

John let Gerlof lead the way when they got outside. Leaning heavily on his cane, Gerlof went out onto the steps, down onto the gravel, and round the corner of the house toward the edge of the quarry.

"What are we going to look at?" asked John.

"It's over here by the edge, something I noticed before I went inside . . . Here."

Gerlof was pointing down into the quarry where the polished stone that looked like a big egg or a misshapen head lay, split into a larger and a smaller piece.

"You recognize it, don't you?" he said to John.

John nodded slowly. "It was the one Ernst called 'the Kant stone,'" he said. "As a joke."

"It's been pushed," Gerlof went on. "Hasn't it?"

"Yes," agreed John. "It looks that way."

"It was propped up behind the house last summer," said Gerlof.

"It was standing here last week when I was here," said John. "I'm sure of that."

"Ernst pushed it over on purpose," said Gerlof.

"You're probably right."

The old friends looked at each other.

"What are you thinking?" asked John.

"I don't really know." Gerlof sighed. "I don't know. But I think Nils Kant might be back."

9

Julia made sure the two grieving old men had a cup of strong coffee. She borrowed Ernst's white porcelain with yellow Öland suns on it, and made each of them a cup in his cottage before they left, with the feeling that she was doing something useful for once. John and Gerlof sat on the sofa, talking quietly about Ernst.

Just little stories and fragments of memories, often without any particular point, about mistakes Ernst had made as a newly employed quarry worker when he first moved to Öland, or about beautiful pieces of sculpture he'd created in his workshop as an old man. Julia realized that Ernst, apart from a few years at sea on the Baltic during the war, had worked with stone all his adult life. When the quarry closed in the 1960s, Ernst had carried on alone. He took the reject stone that had been cast aside by the quarry workers and chiseled and polished and made some kind of art out of it.

"He loved this quarry," said Gerlof, looking out of the window. "I'm sure he would have bought it from Gunnar Ljunger over in Långvik if he'd had the money; he didn't want to live anywhere else. He knew everything about how different kinds of stone should be cut and split and worked."

"Ernst made the best gravestones," said John. "If you walk around Marnäs churchyard, or down in Borgholm, you can see that."

Julia sat quietly looking at a pile of old books about the local area that were lying on Ernst's coffee table. She was listening to John and Gerlof, but it was hard to forget what Ernst had looked like when she found him.

The first police officer to arrive at the scene, Lennart Henriksson, had quickly placed a blanket from his car over Ernst, and led her into the house. He'd stayed with her without saying much, and that had felt good. After the day Jens disappeared, she had heard too many empty words of consolation, words she hadn't asked for.

"Would you be able to drive me home, Julia?" asked Gerlof when both the coffee and the stories had come to an end.

"Of course."

She got up to go into the kitchen to wash up the coffee things, almost annoyed by Gerlof's question.

I found a man crushed underneath a block of stone, she thought, *with blood coming out of his mouth and eyes that had burst out of their sockets. But I've seen blood before, I've seen dead bodies. I've experienced worse.*

And as her thoughts went round and round, she suddenly remembered something that might be important, and turned back to her father.

"He had a message for you," she said. "I forgot."

Gerlof looked up.

"Ernst," she explained. "I met him at the cottage when I arrived in Stenvik, and I was supposed to tell you something . . . He said it just before he left." She stopped speaking and tried to remember. "Something about the fact that it was the thumb that was the most important, not the hand."

"The thumb was the most important?" said Gerlof.

Julia nodded. "Do you know what he meant?"

Gerlof shook his head thoughtfully. He looked at John. "Do you?"

"No idea," said John. "Is it some kind of proverb maybe?"

"That's what he said, anyway," said Julia, and went into the kitchen.

Julia and Gerlof drove back to the campsite in the Ford, and John followed them in his own car. The gray cloud cover had swept in over Kalmar Sound, and now hid the sun. The Stenvik that had been brought to life in the old men's tales, where people lived and worked all year round and where every property and every path had its own name—that Stenvik had gone back to sleep now. All the houses were empty and closed, the sails of the windmill no longer turned, and there were no eel traps laid out in the waters of the sound.

When Julia had turned in and stopped beside the mini-golf course, John parked his car and came over to them. Gerlof rolled down his window, and John looked at Julia:

"Look after your dad."

It was the first time John Hagman had spoken directly to her, she suddenly realized.

Julia nodded. "I'll try."

"Keep in touch, John," said Gerlof beside her. "Let me know if you see anyone . . . any strangers."

Strangers, thought Julia, recalling an incident from her childhood in the fifties, when a black man with a broad smile who spoke poor English and no Swedish at all had turned up in Stenvik one summer, going from house to house with a suitcase in his hand. People in the village had locked their doors and refused to open them—and when somebody finally had the courage to find out what he wanted, it turned out the man wasn't a robber at all, just a Christian from Kenya selling Bibles and hymnbooks. People didn't like strangers in Stenvik.

"We'll speak soon," said John Hagman.

Julia watched him go over toward the house and grab hold of the broom as if it were his most treasured possession. With it in his hand, he headed for the golf course and started waving his arms at his son Anders again.

"John ran the campsite for twenty-five years," Gerlof told Julia. "Now it's Anders's responsibility, but he goes around in a dream most of the time. It's still John who has to sweep and paint and keep the place from falling apart . . . He should take things easier, but he won't listen to me."

He sighed.

"That's that, then," he said. "We can drive over to the cottage now."

Julia shook her head. "I'm taking you back to Marnäs," she said.

"I'd really like to have a look at the cottage," said Gerlof. "While I've got such an excellent chauffeur."

"It's already late," said Julia. "I was thinking of going home today . . ."

"There's no rush, is there?" said Gerlof. "Gothenburg isn't going anywhere."

Afterward Julia couldn't remember whether it was she or Gerlof who'd suggested spending the night in the cottage.

Perhaps it was decided when Gerlof walked into the living room with his coat on and sank down into the room's only armchair with a deep sigh. Or perhaps when Julia went out into the street to turn on the stopcock under the lid of the well, and switched on the electricity in the kitchen. Or when she turned on the lights, put the radiators on, and made them both a cup of elderflower tea. In any event, there was an unspoken agreement between the two of them that they would spend the night in Stenvik. Julia switched on her cell phone so that Gerlof could ring the home and tell the staff what had been decided.

Afterward Gerlof took a stroll around the yard.

"No sign of rats," he reported contentedly when he came back into the house.

Julia looked around the summer cottage's small, dark rooms tentatively, as if she were in a museum. Part of her history was here, all the way back to her childhood, but it felt as if it were shut up in a glass case.

What was there to see in the cottage? Not much. Five cramped rooms, with the furniture swathed in white sheets, six narrow beds without any bed linens, a little kitchen with a window, the dead flies lying like sprawling letters against the glass. There was a bookcase in one corner. An old shipping chart of northern Öland, faded by the sun, hung on one wall, and on a bureau stood a framed black-and-white photograph from the sixties, showing a teenage Julia with a strained smile, her sister Lena beside her. Otherwise the room was almost as lacking in personal possessions as a rental cottage.

There were no rugs on the wooden floor, and it was ice-cold. And there was almost nothing left that Julia remembered from her childhood.

But there had been more personal items, and when Julia pulled out the bottom drawer of the desk in what had been her room when she was a child, she found one of them: a framed photograph of a sunburnt little boy in a white cotton top, smiling shyly at the photographer. For many years it had stood on the desk, but now somebody had hidden it away.

Julia put the photograph back where it ought to be. She studied the picture of her vanished son, and longed for red wine; a few glasses would warm her up and make her forget, make the cottage an easier place to be. But she had no intention of letting Gerlof see that she drank.

Gerlof didn't appear to notice how she was feeling; he was walking slowly around every room as if this were his real home. And it was, in a way. He had spent every summer and every weekend here after he retired, first with Ella and then alone, for as long as Julia could remember. He had stood by the gate waving when the children went back to the mainland after staying for a few weeks in the summer holidays.

It isn't summer and I must leave soon, thought Julia, standing by the door with the car keys in her hand, but what she said out loud to Gerlof was:

"Lena and I used to sleep in bunk beds when we were here . . . I had the top one."

Gerlof nodded. "There wasn't much room in the holidays when everybody was here, but nobody complained, as far as I remember."

"No. I just remember it was great having all our cousins here, all through the summers . . . The sun was always shining, as I recall," said Julia, looking at the clock. "But we'd better get to bed now . . ."

"Already?" said Gerlof, straightening the chart on the wall behind him. "Haven't you got any more questions?"

"Questions?" said Julia.

"Yes . . ." Gerlof pulled the dust sheet off an armchair in the living room and folded it up. "Just ask away," he said.

He sat down slowly, and at that moment Julia's cell phone rang in her jacket pocket out in the darkened hallway.

The digital signal sounded wrong in the silence, and she hastily went to answer it.

"Hello, Julia here."

"Hi. How's it going?" It was Lena—possibly the only person who knew Julia's number. "Have you arrived?"

"Yes . . . Well . . . Yes, I have."

What was Julia supposed to say? She caught sight of her un-easy expression reflected in the darkness of the windowpane, and realized she didn't really want to tell her sister anything about what had happened, about Jens's sandal and the death at the quarry. "Everything's fine," she said at last.

"Have you seen Gerlof?"

"Yes . . . we're at the cottage now."

"The cottage in Stenvik?" said Lena. "Surely you're not going to sleep there?"

"We are," said Julia. "We've turned on the water and the electricity."

"Dad mustn't get cold," warned Lena.

"He won't," said Julia, feeling ashamed, and then feeling ashamed because she felt ashamed. "We're just sitting and chatting . . . What was it you wanted?"

"Well . . . It's the car. Marika rang, and apparently she's going to take some drama workshop in Dalsland next weekend, so she needs the car. I said that would be fine . . . I mean, you're not stay-ing on Öland, are you?"

"I'm staying for a while longer," said Julia.

Marika was the daughter of Lena's husband Richard from his first marriage. Julia had thought the relationship between Marika and Lena was pretty bad, but clearly it was good enough now for her to be lending Julia's car to her stepdaughter.

"For how long?"

"Hard to say . . . A few days."

"Yes, but how long . . . three days?" said Lena. "So you'll bring the car back here on Sunday?"

"Monday," said Julia quickly.

Whichever weekday Lena had said, she would have added another day.

"Come early, then," said Lena.

"I'll try," said Julia. "Lena . . ."

"Great. Love to Dad. Bye, then."

"Lena . . . Was it you who put the photo of Jens in the desk drawer?" Julia asked quickly.

But Lena had already hung up.

Julia turned off her phone with a sigh.

"Who was that?" said Gerlof from his armchair.

"Your other daughter," said Julia. "She sends her love."

"Aha," said Gerlof. "Does she want you to come home?"

"Yes. She's checking up on me."

Julia sat down in the corner opposite Gerlof's armchair. Her elderflower tea with honey was lukewarm, almost cold, but she drank it anyway.

"Is she worried about you?" said Gerlof.

"A bit," said Julia.

Worried about her car, anyway, she thought.

"It's safer here than in Gothenburg," said Gerlof with a smile.

But then he seemed to remember what had happened earlier in the day over at the quarry, and his smile faded. He looked down at the floor. Julia didn't say anything either.

The air in the cottage was slowly warming up. Night was falling outside the windows; it was almost nine o'clock. Julia wondered if there were sheets in the cottage. There ought to be.

"I'm not afraid of death," said Gerlof suddenly. "I used to be when I was young and at sea, for many years—afraid of running aground and mines and storms—but now I'm too old . . . And a lot of the fear disappeared when Ella ended up in hospital. That autumn when she went blind and slowly faded away from us."

Julia nodded without speaking. She didn't want to think about her mother's death either.

Jens had been able to leave the cottage and go out into the fog that September day for two reasons. One had been the fact that Gerlof wasn't at home. And the other reason was that Jens's grandmother Ella had gone for a lie-down and fallen asleep, in the middle of the afternoon. A chronic exhaustion had crept up on Ella that summer, draining away her usual energy. It had seemed totally inexplicable, until the following year when the doctors had established that she was suffering from diabetes.

Jens had disappeared and his grandmother had lived for only

a few years after that. She had wasted away, tortured by grief and a guilty conscience at having fallen asleep that day.

"Death becomes a bit like a friend when you get old," said Gerlof. "An acquaintance, at any rate. I just want you to know that, so you won't think I can't cope with this . . . with Ernst's death."

"Good," said Julia.

But she hadn't really had time to think about how Gerlof might be feeling.

"Life goes on," said Gerlof, and drank his tea.

"In one way or another," said Julia.

There was silence for a minute or so.

"Did you want me to ask you something?" said Julia eventually.

"Yes. Ask away."

"About what?"

"Well . . . Would you like to know what that rounded sculpture was called, the one somebody knocked down into the quarry?" Gerlof looked at Julia. "That shapeless stone . . . Maybe the police officers from Borgholm asked about it? Or Lennart Henriksson?"

"No," said Julia. She thought about it. "I don't think they even saw it; they were looking further away, at the sculpture of the church tower and . . ." She stopped. "I didn't think about that stone either. Is there something special about it?"

"Maybe," said Gerlof. "It's mainly the name, though."

"So what was it called, then?"

Gerlof took a deep breath and leaned back in the armchair. He exhaled with a long drawn-out sigh.

"Ernst wasn't really very happy with it . . ." said Gerlof. "It had cracked and hadn't turned out very well, he thought. So he christened it 'the Kant stone.' After Nils Kant."

Gerlof was looking at Julia as if she ought to react, but she didn't know why.

"Nils Kant," she said.

"Have you heard that name before?" asked Gerlof. "Did anybody mention him when you were growing up?"

"Not that I remember," said Julia. "But I think I've heard the name Kant somewhere."

Her father nodded.

"The Kant family lived here in Stenvik," he told her. "Nils

was the son, the black sheep . . . but when you were born, after the war, he wasn't here anymore."

"Right."

"He'd gone away," said Gerlof.

"So what did Nils Kant do that was so terrible?" asked Julia. "Did he kill somebody?"

Nils Kant is standing with his shotgun pointing at the two foreign soldiers, his finger on the trigger. The wind and the birdsong and all the other sounds on the alvar have fallen silent. The landscape has become blurred; Nils can see only the soldiers and the double barrel of the shotgun which he is keeping trained on them all the time.

The soldiers slowly get to their feet, as if obeying an order. Their legs seem to have no strength; they grab hold of the grass to help them rise, then they raise their arms in the air. But Nils does not lower his weapon.

"What are you doing here?" he asks.

The men merely stare at him, their hands above their heads, and don't reply.

The one at the front moves back half a pace, bumps into the other one, and stops. He looks younger than the one behind him, but both their faces are covered in a mask of gray dust, smears of mud, and faint black stubble, and it's impossible to tell how old they are. The whites of their eyes are bloodshot with fine red lines, and their eyes look a hundred years old.

"Where are you from?" asks Nils.

No reply.

When Nils quickly looks down, he can't see any sign that the soldiers have a pack or any weapons with them. The knees of their gray-green uniforms are threadbare and the seams are frayed, and the soldier in front has a wide rip in the material above the knee.

Nils has his gun, but it doesn't make him feel calm. He tries to breathe in and out slowly through his nose so that his arms won't begin to shake and the gun start wobbling about all over the place. An invisible band of iron is tightening around his head just above his ears; the pain makes it impossible for him to think clearly.

"Nicht schiessen," says the soldier in front once again.

Nils doesn't understand the words, but he thinks the language sounds like Adolf Hitler's language on the radio. That means they're Germans, from the big war. How have they ended up here?

A boat, he thinks. They must have crossed the Baltic in a boat.

"You have to . . . come with me," he says.

He speaks slowly, so the soldiers will understand. He must take command here; he has a gun in his hands after all.

He nods at them.

"Do you understand what I'm saying?"

It feels good to talk, even if they don't understand. It lessens the fear and makes it possible to fight against the paralysis in his head. Nils could take them with him to Stenvik; he would be a hero. What other people in the village think doesn't matter, but his mother would be proud of him.

The soldier in front nods too, and slowly lowers his arms.

"Wir wollen nach England fahren," he says. *"Wir wollen in die Freiheit."*

Nils looks at him. The only word he understands is "England," which sounds the same as in Swedish, but he's sure the soldiers aren't English. He's more or less certain they're Germans.

The soldier at the back lowers one hand toward his pocket.

"No!"

Nils's heart is pounding, he opens his mouth.

The soldier reaches into his pocket. His hands are moving too quickly, Nils can't follow him with his eyes. He has to do something, and he says:

"Han—"

A thundering roar drowns out the rest. The shotgun jerks.

Powder smoke billows out of the barrels, obscuring the men in front of him for a moment.

It wasn't really Nils's intention to shoot, he just squeezed the shotgun a little harder so he could point with it, point upward. But the gun goes off and a hail of lead shot flies out and knocks the soldier in front to the ground as if he's been struck by a mace.

Nils sees him as a shadow behind the powder smoke, a shadow that falls and jerks and remains lying there on the grass.

The smoke drifts away, every sound disappears, but the soldier is still lying there on his side, his jacket ripped to shreds. For a few seconds his body looks completely unharmed, but then the blood begins to seep through the torn fabric like dark, spreading patches. The soldier closes his eyes; he looks as if he's dying.

"Oh shit . . ." Nils whispers to himself.

It's done. He's shot the soldier—even worse, he's shot the wrong one. It wasn't the soldier in front who put his hand in his pocket, but he's the one who's lying there bleeding on the ground.

Nils has shot a human being as if he'd been a hare; *he* shot him, nobody else.

The soldier on the ground blinks slowly, his arms are twitching slightly, and he is struggling to raise his head, but without success.

His breath is coming in short gasps, he coughs, breathes out, but never breathes in. His uniform is covered in blood. His gaze wanders all around, back and forth, and finally stops, his eyes fixed on the sky.

The other soldier is standing behind him, the one who was fumbling in his pocket, his mouth compressed into a thin line, his eyes empty. He is standing utterly still, but he is holding something between his left thumb and his index finger. Something he took out of his pocket just before the shot went off.

Not a gun, something smaller. It looks like a small dark red stone, shining and glittering, although there is no sun on the alvar.

Nils is holding the gun, the soldier is holding his little stone. Neither of them lowers his eyes.

Nils has shot someone, he has killed someone. The initial panic disappears, and an icy calm fills him. He's in control now.

Nils breathes out, takes a step toward the soldier, and nods toward the little stone.

"Give that to me," he says calmly.

10

Gerlof didn't reply to Julia's question about Nils Kant. He simply pointed over her shoulder, toward the darkness outside the window.

"The Kant family lived just down here," he said. "In the big yellow house. They'd been living there for a long time before we built this cottage."

"I remember some old woman lived there when I was little," said Julia.

"That was Nils's mother, Vera," said Gerlof. "She died at the beginning of the seventies. Before that she lived alone for many years. She was rich . . . her family owned a sawmill in Småland, and she owned a lot of land here along the coast, but I don't think she ever got any pleasure from her money. I assume her relatives are still squabbling about what's left of their inheritance, because the house is just falling apart down there. Or maybe nobody dares live there."

"Vera Kant . . ." said Julia. "I've just got a vague memory of her. She wasn't very popular, was she?"

"No, she was too bitter for that, and she bore grudges," said Gerlof. "If your grandfather had done her some injustice, she would hate your mother and you and your dog, for the rest of your life. Vera was stubborn and proud. When her husband died, she went straight back to her maiden name."

"And she never went out in the village?"

"No, Vera was a recluse," said Gerlof. "She spent most of her time sitting in her house, longing for her son."

"So what did he do?" Julia asked again.

"A lot of things . . ." said Gerlof. "When he was young, people suspected that he'd drowned his little brother down by the shore. Evidently only Nils and his brother were there when it happened, and afterward Nils swore it was an accident . . . so we'll never know the truth about that."

"Were you friends? You and Nils?"

"No, no. He was a few years younger than me, and I soon left and went to sea. So I hardly ever ran into him when he was little."

"And when he grew up?"

Gerlof almost smiled, but when it came to Nils Kant, there was nothing to smile about.

"Definitely not when he grew up," he replied. "He left the village, as I said." He raised his hand and pointed toward the narrow bookcase in the corner of the room. "There's a book about Nils Kant over there. At least it's partly about him. It's on the third shelf down, it's got a narrow yellow spine."

Julia got up and went over to the shelves. She looked and finally pulled a book out from the third shelf. She read the title.

"*Öland Crimes.*"

She looked inquiringly at Gerlof.

"That's it," he said. "A colleague of Bengt Nyberg's on the local paper wrote it a few years ago. Read it, it'll fill you in on most things."

"Okay." She looked at the clock. "But not tonight."

"No. Time for bed," said Gerlof.

"I'd like my old room," said Julia. "If that's all right."

It was. Gerlof chose the bedroom next door, the one he and Ella had shared for many years. Their old double bed was gone, but the new beds stood in the same spot. While Gerlof was in the bathroom, Julia made up one of them for him; making beds was something her father could no longer manage.

When Julia had finished and had gone into her own room, Gerlof undressed down to his long johns and T-shirt and got into bed. The mattress here was harder than he was used to nowadays.

He lay there for a while in the darkness thinking, but he no longer felt any more at home here in the cottage than he did in his room up at Marnäs. It had been a big step, admitting he was too old to manage on his own in Stenvik and moving up there, but perhaps it had been the right decision. At least he didn't have to wash dishes and make his own coffee.

Gerlof listened to the wind in the trees for a while, then he fell asleep. And at some point during the night he dreamed he was lying on a bed of hard stones over in the quarry.

The sky up above him was deep blue, the wind was blowing, but oddly enough a thin mist was still hanging above the ground.

Ernst Adolfsson was standing up on the edge of the cliff, looking out across the quarry with black eye sockets.

Gerlof opened his mouth to ask his friend if he was really the one who had pushed the sculpture down into the quarry, and if so, exactly what he'd meant by it—but a whisper made Ernst turn around.

"I killed them all."

It was Nils Kant who had whispered.

"Gerlof . . . your grandson says hello."

Nils Kant had come wandering across the alvar with his smoking shotgun, and now he was standing just around the corner of Ernst's house; soon he would come over. Gerlof lifted his head and held his breath, full of expectation; he would finally get to see what Nils Kant looked like as an adult, as an old man. Did he still have his hair? Was it gray? Did he have a beard?

But it was Ernst who turned and disappeared around the side of the house instead, slipping slowly away in the mist like a silent ghost ship. Gerlof called after him, but Ernst was gone.

The grief he felt over Ernst was crippling when Gerlof finally awoke.

"Turn left," said Gerlof to Julia in the car the following morning.

Julia looked at him, then braked.

"We're going to Marnäs, aren't we?" she asked. "Back to the home?"

"Soon. Not just yet," said Gerlof. "I thought we might have a coffee here in Stenvik first."

Julia studied him a few seconds longer, then turned left. They rolled back down toward the road above the water. Gerlof automatically glanced over to his boathouse to make sure no windows were broken.

"Left again," he said, pointing to a house on the coast road. "That's where we're going."

Julia braked and turned across the road without checking whether anything was coming toward them, or even looking in her rearview mirror.

"An old woman lives here," she said as she pulled up in front of the house. "I saw her the day before yesterday . . . She was out with her dog."

"She's not that old," said Gerlof. "I'd say Astrid Linder is only about sixty-seven, or maybe sixty-eight. She's only recently retired . . . she was a doctor down in Borgholm for many years. But she grew up here."

"And she lives in Stenvik all year round?"

"She does now. I moved out of my summer cottage, but Astrid did the opposite when she was widowed. She moved into hers." Gerlof opened the door, felt the pain in his limbs as he twisted in his seat, and sighed. "Of course, she's a bit fitter than me."

Gerlof managed to swing his legs out, but Julia had to go round and help him to his feet. He gave her a brief nod of thanks and they walked toward the house.

"When I'm back in Stenvik, I pretend there are people living in all the houses all year round," Gerlof said, looking around. "Sometimes I think the curtains move in the cottages. You can see shadows strolling along the village road, just small movements out of the corner of your eye . . . You can see ghosts most clearly out of the corner of your eye."

Julia didn't reply.

There was a wooden gate in the low wall, and Julia opened it. The garden inside was empty, but furnished. On a low limestone terrace in front of the house, four white plastic chairs stood around a small plastic table, and beside them stood a little gray porcelain gnome wearing a green hood and gazing out over the inlet with a fixed smile.

Even before they'd got as far as ringing the doorbell, the sound of excited barking could be heard from inside the house.

"Quiet, Willy!" shouted a woman's voice, but the dog took no notice.

When the door opened, it came hurtling out like a little brown and white bolt of lightning, dashing around Julia's and Gerlof's legs; he had to hang on to her to avoid losing his balance.

"Calm down, you stupid dog!" shouted Astrid again.

She appeared in the doorway, small and white-haired, and, in Gerlof's eyes, very beautiful.

"Hello, Astrid."

Astrid grabbed hold of the fox terrier's leash, held on tight, and looked up.

"Hello, Gerlof, are you back at home?" Then she saw Julia, and asked quickly, "Goodness—have you brought a new girlfriend with you?"

Despite the fact that the sun was shining, the autumn wind sweeping in across the island was persistent and bitterly cold. But still Astrid Linder set the table for morning coffee out on the terrace, fetched a blanket which she wrapped around Gerlof, and put on a thick green woolen sweater.

"I need a sweater," said Gerlof.

"No you don't. It's nice and fresh out here," said Astrid, bringing out the coffee and a plate of cakes—nothing homemade, just four shop-bought muffins. Astrid wasn't fond of baking. She poured the coffee and settled down.

Gerlof had introduced Julia as his youngest daughter; she and Astrid had said hello, chatted a little about Willy's tremendous energy, and watched the dog gradually calm down and settle under the table. None of them had mentioned Ernst.

Gerlof didn't think Astrid remembered who Julia was, so he was surprised when she suddenly said quietly:

"You probably don't remember me, Julia, but . . . I was there on that day, searching along the shore. My husband was there too."

Gerlof saw Julia stiffen on the opposite side of the table; she slowly opened her mouth and searched for the right words.

"Thank you," she said eventually. "I don't remember . . . Everything was so mixed up that day."

"I know, I know." Astrid nodded and drank her coffee. "Everybody was running around all over the place. The police sent boats out into the sound, but nobody knew where they were supposed to be going. One group of villagers was sent southward along the water's edge, and we went north with another group. We walked and walked along the shore and looked in the water and underneath all the boats that had been pulled up onto the shore, and behind every single rock. In the end it got dark and we couldn't see anything anymore, not even a hand in front of our faces . . . so we had to turn back. It was terrible."

"Yes," said Julia, gazing down into her cup. "Everybody searched that evening. Until it got dark."

"It was so dreadful," said Astrid. "And he was neither the first nor the last to disappear in the sound."

There was silence around the coffee table. The wind was blowing gently. Willy sneezed and shuffled uneasily at Astrid's feet.

"The boy's sandal has been found," said Gerlof after a moment.

He was looking at Astrid, but he glimpsed Julia's surprised expression out of the corner of his eye.

"I see," said Astrid. "Was it in the water?"

"No," said Gerlof. "On land. Somebody must have had it for all these years, but so far we don't know who."

"Goodness," said Astrid. "But wasn't it . . . didn't he drown?"

Julia put down her coffee cup, but didn't speak.

"Apparently not," said Gerlof. "It's complicated . . . We don't really know much yet."

"That man you mentioned yesterday, Gerlof," said Julia. "Nils Kant. Might he know something about Jens? Is that what you think?"

"Nils Kant?" said Astrid, looking at Gerlof. "Why are you talking about him?"

"I just happened to mention him yesterday."

Julia looked uncertainly from Astrid to Gerlof, as if she'd said something inappropriate. "I just thought . . . that maybe he was involved. Since he'd obviously caused problems before."

Astrid sighed. "I thought Nils Kant had been forgotten by now," she said. "When he left Stenvik—"

"He is forgotten, by and large," Gerlof broke in. "The fact that Julia had never even heard of him until yesterday proves that, if nothing else."

"He was a year or so older than me," Astrid went on, "but we were still in the same class up at the junior school. And he always seemed to be in a bad mood, I never once saw him looking happy. He was always fighting, and he was a big lad. We girls were afraid of him . . . and so were the boys. Nils was always the one who started a fight, but he always blamed somebody else."

"I missed him in school, I was older than Kant," said Gerlof, "but John Hagman told me about the fights."

"Then he started working in the quarry the family owned," said Astrid, "but that didn't go too well either."

"There was a fight there too. A stevedore nearly drowned." Gerlof shook his head. "Do you remember one of the boats they used to transport the stone caught fire the night after Nils finished there, Astrid? *Isabell,* she was called. She'd been blown into the harbor over at Långvik, and the captain was woken by the fire on board. They only just managed to tow her out past the jetty before she went up. 'Spontaneous combustion' they said at the hearing, but here in Stenvik plenty of people thought Nils Kant was responsible. And that was when it all started."

Julia looked at him inquiringly. "When what started?"

"Well . . . Nils Kant became Stenvik's very own scapegoat," he answered. "Anything bad that happened was blamed on him."

"Not everything," objected Astrid. "Just all the crimes. Fires and thefts and injured animals . . ."

"Accidents too," said Gerlof. "If the windmill sails split or nets broke or boats slipped their moorings and drifted away . . ."

"He deserved all the suspicion," declared Astrid. "And he proved it."

"He had his own story," said Gerlof. "A strict father who died when he was little, and a mother who constantly told Nils he was better than everybody else in the village. It wasn't a healthy up-bringing."

Astrid nodded, but remained silent and pensive for a few moments before asking quietly:

"I heard about the accident on the local radio yester-day . . . When's the funeral, Gerlof?"

She'd quickly changed the subject, he noticed. Unless Astrid too realized that there was some kind of connection between Nils Kant and Ernst's death.

"On Wednesday, as far as I know," he said. "I spoke to John on the telephone this morning, and that's what he thought."

"And it'll be in Marnäs church?"

"Yes," said Ernst, picking up his coffee cup. "Even if it was that bloody church tower that did for him in the end."

"Ernst was always so careful," said Astrid. "I can't understand what he was doing at the cliff edge."

Gerlof shook his head, but said nothing.

"Is that everybody?" asked Julia after their visit to Astrid, when they were in the car on the way back to Marnäs.

"Everybody?" said Gerlof.

"Everybody who lives in Stenvik. Have we met everybody who lives there now?"

"More or less," said Gerlof. "All the real Stenvik people. There are a few who come over on weekends from Borgholm and Kalmar. Probably fifteen or twenty altogether. I don't really know them very well."

"What's it like in the summer?"

"Busy," said Gerlof. "It's packed with summer visitors here . . . hundreds of them. We just get more and more tourists. They keep on building and building. And there are just as many over on John's campsite every week. We end up with almost more people than actually lived here when I was little. But it's even worse over in Långvik, where they've got the marina and the beach hotel."

"I remember what it's like in the summer," said Julia.

Gerlof sighed. "I shouldn't complain. They come over from the mainland with money, after all."

"But it's difficult to know who's who," said Julia, braking to turn off toward Marnäs.

"It's impossible in the summer," Gerlof pointed out. "It gets just like the city where you live, people can come and go as they want."

"They can do that in the autumn too," said Julia. "I mean, there's nobody down in Stenvik who can see—"

She suddenly stopped, as if something had occurred to her.

"Astrid usually keeps an eye open," said Gerlof. Then he noticed Julia's silence. "What is it?"

"I just remembered . . . Ernst said he was expecting a visitor. When I met him at our cottage the day before yesterday. He said,

'You're welcome to come and have a look at my sculptures, but not tonight because I'm expecting a visitor.' Or something like that."

"Is that what he said?" said Gerlof, gazing thoughtfully through the windshield.

"Is this about him too . . . this Nils Kant?"

"Maybe."

There was silence in the car. They drove past Marnäs church, and Gerlof was reminded of Ernst's impending funeral. He wasn't looking forward to it.

"You know more than you're willing to tell me," said Julia after a while.

"A bit more," said Gerlof quietly. "Not much. We have a few theories, John and I."

Of course, Ernst had had a number of theories too, he thought sadly.

"This isn't a game," said Julia, a little sharply. "Jens is my son."

"I know that." Gerlof wished he could ask her to stop talking about Jens as if he were still alive. "And I'll tell you what I think, soon."

"Why did you tell Astrid about the sandal?" said Julia.

"To spread the news," said Gerlof. "Astrid's bound to pass it on, she's good at that." He looked at Julia. "Did you tell the police about the sandal yesterday?"

"No . . . I had other things on my mind. And why should we tell people about it?"

"Well . . . it might bring something out. Bring somebody out."

"Bring who out?"

"You never know," said Gerlof as they arrived at the residential home.

Julia helped him out of the car again.

"What are you going to do now?" he asked.

"I don't know . . . I might go over to the church."

"Good idea. There's a lantern on Ella's grave; you can take a candle to put in it. I've got one up in my room."

"Okay," said Julia, going to the door with him.

"And you can have a look around the churchyard too. When you've lit the candle on your mother's grave, go over to the left-hand wall of the church and have a look at the graves there."

"Right. Why?" said Julia, pressing the button that opened the outside door of the residential home.

"You'll know when you see it," said Gerlof.

11

Julia was standing in Marnäs churchyard looking down at Nils Kant's grave.

It lay over by the west wall, the last in a long row of graves. The name NILS KANT was etched into the gravestone, and the dates 1925–1963. The headstone was small and unassuming, an ordinary piece of limestone that had probably come from the quarry down in Stenvik. Perhaps Ernst Adolfsson had hewn it out. It was over thirty years old, and patches of white lichen had begun to cover the top.

There was dry, yellow grass growing over the grave, but no flowers.

Julia had been wondering why nobody had mentioned Nils Kant as a suspect when Jens went missing. To provide an answer, Gerlof had sent her here, to the deserted churchyard outside Marnäs—and now she could see that Nils Kant couldn't have had anything to do with Jens's disappearance. In 1972 Kant had been dead for almost ten years. The answer to her question was carved into the stone.

So. Another dead end.

Two yards away was another gravestone, also made of limestone, but this one was taller and broader. Names and dates were carved into it: KARL-EINAR ANDERSSON 1889–1935 and VERA ANDERSSON B. KANT 1897–1972. In smaller letters below these names was another one: AXEL THEODOR KANT 1929–1936. That was Nils Kant's little brother who had drowned, and whose body had been lost in the sound.

Just as Julia was about to turn and leave the churchyard, she caught sight of something small and white fluttering behind the stone on Nils Kant's grave. She stopped, took a couple of steps, and bent down.

A white envelope was stirring slightly in the breeze, wedged in between the stems of a couple of dried-up roses.

Somebody had placed the roses behind the gravestone not very long ago, Julia realized, because they still had their dry, dark red petals. When she picked up the envelope, she could feel it was damp. If something had been written on it, the ink had been washed away by the rain.

She looked around. The churchyard was still completely deserted. The white church rose up fifty yards or so away, but the door had been locked when Julia tried it, and nobody was moving behind the narrow church windows.

Quickly she stuffed the envelope in her coat pocket and turned her back on the grave.

She went back to her mother's grave, brushed aside a yellow birch leaf that had blown down onto it during the few minutes she'd been away, and bent down to check that the candle in the little lantern was still burning. It was.

Then she went back to the car to drive the short distance into the center of Marnäs.

When Julia was little, a trip from the summer cottage to Marnäs on the eastern side of the island had been a real adventure. There wasn't just one kiosk here, there were *shops*. You could buy toys.

As she drove into the little village now she was mainly grateful for the fact that you could park free of charge—a big advantage over Gothenburg. You could park outside the ICA supermarket, along the short main street, and down by the harbor. Julia chose the harbor. There was a little bar there, the Moby Dick Restaurant & Pub, and the tables by the windows were all empty, just half an hour or so before lunchtime.

There were neither pleasure boats nor fishing boats in the little harbor. Julia got out of the car and went over to the empty concrete jetty that pointed out toward the horizon. She stood there for a few minutes gazing out over the gray sea, its surface crinkled with ripples. Nothing could be seen on the horizon. Beyond it somewhere to the northeast lay Gotland, and on the other side of the Baltic was Eastern Europe, and the old/new countries that had broken away from the Soviet Union—Estonia, Latvia, and Lithuania. A world Julia had never visited.

She turned away and walked along the main street without meeting a soul. She went past a small clothes shop and a flower shop, then came to a cash machine, where she stopped to take out three hundred kronor. The receipt showed that she was short of money as usual, and she quickly crumpled it up.

Above the next door hung a metal sign that said ÖLANDS-POSTEN. In smaller letters underneath it said: *The daily newspaper for the whole of northern Öland.*

Julia hesitated for a few seconds, then went in.

A little brass bell tinkled above her head as she opened the door. Inside was a small room where the light was good but the air was terrible—it stank of stale cigarette smoke. There was an empty reception desk by the entrance, and behind it an office with two desks covered in newspapers and papers. Two men, not exactly young, sat at humming computers; one of the men had gray hair, the other had no hair at all, and both wore jeans and shirts that needed ironing. There was a nameplate on the bald man's desk: LARS T. BLOHM. There was no plate on the gray-haired man's desk, but Julia recognized him as Bengt Nyberg, the reporter who had been on the scene so quickly over at the quarry. Lennart Henriksson had told her who he was.

On the wall hung a long series of news placards; the one on the far left said TRAGIC FATAL ACCIDENT AT QUARRY in thick black letters.

Weren't all fatal accidents tragic?

"Can I help you?" Bengt Nyberg didn't appear to recognize her; he was peering at Julia through a pair of thick reading glasses as she came over to the desk. "Was it about an advert?"

"No," said Julia, who didn't really know why she'd come in at all. "I was just passing . . . I'm living down in Stenvik at the moment and . . . My son has disappeared."

She blinked. Why had she said that?

"Right," said Nyberg. "But this isn't the police station. That's next door."

"Thank you," said Julia, feeling her pulse rate increase, as if she'd said something embarrassing.

"Or do you want us to write about it?"

"No," said Julia quickly. "I'll go to the police."

"When did he disappear?" asked the other man, Lars Blohm. He had a deep, gruff voice. "What time was it? Was it here in Marnäs?"

"No. It didn't happen today," said Julia. She could feel her face getting redder and redder, as if she were standing there lying to the two newspapermen. "I have to go now. Thank you." She could feel their eyes on the back of her neck as she quickly turned and left the office.

Out on the sidewalk she took a shaky breath in the cold air, and tried to relax. Why on earth had she gone there at all? Why had she mentioned Jens? She wasn't used to meeting people she didn't know. And it was even worse in a small place like this, where everybody knew everybody else and a new visitor was instantly noticed and became the subject of gossip. She longed for Gothenburg, where people treated each other like trees in the forest and met on the sidewalks without so much as a glance.

In order to escape from the blank windows of *Ölands-Posten,* she took a few steps, and noticed another sign next to the newspaper office: POLICE, with the blue and yellow police shield above it.

A note was taped to the door beneath the sign. Julia went up the two steps to the door to read it.

Station manned Wednesdays 10–12, it said on the note in black ink.

It was Friday, so the station was closed. What happened if a crime was committed in Marnäs on a day other than Wednesday? There was no note to answer that question.

She looked at the window and saw a shadow moving about inside.

She walked down the steps and just at that moment the door rattled. A key turned, and Lennart Henriksson appeared in the doorway. He was smiling.

"I saw I had a visitor," he told her. "How are you feeling today?"

"Hi," she said. "I'm fine . . . I didn't think there was anybody here. I read the sign . . ."

"I know, I have to be here for two hours on Wednesdays," said Lennart. "But I'm here at other times too. Although that's a secret—I get more done that way. Come in."

He was wearing a black uniform jacket with a police radio and a revolver in his belt, so she asked, "Are you on your way out?"

"I was going for lunch, but come in for a minute."

He stepped aside to let Julia in.

The room inside looked older than the newspaper office she'd just visited, but it was clean and neat with plants on the windowsill, and there was no smell of stale cigarette smoke. There was just one desk, facing the door, with all the paperwork in tidy piles. A computer, a fax machine, and a telephone were neatly arranged. Above a shelf full of files was a poster with a drawing of a telephone, advertising the police narcotics helpline. On another wall was a big map of northern Öland.

"Nice office," said Julia.

Lennart Henriksson liked everything neat and tidy, and that pleased her.

"Do you think so?" asked Lennart. "It's been here for over thirty years."

"Are you the only one who works here?"

"At the moment, yes. In the summer there are usually more of us, but at this time of year it's just me. There are more and more cutbacks all the time." He looked around the room with a gloomy expression, and added, "We'll see how long this place is allowed to stay open."

"Is it going to close?"

"Maybe. The big bosses are always talking about it, to save money," said Lennart. "Everything should be consolidated in Borgholm, according to them; that will be the best and cheapest arrangement. But I hope I can stay here until I retire in a few years." He looked at Julia. "Have you had lunch?"

"No."

Julia shook her head, thought about it, and realized she was actually quite hungry.

"Shall we eat together?" said Lennart.

"Yes . . . okay."

She couldn't come up with any reason for saying no.

"Great. We'll go over to Moby Dick . . . I'll just shut down the computer and put the answering machine on."

Five minutes later Julia was back by the little harbor, together with Lennart. They went into the best restaurant in Marnäs—both the best and only one in the village, he'd explained.

The décor inside was inspired by the sea, with shipping charts and fishing nets and old, cracked wooden oars hanging on the dark wood-paneled walls. Half the tables were occupied by customers eating lunch, and the room was filled with the low hum of conversation and the sound of dishes clattering in the kitchen. A few curious faces turned toward Julia as she walked in, but Lennart went first as if to protect her and chose a table by the window set slightly apart, with a view over the Baltic.

When had Julia last eaten in a restaurant? She couldn't remember. It felt very strange to sit down at a table in a room full of strangers, but she made an effort to breathe calmly and to meet Lennart's gaze across the table.

"Good afternoon. Welcome."

A man with a huge belly, his shirtsleeves rolled up, came over and handed them two leather-bound menus.

"Hi, Kent," said Lennart, taking the menus.

"And what would you like to drink on a beautiful day like today?"

"I'll have a light beer," said Lennart.

"Iced water, please," said Julia.

Her first impulse was of course to order red wine, preferably a whole carafe, but she suppressed it. She was going to get through this sober. It wasn't dangerous, people had lunch in restaurants all over the world every single day.

"Today's special is lasagna," said Kent.

"Fine by me," said Lennart.

"Me too."

Julia nodded and caught a glimpse of a broad tattoo, dark green and blurred with age, on Kent's upper arm just beneath the sleeve as he reached over for the menus. It looked like letters in some kind of frame. A name? The name of a ship?

"Salad and coffee are included in the price," he said, disappearing into the kitchen.

Lennart got up to fetch some salad, and Julia went with him.

"Lennart!" a man's voice called out from the other side of the room as they were on their way back to the table. "Lennart!"

The police officer sighed quietly.

"Back in a minute," he told Julia in a low voice, turning toward the man who had called him; he was an elderly man with a red, shiny face, wearing some kind of blue farm overalls. Julia sat down at their table and watched the man gesturing wildly, telling Lennart something with a determined expression on his face. Lennart gave him some kind of answer, quietly and briefly, and the man started waving his arms about again.

Lennart came back to the table after a few minutes and had just sat down when Kent arrived with two plates full of bubbling hot lasagna.

Lennart sighed again. "Sorry about that," he said to Julia.

"It's fine."

"He's had a break-in in his barn and somebody's taken a petrol container," he went on. "When you're a country policeman, you're always on duty, you never have any problems deciding what to do in your spare time. Anyway, let's eat."

He bent over the lasagna.

Julia started eating too. She was suddenly hungry now and the lasagna was good, with plenty of meat.

As his plate gradually emptied, Lennart took a sip of his beer and leaned back.

"So you're here visiting your dad?" he asked. "Not to lie in the sun and swim?"

Julia smiled and shook her head. "No," she said, "although Öland is lovely in the autumn too."

"Gerlof seems well," remarked Lennart. "Except for the rheumatism."

"Yes . . . He has Sjögren's syndrome. It's some kind of rheumatic pain in the joints that comes and goes. But there's nothing wrong with his mind. And he can still build ships in bottles."

"Yes, they're quite beautiful . . . I've kept meaning to order one for the police station, but I've never got round to it."

There was a silence again. Lennart emptied his glass and asked quietly:

"And what about you, Julia? Are you all right now?"

"Oh yes . . ." said Julia quickly. It was a lie to some extent, one she was accustomed to telling, but then she realized Lennart might genuinely be interested, and asked, "You mean . . . after yesterday?"

"Well, yes," said Lennart, "partly that. But I was thinking about what happened a long time ago as well . . . over twenty years ago."

"Oh," said Julia.

Lennart knew about it. Of course he did, what had she been thinking? He'd been a police officer here for thirty years, he'd told her that. And just like Astrid, he'd dared to bring up the forbidden topic, calmly and cautiously—a topic her sister had long ago grown tired of, and which several of Julia's relatives had never dared to mention.

"Were you . . . involved?" she asked quietly.

Lennart looked down at the table, hesitating, as if the question had evoked unpleasant memories.

"Yes, I was involved in the search," he said at last. "I was one of the first officers on the scene down in Stenvik . . . I sent people out in search parties along the shore. We were out there all evening; the search was called off an hour or so after midnight. When a child disappears, nobody wants to give up looking . . ."

Julia remembered Astrid Linder saying almost the same thing, and she looked down at the table. She had no intention of starting to cry, not in front of a police officer.

"Sorry," she said to Lennart a second later, as the tears came.

"There's nothing to apologize for," said Lennart. "I've cried too, sometimes."

His voice was low and calm, like the still surface of a pool. Julia blinked and concentrated on his serious face in order to keep her gaze clear. She wanted to say something, anything.

"Gerlof," she said, clearing her throat, "doesn't believe that Jens, my son . . . he doesn't believe he drowned."

Lennart looked at her.

"I see" was all he said.

"He's . . . he's found a shoe," said Julia. "A little sandal, a boy's sandal. Like the one Jens had on when he . . ."

"A shoe?" Lennart was still looking at her. "A boy's sandal. Have you seen it?"

Julia nodded.

"And did you recognize it?"

"Yes . . . maybe." Julia picked up her glass of water. "I was sure about it at first . . . but now I don't really know. It was a long time ago. You think you'll never forget certain things, but you do."

"I'd like to see it," said Lennart.

"I'm sure that'll be fine." She didn't know what Gerlof would make of this, getting the police involved, but it didn't really matter. Jens was *her* son. "Do you think it might mean something?" she asked.

"I don't think we should get our hopes up," said Lennart. He finished off his lasagna and added, "So Gerlof's turned private eye in his old age?"

"Private eye . . . yes, maybe." Julia sighed; it was actually good to talk about this with someone other than Gerlof. "He's got a load of theories, or whatever you like to call them. Vague hypotheses . . . I don't really know what he thinks. He's told me the sandal was sent to him in an envelope through the mail, with no sender's address, and he's been talking about a man called Kant who–"

"Kant?" Lennart interrupted. He was completely still now. "Nils Kant? Is that what he said?"

"Yes," said Julia. "He was from Stenvik, but he wasn't living there when I was born. I was over in the churchyard today and I saw–"

"He's buried in Marnäs churchyard," Lennart interrupted again.

"Yes, I saw the gravestone," said Julia.

The policeman in front of her was staring out the window at the sparkling water. His shoulders drooped, and he suddenly looked very tired again.

"Nils Kant . . . He just refuses to die."

ÖLAND, MAY 1945

A fat, green, shimmering fly comes buzzing across the alvar in the sunshine. It zigzags through the air between juniper bushes and plants, and finally lands heavily in the center of an outstretched palm. The fly's wings stop moving, and it extends its legs and holds on tight, ready to take off at the least sign of danger, but the hand lies motionless on the grass.

Nils Kant is still standing there with his shotgun raised, looking at the fly resting its wings on the German soldier's hand.

The soldier is lying on his back on the grass. His eyes are open, his face is turned to the side, and it's almost possible to believe that he's looking at the fly in surprise. But half the soldier's neck and his left shoulder have been blasted away by Nils's shot, the blood has soaked the jacket of his uniform, and the soldier can't see anything.

Nils breathes out and listens.

Without even the buzzing of the fly, there is absolute silence on the alvar, even though Nils's ears are still ringing slightly from the two blasts of the shotgun. The shots must have echoed far and wide, but Nils doesn't think anyone has heard them. There are no tracks nearby, and people seldom venture this far out onto the alvar. Nils feels very calm.

After the first shot, after the *what-was-that?* shot that felled the first German, it was as if two invisible hands had taken hold of his shaking shoulders and steadied them. The blood had stopped pounding in his fingers, his hands had stopped shaking, and he had felt more secure than ever as he pointed the Husqvarna shotgun at the other German. His gaze was direct, his finger just nudging the trigger, the barrel's aim steady. If this was war, or almost war, it was a lot like hunting hares.

"Give that to me," he said again.

He reached out his hand and the German understood. With a cautious flick of his hand, he passed over the little sparkling gemstone he had been holding.

Nils closed his fingers around the stone without looking down or lowering the gun and pushed it into his back pocket. He nodded to himself and slowly curled his finger around the trigger.

The German raised his hands helplessly and realized at that moment how hopeless the situation was; he bent his knees and opened his mouth, but Nils had no intention of listening to him.

"Heil Hitler," he said quietly, and fired the shotgun.

A final explosion and then silence. It was that simple.

Now both of the soldiers are lying there beside the juniper bushes, one half-thrown backwards with his back arched, lying on top of the other one. The fly crawls up the index finger of the soldier on top, extends its wings, and takes off without any effort whatsoever. Nils follows it with his eyes until it flies around a big juniper bush and is gone.

Nils takes a step forward, places one boot against the soldier on top, and pushes. The body slowly slides off the soldier underneath and settles on the grass. That looks better. He could arrange the soldiers even more nicely, like for a real wake, but that will have to do.

Nils looks at the bodies. The soldiers look old, but they are his own age, and as they lie there he wonders again who they are.

Where do they come from? He didn't understand them, but he's fairly sure they were speaking German. Their uniforms are muddy and ragged, with frayed seams and worn, shiny knees. Neither has a gun, but the one who was lying on top had a green cloth bag over his shoulder which was thrown to one side when he fell. Nils hadn't noticed it until now.

He bends down and picks up the bag, which is dry and almost completely free of blood. He opens the flap and sees a whole pile of different objects: a couple of cans with no labels, a small knife with a worn wooden handle, a bundle of letters tied up with string, half a loaf of dry black bread. A few bits of rope, a couple of grubby brown bandages, a small compass made of unpolished brass.

Nils takes out the knife and puts it in his pocket, as a memento. It probably isn't worth anything.

There's something else in the bag too: a little metal box, slightly smaller than the butt of a gun. Nils picks it up; something rattles inside. He presses it with his thumb and opens the lid.

The box is full of sparkling gemstones. He tips them out into his hand, feeling their hardness and their polished surfaces. Some are as small as gunshot, some as big as teeth, more than twenty altogether. And next to them is something bigger, wrapped in a piece of green cloth. He takes it out and opens up the fabric.

It's a crucifix made of pure gold, as big as the palm of his hand, with a row of glittering red gemstones inlaid in the gold. Beautiful. He looks at the cross for a long time, before wrapping the cloth around it again.

Nils closes the lid of the box and drops his spoils of war in his rucksack. He closes the bag and places it beside its dead owner. There really isn't anything more he can do here. He ought to bury the soldiers, of course, but he has nothing to dig with.

The bodies can lie where they are, protected by the bushes, then maybe he can come back with a proper shovel another day. But he reaches out and closes their eyes, so they at least won't have to lie there staring up at the sky.

Then he straightens his back; it's time to go home. He shrugs on his rucksack, lifts the shotgun, still warm and smelling of powder, and sets off westward toward Stenvik. The sun is shining between the clouds.

After fifty steps or so he turns around for a moment and looks back over the bright grassy plain. The hollow among the juniper bushes is in the shade and the soldiers' green uniforms melt into the landscape, but a motionless white hand is sticking up out of the grass, clearly visible between the crooked trunks of the junipers.

Nils keeps on walking. He starts wondering what he's going

to tell his mother, how he's going to explain the drops of blood on his trousers. He wants to tell her everything, not to have any secrets about what he does out on the alvar, but sometimes he feels there are things she doesn't really want to hear about. Perhaps his battle with the soldiers is one of those things. He needs to think about that.

And so he thinks, but doesn't come up with a good answer. And now he's getting close to the road that leads down to Stenvik. It's deserted, and he walks on.

No, the road is not completely deserted. Somebody is coming toward him just where the road curves, a few hundred yards from the first houses in the village.

Nils's first impulse is to hide, but all he can see behind him are small, stunted juniper bushes. And anyway, why should he run and hide? He's just been part of something big out there on the alvar, something earth-shattering, and he has no need to be afraid of anyone anymore.

Nils stops behind the stone wall a few yards from the village road and watches the figure as it approaches.

Suddenly he sees that it's Maja Nyman.

Maja, the girl from Stenvik that he's looked at and thought about, but never spoken to. He can't talk to her now either, but she's getting closer and closer, smiling as if this were just an ordinary summer's day. She's seen Nils, and although she doesn't increase her pace, it seems to him that she straightens her back, lifts her chin a bit, and sticks out her chest.

Nils stands beside the road as if he were frozen to the spot, and watches Maja stop on the other side of the low stone wall.

She looks at him. He looks back at her but can find no words, not even to say hello. The silence is made all the more unbearable by the joyous song of a nightingale rising from the ditch along by the wall.

In the end Maja opens her mouth.

"Have you shot something, Nils?" she asks cheerfully.

He almost reels backwards at the question. At first he thinks Maja knows everything, but then he realizes she isn't talking about the soldiers. He has a shotgun; he's usually carrying the hares he's shot when he gets back to the village.

He shakes his head. "No," he says. "No hares." He takes a step backwards, feeling the weight of the little metal box in his rucksack, and says, "I have to . . . go now. To my mother, in the village."

"Aren't you taking the village road?" asks Maja.

"No." Nils is still moving backwards. "I can get there quicker across the alvar."

The words are coming more and more easily; he can actually talk to Maja Nyman. He'll talk to her some more another day, but not today.

"Bye, then," he says, and turns away without waiting for an answer.

He can sense that she is standing there watching him, and he walks directly away from the village road, counting up to two hundred steps, then he turns off and heads back down toward the village.

The whole time he can hear the faint rattle of the metal box moving around in the bottom of his rucksack, and he realizes he daren't take it home with him. He must be careful with his spoils of war.

After a few hundred steps more, when the village road has disappeared behind the juniper bushes, a little pile of stones appears in front of him.

The old memorial cairn. It's a marker Nils almost always walks past on his way to and from Stenvik, but now he goes over to it and stops. He looks at the pile of large and small stones, thinks for a moment, and looks around.

The alvar is completely deserted. The only sound is the wind.

An idea is growing within him, and he shrugs off the rucksack and sets it down. He takes out the box containing the gemstones, holds it in his hand, and stands right beside the cairn.

Almost directly to the east lies Marnäs church. Nils can see the church tower sticking up, like a little black arrow on the horizon. He orientates himself by the church tower, positions himself as if he were standing at attention, and takes a big stride away from the cairn. Then he begins to dig.

He lifts the top layer of turf in small pieces and then digs

down into the ground with his hands and the German's little knife.
The rock isn't far below the surface here; the layer of soil is shallow all over the alvar.

Nils scrapes away the soil to make the hole bigger, hacking
and digging and looking around him all the time.

When he has made a broad hole in the ground, about a foot
deep, Nils has already hit the rock, but it's deep enough. He takes
the metal box and places it carefully in the bottom of the hole,
then lifts several flat stones from the cairn and builds a little vault
around it. He quickly fills in the hollow, packing the soil down as
hard as he can with the palm of his hand.

He devotes most of his time to replacing the pieces of turf on
top of the soil—it's important that everything looks the same as
usual around the cairn.

It takes a long time to get the turf right, but in the end he gets
up and looks at the spot from different directions. The ground
looks untouched, he thinks, but his hands are dirty when he puts
his rucksack back on.

He sets off toward home again.

He'll tell his mother about the encounter with the Germans,
he decides, but he'll tell her carefully so she doesn't get worried.
He won't tell her about the gemstones he's hidden. Not yet, that
will be a surprise for her. Right now the spoils of war are hidden
treasure that only he knows about.

He finally climbs over the stone wall and is back on the village road, but closer to the village than when he met Maja. He's
almost back in Stenvik.

Before he reaches home, two men in heavy boots come up
onto the road from the sea and trudge past him. They are eel
fishermen, carrying a freshly tarred hoop net between them, their
hands blackened.

Neither of them says hello; both look away when they are
passing Nils. He doesn't remember their names, but it doesn't
matter. Their rudeness doesn't matter either.

Nils Kant is bigger than them; he's bigger than the whole of
Stenvik. Today he has proved that, during the battle out on the
alvar.

It's almost dusk. He opens the gate to his own house and goes into the silent garden, striding proudly up the stone path. The empty garden is flourishing and turning green. The grass scents the air.

Everything looks just as it did this morning when he left home to hunt for hares—but Nils himself is a new person.

12

Lennart Henriksson was standing next to Gerlof's desk, weighing the plastic bag containing the little sandal in his hand, as if its weight might reveal if it was genuine or not. The fact that the shoe had turned up didn't seem to please him at all.

"You need to tell the police about things like this, Gerlof," he said.

"I know," said Gerlof.

"Something like this needs to be reported straightaway."

"Yes, yes," said Gerlof quietly. "I just didn't get round to it. But what do you think?"

"About this?" The policeman looked at the sandal. "I don't know, I don't jump to conclusions. What do you think?"

"I think we should have been looking in other places, not in the water," said Gerlof.

"But we did, Gerlof," said Lennart. "Don't you remember? We searched in the quarry and all the cottages and boathouses and sheds in the village, and I drove all over the alvar. We didn't find a thing. But if Julia says it's his shoe, then we have to take this seriously."

"I *think* it's Jens's sandal," said Julia behind him.

"And it came in the mail?" asked Lennart.

Gerlof nodded, with the unpleasant feeling that he was in the middle of an interrogation.

"When?"

"Last week. I phoned Julia and told her about it . . . That was partly why she came to visit."

"Have you still got the envelope?" said Lennart.

"No," said Gerlof quickly. "I threw it away . . . I'm a bit absentminded sometimes. But there was no letter with it, and no sender's name, I do know that. I think it just said 'Captain Gerlof Davidsson, Stenvik' on the front, and it had been forwarded here. But the envelope isn't that important, is it?"

"There's something called fingerprints," said Lennart quietly, with a sigh. "There are strands of hair and a lot you can . . . Well, anyway, I'd like to take the sandal with me now. There could be traces on it too."

"I'd really rather–" Gerlof began, but Julia interrupted him and asked, "Are you going to take it to a lab somewhere?"

"Yes," said Lennart, "there's a forensics lab in Linköping. The national police lab. They examine this sort of thing there."

Gerlof didn't say anything.

"Fine, let them have a look at it," said Julia.

"Do we get a receipt?" said Gerlof.

Julia looked annoyed, as if she were embarrassed by her father, but Lennart nodded with a tired smile.

"Of course, Gerlof," he said. "I'll write you out a receipt, then you can sue Borgholm police if the lab in Linköping loses the shoe. But I shouldn't worry if I were you."

When the policeman left a few minutes later, Julia went out with him, but soon returned. Gerlof was still sitting at the desk, holding the receipt Lennart Henriksson had scrawled and staring gloomily out the window.

"Lennart said we shouldn't tell anybody else about the sandal," said Julia.

"Oh, he did, did he."

Gerlof kept on gazing out of the window. He did not look at his daughter.

"What's the matter?" asked Julia.

"You didn't have to tell him about the sandal."

"You said I should tell people."

"Not the police. We can solve this ourselves."

"Solve?" said Julia, her voice rising. "What do you mean, solve it ourselves? What on earth are you thinking? Do you think the person who took Jens away, if somebody did take him away . . . do you think that person's going to turn up here and ask to see the sandal? Is that what you really think? That he's just going to turn up here, after all these years, and tell you what he did?"

Gerlof didn't reply; he was still staring out of the window with his back to her, and that just made Julia even more agitated.

"What did you actually do that day?" she went on.

"You know what I did," said Gerlof quietly.

"Oh yes, I know," said Julia. "Mum was tired and your grand-child needed looking after . . . and you went down to the sea to sort your nets out. Because you were going fishing."

Gerlof nodded. "Then the fog came," he said.

"Yes, a real pea-souper . . . but did you go home then?"

Gerlof shook his head.

"You stayed with your nets," said Julia, "because it was much more enjoyable being alone down by the sea than looking after a small child. Wasn't it?"

"I was listening all the time I was down there," said Gerlof without looking at her. "There wasn't a sound. I would have heard Jens if he'd—"

"That's not what this is about!" Julia broke in. "It's about the fact that you were always somewhere else when you should have been at home. That *everything* was on your terms . . . That's always the way it was, all the time."

Gerlof didn't reply. He thought the sky had grown darker out-side the window. Was the twilight coming already? He really was listening to what his daughter was saying, but he couldn't come up with a good answer.

"I suppose I was a bad father," he said at last. "I was often away, I needed to be away. But if I could have done anything for Jens that day . . . If the whole day could have been changed . . ."

He stopped speaking, struggling with his voice.

There was an unbearable silence in the room.

"I know, Dad," said Julia, eventually. "How can I point the finger at you? I wasn't even on Öland that day. I went into Kalmar and I could see the fog drifting in under the bridge as I drove across the sound." She sighed. "How often do you think I've regretted leaving Jens that morning? I didn't even say goodbye to him."

Gerlof breathed in, then out again. He finally turned and looked at her.

"On Tuesday, the day before Ernst's funeral, I'll take you to the person who sent me the sandal," he said.

Julia didn't speak.

"I know who it was," said Gerlof.

"Are you a hundred percent certain?"

"Ninety-five."

"Where does he live? Here in Marnäs?"

"No."

"In Stenvik?"

Gerlof shook his head. "Down in Borgholm," he said.

Julia was quiet for a while, as if she thought this might be some kind of trick.

"Okay," she said. "We'll take my car."

She bent to pick her coat up from the bed.

"What are you going to do now?" Gerlof asked.

"Don't know . . . I'll probably go down to Stenvik and rake up some leaves around the cottage, or something. Now that the electricity and the water are on I can cook in the cottage, but I'll probably keep sleeping in the boathouse. I sleep well there."

"Good. But stay in close touch with John and Astrid," said Gerlof. "You need to stick together."

"Of course." Julia put her coat on. "I was over in the church-yard, by the way. Lit a candle on Mum's grave."

"Good . . . That means it'll burn for five days, right up to the weekend. The church council looks after the graves. I don't get there very often, unfortunately . . ." Gerlof coughed. "Had they dug a grave for Ernst yet?"

"Not that I noticed." She added, "But I did find Nils Kant's grave by the wall. That was what you wanted me to see, wasn't it?"

"Yes."

"Before I saw the grave, I was thinking Nils Kant should have been a suspect," said Julia, "but now I understand why nobody mentioned him."

Gerlof contemplated whether to say something–perhaps he

should point out that the best cover for a murderer has to be to play dead—but he didn't speak.

"There were roses on the grave," said Julia.

"Fresh roses?"

"Not really," said Julia. "From last summer, maybe. And another thing . . ."

She pushed her hand into her coat pocket and took out the little envelope that had been with the roses. It had dried out now, and she passed it over to Gerlof.

"Maybe we shouldn't open it," she said. "I mean, it's private and not . . ."

But Gerlof quickly slit open the envelope, slid out the little piece of white paper, and read the contents.

" 'We shall all stand before the judgment seat of God.' " He looked at Julia. "That's all it says . . . it's a quote from Saint Paul's letter to the Romans. Can I keep this?"

Julia nodded. "Are there usually flowers and notes on Kant's grave?" she asked.

"Not often," said Gerlof, placing the envelope in one of the desk drawers. "But it's happened a few times over the years . . . flowers, at least. I've seen bunches of roses there."

"So Nils Kant still has friends alive?"

"Yes . . . at least somebody wants to remember him, for some reason," Gerlof said, then added, "People who have a bad reputation sometimes attract admirers, after all."

There was another silence.

"Okay. I'm off to Stenvik, then," said Julia, buttoning her coat.

"What are you doing tomorrow?"

"I might go to Långvik. We'll see."

When his daughter had left the room, Gerlof's shoulders slumped with weariness. He raised his hands and saw that his fingers were shaking. It had been an exhausting afternoon, but he still had one more important thing to do today.

"Torsten, did you bury Nils Kant?" asked Gerlof a few hours later.

He and the old man were sitting at separate tables, all alone in the activity room in the cellar. After dinner Gerlof had taken the elevator down to the activity room and sat there for over an hour waiting for another resident, an old woman from the first floor, to finish her interminable weaving.

His aim was to be alone with Torsten Axelsson, who had worked in Marnäs churchyard from the war years up to the mid-1970s. While Gerlof was waiting, the autumn darkness had thickened outside the narrow cellar windows. It was evening.

Before asking his key questions, Gerlof had sat there chatting to Axelsson about the impending funeral, mainly to keep him in the room. Axelsson too suffered from rheumatism, but his mind was razor sharp and he was usually an entertaining companion. He didn't seem to have the same nostalgic yearning for his work as a gravedigger as Gerlof had for his years at sea, but he'd willingly stayed and chatted about old times.

Gerlof was sitting at a table covered with bits of wood, glue, tools, and emery cloth. He was working on a model of the ketch *Packet,* Borgholm's last sailing ship, which had become a pleasure boat in Stockholm in the sixties. The hull was finished, but he needed to do some more work on the rigging, and of course it wouldn't be completely finished until it was in the bottle, and he could raise the masts and fasten off the final ropes. It all took time.

Gerlof carefully filed a small groove in the top of a mast as he waited for a reply from the retired gravedigger. Axelsson was bent over a table covered with thousands of jigsaw pieces. He was halfway through a huge picture of Monet's water lilies.

He fitted a piece into the black lily pond, then looked up.

"Kant?" he said.

"Nils Kant, yes," said Gerlof. "The grave is still a bit isolated, over by the west wall. And that made me think about his funeral. I wasn't living up here at the time . . ."

Axelsson nodded, picked up a piece of the jigsaw, and pondered. "Yes, I dug the grave and carried the coffin, along with my colleagues from the churchyard . . . Nobody rushed to volunteer as a bearer for that particular duty."

"Weren't there any mourners?"

"His mother was there. She was there all the time. I'd hardly ever seen her before, but she was all skin and bone, dressed in a coal-black coat," said Axelsson. "But as for calling her a mourner—well, I don't know about that. She looked a bit too pleased to me."

"Pleased?"

"Yes . . . Of course, I didn't see her inside the church," said Axelsson. "But I remember glancing at her when we were lowering the coffin into the ground. Vera was standing near the grave, watching the coffin disappear, and I could see that she was smiling beneath her veil. As if she was really pleased with the funeral."

Gerlof nodded. "And she was the only one at the burial? Nobody else?"

Axelsson shook his head. "There were several people there, but you'd hardly call them mourners. The police were there too, but they were standing further away, almost by the church door."

"They probably wanted to see that Kant went into the ground, once and for all," said Gerlof.

"True." Axelsson nodded. "And that's everybody who was there, I think, except for Pastor Fridlund."

"At least he was getting paid."

Gerlof polished away at the ship's little hull for a few minutes. Then he took a deep breath and said:

"What you said about Vera Kant smiling at the graveside, it does make you wonder about what was in the coffin . . ."

Axelsson looked down at his puzzle and picked up another piece.

"Are you going to ask me if it felt strangely light when we were carrying it, Gerlof?" he said. "I've been asked that question several times over the years."

"Well, people do talk about it sometimes . . . the fact that Kant's coffin might have been empty. You've heard that too, surely?"

"You can stop wondering, because it wasn't," said Axelsson. "There were four of us carrying it, both before and after the service, and we definitely needed that many. It was bloody heavy."

Gerlof felt as if he were questioning the old gravedigger's integrity, but he had to persist:

"Some people say there might have been just stones in the coffin, or sandbags," he said quietly.

"I've heard that rumor," replied Axelsson. "I didn't look inside myself, but somebody must have . . . when it arrived here on the ferry."

"I've heard that nobody opened it," said Gerlof. "It was sealed, and nobody had the nerve or the authority to break it open. Do you know if anybody opened it?"

"No . . ." said Axelsson. "I just remember vaguely that there was some kind of death certificate from South America that came with the coffin on one of Malm's cargo ships. Somebody down at the truck depot in Borgholm who knew a bit of Spanish had read it . . . Nils Kant had drowned, it said, and he'd been in the water for a long time before they pulled him out. So I imagine the body didn't look too good."

"Perhaps people were afraid Vera Kant would start making trouble," said Gerlof. "I suppose they just wanted to bury Kant and move on."

Axelsson looked at Gerlof, then shrugged his shoulders.

"Don't ask me," he said, placing another piece of a water lily in the pond on Monet's painting. "I just put him in the ground; I did my job and I went home."

"I know that, Torsten."

Axelsson placed another piece in the jigsaw, looked at the result for a while and then at the clock on the wall. He got up slowly.

"Coffee time," he said. But before he left the room, he stopped and turned his head.

"What do *you* think, Gerlof?" he said. "Is Nils Kant lying in his coffin?"

"I'm sure he is," answered Gerlof quietly, without looking at the old gravedigger.

By the time Gerlof had returned to his room, it was already after seven and there was only half an hour left until coffee time. Routine, everything followed a routine at the senior citizens' home.

But the conversation with Torsten Axelsson in the cellar had been useful, thought Gerlof. Useful. Perhaps he might have been a bit too talkative and insistent toward the end, attracting quizzical looks from Axelsson as a result.

No doubt the gossip had already started in the corridors of

the home about Gerlof's remarkable interest in Nils Kant. It might even spread outside the walls of the home, but so be it. That was what he wanted, wasn't it: to stir the ants' nest and maybe make things happen?

He sat down heavily on the bed and picked up that day's copy of *Ölands-Posten* from the bedside table. He hadn't had time to read the paper that morning, or rather he hadn't had the inclination.

The death in Stenvik was the big news story on the front page, and there was one of Bengt Nyberg's photographs of the quarry with an arrow to indicate exactly where the accident had happened.

It was an accident, according to the police in Borgholm. Ernst Adolfsson had been trying to move a stone statue at the edge of the cliff; the old man had tripped and fallen, and ended up with the huge block of stone on top of him. No crime was suspected.

Gerlof read only the beginning of Bengt Nyberg's article, then leafed through the paper until he found news of less personal significance: a building project that was running well overtime in Långvik, a barn fire outside Löttorp, and the eighty-one-year-old suffering from senile dementia who had left his home in southern Öland a few days earlier to go for a walk, and who was still missing without a trace on the alvar. He was bound to be found, but not alive.

Gerlof folded up the paper and placed it back on the table, then caught sight of Ernst's wallet. He'd put it aside when he got back from Stenvik. Now he picked it up, opened it, and looked at all the cash inside and an even thicker bundle of receipts. He left the money in the wallet, but he slowly went through the receipts.

Most of them related to small purchases from food stores in Marnäs or Långvik, or were handwritten receipts from Ernst's own sales of sculpture last summer.

Gerlof was looking for later receipts, ideally from the same day the sculpture of Marnäs church tower fell on Ernst. He didn't find any.

Almost at the bottom of the pile he found something else: a little yellow entrance ticket for a museum. *Ramneby Wood Museum* was printed on the ticket, along with a little drawing of planks of wood in a stack, and a date stamp in black ink: *Sept. 13.*

He left the ticket on the bedside table. He fastened the rest of the receipts together with a paper clip and pushed them into the desk drawer. Then he sat down at the desk, reached for his notebook, and opened it at the first clean page. He picked up a pencil, thought for a little while, then made two notes:

VERA KANT WAS SMILING WHEN NILS'S COFFIN WAS BURIED.

And:

ERNST VISITED THE KANT FAMILY'S SAWMILL IN RAMNEBY.

Then he placed the museum ticket in the book, closed it, and settled down to wait for his coffee. Routine, everything was just routine when you got old.

13

Julia didn't even remember drinking the first glass of wine. She'd seen Astrid pour it out in front of her at the table in Astrid's kitchen, seen the red liquid swirling around in the glass and had reached out her hand in anticipation—then suddenly the glass was standing empty on the table. She had the taste of wine in her mouth and a warming dose of alcohol spreading through her body, and the feeling that she had become reacquainted with an old, dear friend.

Outside Astrid's kitchen window the sun was going down, and Julia's legs were aching after a long bike ride along the coast.

"Would you like another glass?" asked Astrid.

"Yes, please," said Julia, as calmly and evenly as she could manage. "That was lovely."

She would of course have drunk the wine even if it had tasted of vinegar.

She tried to drink the second glass much more slowly. She took just a couple of sips, then placed it back on the table and breathed out.

"Difficult day?" asked Astrid.

"Quite difficult," said Julia.

But in fact nothing much had happened.

She'd cycled north along the coast to the neighboring village of Långvik and had lunch there. And after that she'd been told by an old egg seller on a little farm that her son Jens had been mur-dered. Not just dead and buried long ago—murdered.

"Quite a difficult day," said Julia again, and emptied her sec-ond glass of wine.

The sky had been clear and full of stars the previous evening as Julia got ready for another night alone in the boathouse.

The stars felt like her only friends here by the deserted shore. The moon dangled like a splinter of gray-white bone in the east, but Julia had stood down on the coal-black shore looking at the stars for half an hour before she went up to the boathouse. From there she could see another reassuring light: the outside light at Astrid's house on the opposite side of the road. The lights of the inhabited houses to the north and south along the coast were dis-tant and almost as faint as the glow of the stars, but Astrid's brightly burning light showed that there were other people out there in the darkness.

Julia had fallen asleep, unusually quickly and calmly, and had woken up feeling rested eight hours later to the sound of the waves moving back and forth on the shore, almost in time with her own breathing.

The rocky landscape was peaceful, and she had opened the door and looked at the waves without thinking of fragments of bone.

She went up to Gerlof's cottage to wash and make some breakfast, and when she took a walk around the yard afterward she found an old bike behind the toolshed. Julia assumed it was Lena's. It was rusty and needed oiling, but there was plenty of air left in the tires.

That was when she had decided to cycle northward to Långvik for lunch. In Långvik she would try to find an old man called Lambert, and apologize for having hit him many years earlier.

The coast road to the north was dusty and stony and full of deep holes, but it was possible to cycle along it. And the landscape was just as beautiful as it had always been, with the alvar on the right and the glittering water a few yards below the edge of the cliff on the left. Julia avoided looking over toward the far end of the quarry when she cycled past; she didn't want to know if the pools of blood were still there.

After that her cycling trip was pure enjoyment, with the sun on one side and the wind at her back.

Långvik was five kilometers north of Stenvik, but it was bigger, and a completely different kind of village. There was a proper area for swimming with a sandy beach, a marina for pleasure boats, several bigger apartment houses in the center, and developments of summer cottages both at the north and south end of the village.

PLOTS FOR SALE it said on a sign by the side of the road. Building was still going on in Långvik: fences and markers and newly laid gravel tracks ran out onto the alvar, coming to an end among huge pallets of tiles encased in plastic and piles of treated timber.

There was also a harbor hotel, of course, running the length of the sandy beach and three stories high, with a big restaurant.

Julia ate her lunch of pasta in the restaurant with a vague feeling of nostalgia. She had danced here at the beginning of the sixties. The hotel had been smaller when Julia was a teenager, cycling there from Stenvik with her friends, but it had felt quite grand even then. There had been a big wooden veranda above the beach, and that was where they'd danced till midnight. American and English rock music, interwoven with the sound of the waves out in the darkness in the gaps between records. The smell of sweat, aftershave, and cigarettes. Julia had drunk her first glass of wine here in Långvik, and sometimes she'd had a lift home on a puttering moped late at night. Full speed through the darkness, no helmet, with a deep conviction that life could only get more and more fantastic.

The veranda was gone now, and the hotel had been enlarged, with bright, spacious conference rooms and its own swimming pool.

After lunch Julia had started to read the book Gerlof had given her, the one with the title *Öland Crimes*. In the chapter entitled "The Murderer Who Got Away," she had read about Nils Kant and what he had done one summer's day in 1945 out on the alvar, and what happened after that:

So who were the two men in uniform that Nils Kant executed in cold blood that beautiful day out on the alvar?

They were presumably German soldiers who had managed to get across the Baltic, fleeing the terrible battles in Kurzeme on the west coast of Latvia during the final phase of World War II. The Germans in Kurzeme were surrounded by the Red Army, and the only way to escape was to set off across the water in some kind of floating craft. The risks were great, and yet both soldiers and civilians chose to attempt to flee to Sweden from the Baltic lands at that time.

Nobody knows for certain, however. The two dead soldiers carried no documents or passports which could identify them, and their grave bore no names.

But they had left several traces. What Kant didn't know when he left the two bodies lying out on the alvar was that a little green-painted motorboat with a Russian nameplate had been found abandoned in an inlet a kilometer or so south of Marnäs that same morning.

In the open boat, partly filled with water, were two German military helmets, dozens of rusty tins of food, a chamber pot, a broken oar, and a little tin containing Dr. Theodor Morell's medical powder for Russian lice, produced in Berlin exclusively for soldiers of the Wehrmacht. Dr. Morell was Hitler's own physician.

The discovery of the boat attracted attention—as does anything unusual that drifts ashore along the Öland coast—and thus many people in Marnäs knew before Kant did that there were strangers in the area. Some of them even set out to search, armed or unarmed.

Nils Kant had not buried the soldiers he had killed, or even covered their bodies. Corpses out on the alvar quickly attract scavengers, and the noise small animals and birds make as they squabble over their spoils can be seen and heard far and wide.

It was therefore only a matter of time before somebody searching out on the alvar found the dead soldiers.

When the waitress came to clear the table, Julia closed the book and looked pensively out over the deserted beach below the hotel.

The story of Nils Kant was interesting, but he was dead and buried, and she still didn't know why Gerlof thought it was so important for her to read about him.

"Can I pay you now?" said Julia to the waitress.

"Yes, of course. That'll be forty-two kronor."

The waitress was young, probably not even twenty yet, and she looked as if she enjoyed her job.

"Are you open all year round?" asked Julia as she handed over the money.

She was surprised that there were still so many people around in Långvik in general and at the harbor hotel in particular, even though it was autumn.

"From November to March we're only open on weekends, for conferences," said the waitress.

She took the money and opened the wallet around her waist to pick out some one-krona pieces.

"Keep the change," said Julia; she glanced again out at the gray water outside the window, then went on: "Another thing I was wondering . . . Do you know if there's anyone here in Långvik called Lambert? Lambert, and then something ending in—son . . . Svensson or Nilsson or Karlsson. Is there a Lambert here?"

The waitress looked thoughtful and shook her head. "Lambert?" she said. "It's a name you'd remember, but I don't think I've heard it."

She was too young to know about Långvik's older residents, thought Julia. She nodded and got up, but the waitress said suddenly:

"Ask Gunnar. Gunnar Ljunger. He's the one who owns this hotel. He knows nearly everybody in Långvik." She turned and pointed. "You go out through the main entrance, then left, then along to the side of the hotel. That's where the office is—he should be there now."

Julia thanked her and left the restaurant. She'd drunk ice water with her lunch today; it was starting to become a habit. It was nice to have a clear head as she walked out into the cold air of the hotel parking lot, even if a wine-induced sense of calm might have helped if she was going to see Lambert again . . .

Lambert Svensson or Nilsson or Karlsson.

Julia ran a hand through her hair and went around the side of the hotel. There was a wooden door with a number of company signs next to it, and the top one said LÅNGVIK CONFERENCE CENTER. She opened the door and walked into a small reception area with a yellow carpet and big green plastic plants.

It was like walking into an office in the middle of Gothenburg. Soft music was playing in the background. A young, smartly dressed woman was sitting at the reception desk, and an equally young man in a white shirt was leaning against it. Both looked at Julia as if she had interrupted an important conversation, but the receptionist was quickest to greet her and smile. Julia said hello back, feeling slightly tense as always when she met new people, and then she asked about Gunnar Ljunger.

"Gunnar?" said the receptionist, looking at the man by her desk. "Is he back from lunch?"

"He is," said the man, nodding to Julia. "Come with me and I'll show you."

Julia followed him along a short corridor with a half-open door at the end. He knocked and pushed it open at the same time.

"Dad?" he said. "You've got a visitor."

"Okay," said a deep male voice. "Come in."

The office wasn't particularly large, but the view over the beach and the Baltic through the picture window was glorious. The hotel owner, Gunnar Ljunger, was sitting at the desk; he was a tall man with a gray beard and bushy gray eyebrows, and he was tapping away on a calculator. He was wearing a white shirt with suspenders, and a brown jacket was draped over the back of the chair behind him. On the table next to the calculator was an open copy of *Ölands-Posten,* and Ljunger appeared to be looking through the paper and doing his calculations at the same time.

"Hi," he said, glancing up at Julia.

"Hi."

"How can I help?"

Ljunger smiled and carried on tapping numbers into his calculator.

"I've just got one question," said Julia, stepping into the room. "I'm looking for Lambert."

"Lambert?"

"Lambert in Långvik . . . Lambert Karlsson, I think his name is."

"That would be Lambert Nilsson," said Ljunger. "There's no other Lambert here in Långvik."

"That's it . . . Nilsson, that's his name," said Julia quickly.

"But Lambert's dead," said Ljunger, shaking his head. "He died five or six years ago."

"Oh."

Julia felt a quick stab of disappointment, but she had partly expected that answer. Lambert had looked old back in the seventies, that afternoon all those years ago when he had come chugging along on his moped to find out what had happened to her son.

"His younger brother Sven-Olof is still alive, of course," added Ljunger. "He lives up on the hill, behind the pizzeria; Lambert used to live there too. Sven-Olof sells eggs, so look for a house with hens in the yard."

"Thanks."

"If you're going there, tell Sven-Olof from me that it's even cheaper now to sign up to the city water supply," said Lunger with a smile. "He's the only one in the whole of Långvik who still thinks a well of his own is best."

"Okay," said Julia.

"Are you staying with us?" asked Ljunger.

"No, but I used to come here to the dances when I was young . . . I'm staying over in Stenvik. My name is Julia Davidsson."

"Related to old Gerlof?"

"I'm his daughter."

"Really?" said Ljunger. "Give him my best, then. He's made several ships in bottles for us, for the restaurant. We'd really like some more."

"I'll tell him that."

"It's lovely over there in Stenvik, isn't it?" mused Ljunger. "Nice and peaceful, with the quarry closed and all those empty cottages." He smiled. "Of course, we've taken a different approach up here . . . expanding, going for tourism and golf and conferences. We think it's the only way to keep the coastal villages in northern Öland alive."

Julia nodded, with some hesitation. "It does seem to be working," she said.

Should Stenvik have invested in tourism as well? Julia wondered about that as she left the hotel office and walked across the windy parking lot. There was no answer, because by now Långvik was so far ahead they'd never catch up. It would be impossible to build a beach hotel or pizzeria in Stenvik. The village would remain more or less deserted for most of the year, livening up for just a couple of months in the summer when the visitors came, and there was nothing that could be done about it.

She walked past a gas station by the harbor and continued along the wide village street past the pizzeria.

The street curved inland and up a hill, and now she had the wind at her back. At the top was a grove of trees and behind it a wall surrounding a yard containing a small whitewashed house and a stone henhouse with its own enclosure.

There was no sign of any hens, but a wooden sign by the gate proclaimed EGGS FOR SALE.

Julia opened the gate and walked along a path made of rough limestone slabs. She passed a water pump painted green, and remembered what Gunnar Ljunger at the beach hotel had said about the city water supply.

The door of the house was closed, but there was a bell. When Julia had pressed it there was silence for a few moments, then a thudding noise. The door opened. An elderly man looked out, thin and wrinkled, with fine, silvery hair combed over his bald pate.

"Afternoon," he said.

"Afternoon," said Julia.

"Did you want some eggs?"

The old man appeared to be in the middle of his lunch, because he was still chewing.

Julia nodded. No problem, she could buy some eggs.

"Is your name Sven-Olof?" she asked, without the usual unpleasant feeling of tension she got whenever she met someone new.

Perhaps she was beginning to get used to meeting strangers here on Öland.

"It is indeed," said the man, clambering into a pair of big black rubber boots standing just inside the door. "How many would you like?"

"Er . . . six should be fine."

Sven-Olof Nilsson walked out of his home, and just before he closed the door a cat slunk silently out behind him like a coal-black shadow. It didn't even bother looking at Julia.

"I'll go and fetch them," Sven-Olof told Julia.

"Fine," she said, but as he set off toward the little henhouse, she followed him. When he opened the green door and stepped onto the earth floor she stayed on the other side of the threshold where there were no hens, just several trays of white eggs on a small table.

"I'll just go and get some new-laid ones," said Sven-Olof, opening a rickety unpainted door at the far end of the room and entering the coop.

The smell of the birds drifted toward Julia and she caught a glimpse of wooden shelves along the walls, but she couldn't see much; the light in the room wasn't switched on, and the room was almost pitch black.

"How many hens have you got?" she asked.

"Not so many these days," said Sven-Olof. "Fifty or so . . . we'll see how long I can keep them."

A tentative clucking could be heard from inside the coop.

"I heard Lambert had died," she said.

"What . . . Lambert? Yes, he died in '87," said Sven-Olof in the darkness.

She couldn't understand why he didn't put the light on, but perhaps the bulb had died.

"I met Lambert once," said Julia, "many years ago."

"Oh yes?" said Sven-Olof. "Well, well."

He didn't seem particularly interested in hearing a story about his late brother, but Julia had no choice but to continue:

"It was over in Stenvik, where I live."

"Oh yes," said Sven-Olof.

Julia took a step over the threshold toward him, into the darkness. The air felt dusty and stale. She could hear the hens moving nervously along the walls, but couldn't see if they were free-range or in cages.

"My mother Ella phoned Lambert," she said, "because we needed . . . we needed help looking for someone who had disappeared. He'd been gone for three days, there was no trace of him anywhere. That was when Ella started talking about Lambert . . . She said Lambert could find things. He was well known for it, Ella said."

"Ella Davidsson?" said Sven-Olof.

"Yes. She phoned and Lambert came over from Långvik on an old moped the very next day."

"Yes, he liked to help out," said Sven-Olof, who by now was just a shadow in the coop. His quiet voice could barely be heard over the muted clucking of the hens. "Lambert found things. He would dream about them, then he would find them. He found water for people too, with a divining rod made of hazel. They often appreciated it."

Julia nodded. "He had his own pillow with him when he came to us," she said. "He wanted to sleep in Jens's room, with Jens's things around him. And we let him."

"Yes, that's what he did," said Sven-Olof. "He saw things in dreams. People who'd drowned and things that had disappeared. And future events, things that were going to happen. Lambert dreamed about the day of his own death for several weeks. He said it would happen in bed in his own room, half-past two in the morning, and that his heart would stop and the ambulance wouldn't get there in time. And that's exactly what happened, on the very day he'd said. And the ambulance didn't make it in time."

"But did it always work?" said Julia. "Was he always right?"

"Not always," replied Sven-Olof. "Sometimes he didn't dream about anything. Or he didn't remember his dream . . . That's the way it is sometimes, I suppose. And he never got any names, everybody in his dreams was nameless."

"But when he saw something?" said Julia. "Was he always right then?"

"Almost always. People trusted him."

Julia took a couple of steps forward. She had to tell him.

"I hadn't slept for three days by that night when your brother turned up on his moped," she said quietly. "But I couldn't sleep that night either. I lay awake listening to him getting into the little bed in Jens's room. I could hear the springs squeaking when he moved. Then it went quiet, but I still couldn't get to sleep . . . When he got up at seven the next morning, I was sitting in the kitchen waiting for him."

The hens clucked uneasily around her, but there was no comment from Sven-Olof.

"Lambert had dreamed about my son," she went on. "I could see it in his face when he came into the kitchen with his pillow under his arm. He looked at me, and when I asked him he said it was true, he'd dreamed about Jens. He looked so sad . . . I'm sure he was intending to tell me more, but I just couldn't cope with hearing it. I struck him and screamed at him to get out. My father Gerlof went out with him to the gate where his moped was, and I stood there in the kitchen sobbing and listening to him drive away." She paused and sighed. "That was the only time I met Lambert. Unfortunately."

The henhouse fell silent. Even the hens had settled down.

"That boy . . ." said Sven-Olof in the darkness. "Was it that terrible tragedy . . . ? The little boy who disappeared in Stenvik?"

"That was my son Jens," said Julia, longing desperately for a glass of wine. "He's still missing."

Sven-Olof didn't answer.

"I'd really like to know . . . Did Lambert ever talk about what he dreamed that night?"

"There's five eggs here," said a voice from the darkness. "I can't find any more."

Julia realized Sven-Olof had no intention of answering any questions.

She breathed out, a deep, heavy sigh.

"I have nothing," she said to herself. "I have nothing."

Her eyes had gradually begun to grow accustomed to the darkness, and she could see Sven-Olof standing motionless in the middle of the coop looking at her, clutching five eggs to his chest.

"Your brother must have said something, Sven-Olof," she said. "At some point he must have said something to you about what he dreamed that night. Did he?"

Sven-Olof coughed. "He only spoke about the boy once."

It was Julia's turn to be silent now. She was holding her breath.

"He'd read an article in *Ölands-Posten*," said Sven-Olof. "It must have been five years after it happened. We were reading it at breakfast. But there was nothing new in the paper."

"There never has been," said Julia, wearily. "There was never anything new to say, but they kept on writing anyway."

"We were sitting at the kitchen table and I was reading the paper first," said Sven-Olof. "Then Lambert read it. And when I saw that he was reading about the boy, I asked him what he thought. And then Lambert lowered the paper and said the boy was dead."

Julia closed her eyes. She nodded silently.

"In the sound?" she asked.

"No. Lambert said it had happened out on the alvar. He'd been killed on the alvar."

"Killed," said Julia, feeling an icy chill sweep across her skin.

"A man had done it, Lambert said. The very day the boy disappeared, a man who was full of hatred had killed him on the alvar. Then he had placed the boy in a grave beside a stone wall."

A hen flapped nervously somewhere by the wall.

"Lambert didn't say any more," said Sven-Olof, when Julia didn't speak. "Not about the boy, or the man."

No names, thought Julia. Everybody was nameless in Lambert's dreams.

Sven-Olof was moving again. He came out of the coop with the five eggs in his arms, looking anxiously at Julia as if he were afraid she might hit him as well.

Julia breathed out.

"So now I know," she said. "Thank you."

"Do you need a box?" asked Sven-Olof.

Julia knew.

She could try and convince herself that Lambert had been wrong, or that his brother had just made it up, but there was no point. She knew.

On the way home from Långvik she stopped on the coast road above the deserted shore, watching the water turn to foam as the waves scurried in down below, and she wept for over ten minutes.

She *knew,* and the certainty was terrible. It was as if only a few days had passed since Jens's disappearance, as if all her internal wounds were still bleeding. Now she was starting to let him into her heart as a dead person, little by little. It had to happen slowly, otherwise the grief would drown her.

Jens was dead.

She knew it. But still she wanted to see her son again, see his body. If that wasn't possible, then she at least wanted to know what had happened to him. That was why she was here.

Her tears dried in the wind. After a while Julia got back on her bike and cycled slowly on her way.

By the quarry she met Astrid, out walking the dog; she invited Julia back for dinner and didn't comment on Julia's eyes, puffy with weeping.

Astrid served cutlets, boiled potatoes, and red wine. Julia ate a little and drank a good deal more, more than she should have done. But after three glasses of wine the idea that Jens had been dead for a long time was not quite so intrusive, it was merely a dull ache in her breast. And there had never been any hope, after all, not after the first days had passed with no sign of life. No hope . . .

"So you went to Långvik today?"

Julia's brooding thoughts were interrupted, and she nodded.

"Yes. And yesterday I was in Marnäs," she said quickly, to get away from the thought of Långvik and Lambert Nilsson's accurate dreams.

"Did anything happen up there?" asked Astrid, tipping the last of the wine into Julia's glass.

"Not much," said Julia. "I went to the churchyard and saw Nils Kant's grave. Gerlof thought I ought to see it."

"Nils's grave," repeated Astrid, lifting her wineglass.

"One thing I was wondering," said Julia. "You might not be able to tell me, but those German soldiers Nils Kant killed on the alvar . . . Did many of them come to Öland?"

"Not that I know of," said Astrid. "There were maybe a hundred or so who managed to make it to Sweden alive from the war in the Baltic countries, but most of them came ashore along the coast of Småland. They wanted desperately to go home, of course, or to travel on to England. But Sweden was afraid of Stalin, and sent them back to the Soviet Union. It was a cowardly thing to do. But you must have read about all this?"

"Yes, a little bit . . . but it was a long time ago," said Julia.

She had a vague memory from her school days of reading about war refugees from Russia, but at the time she hadn't been particularly interested in Swedish history, or the history of Öland.

"What else did you do in Marnäs?" said Astrid.

"Well . . . I had lunch with the policeman there," said Julia. "Lennart Henriksson."

"He's a nice man," said Astrid. "Very stylish."

Julia nodded.

"Did you talk to Lennart about Nils Kant?" asked Astrid.

Julia shook her head, then thought about it and added:

"Well, I did mention that I'd been to see Kant's grave. But we didn't talk about it any more."

"It's probably best not to mention him to Lennart again," said Astrid. "It upsets him a bit."

"Upsets him?" said Julia. "But why?"

"It's an old story," said Astrid, taking a gulp of her wine. "Lennart is Kurt Henriksson's son."

She looked at Julia with a serious expression, as if this should make everything clear.

But Julia just shook her head uncomprehendingly.

"Who?" she said.

"The police constable in Marnäs," explained Astrid. "Or the district superintendent, as he was called in those days."

"And what did he do?"

"He was the one who was supposed to arrest Nils Kant for shooting the Germans," said Astrid.

Nils Kant is sawing the end off his shotgun.

He is standing out in the heat of the woodshed where the birch logs are stacked right up to the roof, his back bent. The pile of wood looks as if it might topple over onto him at any moment. His Husqvarna is lying on the chopping block in front of him, and he has almost sawn right through the barrel. His booted left foot is resting on the butt of the gun and he is working the hacksaw with both hands. Slowly but with determination he saws through the barrel, occasionally waving away the flies that buzz around the shed, constantly trying to land on his sweaty face.

Outside everything is as silent as the grave. His mother Vera is in the kitchen, sorting out his rucksack. A tense air of waiting fills the warm spring air.

Nils keeps on sawing, and at last the blade bites through the final millimeter of steel and the barrel falls onto the stone floor of the woodshed with a brief metallic clang.

He picks it up, shoves it in a little hole near the bottom of the woodpile, and sets the saw on the chopping block. He takes two cartridges out of his pocket and loads the gun.

Then he goes out of the shed and places the shotgun in the shadow by the door.

He's ready.

It's four days since the shooting out on the alvar, and now everybody in Stenvik knows what's happened. GERMAN SOLDIERS

FOUND DEAD—EXECUTED WITH SHOTGUN was splashed across the front page of yesterday's newspaper, *Ölands-Posten*. The headline was just as big as when the forest near the shore outside Borgholm was bombed three years earlier.

The headlines are a lie—Nils didn't execute anyone. He was caught up in a gun battle with two soldiers, and he was the one who won in the end.

But perhaps not everyone will see it that way. For once, Nils went down into the village in the evening, walking along the road past the mill, and he was met by the silent gaze of the millers. He didn't say anything, but he knows they are talking about him behind his back. There's gossip. And stories about what happened out on the alvar are spreading like rippling circles on the water.

He goes into the house.

His mother Vera is sitting there silent and motionless at the kitchen table with her back to him, looking out through the window over the alvar. He can see that her narrow shoulders are tense with anxiety and sorrow beneath her gray blouse.

Nils's own fears are equally wordless.

"I think it's probably time now," he says.

She merely nods, without turning around. The rucksack and the small suitcase are on the table beside her, all packed, and Nils walks over and picks them up. It's almost unbearable; if he tries to say anything else his voice will be thick with tears—so he simply leaves.

"You will come back, Nils," say his mother behind him, her voice hoarse.

He nods, although she can't see it, and takes his blue cap off the peg by the door. His copper hip flask is hidden in the cap, filled with brandy. He pushes it into his rucksack.

"Time to go, then," he says quietly.

He has his wallet with his own traveling money in his rucksack, as well as twenty substantial notes from his mother rolled up and tucked into his back trouser pocket.

He turns around in the doorway. His mother is now standing in the kitchen, her profile toward him, but she still isn't looking at him. Perhaps she can't do it. Her hands are clasped over her stomach, her long white nails digging into her palms; her mouth is trembling.

"I love you, Mother," says Nils. "I'll be back."

Then he walks quickly out of the door, down the stone steps, and into the garden. He stops briefly by the woodshed to pick up his shotgun before going around the house and in among the ash trees.

Nils knows how to leave the village without being spotted. He stoops and moves along the cow paths, through the dense thickets far away from the road, climbing over lichen-covered stone walls and stopping occasionally to listen for whispering voices beyond the humming of the insects in the grass.

He emerges in the sunshine on the alvar southwest of the village, without being discovered.

Out here the danger is past; Nils can find his way here better than anyone, moving rapidly and easily across the grass. He can spot anybody before they see him. He walks almost directly toward the sun, giving a wide berth to the place where he met the Germans. He doesn't want to see if the bodies are still there or have been carted off. He doesn't want to think about them, because they are the ones who are forcing him to leave his mother.

The dead soldiers are forcing him to go away, for a while.

"You need to keep away," his mother said the previous evening. *"Take the train to Borgholm from Marnäs, then take the ferry over to Småland. Uncle August will meet you in Kalmar, and you must do what he tells you—and take your cap off when you're thanking him. You're not to speak to anyone else, and you're not to come back to Öland until all this has settled down. But it will be fine, Nils, if we just wait."*

Suddenly he thinks he hears a muted shout behind him, and he stops. But he hears nothing more. Nils moves more cautiously through the juniper bushes, but he can't go too slowly. The train won't wait.

After a couple of kilometers he reaches the graveled main road. A cart is approaching from the south, and he quickly hurries across the road and hides in the ditch. But the cart is being pulled by a lone horse, its head drooping, and Nils is far away from the road by the time it draws level. He is roughly in the middle of the island now, and he thinks about what he read in the newspaper: it was along this road that the German soldiers are presumed to have sneaked a week or so earlier, when their boat suffered engine failure and drifted ashore to the south of Marnäs.

He's not going to think about them, but for a moment he remembers the little box of gemstones he took from the soldiers, and sees himself burying it deep beneath the memorial cairn. In recent days while he and his mother have mostly stayed in the house, he has almost told her about his spoils of war several times, but something has made him keep silent. He will tell her, he will dig them up and show his mother the treasure, but he intends to leave all that until he comes home again.

After another twenty minutes' walking, the gravel-covered railway track appears ahead of him. It's the narrow-gauge track between Böda and Borgholm, and he turns north and walks alongside it toward the station in Marnäs. The two-story wooden station house stands alone just to the south of the village. It's a post office and railway station combined, and he catches sight of the house just as the two tracks divide and become four just ahead of him.

The track is empty. His train hasn't arrived yet.

Nils has been to Borgholm and back three times before, and knows how a traveler should behave. He walks into the station, where everything is quiet, goes over to the window, and buys a single ticket to town.

The miserable-faced woman with glasses behind the iron grille looks up at him, then hastily looks down at the desk as she issues the ticket. The steel nib of her pen rasps across the paper.

Nils waits anxiously, feeling as if he's being watched, and looks around. Half a dozen people, mostly men in neatly buttoned suits, are sitting on the wooden benches in the waiting room. They are waiting alone or in groups, and several have black leather bags with them. Nils is the only one with both a rucksack and a suitcase.

"There you are. Last carriage, number three."

Nils takes the ticket, pays, and walks out onto the platform, his rucksack over his shoulder and his suitcase in his hand. After just a few minutes he hears the screech of a train whistle, and the train chugs slowly into the station with its three red-painted wooden carriages.

There is an enormous power in the black, puffing steam engine as it slows down in front of the station house, its brakes squealing.

Nils climbs aboard the last carriage. The stationmaster calls out something behind him; the doors of the station house open and the other travelers emerge.

Nils turns around on the top step and stares silently at them; they choose to go toward the other carriages.

The compartment is dark and completely empty. Nils lifts his suitcase onto the luggage rack and sits down on a leather-covered window seat with a view over the alvar, his rucksack beside him. The train jolts, heavy and steady, and begins to move. Nils closes his eyes and breathes out.

The train stops again, with a dull hiss. The carriages remain still.

Nils opens his eyes, waits. He's still alone in the carriage.

A minute passes, then two. Is something wrong?

Somebody shouts something outside, and at last he feels the train begin to move again. It slowly picks up speed, and Nils sees the station house slip past and disappear behind him. Cool air blows into the carriage through gaps in the windows; it feels like a sea breeze on the shore at Stenvik.

Nils's shoulders slowly drop. He places a hand on his rucksack, opens it, and leans back in his seat. The train's speed is increasing all the time. The whistle screams.

Suddenly the door of his compartment opens.

Nils turns his head.

A well-built man wearing a black police uniform with shiny buttons and a police cap walks in. He looks Nils straight in the eye.

"Nils Kant from Stenvik," says the man, his expression serious.

It isn't a question, but Nils nods automatically.

He's sitting there as if he were nailed to the seat as the train races across the alvar. The greenish brown landscape outside the window, blue sky. Nils wants to stop the train and jump off, he wants to get back out onto the alvar. But the train is moving swiftly now, the wheels pounding along the track, the wind howling.

"Good."

The man in the uniform sits down heavily on the seat diagonally opposite Nils, so close that their knees are almost touching. The man straightens his coat, which is buttoned up despite the heat. His forehead is shiny with sweat beneath the brim of his cap. Nils recognizes him, vaguely. Henriksson. He's the district police superintendent in Marnäs.

"Nils," says Henriksson, as if they knew each other, "are you going to Borgholm?"

Nils nods slowly.

"Are you going to visit someone down there?" asks Henriksson.

Nils shakes his head.

"What are you going to do, then?"

Nils doesn't answer.

The police officer turns his head and looks out of the window.

"Anyway, we can travel together," he says, "and we can have a little chat in the meantime."

Nils says nothing.

The police officer goes on:

"When they phoned and told me you were here, I asked them to hold the train for a few minutes so that I could come along and join you." He turns his gaze back to Nils almost reluctantly. "I'd really like to talk to you, you see, about all those long walks on the alvar . . ."

The train begins to slow down again at one of the stations between Marnäs and Borgholm. A little cottage surrounded by apple trees slips past Nils's window. He imagines he can smell the aroma of pancakes through the window; his mother had made him fresh pancakes with sugar the previous evening.

Nils looks at the policeman.

"The alvar . . . there's nothing to talk about," he says.

"I can't really agree with you there." The police officer takes a handkerchief out of his pocket. "I think we do need to talk about it, Nils, and many other people agree with me. The truth will always come out."

The policeman holds Nils's gaze as he slowly wipes the sweat from his face. Then he leans forward.

"Several people from Stenvik have got in touch with us over the past few days. They've said that if we want to know who's been shooting out on the alvar with a shotgun, we ought to talk to you, Nils."

Nils can see the two dead soldiers lying out there on the alvar; he can see their staring eyes inside his brain.

"No," says Nils, shaking his head.

There's a rushing sound in his ears. The train begins to brake.

"Did you meet the foreigners out on the alvar, Nils?" asks the policeman, putting his handkerchief away.

The train stops, jolting the carriages slightly. After only half a minute or so it begins to move again.

"You did, didn't you?"

All the time the policeman is looking at him and waiting for a reply. His steady gaze sears Nils's face.

"We've found the bodies, Nils," he says. "Was it you who shot them?"

"I didn't do anything," says Nils quietly, his fingers fumbling with the opening of his rucksack.

"What did you say?" asks the policeman. "What have you got there?"

Nils doesn't reply.

The wheels begin to pound again, the whistle screams, his fingers tremble and search and burrow into the rucksack, which falls over on its side. His right hand gropes among his clothes and possessions.

The police officer half gets up from his seat; perhaps he has realized that something is about to happen.

The train whistle screams in terror.

"Nils, what have you got–"

Inside the rucksack, Nils's fingers close firmly around the sawn-off shotgun. He presses the trigger and the gun jerks among the clothes inside the rucksack.

The first shot shreds the bottom of the rucksack, ripping up the seat beside the policeman. Splinters of wood spray up toward the ceiling.

The police officer jumps at the noise, but doesn't try to take cover.

He has nowhere to go.

Nils quickly lifts the torn rucksack and fires again, without even looking where he's shooting. The rucksack is ripped apart.

The second shot hits the policeman. His body is flung back against the wall so hard that Nils can hear the crack, he falls heavily, his back rolls across the shattered seat and crashes down on the carriage floor.

The wheels pound against the rails, the train hurtles across the alvar.

The police officer is lying on the floor in front of Nils, his arms twitching slightly. Nils keeps hold of the shotgun, but lets go of the torn rucksack and stands up, his legs unsteady.

Shit.

"Take the train to Borgholm," he hears his mother saying inside his head.

Her plan is ruined now.

Nils gazes around, and sees the landscape racing past the window.

The alvar is still there, and the sunshine.

He turns the rucksack upside down and ripped clothes stinking of gunpowder come tumbling out: socks, pants, a woolen sweater. But there's a little bag of butter toffees right at the bottom, and his wallet and hip flask full of brandy are undamaged. He picks up the flask, takes a quick swig of lukewarm brandy, and slips the flask into his back pocket. That feels better.

The money, the sweater, the flask, the gun, and the toffees. He can't take anything else with him. He'll have to leave the suitcase of clothes.

Nils climbs over the policeman's motionless body, opens the door, and makes his way out into the thundering din between the carriages.

The train rolls on across the alvar. The wind tugs at him, he screws up his eyes against it. Through a window he can see into the carriage in front of him; a man in a black hat is sitting with his back to him, swaying in time with the train's movement. The sound of the shots was deadened by the clothes in the rucksack— the train thunders on along the track, and no one seems to have heard a thing.

Nils opens the side door, catches the scent of the plants on the alvar and sees the gravel on the track hurtling past beneath him like a pale gray river. He climbs down onto the last step above the ground, sees that the track behind is empty, and jumps.

He tries to jump through the air and hit the ground with his legs moving, but the impact knocks his feet from underneath him. The wheels of the train thunder on, the world spins around. He is hurled to the ground, takes a hard blow on the forehead, and tenses his body, aware of the risk that he might die beneath the train. But the track knocks him out of the way.

He raises his head and sees the train moving away, sees the last carriage, the one he has just left, growing smaller and smaller along the track.

The train disappears in the distance. There isn't a sound.

He made it.

Slowly he gets up and looks around. He's back out on the alvar, his shotgun still in his hand.

No buildings are in sight, no people. Just the endless grass and the blue sky.

Nils is free.

Without a single glance back toward the railway line, he quickly strides out onto the alvar, toward the west coast of the island.

Nils is free, and now he's going to disappear.

He's already disappeared.

14

"*That was a story* in the twilight hour," said Astrid quietly.

By the time she'd finished telling the story of Nils Kant, the wine bottle was empty. The glow of the sun had gradually disappeared outside the kitchen window and had become a narrow, dark red line on the horizon.

"So the policeman on the train . . . he died?" asked Julia.

"The conductor came into the compartment and found him lying there dead," answered Astrid. "Shot in the chest."

"Lennart's father?"

Astrid nodded.

"Lennart must have been eight or nine when it happened, so he probably doesn't remember much about it," she said, and added, "But it must have had a terrible effect on him . . . I know he never wants to talk about how his father died."

Julia looked down into her wineglass. "I understand why he didn't want to talk about Nils Kant either," she said. Thanks to the intoxicating effect of the wine, she was beginning to feel a blossoming sense of closeness to Lennart Henriksson—he had lost a father, she had lost a son.

"No," said Astrid. "And these rumors about Nils Kant still being alive don't make it any easier for him."

Julia looked up at her. "Who's saying that?" she asked.

"Haven't you heard people talking about it?"

"No. But I have seen Kant's grave in Marnäs. There's a gravestone and the date and . . ."

"There aren't many left who remember Nils Kant any longer, but those who do, the older ones . . . Some of them believe the coffin contained nothing but stones when it came home from overseas," said Astrid.

"Is that what Gerlof thinks?"

"He's never said," replied Astrid. "Not that I've heard. Gerlof's an old sea captain after all, so he's probably never given much credence to rumors. And that's all this talk about Nils Kant is . . . just rumors and gossip. Some people say they've seen Nils Kant standing by the side of the road in the autumn fog, watching the cars, with a shaggy beard and gray hair . . . and others have seen him wandering around out on the alvar, as he did when he was young, or in amongst the crowds in Borgholm in the summer." Astrid shook her head. "I've never seen hide nor hair of Kant. He must be dead."

She picked up their wineglasses and got up from the table. Julia stayed where she was, wondering whether she and her mother, Ella, would have sat chatting like this in Stenvik, if Ella had still been alive. Probably not; her mother had hardly ever given away what she was thinking.

Then Julia felt something soft and warm against her trouser leg and gasped, but it was only Astrid's fox terrier Willy, who had padded over to her under the table. She reached down and scratched the coarse hair at the back of his neck, gazing pensively out of the kitchen window at the red afterglow of the sun on the mainland.

"I wish I could stay here," she said.

Astrid turned from the sink. "You stay right there," she said. "You don't need to go, it's not that late. We can talk some more."

Julia shook her head. "I mean . . . I wish I could stay in Stenvik."

And she did. It might just have been the wine, but at that moment she could feel the memory of all those childhood summers in the village, like the echo of a beautiful melody in her head, an Öland folk song, as if it were here in Stenvik that she really belonged. Despite the pain associated with Jens's disappearance, despite Ernst's death.

"Well, can't you stay here?" said Astrid. "You're going to Ernst's funeral up in Marnäs, aren't you?"

"I need to get the car back to my sister." It was a very feeble reason; she was the joint owner of the Ford after all, but it was all she could come up with. "I'll probably go tomorrow evening, or the day after."

She got up from the table, with a certain amount of difficulty. Her legs were unsteady after the wine.

"Thank you so much for dinner, Astrid," she said.

"It was a pleasure," said Astrid, smiling broadly for once. "We must try and meet up again before you go. Or next time you come to Stenvik."

"We will," promised Julia. She patted Willy and went out through the kitchen door.

It wasn't yet night outside, only early evening, and she didn't need to feel her way home through the pitch darkness.

"Come over to me if you get scared in the dark," called Astrid behind her. "Just think—there's only us left in Stenvik now, you and me and John Hagman. There were three hundred people living here at one time. There was a temperance society and a mission house and rows of mills down by the sea. Now there's only us left."

Then she closed the kitchen door, before Julia had time to answer.

The intoxication which had been so noticeable in Astrid's kitchen began to subside out in the fresh air—at least Julia thought so. The evening was clear and cold, and faint lights glimmered far away on the mainland, on the other side of the sound. To the north and south along the Öland coast, more lights glowed from houses and lamps too far away to be visible in daylight.

Julia had kept the key to Gerlof's cottage, and after a few hundred yards she turned inland. She walked along the village road, striding out as best she could; she glanced into Vera Kant's garden, and wondered briefly if old Vera had managed to see her beloved son Nils before he died, or not.

The garden was silent and full of shadows. Julia kept walking up to the summer cottage, unlocked the outside door, and switched on the light in the hallway.

No shadows here. Jens was in the cottage, but only as a vague memory. Jens was dead.

She used the cottage bathroom to wash, go to the toilet, and brush her teeth.

When she'd finished, she turned off the hall light, but the last thing she did was to pick up the cell phone, which had been charging all day in the cottage. Standing in the hallway in front of the big window, she dialed Gerlof's number at the residential home. He answered after three rings.

"Davidsson . . ."

"Hi, it's me."

She always had a guilty conscience when she spoke to Gerlof when she wasn't entirely sober, but there was nothing she could do about that.

"Hello," said Gerlof. "Where are you?"

"In the cottage. I had dinner at Astrid's, and now I'm going back to the boathouse and I'm going to bed."

"Good. So what did you two talk about?"

Julia thought for a moment. "We talked about Stenvik . . . and about what happened to Nils Kant."

"Haven't you read about it yet, in the book I gave you?" asked Gerlof.

"I haven't finished reading it yet," replied Julia, then changed the subject. "Shall we go to Borgholm soon?"

"I've been thinking it would be a good idea to go on Tuesday," said Gerlof, "if I can get out of here. I think we'll soon need written permission from Boel to leave the premises."

This was typical of Gerlof's sense of humor.

"If you can get permission," retorted Julia, "I'll come and pick you up at half past nine on Tuesday."

Then her breath caught in her throat and she leaned against the window.

She could see something out there, a pale light . . .

"Hello?" said Gerlof. "Are you still there?"

"Is anybody living in the house next door?" asked Julia, her eyes fixed on the window.

"What do you mean, next door?"

"In Vera Kant's house."

"Nobody's lived there for over twenty years. Why?"

"I don't know . . ."

Now she couldn't see any lights over there. And yet she was

still certain she'd seen a light flicker in one of the rooms on the ground floor.

"So who owns that house?" she asked.

"Er . . . it must be distant relatives, I suppose," said Gerlof. "Second cousins of Vera Kant's, I think. At any rate, nobody's shown the slightest interest in maintaining it. You've seen the state it's in . . . and it was already in a mess when Vera died in the seventies."

Everything was still dark outside the window.

"Okay," said Gerlof, "see you tomorrow. And then on Tuesday, we'll go to Borgholm."

"So are we going to find the man who took Jens away?"

"I never said that," said Gerlof. "All I promised to do was to show you the person who sent the sandal to me. That's all."

"Isn't that the same person?"

"I don't think so."

"Can you explain why?"

"I'll do that in Borgholm."

"Okay," said Julia, who knew he wouldn't say more, no matter how hard she implored him. "Tomorrow, then."

She switched off her cell phone.

On the way down the village road, Julia slowed as she walked past Vera Kant's house this time. It was dark beneath the dense old trees, and she kept staring up at the big, empty windows. They were all dark. The derelict house formed a big, black shadow against the night sky. The only way to find out if anyone was hiding in there was to . . . go into Vera's house and have a look for herself.

But it would be insane to do it, Julia knew that. At least to do it all alone. Vera Kant's was a ghost house nowadays, but . . .

What if Jens had gone in there on that day? What if he was still in there?

Come inside, Mummy. Come inside, come and get me . . .

No. She mustn't think like that.

Julia walked quickly down to the boathouse, opened the door, and went in. She locked the outside door behind her.

15

Tuesday morning was cold and windy, and it was humiliating for Gerlof not to be able to walk out to the car on his own. He was forced to lean on both Boel and Linda as he made his way out of the home to Julia's Ford out at the front.

Gerlof could feel how hard both women were working to make his heavy, unwilling body move forward. All he could do was grip his cane tightly with one hand and his briefcase with the other, and allow himself to be led.

It was humiliating, but there was nothing to be done about it. Some days he could walk without too much difficulty, other days he could hardly move. This autumn day was cold, and that made everything worse. It was the day before Ernst's funeral, and Gerlof and his daughter were off on an excursion.

Julia opened the passenger door from the inside, and he got in.

"Where are you off to?" asked Boel beside the car. She always liked to keep tabs on him.

"South," said Gerlof. "To Borgholm."

"Will you be back for dinner?"

"Probably," said Gerlof, closing the door. "Right, off we go," he said to Julia, hoping she wouldn't comment on the wretched state he was in this morning.

"She seems to care about you," said Julia as she drove away from the home. "Boel, I mean."

"It's her responsibility, she doesn't want anything to happen to me," said Gerlof, and added, "I don't know if you heard, but a pensioner has disappeared in the south of Öland . . . The police are looking for him."

"I heard it on the car radio," said Julia. "But we're not going out onto the alvar today, are we?"

Gerlof shook his head. "Like I said, we're going to Borgholm. We're going to see three men. Not all at the same time. One after another. And one of them sent Jens's sandal to me. You want to talk to him, don't you?"

"And the others?"

"One of them is a friend of mine," said Gerlof. "His name's Gösta Engström."

"And the third man?"

"He's a little bit special."

Julia braked as they approached the stop sign at the intersection with the main road.

"You always have to be so secretive, Gerlof," she said. "Is it because you want to feel important?"

"No, it isn't," said Gerlof quickly.

"Well, that's what *I* think," said Julia as she turned onto the main road to Borgholm.

Maybe she was right, thought Gerlof. He'd never really considered what it was that motivated him.

"I'm not self-important," he said. "I just think it's best to tell stories at their own pace. Before, people always took their time over telling stories, but now everything has to be done so quickly."

Julia didn't say anything. They drove south, past the turning for Stenvik. A few hundred yards further on, Gerlof could see the old station house on the horizon to the west. This was where Nils Kant had walked that summer's day after the end of the war, the day that ended with him shooting District Superintendent Henriksson dead on the train.

Gerlof could still remember the commotion. First two German soldiers shot dead on the alvar, then the murder of a policeman, and a murderer on the run—a sensation that merited plenty of news coverage, even during the final bloody and dramatic months of the Second World War.

Reporters had come from far and wide to write about the violence and the horrifying events on Öland. Gerlof himself had been in Stockholm at the time, trying to resume his civilian maritime career, and had only been able to read about the drama in the newspaper. The police had called in reinforcements from all over southern Sweden to search the island for Kant, but he had jumped off the train and managed to get away.

There were no trains on Öland now; even the railway tracks had been pried up, and the Marnäs train station had become someone's home. A summer home, of course.

Gerlof looked away from the station house and leaned back in his seat; a few minutes later something suddenly started bleeping persistently somewhere inside the car. He looked around quickly, but Julia remained calm and, as she was driving, slid a cell phone out of her purse. She spoke quietly, answering in monosyllables, then switched off the phone.

"I've never understood how those things work," said Gerlof.

"What things?"

"Cordless phones. Cell phones, as they call them, whatever a cell is."

"All you have to do is switch them on and make a call," said Julia. Then she added, "That was Lena. She says hello."

"That's nice. What did she want?"

"I think she mainly wants her car back," said Julia tersely. "This one. She keeps calling me about it." Her grip on the steering wheel tightened. "I own it jointly with her, but that doesn't seem to bother her."

"Right," said Gerlof.

His daughters obviously had points of disagreement between them that he knew nothing about. Their mother would doubtless have done something about it if she'd been alive, but unfortunately he had absolutely no idea what he ought to do.

Julia sat in silence behind the wheel after her telephone conversation, and Gerlof couldn't come up with any way of breaking the silence.

After a quarter of an hour Julia turned off onto the exit road to Borgholm.

"Where are we going now?" she asked.

"First of all we're going to have our morning coffee," replied Gerlof.

It was warm and comfortable in the Engströms' apartment on the southern outskirts of Borgholm. Gösta and Margit had a fantastic view of the ruined castle from their balcony in the low apartment block. On the far side of a narrow, deserted meadow was a long steep hillside with huge deciduous trees clinging to it, and on the plateau above the hillside rose the medieval castle. One of Borgholm's many mysterious fires had ravaged it at the beginning of the nineteenth century, and now both the roof and the wooden beams were gone. Great black openings gaped where the windows had been.

The burnt-out windows up there always made Gerlof think of a skull with empty eye sockets. Some of those who lived in Borgholm had never liked the castle, he knew, at least not until it was transformed from a showy, dilapidated wreck into a historic ruin that brought in the tourists. Centuries ago, the inhabitants of Öland had been forced to build the castle, but it had been yet another royal command that brought nothing but blood and sweat and disappointment for them. The people of the mainland had always tried to suck the island dry.

Julia stood in silence on the balcony contemplating the ruin, and Gerlof turned to her.

"In the Stone Age they used to throw the old people who were sick off that cliff," he said quietly, pointing toward the ruin. "That's what they say, anyway. Of course, that was before the castle was built. And long before those who govern us started building old people's homes . . ."

Margit Engström bustled toward them. She was carrying a tray of coffee cups and wearing an apron that proclaimed THE BEST GRANNY IN THE WORLD!!!

"In the summer they have concerts in the ruin," she told them, "and it can get a bit noisy here. Otherwise it's really nice living below a castle."

She set the tray on the table in front of the television and poured coffee for them all before fetching a basket of buns and a plate of cookies from the kitchen.

Her husband Gösta was wearing a gray suit with a white shirt and suspenders, and was smiling the whole time. He had looked happy when he was a sea captain too, Gerlof remembered—at least as long as people were doing what he told them to do.

"Nice to see you both," said Gösta, picking up a steaming cup of coffee. "Of course we're coming up to Marnäs tomorrow. You're going too, I presume?"

He was talking about Ernst's funeral. Gerlof nodded.

"I am, at least. Julia might have to get back to Gothenburg."

"What's happening to his house?" said Gösta. "Have they said?"

"No, I suppose it's too early to decide," said Gerlof. "But I imagine it will end up as a summer cottage for his family in Småland. Not that northern Öland needs any more summer cottages . . . but I expect that's what it will be."

"Yes, things will have to change a good deal before anybody moves in to live there all year round," said Gösta, taking a sip of his coffee.

"We're so happy down here in town, with everything close by," said Margit, placing the generously filled dishes on the table. "But of course we're members of the Marnäs local history association."

Her husband smiled lovingly at her.

They didn't stay long at the Engströms', no more than half an hour.

"Okay," said Gerlof once they were back in the car, "you can drive over to Badhusgatan now. We'll stop off at Blomberg's car lot and do a little shopping before we head off down to the harbor."

Julia looked at him before she started the car.

"Was there any point to this visit?"

"We got coffee and cookies," said Gerlof. "Isn't that enough? And it's always nice to see Gösta. He was the captain of a Baltic cargo ship, just like me. There aren't many of us left now . . ."

Julia turned onto Badhusgatan and drove past the empty sidewalks. They hardly met any cars either. Ahead of them at the end of the street was the white harbor hotel.

"Turn in here," said Gerlof, pointing to the left.

Julia blinked, then turned onto an asphalt area where a sign saying BLOMBERG'S AUTOS hung in front of a low building housing both a workshop and a used-car lot. A few newer Volvos had the

honor of being positioned inside behind glass, but most of the vehicles were parked outside. Handwritten signs behind each windshield showed the price and mileage.

"Come on," said Gerlof when Julia had pulled up.

"Are we buying a new çar?" she asked, bewildered.

"No, no," said Gerlof, "we're just going to pop in and see
Robert Blomberg for a few minutes."

His joints had grown warmer and coffee with the Engströms
had perked him up. His aches and pains had subsided somewhat,
and he was able to walk across the asphalt with only his cane for
support, although Julia did go ahead of him to open the door of
the workshop.

A bell rang, and the smell of oil hit them.

Gerlof knew a lot about boats but far too little about cars, and
the sight of engines always made him feel unsure of himself. There
was a car standing on the cement floor, a black Ford surrounded
by welding gear and various tools, but nobody was working on it.
The place was deserted.

Gerlof walked slowly over to the little office inside the workshop, and looked in.

"Good morning," he said to the young mechanic in grubby
overalls who was sitting at the desk, intent on the cartoon page of
Ölands-Posten. "We're from Stenvik, and we'd like to buy some oil
for the car."

"Oh? We actually sell that in the other place, but I can get it
for you."

The mechanic got up; he was a little taller than Gerlof. This
must be Robert Blomberg's son.

"We'll come with you and have a look at the cars," said
Gerlof.

He nodded to Julia and they followed the young man through
a door to the sales area.

There was no smell of oil here, and the floor was spotless
and painted white. Rows of shining cars were parked in the showroom.

"Motor oil?" the mechanic asked.

"That'll be fine," said Gerlof.

He saw an older man come out of a small office and position
himself in the doorway of the showroom. He was almost as tall

and broad-shouldered as the mechanic, and he had a wrinkled face with cheeks flushed red by broken blood vessels.

They had never spoken to one another, because Gerlof had always conducted any business involving cars in Marnäs, but he knew immediately that this was Robert Blomberg. Blomberg had come over from the mainland and opened his car workshop and small showroom in the middle of the 1970s. John Hagman had had some dealings with the old man, and had told Gerlof about him.

The older Blomberg nodded to Gerlof without saying anything. Gerlof nodded silently back. He'd heard that Blomberg had had some problems with alcohol a while ago, and maybe he still did, but it was hardly a promising topic of conversation.

"There you go," said the young mechanic, handing over a plastic bottle of engine oil.

Robert Blomberg slowly withdrew from the doorway and went back into the office. He was swaying slightly, Gerlof realized.

"I didn't need any oil," said Julia when they were back in the car.

"It's always good to have some spare oil," said Gerlof. "What did you think of the repair shop?"

"It looked like any other repair shop," said Julia, pulling out onto Badhusgatan. "They didn't seem to have that much to do."

"Drive toward the harbor." Gerlof pointed. "And the owners . . . the Blombergs? What did you think of them?"

"They didn't say much. Why?"

"Robert Blomberg was at sea for many years, or so I've heard," said Gerlof. "Sailing the seven seas, all the way down to South America."

"Right," said Julia.

It was quiet in the car for a few seconds. They were approaching the harbor hotel at the bottom of Badhusgatan. Gerlof looked at the harbor beside the hotel, and felt a quiet sorrow.

"No happy ending," he said.

"What?" said Julia.

"Many stories have no happy ending."

"The most important thing is that they have an ending, isn't it?" said Julia. She looked at him. "Are you thinking about anyone in particular?"

"Yes . . . I suppose I'm thinking mostly about seafaring and Öland. It could have turned out better. It ended too quickly."

Borgholm harbor had just a few concrete quays, and they were completely empty. Not one single fishing boat was in. A huge anchor, painted black, had been propped up on the asphalt beside the water, possibly as a reminder of livelier times.

"In the fifties the cargo boats would be lined up here," said Gerlof, looking out the window at the gray water. "On a day like this in the autumn they would have been loading up or having maintenance work done, there would have been people all around them. The air would have been filled with the smells of tar and varnish. If it was sunny, the captains would have hoisted the sails to air them in the breeze. Ivory-colored sails all lined up against a blue sky, it was a beautiful sight . . ."

He fell silent.

"So when did the ships stop coming here?" asked Julia.

"Oh . . . in the sixties. But they didn't stop coming here—it was more that they stopped sailing from here. Most captains on the island needed to exchange their boats for more modern ships around that time, so they could compete with the shipping companies on the mainland, but the banks wouldn't approve any loans. They didn't believe in seafaring on Öland anymore." He stopped speaking, then added, "I couldn't get a loan either, so I sold my last schooner, *Nore* . . . Then I went to evening classes to learn about office administration, to make the time pass in the winter."

"I don't remember you being at home in the winter," said Julia. "I don't remember you being home at all."

Gerlof looked away from the empty quays, at his daughter.

"Oh, but I was at home. For several months. I'd intended to get a job as a captain on an oceangoing ship the following year, but then I got an office job for the local council, and there I stayed. John Hagman, who had been my first mate, bought his own boat when I came ashore, and he had that for a couple more years. It was one of Borgholm's very last ships. It was called *Farewell,* appropriately enough."

Julia had allowed the car to roll slowly forward, away from

the quays and toward the imposing wooden houses that lay to the north of the harbor, behind neat wooden fences. The house nearest to the harbor was the biggest, wide and painted white and almost as big as the harbor hotel.

Gerlof raised his hand.

"You can stop here," he said.

Julia pulled in at the side of the road in front of the houses, and Gerlof leaned slowly forward and opened his briefcase.

"The Öland boat owners were too stubborn," he said, taking out a brown envelope and the slim volume he had brought with him from his desk. "We could have got together enough capital between us to buy new, bigger ships. But that wasn't for us. Strength lies in working alone, I suppose we thought. We didn't dare to make a big investment."

He handed the book over to his daughter. *Malm Freight—Forty Years* was the title, and on the cover was a black-and-white aerial picture of a big motorized ship plowing through an endless ocean in the sunshine.

"Malm Freight was the exception," said Gerlof. "Martin Malm was a captain who had the courage to invest in bigger ships. He built up a small fleet of cargo ships that sailed all over the world. He made money, and bought more ships with his profits. Martin became one of the richest men on Öland by the end of the sixties."

"Did he?" said Julia. "Great."

"But nobody knows where he got the capital from to start up," said Gerlof. "He didn't have any more money than any other skipper, as far as I know." He pointed at the book. "Malm Freight published this memoir last spring. Turn it over, I want to show you something."

On the back was a short text explaining that this was an anniversary publication about one of Öland's most successful shipping companies. Beneath the text was a logo, consisting of the words MALM FREIGHT with a silhouette of three seagulls hovering above them.

"Look at the seagulls," said Gerlof.

"Right," said Julia. "A drawing of three seagulls. And?"

"Compare it with this envelope," said Gerlof, passing her the brown envelope. It had a Swedish stamp with a blurred postmark, and was addressed to him at the Marnäs Home, Marnäs, in shaky handwriting in black ink. "Somebody has torn off the right-hand corner, just there. But there's still a little bit of the right seagull's wing . . . can you see it?"

Julia looked, then nodded slowly. "What is this envelope?"

"The sandal arrived in it," said Gerlof. "The boy's sandal."

"But you threw that envelope away. That's what you told Lennart."

"A white lie. I thought it was enough that he was taking the sandal." Gerlof quickly went on: "But the important thing is that this envelope came from Malm Freight. So it was Martin Malm who sent Jens's sandal. I'm sure of it. And I think he's phoned me too."

"Phoned you?" said Julia. "You didn't tell me that."

"He *might* have phoned." Gerlof looked out at the big houses. "There wasn't much to say about it, just that somebody has called me this autumn on a few evenings. It started after I got the sandal. But the person who called never said a word."

Julia lowered the envelope and looked at him. "Are we going to see him now?"

"I hope so." Gerlof pointed at the big white wooden house. "He lives there."

He opened the car door and got out. Julia stayed where she was for a few seconds, motionless at the wheel, then she got out of the car as well.

"Are you sure he's at home?"

"Martin Malm is always at home," said Gerlof.

A cold wind from the sound was blowing around them, and Gerlof glanced back over his shoulder at the water. Once again he wondered about Nils Kant—how he'd somehow got across this sound, almost fifty years earlier.

Nils Kant is sitting in a grove of trees on the mainland, looking out across the water to Öland, which is a narrow strip of limestone along the horizon. His expression is full of sorrow, and the sighing of the wind is melancholy in the tops of the pine trees above him. The island on the opposite side of the sound is illuminated by the morning sun; the trees are bright green, the long beaches shimmer like silver.

His island. And Nils will return to it. Not now, but as soon as he can—that's for certain. He knows he has done things for which no one will forgive him for a very long time, and Öland is dangerous for him right now. And yet none of this is really his fault. Things have simply happened, there was nothing he could do about them.

The fat district superintendent crept up on him on the train and tried to capture him, but Nils was too quick for him.

"Self-defense," he whispers toward the island that is his home. "I shot him, but it was self-defense . . ."

He stops and clears his throat noisily to get rid of the tears.

Twenty hours have passed since Nils jumped off the train out on the alvar. He escaped by making his way quickly south on the island, staying far out on the alvar where he feels at home, avoiding all roads and villages.

A few miles south of Borgholm, where the sound is at its narrowest, he went down to the water through the forest. There he found a half-rotten dried-out tar barrel with the top part cut away, and he placed his few possessions inside it. Nils waited in the forest until darkness fell, then he undressed and pushed the barrel out into the cold water. He wrapped his arms and upper body around it, clinging on tightly, then began to kick his way across the sound, toward the black strip that was the mainland.

It must have taken a couple of hours to get across, but there were no boats in the vicinity when he passed the channel, and nobody appeared to have spotted him. When he finally reached Småland, naked and with frozen legs, he barely had the strength to lift his possessions out of the barrel and crawl in beneath the trees, where he immediately fell into a deep sleep.

Now he's wide-awake, but it's still early in the morning. Nils stands up; his legs are still aching after the swim, but it's time for them to get to work again. He isn't far from Kalmar, he realizes, and he needs to get away from the town. There are bound to be lots of policemen patrolling the streets.

His clothes are dry and he puts on a shirt, sweater, socks, and boots, and slips his wallet into his pocket. He must definitely hang on to the money his mother gave him; without it he's lost, and won't be able to stay in hiding.

He no longer has the Husqvarna shotgun—it's at the bottom of the sound. When he was about halfway between the island and the mainland, he took it out of the barrel, held it by the sawn-off barrels, and dropped it into the water with a feeble splash. And it was gone.

There were no cartridges left in the gun anyway, but Nils will miss its reassuring weight.

He thinks about his rucksack, shot to pieces, and misses that too. He has to carry everything in the pockets of his trousers now, and in a little bundle made from a handkerchief, so he can't take much with him.

He starts to walk northward in the morning sun. He knows where he's heading, but it's a long way, and it takes most of the day. He keeps to the coast, avoiding all villages. He crosses the roads through the forest as quickly as possible; he feels safe among the trees. Twice he sees deer in the forest, so quiet that they surprise him. He can hear people approaching when they're several hundred yards away, and can easily avoid them.

Nils knows perfectly well where Ramneby is; he's been there several times while he was growing up, and his last visit was the previous summer. He doesn't need to go into the village or around it, because the sawmill his Uncle August owns and runs lies to the south of the community.

He can hear the sound of whining saws from far away as he approaches, and soon he can smell the familiar aroma of newly sawn timber mixing with the seaweed from the waters of the Baltic.

Nils creeps cautiously out of the forest in the shelter of a big barn filled with planks of wood. He's visited the place a few times, but isn't sure how to get to the office. And he couldn't show himself in the open anyway. A few hundred yards to the south of the sawmill is Uncle August's wooden house, but Nils daren't go there either. There are children there, chauffeurs, servants—people who might tell the police if they see him. He is forced to wait by the barn, concealed by a dense lilac bush whose heavily scented flowers attract countless insects.

Nils's watch stopped when he was swimming across the sound, but he's sure that at least half an hour passes before the first people come into view. Three workers from the mill pass the barn laughing, without even glancing in his direction.

He waits.

A few minutes later another person comes plodding along. It's a boy, maybe thirteen or fourteen years old, but almost as tall as Nils. He has a thick cap pulled down over his forehead, and his hands are thrust deep into the pockets of his oil-stained trousers.

"Hey!" calls Nils from behind the bush.

He calls out quietly, and the boy doesn't react. He keeps on walking.

"You! With the cap!"

The boy stops. He looks around suspiciously, and Nils cautiously stands and waves to him. "Over here."

The boy changes course and takes a few steps toward the bush. He stands there staring at Nils, without saying a word.

"Do you work here at the sawmill?" asks Nils.

The boy nods proudly. "It's my first summer."

His voice very nearly cracks, and he speaks with the Småland dialect.

"Good," says Nils. He is making a real effort to sound calm

and friendly. "I need some help. I want you to fetch August Kant. I need to talk to him."

"The boss?" asks the boy in surprise.

"August Kant, the boss, that's right," says Nils. He holds the boy's gaze and extends his hand to show that he is holding a whole one-krona coin between his fingers. "Tell him Nils is here. Go to the office and tell the boss he has to come."

The errand boy nods, without any reaction to the name Nils, and quickly grabs the coin. Then he turns away, without any great hurry. He pushes the coin deep into his pocket.

Nils breathes out and settles back down behind the bush. That's it, everything will be all right now. His uncle will look after him, hide him until everything has calmed down. No doubt he'll have to stay out of the way here in Småland for the rest of the summer, but he'll just have to put up with that.

He has to wait again, for far too long. At last he hears steps approaching the barn. Nils raises his head, smiling, and takes a step forward—but it isn't his Uncle August. It's just the boy with the cap again.

Nils looks at him. "Wasn't he in the office . . . the boss?" he asks.

"Yes." The boy nods. "But he doesn't want to come."

"Doesn't want to?" says Nils uncomprehendingly.

"I'm to give you this," says the boy.

He is holding a small white envelope in his hand.

Nils takes it, turns his back on the boy, then opens it.

There is no letter in the envelope, just three bills. Three one-hundred-krona bills, folded up.

Nils closes the envelope and spins around.

"Was that all?" he asks.

The boy nods.

"The boss didn't say anything . . . He didn't send a message?"

The boy shakes his head. "Just the letter."

Nils lowers his eyes and stares at the bills.

Money, that's all he got. Money to get away, and it's a very clear message.

His uncle doesn't want anything to do with him.

He sighs and looks up again, but the boy is gone. Nils catches a glimpse of him as he disappears around the corner of the barn.

Nils is alone again. He'll have to manage on his own.

So he has to get away. Where to?

Away from the coast, first and foremost. After that, something will turn up.

Nils looks around. The insects are humming, the scent of lilac fills the air. Everything is green, the dark rich green of summer. To the northeast he can see a little strip of blue water.

He will come back. They might be able to chase him away right now, but he will return. Öland is *his* island.

Nils looks at the water for one last time, then turns and strides back into the safety of the fir trees in the forest.

16

A broad path made of large limestone slabs led up to Martin Malm's big white house; Julia looked at the building and thought of Vera Kant's house in Stenvik. It was about the same size, but of course this one had been painted and was well looked after, and somebody lived here. But who lit a candle in Vera Kant's house late at night? Julia couldn't stop wondering—had she really seen the light at the window?

She held on to Gerlof's arm as they opened the heavy iron gate and made their way over the rough stones. Maybe he was supporting her as much as she was supporting him, thought Julia, because she was feeling nervous now.

For her, this was a meeting with Jens's murderer. If Martin Malm had definitely sent the sandal, then he must be the murderer—whatever reservations Gerlof might have.

The path stopped at steps leading up to a broad mahogany door with an iron nameplate that said MALM. In the middle of the door beneath a small stained glass window was a bell, shaped like a little key.

Gerlof looked at Julia. "Ready?"

Julia nodded, and reached out toward the bell.

"Just one more thing," said Gerlof. "Martin had a brain hemorrhage quite a few years ago. He has good days and less good days, more or less like I do. If this is a good day, we can talk to him. If not . . ."

"Okay," said Julia, her heart pounding.

She twisted the bell and a muted but prolonged ringing could be heard from inside the house.

A shadow appeared behind the glass panel after a moment, and the door opened.

A young woman was standing in front of them. She was small and blonde and slightly wary.

"Hello," she said.

"Good afternoon," said Gerlof. "Is Martin home?"

"Yes," said the girl, "but I don't think he—"

"We're good friends," said Gerlof quickly. "My name's Gerlof Davidsson. From Stenvik. And this is my daughter. We wanted to call on Martin."

"Okay," said the girl. "I'll check."

"Could we come into the warmth in the meantime?" asked Gerlof.

"Of course."

The girl stepped back.

Julia helped Gerlof over the threshold and across the marble floor of the hallway. It was spacious, with dark wooden panels on the wall, showing off framed photographs of old and modern ships. Three doors led off into the house, and a wide staircase led to the upper floor.

"Are you a relative of Martin's?" asked Gerlof when they had closed the front door behind them.

"I'm a nurse from Kalmar," the girl said, shaking her head and walking toward the middle door.

She opened it and Julia tried to see what lay beyond, but there was a dark curtain on the other side.

She and Gerlof remained where they were, in silence, as if the big house with its closed doors didn't invite conversation. Everything was as hushed and solemn as in a church—but when Julia listened carefully she thought she could hear someone moving about upstairs.

The middle door opened and the nurse came back out.

"Martin isn't feeling too well today," she told them quietly. "I'm sorry. He's tired."

"Oh dear," said Gerlof. "That's a shame. We haven't seen each other for several years."

"You can come back another time," said the nurse.

Gerlof nodded. "We'll do that. But we'll call first."

He was moving backwards toward the front door, and Julia reluctantly went with him.

Outside the air seemed even colder than before, Julia thought. She walked beside Gerlof in silence, opened the iron gate, and then looked back at the big house.

She could see a pale face staring at her through one of the broad windows on the upper floor. It was an elderly woman, standing up there and gazing intently down at them through the window.

Julia opened her mouth to ask if Gerlof recognized the woman, but he was already at the car. She had to move quickly to get the door open for him.

When she looked at the house again, the woman at the window had vanished.

Gerlof settled into his seat and looked at his watch.

"Half past one," he said. "Maybe we should get something to eat. Then we need to pop down to the liquor store. I promised some of my neighbors at the home I'd make a few purchases. Is that okay?"

Julia got behind the wheel.

"Alcohol is a poison," she said.

They ate the pasta dish of the day at one of the few restaurants in Borgholm that was open during the winter. The dining room was almost empty, but when Julia tried to get Gerlof to discuss the visit to Martin Malm, he just shook his head and concentrated on the food. Afterward he insisted on paying, then they went off to the liquor store, where Gerlof bought two bottles of schnapps flavored with wormwood, a bottle of advocaat, and six cans of German beer. Julia had to carry it all.

"Time to go home now," announced Gerlof when they were back in the car.

He had the carefree tone of someone who had enjoyed a successful day in town, and it annoyed Julia. She slammed the car into gear and pulled out onto the street.

"Nothing happened," she said once they were on their way and had stopped at a red light east of Borgholm.

"What do you mean?" said Gerlof.

"What do I mean?" said Julia, turning north onto the main road. "We achieved nothing today."

"But we did. First, and most important, we had delicious cakes at Margit and Gösta's," said Gerlof. "Then I got a closer look at Blomberg the car dealer. And we also got—"

"Why did you want to do that?" interrupted Julia.

Gerlof didn't reply at first.

"For various reasons," he said eventually.

Julia took a deep breath.

"You need to start telling me things, Dad," she said, staring fixedly through the windshield. She felt like stopping the car, opening the door, and throwing him out on the alvar. It felt as if he were teasing her.

Gerlof was silent for a while longer.

"Ernst Adolfsson got an idea in his head last summer," he said. "A theory. He believed that my grandchild, our Jens, went out onto the alvar in the fog that day, not down to the sea. And he believed that Jens met a murderer out there."

"Who?"

"Nils Kant, perhaps."

"Nils Kant?"

"Nils Kant who's dead, yes. He'd been dead and buried for ten years at the time . . . You've seen his gravestone, after all. But there were rumors . . ."

"I know," said Julia. "Astrid told me about them. But where did the rumors come from?"

Gerlof sighed. "There was a mailman in Stenvik . . . Erik Ahnlund. There was a story he used to tell after he'd retired, to me and Ernst and anybody else in the village who was prepared to listen to him; he said Vera Kant used to receive postcards with no sender's name on them."

"So?"

"I don't know when they started to arrive, but according to Ahnlund she kept getting postcards from different places in South America in the fifties and sixties. Several times a year. Every one with no sender's name."

"Were they from her son?"

"Presumably. That's the most likely explanation." Gerlof

looked out across the alvar. "Then of course Nils Kant came home in a coffin and was buried in Marnäs."

"I know," said Julia.

Gerlof looked at her.

"But the postcards kept on coming even after the funeral," he said. "From abroad, with no sender's name."

Julia glanced quickly at him. "Is that true?"

"I think it probably is," said Gerlof. "Erik Ahnlund was the only one who actually saw the postcards addressed to Vera, but he swore they kept arriving for several years *after* Nils's death."

"And that made people in Stenvik think Kant was still alive?"

"Definitely," said Gerlof. "People have always sat around chatting in the twilight hour. But Ernst wasn't much of a one for gossip, and he thought the same thing."

"And what do you think?"

Gerlof hesitated.

"I'm like the apostle Thomas," he said. "I want proof that he's alive. I haven't found it yet."

"So why did you want to see this Blomberg?" asked Julia.

Gerlof hesitated again, as if he were afraid of appearing old and gaga.

"John Hagman thinks Robert Blomberg might be Nils Kant," he said at last.

Julia stared at him. "But surely you don't think that?"

Gerlof slowly shook his head. "It seems a bit far-fetched," he said. "But John made a number of points. Blomberg was a seaman, as I said. He grew up in Småland and went to sea as an engineer when he was just a teenager. He was away for many years . . . twenty or twenty-five years, or more. Eventually he came home and moved to Öland. He got married here, and had children. I think his son is the one who was in the workshop today."

"That doesn't sound particularly suspicious," said Julia.

"No," agreed Gerlof, "the only odd thing really is that he was away for so long. John's heard rumors that Blomberg was kicked off his ship, then drifted around some port in South America as a down-and-out alcoholic until some Swedish captain finally brought him home."

"But Blomberg can't be the only person who's moved to Öland?"

"Oh no," said Gerlof. "Hundreds of people have moved here from the mainland."

"And does John suspect them all of being Nils Kant?"

"No. And I didn't think Blomberg was anything like him either," said Gerlof. "But you see what you want to see, don't you? My mother—your grandmother Sara—saw a goblin once when she was young . . . Do you remember? She used to refer to him as 'a gray man' . . ."

"Yes, I've heard that story," said Julia, "you don't need to—"

But there was no stopping Gerlof.

"Whatever it was, she saw him one spring day toward the end of the nineteenth century as she was standing down by Kalmar Sound doing her washing, outside Grönhögen. She suddenly heard rapid footsteps behind her, and he came rushing out of the forest . . . A little man, about three feet tall, in gray clothes. He didn't say a word, just ran toward the sound, straight past Sara without even looking at her. And when he reached the water, he didn't stop . . . Mother called out to him, but he kept on going, straight out into the water, until the waves washed over him and he sank beneath the surface. Then he was gone."

Julia gave a brief nod. It was a bizarre tale—maybe the strangest of all the stories told by her family on Öland.

"A goblin who commits suicide," she said, a little sarcastically. "Now, there's a thing you don't see every day."

"Obviously the story isn't true," Gerlof went on. "But I believe it. I *believe* my mother saw a goblin, or at least some kind of natural force or unknown phenomenon that she interpreted as a goblin. And at the same time, I know goblins and trolls don't exist."

"They don't appear so often nowadays, at any rate," said Julia.

"No," said Gerlof slowly, "and it's probably the same with Nils Kant. Nobody talks about him, nobody sees him. The police have got him down as being dead, and he's buried in Marnäs churchyard with a gravestone anybody can go and look at. And yet there are still certain people in northern Öland who believe Nils Kant is still alive. At least among those who are old enough to remember him."

"What do you think?" asked Julia again.

"I think it would be a good thing if all the strange things surrounding Nils Kant could be sorted out," said Gerlof.

"I'd rather find my son." Julia said it quietly. "That's why I came here."

"I know," said Gerlof. "But there might be a connection between the two stories."

"Nils Kant and Jens?"

Gerlof nodded. "I already know they are connected to some extent, in fact. Through Martin Malm."

"But how?"

"Malm had Jens's sandal," said Gerlof. "And it was one of Malm Freight's ships that brought Nils Kant's coffin home to Sweden."

"Was it? How do you know that?"

"It's no secret. I was down at the harbor myself when the ship with the coffin came in. An undertaker in Marnäs took care of it."

Julia gave this some thought as they were approaching Marnäs. She braked and turned.

"But we didn't get to speak to the person who sent the sandal today," she pointed out.

"No, but you did see his house," said Gerlof. "Martin was bad today, but sooner or later we'll be able to speak to him. Next week, maybe."

"I can't stay here just for that," said Julia sharply. "I have to get back to Gothenburg."

"So you say," said Gerlof. "When are you leaving?"

"I don't know. Soon . . . tomorrow, maybe."

"Tomorrow's the funeral in Marnäs church," said Gerlof. "Eleven o'clock."

"I don't know if I'm going to go," said Julia, turning into the entrance to the home. "I didn't even know Ernst, after all. His death is tragic and I'll never forget the morning I found him . . . but I didn't know him."

"Try to come anyway," said Gerlof, opening the car door.

Julia got out to help him. She carried the bag of liquor and his briefcase.

"Thank you," said Gerlof, leaning on his cane. "My legs are much better now."

"See you soon," said Julia when she'd walked him as far as the elevator. "Thanks for today."

She watched Gerlof open the elevator door and step in without falling over.

Then she returned to the car and turned out onto the road again, heading east. She decided to buy some groceries in Marnäs before she went down to the boathouse.

It was slowly beginning to grow dusk now; it was twenty past four. Normal people, people who had jobs, were no doubt on their way home from work.

But some people hadn't gone home yet. As she drove past the little police station in Marnäs, she could see there was a light on inside.

Julia stopped at the grocery store and bought milk and bread and something to put on it. She didn't have much money left in her account, and there was over a week left until her next benefit payment.

When she came out of the store, she noticed the light in the windows of the police station again. She thought about Lennart Henriksson, and about what Astrid had told her about him. Lennart too had been affected by a great tragedy in his life.

Julia stopped, looking at the light in the windows. She put the food in the trunk of the Ford and locked it. Then she crossed the road and knocked on the door of the police station.

17

"*I've always blamed my mother,*" said Julia. "She fell asleep that afternoon and left him by himself."

She blinked the tears away and went on:

"I've blamed my father even more . . . because he went down to the sea to mend his nets. If Gerlof had been at home, Jens would never have left the house—Jens loved his grandfather."

Julia sniffled and sighed.

"I've blamed them for many years," she said, "but it was actually my fault. I left Jens and went to Kalmar to meet a man. Although I knew it was a waste of time. He didn't even turn up." She stopped speaking, then she said, softly, "It was Michael . . . Jens's father. We'd split up and he was living in Skåne, but he'd talked about catching the train and coming up to see me . . . I'd thought we might be able to try again, but he wasn't interested." She sniffled again. "So of course Michael was absolutely no help either when Jens disappeared, he was still in Malmö . . . But the main person who was to blame was me."

Lennart sat in silence on the opposite side of the table, listening—he was a good listener, thought Julia—and letting her talk. Now he said:

"It was nobody's fault, Julia. It was simply, as we say in the police . . . a series of unfortunate circumstances."

"Yes," said Julia. "If it was an accident."

"What do you mean?" asked Lennart.

"I mean . . . unless Jens went outside and met somebody who took him away."

"But who?" said Lennart. "Who would do such a thing?"

"I don't know," said Julia. "A madman? You know more than I do about these things, you're a policeman."

Lennart shook his head. "Such a person would need to be disturbed . . . extremely disturbed. And they would almost certainly have come into contact with the police already for other violent crimes. There was nobody like that on Öland at the time. Believe me, we looked for suspects . . . We knocked on doors, we went through our records."

"I know," said Julia. "You did what you could."

"Our assumption was that Jens went down to the water," said Lennart. "It's only a few hundred yards, and it would have been easy to get lost in the fog that day. Many people who have drowned in Kalmar Sound have disappeared forever, both before and since . . ." He stopped. "It must be difficult for you to talk about this, and I don't want to . . ."

"It's fine," said Julia quietly. She thought for a moment, then added, "I didn't think it would be a good thing to come here in the autumn and face it all again, but it has been. I've started to get over Jens . . . and I know he isn't coming back." She made an effort to sound absolutely certain: "I have to move on."

It was Tuesday evening in Marnäs. Julia had intended to call in briefly to see Lennart in the police station, but she was still there. And Lennart had obviously been about to finish work for the day, turn off the computer, and go home, but he'd stayed.

"So you're not on duty tonight?" Julia had asked.

"I am, but not until later," said Lennart. "I'm on the building committee and we've got a meeting tonight, but not until half past seven."

Julia wanted to ask what political party he represented, but there was always the risk that she wouldn't like the answer. Then she wanted to ask if he was married, but she might not like that answer either.

"We could order a pizza from Moby Dick," said Lennart. "Would you like one?"

"That would be nice," said Julia.

There was a kitchen in the office at the police station. Although the offices were impersonal, there was a certain level of home comfort in the kitchen in the form of curtains, red rag rugs on the floor, and even a couple of pictures on the walls. A spotlessly clean coffee machine stood on the equally spotless counter. There was a low table with armchairs in one corner, and when the pizzas topped with ham had been delivered from the bar down by the harbor, Lennart and Julia ate them there.

As they were eating they began to talk—and their conversation centered on sorrow and loss.

Afterward Julia couldn't remember which of them had first started to make things so personal, but she assumed it was her.

"I have to move on," said Julia. "If Jens disappeared in the sound, I have to accept it. It's happened before, as you say." She added after a pause, "It's just that he was afraid of the water, he didn't even like playing on the shore. So I've sometimes thought he went the other way, out onto the alvar. I know how it sounds, but . . . Gerlof thinks the same."

"We looked on the alvar too," said Lennart quietly. "We looked everywhere over the next weeks."

"I know, and I've been trying to remember . . . Did we meet at the time?" asked Julia. "You and I, did we meet?"

The police officers who had turned up and asked questions when Jens disappeared were just a nameless row of faces to her. They had asked their questions, she had answered, frantically at first, and then numbly. Who they were had been irrelevant, just as long as they found Jens.

Much later she had realized that some of their questions had focused on the possibility that she herself—for some unknown reason, insanity perhaps—had killed her own son and hidden his body.

Lennart shook his head.

"You and I never met . . . at least, we never spoke," he replied. "Other officers were responsible for the contact with you and your family, and as I said, I was one of those leading the search. I assembled volunteers down in Stenvik who spent the entire evening searching along the shore, and I drove round in my patrol car, all along the roads around Stenvik and out on the alvar. But we didn't find him . . ."

He stopped speaking, and sighed.

"Those were terrible days," he went on, "particularly as I'd . . . I'd been involved with something similar before, in my private life. My father had . . ."

He stopped again.

"I know something about that, Lennart," said Julia gently. "Astrid Linder told me what happened to your father . . ."

Lennart nodded. "It's no secret," he said.

"She told me about Nils Kant," said Julia. "How old were you when . . . when it happened?"

"Eight. I was eight years old," said Lennart, his eyes fixed on the floor. "I'd started school in Marnäs. It was almost the end of term, a beautiful, sunny day. I was happy . . . looking forward to the summer holidays. Then a rumor started going round among the pupils—there had been a shooting on the train to Borgholm, somebody from Marnäs had been shot . . . but nobody knew anything definite. It wasn't until I got home that I found out. My mother was at home and her sisters were there. They sat there in silence for a long time, but in the end my mother told me what had happened . . ."

Lennart stopped, lost in the past. In his eyes Julia thought she could see the shocked, unhappy eight-year-old he had been that day.

"Are policemen not allowed to cry?" she asked tentatively.

"Oh yes," said Lennart quietly, "but I suppose we're better at keeping the lid on our feelings." He went on: "Nils Kant . . . I didn't even know who he was. He was more than ten years older than me, and we'd never met, although we lived just a few kilometers from each other. And suddenly he'd shot my father dead."

There was silence once again.

"What did you think of him afterward, then?" asked Julia eventually. "I mean, I can understand it if you hated him . . ."

She was thinking of herself, the number of times she'd wondered how she would react if she ever met Jens's murderer. She still didn't know what she would do.

Lennart looked out of the window through the darkness at the back of the police station.

"Yes, I hated Nils Kant," he said. "Deeply and intensely. But I was afraid of him too . . . Particularly at night, when I couldn't sleep. I was terrified he'd come back to Öland and kill me and my mother too." He paused. "It took a long time before those feelings went away."

"Some people say he's still alive," said Julia quietly. "Have you heard that?"

Lennart looked at her. "Who's still alive?"

"Nils Kant."

"Alive?" said Lennart. "That's impossible."

"No. I don't believe it either . . ."

"Kant is not alive," said Lennart, cutting into his pizza. "Who says he is?"

"I don't believe it either," repeated Julia quickly. "But Gerlof has been talking about him ever since I got here . . . It feels as if he's trying to get me to believe that Nils Kant is behind Jens's disappearance. That Jens met Kant that day. Although he must have been dead for ten years by then."

"He died in 1963," said Lennart. "The coffin arrived in Borgholm harbor that autumn." He set down his knife and fork. "And I don't know if it would be a good idea if this came out . . . but the coffin was opened up by the police in Borgholm. Very discreetly, for some reason, perhaps out of fear or respect for Vera Kant, I mean, she did have a lot of money and she owned a considerable amount of land . . . but it was opened."

"And there was a body in it?"

Lennart nodded. "I saw it," he said in a low voice, adding, "This isn't exactly official either, but when the coffin came ashore . . ."

"From one of Malm Freight's ships," Julia interposed.

"That's right. Is it Gerlof who's filled you in on all this background stuff?" he asked, then went on without waiting for her reply: "I'd just started as a police constable in Marnäs, after a couple of years in Växjö, and I asked if I could go down to Borgholm to be there when they opened up Kant's coffin. Of course, my reasons were entirely personal, nothing to do with the police, but my colleagues understood. The coffin was in one of the sheds down by the harbor, waiting for the undertaker. It was a wooden box that was nailed shut, with documents and stamps from some Swedish consulate in South America." He paused. "One of the older constables broke open the lid. And it was Nils Kant's body lying in there, partly dried out and covered in furry black mold. A doctor from the hospital in Borgholm was there and confirmed that he'd drowned in salt water. He'd obviously been in the water for quite some time, because the fish had started . . ."

Lennart's expression had become absent as he was telling the story, but suddenly he looked down at the table and seemed to remember that they were eating pizza.

"Sorry about all the details," he said quickly.

"It's fine," said Julia. "But how did you know it was Kant? Fingerprints?"

"There were no confirmed fingerprints of Nils Kant on record," said Lennart. "No dental records either. But he was identified because of an old injury to his left hand. He'd broken several fingers during a fight at the quarry in Stenvik. I've heard that myself from several people who lived in Stenvik. And the body in the coffin had exactly the same injury. So that decided it."

There was silence in the kitchen for a few seconds.

"How did it feel?" asked Julia eventually. "Seeing Kant's body, I mean."

"I didn't actually feel anything. It was the living Kant I wanted to meet. You can't hold a dead body responsible for anything."

Julia nodded pensively. There was something she'd been thinking of asking Lennart to do for her.

"Have you ever been inside Kant's house?" she asked. "Did the police ever look for Jens in there?"

Lennart shook his head. "Why would we have looked in there?"

"I don't know . . . it's just that I've been trying to work out where Jens could have gone. Perhaps if he didn't go down to the sea, and he didn't go out onto the alvar, he might have gone into one of the neighbors' houses. And Vera Kant's house is only a couple of hundred yards from our cottage . . ."

"Why would he have gone in there?" said Lennart. "And why would he have stayed?"

"I don't know. If he'd gone in and fallen, or . . ." said Julia, thinking, Who knows, perhaps Vera Kant was just as crazy as her son.

Maybe you went in there, Jens, and Vera locked the door behind you.

"I know it's a long shot . . . but would you take a look in there? With me?"

"Take a look . . . You mean go inside Kant's house?"

"Just a quick look, before I go back to Gothenburg tomorrow,"

Julia went on, her eyes holding his dubious gaze. She wanted to tell him about the light she'd seen inside the house, but decided against it in case she'd been imagining things. "I mean, it can't be breaking and entering if the house is empty, can it?" she asked. "And you must be able to go in anywhere you want to, as a police officer?"

Lennart shook his head. "There are very strict regulations. As the only policeman in a country posting, I've been able to improvise a little bit, but—"

"But nobody's going to see us," Julia interrupted him. "Stenvik is practically empty, and the houses all around Vera Kant's are summer cottages. Nobody lives nearby."

Lennart looked at his watch. "I've got to go to this meeting," he said.

At least he hadn't said no to her suggestion, thought Julia. "And after that?"

"You mean you want to go in there tonight?"

Julia nodded.

"We'll see," said Lennart. "These meetings can drag on a bit. I can phone you if it finishes early. Have you got a cell phone?"

"Yes, ring me."

There were a couple of pencils on the kitchen table, and Julia tore off a piece of the pizza box and wrote down her number. Lennart tucked it in his breast pocket and stood up.

"Don't do anything on your own," he said, looking down at her.

"No, I won't," she promised.

"Vera Kant's house looked as if it was about to fall down last time I went past."

"I know. I won't go in there on my own."

But if Jens was there, all alone in the darkness—would he ever forgive her if she didn't go and look for him?

The streets of Marnäs were completely empty when they emerged from the station. The shops were dark, and only the kiosk over in the square was open. The damp air felt almost as if it were starting to freeze.

Lennart switched off the light and locked the station door behind them.

"So you're going back to Stenvik now?" he asked.

Julia nodded. "But we might meet up later?"

"Maybe."

Julia thought of something else.

"Lennart," she said, "did you find out anything about the sandal? The one Gerlof gave you?"

"No, unfortunately," he said. "Not yet. I sent it to Linköping, to the national forensic lab there, but I haven't had a reply yet. These things take time. I'll give them a ring next week. But perhaps we shouldn't hope for too much. I mean, so much time has passed, and we're not even sure it's the right—"

"I know . . . It might not even be his shoe," said Julia quickly.

Lennart nodded. "Take care, Julia."

He held out his hand, which seemed like a rather impersonal way to say goodbye after everything they'd revealed about themselves that night. But Julia wasn't much of a one for hugging either, and she took his hand.

"Bye, then. Thanks for the pizza."

"You're welcome. I'll phone you after the meeting."

His gaze lingered on her face for a moment longer, in the way you can interpret however you like afterward. Then he turned away.

Julia crossed the street to her car. She drove slowly out of the center of Marnäs, past the residential home, where Gerlof was perhaps sitting and drinking his evening coffee, past the dark church and the graveyard.

Was Lennart Henriksson married or a bachelor? Julia didn't know, and hadn't dared to ask.

On the way down to Stenvik she pondered over whether she had revealed too much about herself and her feelings of guilt. But it had been good to talk and to get some perspective on this remarkable day in Borgholm, when Gerlof had shared his new theories: that the man who'd murdered Jens was lying there ill in a luxury villa in Borgholm, and that Nils Kant, who'd murdered District Superintendent Henriksson all those years ago, might be alive and working as a car salesman in the same town. It was difficult to know if her father was teasing her or not.

No. He wouldn't joke about these things. But she didn't feel that his ideas were moving them forward, somehow.

Might as well go home.

She decided to go back to Gothenburg the following day. First she would go to Ernst Adolfsson's funeral, then she'd say goodbye to Gerlof and Astrid—and in the afternoon she'd drive home and try to live a better life than before. Drink less wine, swallow fewer pills. Get back to work as soon as possible. Stop clinging to the past and brooding over riddles that could never be solved. Live a normal life and try to look to the future. Then she could come back and visit Gerlof—and perhaps Lennart too—in the spring.

The first houses in Stenvik appeared, and she slowed. At Gerlof's cottage she stopped the car, got out in the darkness and opened the gate, then drove in. She would spend this last night in her room at the cottage, she decided. She would sleep close to all the good and bad memories for one last time.

Inside, she switched on some lights. Then she left the cottage and went down to the boathouse to collect her toothbrush and everything else she'd left down there—including the bottles of wine she'd brought with her from Gothenburg, and never opened.

She was very aware of Vera Kant's house in the darkness on her left as she walked along the village road, but she didn't turn her head. She merely glanced in passing at the lights in Astrid Linder's house and in John Hagman's to the south before she went down to the boathouse.

When she'd collected all her belongings, she caught sight of the old paraffin lamp hanging in the window; after a second's hesitation, she unhooked it and took it up to the cottage with her. To be on the safe side.

On the way back she did look up at Vera's house behind the tall hawthorn hedges: big and black. There were no lights to be seen at the windows now.

"We never looked in there," Lennart had said.

And why should the police have gone in? Vera Kant was hardly suspected of having abducted Jens.

But if Nils Kant had hidden himself in there in secret, if Vera had been protecting him . . . If Jens had gone out onto the village road in the fog and down toward the sea, and stopped at Vera Kant's gate and opened it and gone in . . .

No, it was impossible.

Julia kept walking. She went back inside the summer cottage, into the warmth, and switched on the lamps in every room. She took one of the bottles of wine out of her bag, and since this was her last evening on Öland, she opened it in the kitchen and filled a glass. When she'd drunk that, standing by the kitchen counter, she quickly refilled the glass. She took it into the living room.

The alcohol spread through her body.

But—just a quick look. If Lennart's meeting up in Marnäs finished early, and if he phoned . . . she'd ask him again if he'd come down. Did he really not want to take a look inside the house where his father's murderer had grown up? Just a quick look?

It was like a fever that Gerlof had infected her with—Julia couldn't stop thinking about Nils Kant.

The first summer following the six-year-long world war is bright and warm and full of optimism for the future. In the city of Gothenburg, whole new residential areas are planned, and old ramshackle wooden houses are being torn down. Nils Kant sees several excavators working as he wanders through the streets of the city.

WORLD PEACE Nils read on the cream-colored posters on the walls in the city center at the beginning of August. A day or so later he buys a newspaper and reads the headline ATOM BOMB— NEW WORLD SENSATION on the front page. Japan has surrendered unconditionally; the Americans' new bomb brought the war to an end. It must have been quite some bomb to achieve such success, according to what Nils has heard people saying on the trams, but when he sees a picture in the newspaper of the great mushroom cloud rising toward the sky, for some reason it makes him think about the bluebottle fly sitting on the dead soldier's hand.

As far as Nils is concerned, there is no peace—he's still a wanted man.

It's late afternoon. Nils is standing under a tree in a little park on the outskirts of the city, watching a young man in a suit approaching rapidly from one of the streets.

Nils himself is wearing a dark suit that he bought secondhand in a shop in Haga; it's neither new nor noticeably shabby. On his head he wears a hat, pulled well down, and he has stopped shaving and cultivated a beard, a thick dark beard that he trims each morning in front of the mirror in his little rented room in Majorna.

As far as he knows, there is only one photograph of him in existence, and it's six or seven years old: a group photograph from school, with Nils standing in the back row, his eyes shadowed by his cap. It's blurred and Nils doesn't even know if the police have it, but he still wants to make sure he's completely unrecognizable.

The street below the park is above the docks, and is one of the most miserable in Gothenburg, more mud and dust than cobbles, and the unpainted wooden houses seem to be leaning on each other to avoid falling down. Nils Kant fits in here, with his beard and his secondhand suit and his slicked-back hair. He looks poor, but he doesn't look like a criminal. At least he hopes not.

Much of his flight from Öland has been about fitting in, preferably not being seen, and definitely not drawing attention to himself.

Nils found it difficult to leave the Baltic coast, where he could catch glimpses of his island through the fir trees. He hung around close to Uncle August's sawmill, and it wasn't until the third morning, when he saw a police car parked outside the office, that he set off toward the west.

Straight into the dense forest.

He was used to walking long distances from his time out on the alvar, and good at finding the right direction with the help of the sun and his intuition.

During June he walked through the countryside, one of many young men on their way to bigger towns and new opportunities after the war, and he didn't attract much attention. Few people even saw him. He avoided the roads, moved through the forest, ate berries and drank water from the streams, and slept under a tree or in a barn if it was raining. Sometimes he found apples growing wild; sometimes he sneaked onto a farm and stole some eggs or a jug of milk.

His stock of Vera's butter toffees had run out by the third day.

In Huskvarna he stopped for a few hours to have a look at the town where his shotgun had been made, but he couldn't find the gun factory, and didn't dare ask anyone where it was. Huskvarna felt almost as big as Kalmar, and the neighboring town of Jönköping was even bigger. Even though his suit smelled of sweat and the forest, there were enough people out on the streets for him to walk around without anyone staring at him.

He even dared to eat in a restaurant and buy a new pair of walking shoes. A good pair of shoes cost exactly thirty-one kronor from the reserve of money his mother had given him, topped up by his Uncle August. His cash was dwindling, but he still went into a little bar near the railway and ordered a big steak, a pilsener, and a small glass of Grönstedt's cognac, which cost two kronor and sixty-three öre altogether. Expensive, but Nils felt he'd earned it after his long trek.

Fortified by his visit to the bar, he left Jönköping behind him and kept moving west through the forests of Västergötland for a few more weeks. Finally, he reached the coast.

Gothenburg is Sweden's second-largest city; Nils learned that at school. Gothenburg is enormous: block after block of tall buildings along the river Göta, hundreds of vehicles on the streets, and all kinds of people. At the beginning all the people around him almost made Nils panic, and for the first few days he kept getting lost. On the streets around the docks he has heard foreign languages, from seamen from England, Denmark, Norway, and Holland. He has watched ships set sail for foreign ports, or slowly heave to at the quayside, laden with cargoes from other lands. For the first time in his life he has eaten a banana; it was almost black and slightly rotten, but it still tasted good. A banana from South America.

Everything on the docks is huge compared with the harbors on Öland, big and different. Rows of derricks for loading and unloading cargo are silhouetted against the sky like great black prehistoric creatures, and tugboats churn out thick gray smoke as they move between the great white Atlantic steamers out in the channel. In the port of Gothenburg, sails and masts have more or less disappeared; now ranks of propeller-driven cargo ships line up at the quays.

Nils has walked by the waterside, studied the long hulls, and thought about the bananas in South America.

He spends as little time as possible in the scruffy room at the boardinghouse for single men; he comes home late and gets up early. He doesn't miss the bitterly cold nights lying on moss and twigs in the forest, but when he is lying in bed the walls around him feel like a cell, and he is listening for the heavy tread of the police on the stairs the whole time.

One night the door of his room opened, and the substantial figure of District Superintendent Henriksson walked into the room in full uniform. His clothes were soaked in blood. He stretched out his hand, dripping red with blood, toward the bed.

You murdered me, Nils. And now I've found you.

Nils shot out of bed, his teeth clenched. The room was empty.

He has sent just one postcard to Vera during his time in Gothenburg. A black-and-white card with a picture of Vinga lighthouse on the front. Nils sent it all the way across the country to Stenvik, without putting his name on it, or even writing a message. He daren't let his mother know anything more than the fact that he's still free and somewhere on the west coast, but he thinks that's enough.

A young man has come into the park now. He's about the same age as Nils, and his name is Max.

The first time Nils saw him was three days earlier at a little café by the docks; Max was sitting in a corner a couple of tables away from Nils. It was easy to spot him, as he was smoking cigarettes from a gold case and talking loudly in a broad Gothenburg accent, to the waitresses, to the smiling owner of the café, and to other customers. Everybody called him Max. Sometimes visitors came in off the street and sat down at his table, young and elderly men who spoke quietly. Then Max lowered his voice as well, and the conversation was conducted with gestures and a rapid exchange of sentences.

Max was selling something, that much was obvious, and since he never handed anything over to those who visited his table, Nils guessed that he was selling information and good advice. So after an hour or so Nils got up and went over to the corner table himself. Closer, he could see that Max was even younger than he was, with greasy hair and a spotty face. But his expression was alert as he listened to Nils.

It felt strange to sit and talk to a stranger after such a long time alone, but it was all right. Just as quietly as the others who had sat at the table, without giving his name, he asked for some particularly good advice. And he wanted Max to do something for him—something important. Max listened and nodded.

"Two days," he said.

That was the time he needed to carry out the important task.

"I'll give you twenty-five kronor," said Nils.

"Thirty-five would be better," the young man said quickly.

Nils thought about it. "Thirty, then."

Max nodded and leaned forward. "We won't meet here again," he said, even more quietly. "We'll meet in a park . . . a good park I often use."

He told Nils where to find it, then got up and quickly left the café.

And now Nils is standing in the park, waiting. He's been here for half an hour, walked round and checked that the park is completely empty, and found two different escape routes in case something should go wrong. He never told his new acquaintance his name, but he's sure Max quickly realized that Nils is wanted by the police.

The young man comes straight up to him without glancing around or signaling to any unseen observers.

This doesn't make Nils relax, but he doesn't run away either. He stares at Max, who has stopped a yard or so in front of him.

"*Celeste Horizon,*" he says. "That's your ship."

Nils nods.

"She's English." Max sits down on a rock among the trees and takes out a cigarette. "But the captain is Danish, his name's Petri. He wasn't particularly interested in who was coming aboard, he just wanted to know about the money."

"We can talk about that," says Nils.

"They're loading timber at the moment, and she sails in three days," says Max, blowing out smoke.

"Where to?"

"East London. They'll unload the timber there, then go on to Durban to pick up coal, then on to Santos. You can go ashore there."

"I want to go to America," says Nils quickly. "To the USA."

Max shrugs his shoulders. "Santos is in Brazil, south of Rio," he says. "Get another ship from there."

Nils thinks about it. Santos is in South America? That might be a good starting point for more travels, before he comes back to Europe.

He nods. "Fine."

Max gets up quickly. He reaches out his hand.

Nils places five heavy two-krona pieces on his palm. "I want to meet this Petri first," he says. "You'll get the rest later. You can show me where to find him."

Max smiles. "You're going 'on the lump,' as they say."

Nils stares uncomprehendingly at him, and Max goes on:

"Men looking for work come to the docks early in the morning and wait for the day's jobs. Some get work, some have to go back home. You're to go down and stand with them early tomorrow morning . . . then you'll be picked to join the *Celeste Horizon*."

Nils nods again.

The young man quickly stuffs the coins in his pocket.

"My name's Max Reimer," he says. "What's yours?"

Nils says nothing. Hasn't he paid to avoid questions? The pulse in his neck begins to throb a little faster as his anger slowly stirs to life.

Max smiles pleasantly at him; he doesn't appear to feel threatened.

"I think you're from Småland," he says, crushing his cigarette under his heel. "That's what it sounds like when you talk."

Nils still doesn't say anything. He knows he can flatten Max— Max is smaller than him, and it would be easy. Knock him down and give him a good kicking. Use a heavy stone to finish him off, then hide the body in the park.

It would be very easy.

But what about afterward? Max might come back at night, just like the dead district superintendent.

"Don't ask too many questions," he says to Max, and starts walking away through the park, toward the docks. "You might not get your money."

18

Lennart didn't call.

Julia sat there waiting in the summer cottage for several hours. It got to eight-thirty on Tuesday evening, then nine o'clock, but he never rang.

By this time Julia had finished off the bottle of red wine; it wasn't difficult. And the temptation to go inside Vera Kant's house had become so obsessive that it didn't actually matter whether Lennart turned up or not.

She thought about phoning Gerlof and telling him what she was intending to do, but decided against it. She couldn't do any more packing or cleaning to make the time pass. She was restless and curious.

Darkness and silence pressed against the walls of the cottage. At a quarter to ten Julia finally stood up, slightly tipsy, but more determined than drunk.

She put an extra sweater on under her coat, and thick socks. There was an old brown woolly hat in the wardrobe by the front door; she tucked her hair inside it and glanced at herself in the hall mirror. Had the furrows of anxiety etched on her forehead smoothed out slightly since her conversation with Lennart?

Maybe—or then again, it could be the wine.

She put her cell phone in her pocket, picked up the old paraffin lamp, and switched off the light in the cottage. She was ready.

Just a quick look.

The evening had turned clear and cold, with only a faint breeze in the trees. When she came out onto the village road, the darkness closed around her instantly, but she could see glimmering points of light on the mainland.

She stopped after a few moments, listening for noises among the shadows: rustling leaves or creaking branches. But there wasn't a sound—nothing was moving.

Stenvik was deserted. The gravel crunched faintly beneath her feet as she made her way down to Vera Kant's house.

There she stopped again. The gate glowed pale and white in the moonlight, and it was closed as usual. Julia slowly reached out and touched the cold iron latch. It was rough with rust, and was stuck fast.

She pushed. The gate groaned slightly, but didn't open. Perhaps the hinges had rusted up.

Julia put the paraffin lamp on the gravel, stood close to the gate with both hands on the top, and lifted it up and inward. It moved a few inches before sticking again. But now she could squeeze through the opening.

The intoxication from the wine was holding her fear of the dark at bay, but only just.

The garden was surrounded by tall trees and was full of black shadows. Julia stood still, allowing her eyes to become accustomed to the gloom. Slowly she began to discover details in this new darkness: a winding path made of limestone slabs that led further into the garden like a silent invitation, a round well lid beside the path, covered in leaves and patches of black mold, and overgrown grass everywhere. On the far side of the well stood a rectangular woodshed, the roof of which seemed to be on the very edge of collapse, like a badly erected tent.

Julia took a tentative step into the dark garden. And another. She listened, then took a third step. It was getting more and more difficult to move forward.

Her cell phone suddenly started bleeping; the ringtone made her heart jump. She hastily pulled the phone out of her coat pocket, as if it might disturb someone or something in the darkness, and pressed the reply button.

"Hello?"

"Hello . . . Julia?"

It was Lennart's calm voice on the other end.

"Hi," she said, making an effort to sound sober. "Where are you?"

"I'm still in the meeting. And we're not quite finished yet . . . it went on a bit. But I was thinking of going straight home afterward."

"Okay," she said, taking a couple more steps along the path. Now she could see one corner of Vera Kant's house. "That's fine. At least I know . . ."

"It's just that it's the funeral tomorrow, and I have to put in a few hours' work before that," Lennart went on. "I don't really think I can manage to get to Stenvik tonight . . ."

"No, I understand," said Julia quickly. "We can do it some other time."

"Are you outdoors?" asked Lennart.

There was no hint of suspicion in his voice, but Julia was still tense as she came out with the lie in a relaxed voice:

"I'm just out on the ridge. I'm taking a little evening stroll."

"Oh, right . . . Will I see you tomorrow? In church?"

"Yes . . . I'll be there," said Julia.

"Fine," said Lennart. "Good night, then."

"Good night . . . sleep well," said Julia.

Lennart's voice vanished with a click. Julia was completely alone once more.

Half a dozen steps in front of her, the path came to an end at the bottom of a flight of broad stone steps, leading up to a white wooden door and a glassed-in veranda decorated with ornate carvings that the wind and rain had done their best to splinter and wear away.

The house loomed above Julia. The black windows made her think of the burnt-out ruined castle she'd seen that morning in Borgholm.

Are you there, Jens?

Not even the darkness could disguise the state of decay. The panes of glass on either side of the front door were cracked, and the paint was flaking off the window frames.

The veranda inside was pitch-black.

Julia walked slowly to the end of the path. She listened. But who was she actually creeping up on? Why had she almost whispered when she was talking to Lennart on the telephone?

She realized how ridiculous it was to try and be quiet when nobody could hear—but still she couldn't relax. She went up the stone steps with stiff legs, her heart pounding.

She tried to reason like Jens, feel as Jens would have if he'd been here the day he disappeared. If he'd gone into Vera Kant's garden—had he been brave enough to go up the steps to the front door, and knock? Perhaps.

The iron handle on the door to the veranda was pointing downward, as if someone were just opening it from the inside. Julia assumed it was locked and didn't even bother reaching out for the handle—until she realized the door was slightly ajar. A piece of wood had been hacked or whittled out of the doorframe so that the barrel of the lock had nothing to click into. All someone had to do was open the door and walk in.

So somebody had broken into Vera Kant's house.

Burglars, perhaps? They came out to rural areas in the winter so that they could work undisturbed in the empty summer cottages. An abandoned property that had belonged to one of the richest women in northern Öland was bound to have been of interest to them.

Or was it someone else?

Julia reached out silently and pulled at the door. It didn't move, and when she looked down she could see why. A small wooden wedge had been pushed under the door.

Presumably somebody had put it there so that the door wouldn't be battered by the wind, with the lock being broken. Would a burglar be so considerate?

No.

Julia nudged the wedge out with her foot and pulled at the handle again. The hinges were stiff, but the door opened.

The darkness inside made her feel even more nervous, but she couldn't turn back now. *Curiosity killed the cat*.

But the person who had put the wedge there had done it from the outside, so they weren't still inside the house. Unless of course there was another way out.

Julia walked across the threshold of Vera Kant's house.

It felt even colder inside than outside, and as dark and still as in a cave. She couldn't see a thing, and then she remembered that she was carrying the paraffin lamp.

She took a box of matches out of her pocket, struck one, and lifted the glass. The broad wick began to burn with a small, flickering flame, which grew bigger and brighter when Julia lowered the glass over it. There was enough light to illuminate the empty veranda with a thin gray glow, even though the darkness remained, in the form of shadows creeping around the corners of the room.

She raised the lamp and made her way through the veranda toward the inside door. It was closed but not locked, and Julia opened it.

Vera's hallway. It was narrow and long, with flowery wallpaper faded by the sun, and it was just as empty as the veranda. Julia wouldn't have been surprised to find a hall stand with Vera's black coats still hanging there, or a row of narrow ladies' shoes, but the floor was completely bare. Along the walls and from the ceiling hung white curtains made of cobwebs.

There were four doors leading off the hallway. They were all closed.

She reached out for the nearest door along the long wall, and opened it.

The room inside was small, only a few square yards, and completely empty except for some glass jars on the floor, containing something moldy. A storeroom for cleaning materials.

She closed the door carefully, and opened the next one.

This was Vera's kitchen, and it was huge.

Julia could see a brown linoleum floor that changed to polished stone in the center of the room, where an enormous black iron stove stood resplendent against the wall. Straight ahead were two big windows looking out from the back of the house, and Julia knew that the summer cottage lay behind the trees, just a few hundred yards away. It made her feel less alone, and gave her the courage to step into the room.

To the left along the wall, a narrow, steep wooden staircase with a rickety banister led to the upper floor. A faint smell of rotting vegetation hung in the dark, motionless air. Dust and dead flies lay in drifts on the floor.

This is where Vera Kant must have stood in the evenings,

bending over her steaming pots and pans. This was the room Nils Kant had left with his shotgun hidden in his rucksack one beautiful summer's day after the war.

I'll be back, Mother.

Had he promised her that?

There was a half-open door under the stairs, and when Julia took a couple of silent steps toward it, she saw a steep drop on the other side.

It was the staircase down into the cellar. The cellar would be a good place to start if she was looking for . . .

A dead body, hidden away. But she wasn't. Was she?

Just a quick look.

Julia could feel the weight of her cell phone in her pocket. Lennart's number was in the memory, and she could ring him any time she wanted to—some small consolation.

She leaned in through the doorway under the stairs, holding the paraffin lamp up in front of her.

The staircase leading underground was made of rough-hewn planks of wood. At the foot of the steps below was a hard-packed earth floor, black and moist and glistening in the glow of the lamp.

But—something was wrong.

Julia went down a couple of steps so that she could see more clearly. She bent her head to avoid catching it on the sloping ceiling, and stared downward.

The earth floor in the cellar had been dug up.

The patch at the bottom of the steps had been left untouched, but somebody had made little holes all over the place along the stone walls. And there was a spade leaning against the staircase, as if the person who'd been digging had just gone for a short break.

Patches of dried mud from a pair of boots led up the cellar stairs toward her.

Earth was piled up in a little heap along the wall, and a couple of full buckets stood a little further away. Somebody was in the process of methodically digging up the entire cellar.

What was going on?

Julia moved backwards up the stairs. She moved as noiselessly as she could until she was back in the kitchen, holding her breath while she listened, her heart thudding in her ears.

Everything was still silent.

She could phone Lennart now—but she didn't want to be heard, or seen.

She reached carefully into her pocket and took out her cell phone. She started to walk across the kitchen taking small steps, switching on the cell phone and retrieving Lennart's number from the memory as she did so. Then she let her thumb rest on the call button.

If something happened, if . . .

She tried to convince herself that her son was with her in this dark house, even if he was dead, and that he wanted her to look for him. She kept on walking.

Piles of fluff swirled noiselessly away from her shoes and scuttled along the walls to hide as she walked across the linoleum in the kitchen, onto the stone floor and past the iron stove.

Then she went up the first flight of stairs to the upper floor, her heart pounding.

The wood creaked beneath her feet, but only faintly. Julia allowed her right hand, clutching the cell phone, to rest lightly on the banister so that she could feel the solid security of the wall, and continued moving upward, where the light of the paraffin lamp didn't reach. When another stair creaked, she placed her foot on the one above instead.

It was utterly dark above her.

Halfway up the staircase she stopped, breathed out, and listened once more. Then she set off again.

The banister ended by an opening without a door, and Julia stepped cautiously onto the wooden floor of the upper story.

She was in a corridor, just as narrow as the hallway downstairs, and with a closed door at either end.

Fear and indecisiveness made her stop once more.

Right or left? If she stood still for long, it would be impossible to move, so she chose the left side of the corridor. It seemed less dark, somehow. She kept going, moving through yet more balls of fluff and the black corpses of flies.

Paler rectangles were visible on the walls—the traces of pictures that had once hung there.

She had reached the end of the corridor. She pushed open the door, holding the lamp in front of her.

The room inside was small and unfurnished, like the rest. But it wasn't completely empty. Julia stepped inside and stopped when she saw a dark figure lying by the wall next to the room's only window.

No. It wasn't a person lying there, she could see that now. It was a sleeping bag, unrolled like a black cocoon. It was lying below a collection of newspaper cuttings stuck up on the wall.

Julia took another step forward. She saw that the cuttings were old and yellow, attached to the wallpaper with pins.

GERMAN SOLDIERS FOUND DEAD—EXECUTED WITH SHOTGUN was printed in black on one of them. On another:

POLICE KILLER HUNTED NATIONWIDE

And on a third, slightly less yellow:

BOY VANISHES IN STENVIK

In the slightly blurry picture beside the headline, a little boy smiled his carefree smile at her, and Julia was seized by the same feeling of despair that overwhelmed her every time she saw her son. There were more cuttings, but she didn't stay to read them. She quickly looked away and backed out of the room.

Then she stopped. In the light of the paraffin lamp she saw that the door at the other end of the corridor was now open.

It had been closed before, she was certain of it, but now the threshold leading into the darkness of the room beyond was visible. This room wasn't just dark, it was pitch-black.

And it wasn't empty. Julia could feel that there was someone waiting in there. An old woman. She was sitting on a chair by the window.

This was her bedroom. A cold bedroom, full of loneliness and waiting and bitterness.

The woman was waiting for company, but Julia stood there in the corridor, rooted to the spot.

She heard a scraping noise from within the darkness. The woman had got up. She was moving slowly toward the door. Dragging footsteps were moving closer . . .

Julia had to get away. She had to get back downstairs.

Julia ran.

Onto the landing and then down.

She thought she could hear footsteps above her, and she felt the old woman's cold presence behind her.

He deceived me!

Julia felt the hatred like a hard push in her back. She ran blindly forward in the darkness, missed the next step, and lost her balance, three or four yards above the stone floor.

Her arms flailed in the air, both the cell phone and the paraffin lamp went flying.

The lamp and the cell phone smashed onto the kitchen floor down below. Flames shot up from the paraffin—and Julia knew that she too would very soon land on the stone floor down below.

She gritted her teeth against the pain.

19

On the day that Ernst Adolfsson was to be buried, Gerlof woke up in the cold, gray dawn feeling as if he'd been hurled onto the floor from a great height. The pain in his arms and knees was agonizing.

It was stress: Sjögren's syndrome had come calling again—it was such a bloody nuisance. He was going to need a wheelchair to be able to get to the church at all.

The rheumatic condition Sjögren's syndrome was a companion, not a friend—despite the fact that Gerlof had tried to welcome and disarm him many times, simply by relaxing and trying to be pleasant when he turned up. Sjögren had open access to his body, just help yourself, but it was no use. The syndrome was always equally merciless when it came, hurling itself at him and burrowing deep into his joints, tugging and pulling at his nerves, making his mouth dry and his eyes sore.

Gerlof allowed the pain to continue until it grew tired. He laughed in Sjögren's face.

"I'm back in the pram," he stated after breakfast.

"You'll soon be back on your feet, Gerlof."

Marie, his helper for the day, placed a small cushion behind his back for support and folded down the wheelchair's footplates beneath his best shoes.

With Marie's help, Gerlof had laboriously put on his only black suit, which was shiny and much cleaned. He had bought it for his wife's funeral, then worn it to twenty or so since then: a long series of friends' and relatives' funerals in Marnäs church. Sooner or later he would be wearing the suit to his own funeral.

Over the suit he put on his gray overcoat, with a thick woolen scarf around his neck and a fedora pulled well down over his ears. The temperature had dropped to near freezing on this gloomy day in the middle of October.

"Ready?" said Boel when she came out of the office. "How long will you be away?"

Always the same old question.

"That depends on how inspired Pastor Högström is today," replied Gerlof.

"We can warm up your lunch in the microwave," said Boel, "if need be."

"Thank you," said Gerlof, who doubted if he would be particularly hungry after Ernst's funeral.

He thought Boel should be happy now that Sjögren had forced him into a wheelchair and made it easy to keep an eye on him; she liked to be in control of things. But he would soon be back on his feet again, when the syndrome subsided. Once he could walk again, he would find the person who murdered Ernst.

Marie pulled on a pair of gloves and grabbed hold of the wheelchair's handles.

Off they went. Into the elevator, slowly down, then out into the bright cold air, down the ramp, and onto the turning area for cars. The frosty gravel crunched beneath the wheels of the chair as they set off along the empty track to the church.

Gerlof gritted his teeth. He hated feeling so helpless in the wheelchair, but he tried to relax and let go of the responsibility.

"Are we late?" he asked.

It had taken far too long to get into his suit.

"Not much," said Marie. "A bit, but that's my fault . . . Good thing the church is nearby."

"I don't think we'll get a detention," said Gerlof, and Marie laughed politely.

He was pleased about that—not all the helpers at the Marnäs home realized it was the duty of the young to laugh at the wit of the old.

They rolled along toward the church, and Gerlof leaned

forward slightly in an attempt to protect his face from the biting wind blowing in off Kalmar Sound. He could tell it was a strong, steady southwesterly, which would have made it possible to sail a ketch close-hauled straight up the Swedish coast, all the way up north to Stockholm—but he had no desire to be out at sea on a day like this. The wind would have been whipping the waves up over the gunwale, and the cold would have covered the thwarts with ice. After more than thirty years ashore, Gerlof still felt like a seaman, and no sailor wants to go to sea in the winter.

The bell started to toll as they passed the bus stop by the church and turned in along the track. The sound was desolate and long drawn out, echoing over the flat countryside, and it made Marie walk faster.

Gerlof was in no hurry to get to the funeral—he regarded it mostly as a ritual for other mourners. He himself had said his goodbyes to Ernst the week before, down at the quarry. The sense of loss he felt for his friend had mingled with his sorrow over Ella, and that would remain with him for as long as he lived. And at the same time he had an unpleasant feeling that Ernst wasn't resting in peace; his old friend was waiting impatiently for Gerlof to put together all the pieces of the puzzle he'd left behind.

There were at least a dozen cars parked in the narrow space in front of the church. Gerlof looked for Julia's red Ford, but couldn't see it. But he noticed that Astrid Linder's Volvo was there, and decided she'd given Julia a lift from Stenvik. If his daughter was at the funeral at all.

The whitewashed church rose up against the gray sky. For almost a thousand years Christians had stood in the same place. This was the third church, built in the nineteenth century when the medieval church became too small and in need of too many repairs.

They entered the churchyard and rolled quickly up the wide stone path, before Marie slowed and pulled the wheelchair backward over the low step and in through the open door of the church.

Gerlof took off his hat as soon as they entered the porch. It was dark and empty, but the body of the church inside was full of people dressed in black. There was a faint hum of conversation in the air; the service hadn't started yet.

Many lowered heads turned discreetly to look at Gerlof as he was wheeled up the left aisle. He realized how feeble and wretched he must look to people, and of course they were right. He *was* feeble and wretched, but his mind was clear—that was the most important thing.

Some people only went to funerals to see who looked as though they might be the next one to end up in a coffin. *You keep looking,* thought Gerlof, *this is as good as it gets.*

He would be up and walking, soon.

A slender white hand appeared from one of the pews at the front and waved to him. It was Astrid Linder, wearing a black hat with a veil. There was an empty seat beside her in the fourth row, and she didn't seem to notice that Gerlof was in a wheelchair.

Marie stopped, and with her help Gerlof heaved himself out of the chair and into the pew next to Astrid.

"You haven't missed a thing," Astrid whispered in his ear. "It's been *so boring.*"

Gerlof merely nodded, after glancing at the seat on the other side of Astrid and noticing that Julia wasn't there.

Marie moved to the back of the church and at the same time the conversation died beneath the vault of the nave as the cantor began to play the traditional funeral psalm. Gerlof had heard the melancholy hymn at more funerals than he cared to recall. He relaxed to the music and looked discreetly around.

The congregation filling the church was on the elderly side. Of a hundred or so people, only a few were under fifty.

Ernst's murderer was there, hidden among the mourners— Gerlof was certain of it.

Beside Astrid sat her brother Carl, Marnäs's last stationmaster, who had changed careers and become an ironmonger when the station closed in the mid-1960s. He was retired nowadays. It was Carl's older colleague Axel Månsson who had waved off Nils Kant's train that summer's day just after the war, but Carl had been there too. He was an errand boy at the station at the time, and had told Gerlof how he saw Margit, the ticket clerk, telephone the police in Marnäs and tell them in a whisper that the wanted man, young Kant, had just bought a ticket to Borgholm. Carl had also seen District Superintendent Henriksson hurry over from Marnäs a few minutes later, lumbering across the platform with his big belly to catch up with the suspected double murderer.

Carl was perhaps the last living person on Öland who had seen the adult Nils Kant at close quarters, but when Gerlof once asked him what Kant looked like, Carl had just shaken his head– he had a bad memory for faces.

Further along the pew sat several more Marnäs pensioners: Bert Lindgren, the former chairman of the local community hall, who had been away at sea for several years in the fifties and sixties, traveling all over the world, and next to him Olof Håkansson the eel fisherman, then Karl Lundstedt, an army colonel who had moved to his summer home in Långvik when he retired.

It wasn't unusual for pensioners to move to Marnäs, but at the same time Gerlof knew that what northern Öland needed wasn't more old folk but young workers and more jobs.

The organ fell silent. Pastor Åke Högström, who had been in Marnäs for a decade, positioned himself in front of the white wooden coffin adorned with roses. He had a large brown leather-covered Bible in his hands, and his expression was serious as he looked at the congregation through his round spectacles.

"We are gathered here today to bid farewell to our friend Ernst Adolfsson . . ." The pastor paused, adjusted his spectacles, then began his funeral oration with an important question: "For who among men knows the thoughts of a man, except the man's own spirit within him?"

Saint Paul's first letter to the Corinthians, chapter two, Gerlof noted.

"We human beings know so little about each other," proclaimed the pastor, "and only God knows everything. He sees all our faults and shortcomings, and yet He still wants to grant us all eternal peace . . ."

From somewhere toward the back of the church came the sound of a hacking cough.

Gerlof closed his eyes and listened, his mind at peace, and only nodded off once. When the congregation sang hymn 113, the one about the rose, he joined in as best he could. Then came prayers led by the pastor, more quotations from the Bible and psalms, then the beautiful song "Where Roses Never Die."

Although he had already said goodbye to Ernst down at his

house by the quarry, Gerlof still felt a growing knot of dark sorrow in his breast when he saw six serious-faced men stand up during the final piece of organ music, ready to step forward and carry the coffin out. Among them were his friends Gösta Engström from Borgholm, and Bernard Kollberg, who for several decades had run the store in the village of Solby, south of Stenvik, and had often delivered things to Ernst. The remaining bearers came from among Ernst's family in Småland.

Gerlof would have liked to get to his feet and shoulder Ernst's coffin himself, but instead he had to stay in his seat until everybody else started to get up. Marie came along with the wheelchair.

"I think I can walk now," he said to her, but of course he couldn't.

Marie helped him back into the chair, but when he was settled Astrid leaned forward and tapped her on the shoulder.

"I'll help Gerlof," she said firmly, taking the handles.

Marie looked hesitantly at Astrid, who was several inches shorter than her and as thin as a rake, but Gerlof smiled encouragingly.

"We'll be fine, Marie," he assured her.

Marie nodded and Astrid pushed the wheelchair down the aisle with her brother Carl beside her.

"There's John," she said.

Gerlof turned and saw John Hagman leaving the church along with his son Anders.

Gerlof fastened his coat as the cold and the bitter wind hit them outside the church door, and he felt a flat object in his pocket. He remembered he'd brought Ernst's wallet with him.

He took it out, feeling the worn leather with his fingertips, and asked Astrid:

"Have you seen my daughter today?"

"Not today," said Astrid. "But wasn't she going back to Gothenburg? Her car wasn't on the ridge when I drove past."

"I see," said Gerlof.

So Julia must have left this morning. She could have come to the funeral, he thought, and she should at least have called to say goodbye to him. But that's the way Julia was. Especially after Jens disappeared. He'd managed to keep her on Öland longer than she'd intended, and even if they hadn't made a great deal of progress, Gerlof still thought the visit had been good for her. He'd call her in Gothenburg soon.

"Isn't that Ernst's money?" asked Astrid.

Gerlof nodded. "I'm going to give it to his family from Småland," he said.

They could have everything that was in it as well, except for the receipt from Ramneby Wood Museum, which Gerlof had hidden in his desk.

"You're an honest man, Gerlof," said Astrid.

"A place for everything, and everything in its place," he said. "I don't like loose ends."

They were among the graves now, moving slowly among all the familiar gravestones. Ernst had carved many of the most beautiful ones before he retired—Ella's broad headstone, among others. It was clean and attractive, and there was plenty of room for Gerlof's name and dates beneath those of his wife.

Ernst's newly dug grave was in a row of Stenvik residents who had been buried in the churchyard. The congregation had gathered around it in a semicircle, and Astrid pushed Gerlof firmly in among the mourners. He saw the deep hole in the ground opening up in front of his wheelchair. The grave was black and cold and impossible to get out of if you fell into it. He had no desire to end up down there himself, despite the fact that Sjögren was tearing at his joints in the cold air.

The pallbearers had paused by the grave, and now they began to lower the coffin carefully into the ground. Out here Gerlof could see several familiar faces: Bengt Nyberg, the editor of the local newspaper, was standing on the opposite side of the grave, without a camera in his hand for once, and Gerlof tried to remember how long he'd been living and working in Marnäs. Fifteen or twenty years. He'd come from the mainland, like so many others.

Beside him stood Örjan Granfors, the farmer who'd had some cows taken away from him once in the eighties, from his farm northeast of Marnäs. He'd been convincted of cruelty to animals, Gerlof recalled.

Standing close together, next to Granfors, were Linda and Gunnar Ljunger, the hotel owners from Långvik. They were talking quietly to each other, presumably about new building going on down in the holiday village. And next to them stood Lennart

Henriksson, the policeman. He was wearing a black suit today, not his uniform.

Gerlof looked down into the grave again. What did Ernst want him to do? How should he move forward with this?

Ernst had kept returning to the subject of Nils Kant and little Jens several times during his visits to Gerlof earlier that autumn, as he was going over and over both mysteries, convinced they were linked by something nobody else could see.

As the years had gone by, Gerlof had come to terms with the fact that Jens had disappeared without a trace, in the same way that he had come to terms with Ella's death, as far as possible.

But Ernst had come to the home in Marnäs to talk to Gerlof at the beginning of September. He'd brought with him a slim book with a soft cover.

"Have you seen this, Gerlof?" he'd asked.

Gerlof had shaken his head and leaned forward.

It was the book celebrating the anniversary of the Malm Freight company. Gerlof had seen in *Ölands-Posten* that it had been published a month or so earlier, but he hadn't read it.

"You know Martin Malm, don't you?" Ernst had asked. "This is an old photo of him from the end of the fifties, at the Kant family's sawmill in Småland."

"I don't know Martin particularly well," Gerlof had replied, taking the book from Ernst with some surprise. "We met mostly in various ports, when we were skippers."

"And after that, when you came ashore?"

"Very rarely. Three or four times, maybe. The odd dinner for old sea captains."

"Dinner?" said Ernst.

"In Borgholm."

"Do you know where Martin got the money from for his first oceangoing ship?" asked Ernst.

"Yes . . . no. I don't think I do," said Gerlof. "From the family?"

"Not his own," said Ernst. "It came from the Kant family."

"Does it say that in the book?" said Gerlof.

"No, but that's what I've heard," said Ernst. "And look at this picture. August Kant is standing there with his arm around Martin. Would you do that?"

"No," Gerlof had said.

But it was true: August Kant, the dour company boss, had his hand resting amicably on the shoulder of the equally sour-faced sea captain Martin Malm. Strange.

Ernst didn't want to say any more, but there was no doubt that he knew things he didn't want to talk about. He'd seen something, or heard something, which had given him new ideas. He'd gone to Ramneby Wood Museum to look for something, without telling Gerlof. And a few weeks after that, he'd arranged to meet someone at the quarry, presumably for some kind of discussion that Gerlof wasn't to be told about either.

"Would you like to go and say goodbye, Gerlof?"

Astrid's question in the churchyard jerked him back from a sea of thoughts. He shook his head briefly.

"I've already done that," he said.

The last roses were tossed down onto the lid of Ernst's coffin, and the funeral was over. Everyone began moving toward the community center next to the church for a short gathering.

"It'll be nice to have a cup of coffee," said Astrid.

She moved backward, pulling the wheelchair, and set off toward the center.

Despite the fact that Sjögren was biting the back of his neck, Gerlof stretched sideways to look across the churchyard in the direction of an old gravestone by the west wall.

Nils Kant's grave.

Who was actually lying in there?

The town by the water is dark and noisy, and stinks of mud and dog piss.

Nils Kant has turned his back on it. He is sitting at his usual table on the veranda of Casa Grande, the harbor bar, with a bottle of wine in front of him; his face is turned toward the sea, the Caribbean outside Costa Rica. Even if the smell of silt and rotten seaweed isn't much better than the stench that hangs over the narrow streets of the town, at least the water is not close.

During the day he often stands on one of the quays, gazing out over the sea as it sparkles in the sun.

The way home. The sea is the way to Sweden. When he has enough money, all Nils has to do is go home.

Worth a toast.

He picks up his glass of warm red wine and takes a deep draft, to forget the major problem regarding his journey home. Because the truth is that he no longer has enough money. It's almost gone. He loads bananas and oil drums down in the harbor a couple of days a week, but that gives him just about enough for food and rent. He should really work more, but he doesn't feel very well.

"*Estoy enfermo,*" he mutters into the night.

He often has stomach pains and headaches, and his hands have become shaky.

How many toasts to Sweden has he drunk on the veranda

of the Casa Grande? To Öland? To Stenvik? And to his mother, Vera?

It's impossible to count the toasts and the bottles he has emptied. This evening is like all the others in the bar, except for the fact that tonight Nils is celebrating his thirtieth birthday. But there isn't actually anything to celebrate—he knows that, and it makes him feel even worse.

"Quiero regresar a casa," he whispers into the darkness.

He has slowly learned to speak Spanish, and a fair amount of English, but it is Swedish that is still most alive within him.

He has been on the run for more than ten years now, ever since he sneaked aboard the cargo ship *Celeste Horizon* in the port of Gothenburg the summer after the war.

On board the *Celeste Horizon* he was given a cabin that was as narrow as a coffin, a coffin made of steel.

He has sailed on several old ships along the coasts of South America since then, but *Celeste* was definitely the worst. There wasn't a single dry patch on board; the moisture from the sea penetrated everywhere, and anything that wasn't wet and moldy was either broken or had fallen to pieces with rust. Water trickled or dripped from every surface. The light didn't reach through the porthole in his cabin for over a month, because it was on the port side, and the constant leaks made the whole ship list to that side.

The engines throbbed day and night. Nils lay half dead from seasickness on a berth in the darkness, and District Superintendent Henriksson often stood mutely beside him with dark blood pouring from his chest; when that happened Nils would close his eyes and wish that the ship would hit a mine. The sea was full of them, despite the fact that the war was over—that bastard Captain Petri had reminded Nils of this fact several times. He had also made it clear that if the *Celeste Horizon* went down, Nils would be last in line for the lifeboat.

While the ship was loading in England, he'd had to stay in his cabin day and night for two weeks, and the isolation had almost driven him crazy before they finally set sail westward across the Atlantic.

At sea outside Brazil he had seen an albatross: a gigantic bird gliding above the crest of the waves with its wings outstretched, carefree and unrestrained in the warm air around the ship. Nils had taken it as a good sign, and decided to stay in Brazil for a while.

But in the port of Santos he had seen *the bums* for the first time, and they had filled him with terror. Pathetic creatures who came stumbling along the quay even before the *Celeste Horizon* had reached her mooring, with empty eyes and ragged clothes.

"Bums," said a Swedish sailor contemptuously at the gunwale beside Nils, and added a piece of advice: "Throw lumps of coal at them if they come too close."

The bums were the forgotten men, the alcoholics, who were at home neither on land nor at sea. Sailors from Europe who had drunk one round too many and been left behind when their ships sailed.

Nils was no bum, he could afford to stay in a hotel every night, and he remained in Santos for a few months, leaving the *Celeste Horizon* and Petri the madman without a single regret. He drank wine in bars the bums couldn't afford to frequent, he wandered along the chalk-white beaches outside the town, learned a little Spanish and Portuguese, but didn't speak to any more people than necessary. He lost some weight, but was still tall and powerful, and nobody ever tried to rob him. He constantly longed for his home on Öland. He sent his mother a postcard every month, with no sender's name, to show her he was alive.

He traveled on up to Rio with a Spanish ship; there were more people there, poorer people, wealthier people, fatter cockroaches, and more bums in the port and on the beaches. And everything was repeated: the aimless wandering, the wine drinking, the longing for home, and finally a new ship away from it all. He made his money last longer by cleaning and washing up on board.

Nils visited a whole series of ports: Buenaventura; La Plata; Valparaiso; Chañaral; Panama; Saint Martin in the Caribbean, which was full of Frenchmen and Dutchmen; Havana in Cuba, which was full of Americans. And none of them was one iota better than the ones he'd left behind.

He sent a postcard to his mother as soon as he came ashore in a new place. No message or name; she just needed to know that Nils was alive and thinking about her. He kept out of trouble, didn't throw money away on women, and almost never fought.

He wanted to get to the USA, and got a berth on a French boat across the gulf to the humidity of Louisiana. The lights of the bars in New Orleans were warm and golden—but he wasn't allowed into the USA without a Swedish passport, that was just the way it was. He couldn't afford to bribe anyone anymore, and had to travel south again on the ship.

He couldn't stand the thought of returning to South America, and in any case it was getting more and more difficult to get across the borders there too. So he went ashore in Costa Rica, in the port of Limón. And stayed there.

He has lived in Limón for more than six years, between the sea and the jungle. In the steaming forests beyond the town there are banana trees and azaleas as big as apple trees, but he never goes out there. He misses the alvar. The tropical jungle smells like a moldy compost heap, and it suffocates him. Every time there's a cloudburst, the arrow-straight streets of Limón turn into strips of mud, and the sewers overflow.

The days, the weeks, and the months have simply trickled away.

After a year or so in Limón, he wrote a proper letter to his mother for the first time, telling her something of what had happened to him and giving her his address in the town.

He got a reply with a little money enclosed, and wrote again. He asked his mother to help him get in touch with Uncle August. Nils wants to come home now. He has been away from Öland for more than ten years, and that must be punishment enough.

If anyone can get Nils home, it's Uncle August. His mother wants him home, but she would never be able to organize his journey on her own.

It took time, but now Nils is sitting with an envelope on the table in front of him next to his wine, with his address in Limón written on it in ink, and a Swedish stamp worth forty öre. The letter arrived from Sweden three weeks ago, with a check for two hundred dollars, and he has read it over and over again.

It's from his uncle August in Ramneby in Småland. August has heard from his sister Vera that Nils is in Latin America, and wants to come home.

You can never come home, Nils.

That's what Uncle August writes. The letter is only one page long and consists almost entirely of scolding, but that short sentence is the one Nils reads over and over again.

You can never come home.

Nils tries to forget those words, but it's impossible.

He reads the sentence again and again, and it feels as if dead District Superintendent Henriksson is standing behind him, smiling and reading over his shoulder.

Never, Nils.

He pours more wine from the bottle. Mosquitoes as big as a Swedish one-krona coin are humming above the beach, and a shiny cockroach is crawling along the wooden balustrade.

Loud laughter can be heard in the darkness from inside the bar; puttering motorbikes chug along the muddy streets of the town. It is never silent in Limón.

Nils drinks and closes his eyes. The world spins around; he's ill.

"Quiero regresar a casa," he mutters into the darkness.

Never.

Nils is only thirty—he's still young.

He won't listen to Uncle August. He'll keep on writing to his mother instead. Beg her, plead with her. She'll look after him.

You can come home now, Nils.

Those are the words he's waiting for in a letter from her.

And they must come, soon.

20

Gerlof was sitting in his wheelchair on the way across the churchyard, pondering. Ernst had failed to reach an agreement with somebody when he died, Gerlof believed—but an agreement about what?

Ernst had never been particularly interested in money, as far as Gerlof knew—he'd been perfectly happy working in the quarry and selling a sculpture to a tourist now and again to earn money for food and rent. That was enough for him. So why hadn't he wanted to share his ideas about Jens's disappearance with Gerlof?

He'd chosen the Kant stone. He'd definitely done that. And what did it mean?

Gerlof could spend ages thinking about all these questions, going round and round in circles. He still kept coming back to the same thing: if Nils Kant wasn't dead, if he'd somehow arranged to fake his death and managed to return to Sweden under another name, as John believed, then the people who were trying to find out the truth would be a danger to him.

"Ready, Gerlof?" asked Astrid behind him as they reached the community center.

He nodded.

"In we go, then," she said, pushing the chair up the ramp.

There weren't as many people inside as there had been at the burial itself, but Gerlof and Astrid still had to weave their way through them. A few bent down to ask Gerlof how he was feeling, but after three such condescending conversations, he forced himself to his feet. He wanted to show that he could actually walk in spite of the pain, he wasn't an invalid.

Astrid pushed the wheelchair to one side, and Gerlof leaned on his cane as he greeted various acquaintances. Thank goodness Gösta Engström from Borgholm wasn't interested in his health, and even better was the fact that Margit wasn't with him when Gerlof made his way over on shaky legs. They had a quiet conversation about the events of the autumn, and eventually Gerlof told him what he thought about Ernst's death.

"Not an accident?" said Gösta.

Gerlof shook his head.

"You mean—murder?"

"Somebody pushed him into the quarry, then tipped that sculpture on top of him," said Gerlof. "That's what John and I think."

He was afraid Gösta would laugh at him, but Gösta's expression was grim.

"Who would do such a thing?" he asked.

Gerlof shook his head again. "That's the question."

Then Margit Engström came over to say hello; Gerlof shook hands with her, and tottered off.

He bumped into Bengt Nyberg from *Ölands-Posten,* who was fishing for news as usual:

"I've heard they're short-staffed up at the home in Marnäs these days. Is that true? Are the residents having problems with the service?"

Gerlof had nothing to tell him. It seemed as if everybody in the room wanted something from him. Before he'd even made it to the buffet tables, he met Gunnar Ljunger and his wife from Långvik. Gunnar got straight to the point as usual.

"I need six more, Gerlof," said the hotel owner. "Has your daughter spoken to you? She was in the hotel in Långvik the other day and I asked her to mention it to you: six more."

He was talking about ships in bottles, of course.

"Isn't it getting a bit crowded on your shelves?" asked Gerlof.

"We're expanding," said Ljunger quickly. "They're going to go in the windows in the new part of the restaurant."

He took out a notebook and a pen with the slogan SHOP AND ENJOY IN LÅNGVIK! and jotted down some figures on a piece of paper, which he passed over to Gerlof.

"That's what I'll pay," he said. "For each ship."

Gerlof looked at the piece of paper. He wasn't happy about what the Ljungers were doing up in Långvik, it was pure exploitation of the area—but this four-figure sum was enough to maintain both the cottage and the boathouse in Stenvik for at least another year.

"I've got two ships ready now," he said quietly. "The others will take a while—maybe till spring."

"That's fine." Ljunger straightened happily. "I'll buy them then. Come down to Långvik and have a meal sometime."

Gerlof shook his hand, his wife smiled at Gerlof, and the two moved on. Gerlof could finally make his way to the tables to have a cup of coffee and a slice of carrot cake.

Astrid and Carl were already sitting there, and when Gerlof had sat down, with some difficulty, and had a cup of coffee in front of him, another man sat down on the other side of the table. It was Lennart Henriksson.

"So that's that, then," the policeman said to Gerlof.

Gerlof nodded. "But of course the sorrow is still with us."

"Indeed. And you daughter . . . is she here?" asked Lennart.

"No. She's gone back to Gothenburg."

"Did she leave yesterday?"

Gerlof shook his head. "I assume she left this morning."

Lennart looked at him. "Didn't she call in to say goodbye?"

"No. But that doesn't particularly surprise me."

He could have added that he and Julia hadn't succeeded in getting all that close to each other during her stay on Öland, but Lennart could work that out for himself.

Lennart sat gazing down into his coffee cup. He wore a troubled frown, and was drumming faintly on the table with the fingers of his right hand.

Then he looked up at Gerlof. "But you're *sure* she's gone?"

"Astrid said the car had gone."

"There was nothing on the ridge," Astrid said. "And the blinds were pulled down in the boathouse, weren't they, Carl?"

Her brother nodded.

"Did she say goodbye to you?" Lennart asked Astrid.

Gerlof couldn't understand why he was so worried.

"Well, no," said Astrid. "But you don't always have time to get round to that sort of thing . . ."

"I'll call her," said Lennart firmly. "Is that okay with you, Gerlof?"

"Of course," said Gerlof. "Did you want her for anything special?"

"No," said Lennart, taking out his cell phone.

"Have you got her number?"

"Yes." Lennart punched in the numbers. "I just want to check where she is. She said she might . . ."

He stopped speaking, holding the phone to his ear.

"I don't understand those phones," Astrid whispered to Gerlof. "How do you use them?"

"No idea," said Gerlof, then asked Lennart, "Is she there?"

Lennart lowered the phone. "The subscriber cannot be reached . . . it's just her voice mail." He looked at Gerlof and added, "You can turn phones off, of course . . . if you don't want to be disturbed."

"Then I'm sure that's what Julia's done," said Gerlof. "She'll be driving through Småland now."

Lennart nodded reluctantly, but still didn't seem satisfied. He kept drumming his fingers on the table, and then he stood up abruptly.

"You'll have to excuse me," he said. "I . . . just need to go and check something."

Then he picked up his coffee cup and walked away.

Gerlof watched the policeman hurrying toward the door, and wondered if his daughter and Lennart Henriksson had some project on the go that he didn't know about—but just a few seconds later a spoon was tapped tentatively against a coffee cup across the room. A chair scraped, and someone stood up.

Gerlof saw to his surprise that it was John Hagman. Both he

and his son Anders looked equally uncomfortable in their black suits.

John cleared his throat, red in the face, his fingers scrabbling nervously at the sides of his black jacket. Then he began to speak:

"I . . ." he said. "I don't usually do this sort of thing . . . not really . . . But I'd just like to say a few words about my friend and yours, Ernst Adolfsson, and the village of Stenvik. It will be a darker and lonelier place now that . . ."

An hour later Gerlof was back at the home in Marnäs—thanks to Astrid and Gösta—and could relax. He ate a late lunch, warmed up for him by Boel. On one of the tables in the empty dining room was that day's edition of *Ölands-Posten,* and Gerlof noticed a headline on the front page: MISSING PENSIONER FOUND DEAD.

Even more bad news. The article was about the elderly man who had left his home in southern Öland a week or so earlier, and had now been found in a copse out on the alvar, frozen to death.

The police did not suspect any crime, the paper reported. The man was old and senile, and appeared to have got lost less than a kilometer from the village where he'd lived all his life.

Gerlof didn't know the dead man, but he still felt the newspaper article was a bad omen.

For the rest of the afternoon he stayed in his room, and didn't bother going for coffee. He didn't come out until dinner, which consisted of Öland dumplings, badly seasoned and with far too little meat—not a bit like the delicious dumplings Ella used to make once a month or so—but Gerlof ate a couple anyway.

"Did you manage all right over in the church without me?" asked Marie as she was serving up his dumplings.

"No problem," said Gerlof.

"So Ernst Adolfsson is in the ground now?" said Maja Nyman on the other side of the table.

Of course, Maja was from Stenvik, too, thought Gerlof, even if she hadn't lived there for forty years.

He nodded. "Yes, Ernst is resting next to the church now."

He picked up his fork and began to eat, grateful as ever that his teeth were good. And thank heavens Sjögren had finally settled down.

"Was it a nice coffin?" asked Maja.

"It was," said Gerlof. "White-painted wood, polished and beautiful."

"I'd like mahogany," said Maja. "If it's not too expensive . . . Otherwise I suppose it'll be cheap wood and a cremation."

Gerlof nodded again politely, took another bite of his dumplings, and was just about to say that cremation was definitely preferable, when somebody touched him on the shoulder. It was Boel.

"Telephone call, Gerlof," she said quietly.

"In the middle of dinner?"

"Yes. It's obviously important. It's Lennart Henriksson . . . from the police."

Gerlof felt a sudden icy chill in his stomach, a chill that woke Sjögren from his evening nap and made him seize Gerlof's joints again. Stress always made his rheumatism worse.

"I'd better take it, then," he said.

Julia? It was almost certainly about Julia, and it was almost certainly bad news. He struggled to his feet.

"You can use the telephone in the kitchen," said Boel.

He made his way into the kitchen, leaning on his cane. There was a red plastic telephone on the wall, and Gerlof picked up the receiver.

"Davidsson," he said.

"Gerlof . . . it's Lennart." His voice sounded extremely serious.

"Has something happened?" asked Gerlof, although he already knew the answer.

"Yes . . . It's Julia. She hadn't gone to Gothenburg."

"Where is she?" Gerlof heard the wobble in his voice.

"Down in Borgholm," said Lennart. "In the hospital."

"Is it bad?"

"Pretty bad. But it could have been much worse. She's knocked herself about a bit. They're putting her in plaster at the hospital . . . I'll go down there and pick her up tonight."

"What happened?" said Gerlof. "What's she done?"

Lennart hesitated, took a deep breath, then replied:

"She broke into Vera Kant's house yesterday evening and fell down the stairs from the upper floor. She was a bit . . . well, she was very confused when I found her. She kept saying the house is occupied. That Nils Kant lives there."

21

Julia was awakened from the warmth of sleep by a squeaking noise, and after a few seconds she remembered where she was: in Vera Kant's big house in Stenvik.

She was shivering. The pain in her broken body had made her drowsy, and after a long night lying awake on the floor, she had closed her eyes and dreamed about that last summer with Jens, when the sun seemed to shine on Öland without interruption. When the autumn was far away.

She saw a dusty, dirty floor underneath her, and realized it was daylight.

The squeaking noise was coming from the outside door, which was being pushed open.

"Julia?" an echoing voice called out above her.

A pair of hands raised her head and pushed a rolled-up jacket or sweater under the back of her neck.

"Can you hear me? Julia, wake up!"

She turned her aching face up toward the ceiling. She could only use her left eye—the right one was swollen shut.

It was Lennart's calm voice—she recognized it even before she saw that it really was him. He wasn't wearing his uniform; he was in a black suit and shiny shoes. They were covered in dried mud from Vera Kant's garden, but he didn't seem to care about that.

"I can hear you," she said.

"Good." He didn't sound annoyed, just tired. "Good morning, in that case."

"I came in here and . . . fell down the stairs," she went on faintly, lifting her head from the floor. "It was stupid."

"Gerlof said you'd gone home," said Lennart. "But I thought you might be here."

Julia was lying on the veranda; that was as far as she'd managed to crawl during the night when she'd finally regained consciousness on the kitchen floor, among the remains of her cell phone and the broken lamp. The paraffin had leaked out and ignited, but the fire had gone out on the stone floor.

It had been impossible to stand, because somebody had driven a red-hot nail through her right foot. So she had begun to crawl laboriously toward the outside door, just to get out of the kitchen, and in the darkness out on the veranda she'd collapsed again. She could hear the wind blowing outside, and had no strength left to set off out into the night. She had collapsed by the door, constantly terrified that she might hear footsteps approaching from inside the house.

"Stupid," Julia repeated quietly. "Stupid, stupid . . ."

"Don't think about that now. I should have come over last night, but the meeting . . ." Lennart stopped speaking, and she felt his hands under her arms. He tried to lift her up, carefully. "Can you stand up?" he asked her.

She hoped he wouldn't be able to tell she'd been drinking. The intoxication was still with her like a revolting aftertaste.

"I don't know . . . I've broken something . . . some bones."

"Are you sure?"

Julia nodded wearily. "I'm a nurse."

And she was, in fact. And the diagnosis she had reached even before she'd started crawling out of the kitchen was a fractured wrist, broken collarbone, and possibly also a broken right foot.

The foot could of course just be very badly sprained, it was difficult to tell. Julia had had patients who'd been unable to put their weight on a sprained ankle for several weeks—while others had broken theirs and walked around almost normally afterward, assuming it would soon get better.

She had no idea what her face might look like. Terrible, no doubt. Her nose might be bleeding as well, because it felt stuffed up.

"Try and get up, Julia," said Lennart.

She liked the fact that his voice remained calm, not annoyed, not stressed.

"Sorry," she said, her voice thick.

"For what?" Lennart lifted her gently under the arms.

"Sorry I came in here without you."

"Don't think about it," said Lennart again.

But Julia didn't want to keep quiet, she wanted to tell him everything.

"I was looking for Jens. I saw a light in the window one night and I think . . . He's living here."

"Living here? Jens?"

"Nils . . ." said Julia. "Nils Kant, Vera's son. He's got a sleeping bag upstairs. I saw it. And old newspaper articles."

"Can you walk?" asked Lennart.

"He's been digging in the cellar too . . . I don't know why. Is that where Jens's body is, down there? Do you think it might be, Lennart? Has he hidden him down there?"

"Come."

Lennart began to lead her slowly through the door, out into the chill wind, and down the steps. It wasn't easy, she couldn't put her weight on her right foot, but Lennart supported her all the time.

When they reached the stone path, Julia saw a dark green car parked outside the gate.

"Is that yours, Lennart?" she said.

"Yes."

"Haven't you got a police car? You ought to have a police car."

"That's my own car . . . I've been to the funeral today."

"Oh . . . of course."

Ernst's funeral. Julia remembered now. She'd missed it.

The old gate was just as difficult to open as it had been the night before, and Lennart had to leave her balancing on one foot while he dragged and kicked it open enough for them to get through.

She got into the car with enormous difficulty, as if she were ninety years old.

"Lennart," she said quickly, before he had time to close the door. "Could you just go into the house and take a look? I just have to know that . . . that I saw what I saw last night. Upstairs and down in the cellar."

He looked at her for a few seconds. Then he nodded.

"I assume you'll wait here?" he said.

She nodded. "Lennart . . . have you got a gun?"

"A gun?"

"Yes . . . in case there's anyone there now . . . inside. I don't think there is, but . . ."

Lennart gave a short laugh. "I haven't got a gun with me, just a flashlight," he said. "There's no danger, Julia, I'll be fine. I'll be right back."

Then he closed the car door and got the flashlight out of the trunk. Julia watched him go into the garden and disappear behind the dilapidated woodshed.

She breathed out in the silence of the car, leaned back cautiously in her seat, and stared blankly at the ridge and the gray sea at the end of the village road.

Lennart wasn't away long, perhaps between five and ten minutes. Julia had begun to feel anxious as soon as he disappeared, and felt relieved when she saw him coming back through the gate.

He opened the driver's door, got in, and nodded at her.

"You were quite right," he said. "Somebody has been there. Very recently, too."

"Yes," said Julia, "and I think–"

Lennart quickly held up his hand. "Not Nils Kant," he interrupted her.

Then he placed a small object in front of her on the dashboard.

"I found this in the cellar. There were several on the floor down there."

It was a snuff tin, one of the round ones that can only be used once.

"Somebody who takes snuff," she said.

"Yes, he takes snuff . . . whoever it is who's been here," said Lennart, turning the key in the ignition. "And now we're going to the hospital."

———

At the hospital in Borgholm they cut off Julia's clothes, both her sweater and her pants, and gave her an injection to ease the pain. A young male doctor came in to examine her, and asked how her injuries had happened.

"It was an accident—she had a fall last night," said Lennart, who was standing by the door of the examination room. "Up in Stenvik."

"On the shore?"

Lennart hesitated only for a second before nodding. "On the shore, yes."

Then Lennart left, and the doctor began to palpate her back and stomach, and to pull at her legs and arms, and the nurses took a series of X-rays. Then they began to apply the wet, cold plaster bandages. Julia didn't protest, she knew the procedures. She just wanted to get it all over with.

There were more important things to think about. She had made an important discovery in Vera Kant's house, she was sure of it.

Nils Kant was alive. He was alive and living in his mother's old house, just like that man in that horrible Hitchcock film. He was hiding in the house and Jens had crept in there and Kant had been forced to kill him. Unless they'd met in the fog on the alvar. Perhaps Nils Kant liked walking out there.

Julia didn't want to stay in the hospital. She asked to borrow a telephone, and she called Astrid in Stenvik. She told her what had happened and asked a question.

Of course Julia could stay with her for a few days, Astrid said. It was always nice to have some company.

Lennart came back to fetch her after an hour.

"You need to be careful of all those stones and rocks on the shore," said the young doctor when he'd checked the plaster once more. "Especially when it's dark."

"Did you have things to do in town?" asked Julia as they were driving back north.

"I was over at the police station," said Lennart. "Their computers are faster than mine up in Marnäs, so I wrote up a few reports." He looked at her. "Including one about a break-in in Stenvik."

"Oh," said Julia.

"It wasn't about you," said Lennart. "I reported that some-body had broken into the Kant house and was sleeping there. You've never been in there, don't forget. You saw a light there one night. The following day you called me and reported it. Isn't that what happened?"

Julia stared back at him.

"Okay," she said. "I stumbled and fell on the shore. In the dark."

"Exactly," said Lennart.

"But I still think Nils Kant has been in there," she added qui-etly. "I don't believe he's dead."

"You can believe what you like," said Lennart tersely. "Kant is dead."

But at the same time Julia could see, or thought she could see, a shadow of doubt in his eyes.

The sun has disappeared, darkness has fallen over the eastern coast of Costa Rica. In the shadows on the little sandy beach below the veranda bar of the Casa Grande, someone coughs quietly and then begins to whistle to himself, a cheerful, carefree melody that rises and falls almost in time with the rhythmic swell of the sea as the waves break on the shore. From inside the bar comes the sound of laughter and clinking glasses.

Silent flashes of white lightning illuminate the horizon, followed by a muted rumbling. It's a night thunderstorm far out over the Caribbean, a storm which is slowly coming closer to the land.

Nils Kant is sitting at his usual table at the far end of the veranda, alone as always beneath the small red lanterns. He stares down into his half-empty glass for a while, then empties it in one gulp.

Is that his sixth or seventh glass tonight?

He can't remember, it doesn't matter. He hadn't intended to drink more than five glasses of lukewarm red wine tonight, but it doesn't matter. Soon he'll order another. There's no reason to stop drinking, none at all.

He puts down the empty glass and scratches his left arm. It's red and swollen. These last few years he's begun to get painful inflamed patches of skin on his arms and legs, from the sun. White flakes of skin peel away in drifts, the skin breaks, and his sheets are spotted with blood each morning when he wakes up. And there are always hairs on the pillow; he's begun to get a bald patch on the top of his head.

It's the sun, it's the heat, it's the humidity. Nils is falling to pieces bit by bit. Nothing he can do about it.

Nothing but keep drinking. He's been drinking cheap wine for a few years now, because the stream of money from his mother has steadily diminished since the middle of the fifties.

All his mother has written by way of explanation is that the family quarry has been sold and closed down. She hasn't told him how much money she has left. And Uncle August hasn't written from Småland for many years.

Nils hasn't had a fight with anyone or seriously injured anyone since he left Öland. But still District Superintendent Henriksson stands by his bed some nights, silent and bleeding. One small consolation is that it happens less often now.

Nils clutches his wineglass and leans forward to get up and go inside for a top-up—and at that very moment he realizes that he actually recognizes the melody someone is whistling in the darkness down below.

He stops and listens more carefully.

Yes, he's heard it before, many years ago. It was played on the radio quite a bit during the war, and it was in his mother Vera's collection of 78s.

Hej mina lustiga bröder . . .

A cheerful, bold song. He doesn't remember what it's called, but he remembers the words.

Hey, if you want, just say the word,
and we'll go home to Söder . . .

He hasn't heard it since he left Stenvik—it's a Swedish tune. Nils gets up. He peers cautiously over the balustrade, seven or eight feet above the ground.

Shadows.

But isn't there someone sitting down there on the sand, right next to the poles supporting the veranda?

"Hello?" he calls quietly in Swedish.

The whistling stops at once.

"Hello yourself," replies a calm voice from the darkness.

As his eyes grow accustomed to the darkness, Nils sees a figure sitting down below. It's a man in a hat. He's stopped whistling, and he isn't moving.

Fine drops of cold drizzle begin to fall as Nils goes over to the steps at the other end of the veranda. He places his hand on the banister and makes his way down on unsteady legs.

Down into the darkness, step by step, until he feels soft sand, still warm, beneath his leather sandals.

Nils has sat up on the veranda in the evenings for years, but he has never been down on the beach in the dark before. There might be rats there, big, hungry rats.

He cautiously approaches the sturdy poles that hold the veranda up.

The figure who answered him is still sitting over there, leaning back comfortably in a deck chair that can be rented for a few colónes in the shop a couple of hundred yards away.

It's a man, Nils sees, with his shirtsleeves rolled up and some kind of sun hat shading his face. He's humming to himself, the same cheerful melody as before.

Just say the word,
and we'll go home . . .

Nils takes a couple more steps and stops. He stands still, his body swaying with the wine, but also with nervousness.

"Good evening," says the man.

Nils clears his throat.

"Are you . . . from Sweden?" he asks.

The Swedish words feel strange in his mouth.

"Can't you tell?" says the man in the deck chair, just as a flash of lightning illuminates the horizon.

In the sudden burst of light, Nils catches a brief glimpse of the Swede's white face. A few seconds later a faint rumble comes from the sea.

"I thought it was best if you came down to me in the darkness, rather than the other way round," says the Swede.

"What?" says Nils.

"I went to look for you in your room, but your landlady said you're usually here in the bar drinking in the evenings. Perhaps there isn't much else to do in Costa Rica."

"What do you want?" asks Nils.

"It's more important to talk about what *you* want, Nils."

Nils says nothing. For a brief moment he has the feeling that he's seen this man before, when he was young.

But when? In Stenvik?

He can't remember.

The Swede grabs hold of the arms of the chair and gets up. He glances at the sea, then looks straight at Nils.

"Do you want to go home, Nils?" he asks. "Home to Sweden? To Öland?"

Nils nods slowly.

"Then I can make that happen," says the Swede. "We're going to give you a whole new life, Nils."

22

"I'm not accusing you of anything, Gerlof," said Lennart slowly, "but you've obviously made your daughter believe that Nils Kant is still alive. That he's living in his mother Vera's old house. And that he stole her son away out on the alvar."

It was late afternoon at the home in Marnäs, and Gerlof was sitting at his desk. He was gazing at the floor like a schoolboy who's been found out.

"I might have hinted at something along those lines," he said eventually. "Not that Nils is hiding in Vera's house, I never said that, but that he might possibly be alive . . ."

Lennart just sighed. He was standing in front of Gerlof in the middle of the room, dressed in his uniform. He'd come to the home to tell Gerlof that Julia was now resting at Astrid's cottage down in Stenvik, after being treated at the hospital in Borgholm the previous day.

"How is she?" asked Gerlof.

"Sprained right foot, broken wrist, broken collarbone, severe nosebleed, lots of bruises, and concussion," said Lennart; he sighed again, then added, "As I said, it could have been worse, I mean she could have broken her neck. It could have been better, too . . . She could, for example, have decided not to break into Vera Kant's house."

"Will she be charged?" said Gerlof. "With the break-in?"

"No," said Lennart. "Not by me. And the owners are hardly likely to do it either."

"Have you spoken to them?"

Lennart nodded. "I managed to find a nephew of Vera's in Växjö," he said. "I called him before I came here. A younger cousin of Nils's . . . He hasn't been to Stenvik for many years, and was pretty sure nobody else in the family has either. The house is owned by several cousins in Småland, but they obviously can't decide whether to renovate it or sell it."

"I suspected it was something like that," said Gerlof. Then he shook his head and looked at the policeman. "I never told Julia that *I* believe Nils Kant is still alive, Lennart," he said. "I only said that *some* people believe it."

"Like who?" asked Lennart.

"Well . . . Ernst," said Gerlof, not wanting to get John Hagman mixed up in police business. "Ernst Adolfsson. I think he believed Nils Kant was alive and that Kant had killed Jens out on the alvar. So Ernst tried to get me to . . ."

Lennart looked at him wearily.

"Private eyes," he interrupted. "Some people think they know better than the police how crimes should be solved."

Gerlof considered coming out with a dry witticism, but couldn't think of anything.

"There's another thing, of course; somebody has actually been inside Vera Kant's house," Lennart went on.

Gerlof looked at the policeman in surprise.

"Really?" he said.

"The door has been forced. And there were traces upstairs. Newspaper cuttings pinned on the wall, stale food . . . a sleeping bag. And the cellar has been dug up."

Gerlof thought it over.

"Have you examined the house?" he said.

"Only briefly," said Lennart. "My priority was getting your daughter to the hospital."

"Good. Her father thanks you for that," said Gerlof.

"This morning I went into Vera Kant's house again before I came here," the policeman went on. "Julia was lucky: the paraffin lamp smashed on the stone floor when she dropped it. If it had ended up by the wall, the whole place could have burnt down."

Gerlof nodded. "But what's this about the cellar? Have they dug things up? Or buried them?"

"It was hard to see. Dug up, I should think. Or just dug."

"People who break in don't usually start digging for things," said Gerlof. "And they don't usually stay the night."

Lennart looked tiredly at him. "Now you're playing private eye again."

"I'm just thinking out loud. And I'm thinking . . ."

"What?" pressed Lennart.

"Well . . . I'm thinking it must be somebody from Stenvik who's been in the house."

"Gerlof . . ."

"You can do plenty of things up here on Öland without being disturbed. You know that too. There's hardly anybody around to see you . . ."

"Do feel free to write a letter to the paper about the shortage of police officers," said Lennart sharply.

"But one thing people always see," Gerlof went on quietly, "is strangers. Strangers with shovels, strange cars parked outside Vera Kant's house—people in Stenvik would have noticed something like that. And they haven't, as far as I know."

Lennart thought about it.

"Who actually lives in Stenvik all year round?" he asked eventually.

"Not many people."

Lennart didn't speak for a few seconds.

"I might need your help, Gerlof," he said, and quickly added, "Not as a private eye, but just to check out a few facts. I found something in the cellar." He put his hand in his pocket. "There were several snuff tins on the windowsill in the cellar and under the stairs. All empty. They're hardly from Vera Kant's day."

He pulled out a snuff tin, along with a notepad. The tin was in a small plastic bag.

"I don't take snuff," said Gerlof.

"No. But do you know anybody down in Stenvik who does?"

Gerlof hesitated for a few seconds, then nodded. There was no point in hiding things the police could find out anyway.

"Just one person," he said.

Then he gave Lennart a name. The policeman wrote it down on his pad and nodded.

"Thanks for your help."

"I'd like to come with you," said Gerlof. "If you're going to see him." Lennart opened his mouth, and Gerlof added quickly, "I feel fine today, I can walk on my own. He'll relax and be more ready to talk if I'm there. I'm almost sure of it."

Lennart sighed.

"Put your coat on, then," he said "and we'll go for a little ride."

"That was a fine speech, John," said Gerlof. "At Ernst's funeral, I mean."

John was sitting on the other side of the table in his little kitchen in Stenvik, and nodded briefly without replying. He leaned back for a few seconds, then forward again. He was tense, Gerlof could see that very clearly, and it wasn't difficult to see the reason either: the third person at the table was Lennart Henriksson, still dressed in his uniform. It was a quarter to six in the evening, and it was dark outside.

The empty snuff tin was on the table between them.

"So you're reopening the case?" John asked Lennart.

"Well, I don't know about reopening . . ." said Lennart, shrugging his shoulders. "We'd like to talk to Anders, if this actually is his snuff tin. Because that means he's definitely the person who's slept at Vera Kant's house and been digging in the cellar and tacked up several newspaper cuttings about Nils Kant and Jens Davidsson. And we'd also really like to find out where Anders was the day little Jens disappeared."

"You don't need to ask Anders about that," said John. "I can tell you."

"Okay," said Lennart. He took out a notepad and pen. "Tell me."

"He was here," said John tersely.

"In Stenvik?"

John nodded.

"And you were here too? Can you give him an alibi for that day?"

John shrugged his shoulders. "It's a long time ago," he said.

"I don't remember . . . but in the evening we were out searching along the shore. Both of us. I do remember that."

"So do I," said Gerlof.

Even if many other memories of that evening were very hazy, he had a picture in his head of John and his son, who must have been around twenty at the time, walking side by side southward along the shore.

"And in the afternoon?" said Lennart. "What was Anders doing then?"

"Don't remember," said John. "He might have been out. But he certainly wasn't up near Gerlof's cottage." John looked at Gerlof. "There's no evil in my son, Gerlof."

Gerlof nodded. "Nobody thinks there is."

"Anyway, we need to talk to him," Lennart said. "Is he here?"

"He's in Borgholm," said John. "He went down yesterday after the funeral."

"Does he live there?"

"Sometimes he does . . . with his mother. Sometimes he lives here with me. He pleases himself. He doesn't drive, so he catches the bus there and back."

"How old is he now?"

"He's forty-two."

"Forty-two . . . and he lives at home?"

"It's no crime." John pointed over his shoulder with his thumb. "And he's got his own cottage, just behind mine."

"I think," Gerlof interjected tentatively, ". . . that we might say Anders is a little bit special. Don't you agree, John? He's kind and helpful, but he's a little bit different."

"I've met Anders a couple of times," said Lennart. "He seemed perfectly capable to me."

John looked straight ahead, his neck rigid. "Anders keeps himself to himself," he said. "He thinks a lot. Doesn't talk much, not to me and not to anybody else. But there's no evil in him."

"And his address?" said Lennart.

John gave them the address of an apartment on Köpmansgatan. Lennart wrote it down.

"Good," he said. "Well, we won't disturb you any longer, John. We'll get back to Marnäs now."

The last sentence was directed at Gerlof. He had seen the

blind fear beginning to grow in John's eyes during the conversation. The fear that Authority, circling high above like a bird of prey, had finally spotted him and his only son up in the desolation of northern Öland, and would never let go of them again.

"There's no evil in my son," John repeated, despite the fact that Lennart was on his way to the door.

"There's nothing to worry about, John," said Gerlof quietly, not sounding in the least convincing. "We'll have a chat on the phone tonight? Would that be okay?"

John nodded, but he was still looking tensely at Lennart, who stood waiting in the doorway.

"Come on, Gerlof," he said.

It sounded like an order. Gerlof didn't even feel like a policeman any longer, more like a lapdog—but he got up obediently and followed Lennart outside. He would really have liked to go and visit his daughter at Astrid's, but that would have to wait until another time.

Gerlof's muscles were trembling more than usual as he walked back to his room; the pain in his joints was also worse than usual. Lennart had brought him back to the home.

He could hear the telephone ringing through the door, and didn't think he'd get there in time, but it kept on ringing.

"Davidsson?"

"It's me."

It was John.

"How are things?"

Gerlof sat down heavily on the bed.

John didn't say anything.

"Have you spoken to Anders?" asked Gerlof.

"Yes. I phoned him in Borgholm. I've spoken to him."

"Good. Maybe you shouldn't tell him that the police want to—"

"It's too late," John broke in. "I told him the police had been here."

"Right," said Gerlof. "And what did he say?"

"Nothing. He just listened."

Silence.

"John . . . I think we both know what Anders was doing at Vera Kant's. What he was looking for in the cellar," said Gerlof.

"The soldiers' treasure. The spoils of war everybody believed they had with them when they came ashore on Öland."

"Yes," said John.

"The treasure Nils Kant took from them," Gerlof went on, "if that's what happened."

"Anders has been talking about it for many years," said John.

"He's not going to find it," said Gerlof. "I know that."

John was silent again.

"We need to go to Ramneby," Gerlof went on. "To the saw-mill and the wood museum. We can go tomorrow."

"Not tomorrow," said John. "I have to go to Borgholm to get Anders."

"Next week, then. When the museum is open. And afterwards maybe we can stop off in Borgholm and see how Martin Malm is."

"Fine," said John.

"We're going to find Nils Kant, John," Gerlof told him.

It was almost nine o'clock that same evening. The corridors of the home were hushed and empty.

Gerlof was standing outside Maja Nyman's closed door, lean-ing on his cane. There wasn't a sound from her room. On the door was a little handwritten note, which said: PLEASE KNOCK! JOHN 10:7.

" 'Truly I say unto you: I am the door of the sheep-fold,' " murmured Gerlof to himself.

He hesitated for a moment, then raised his right hand and knocked.

It took a while, but eventually Maja opened the door. They had seen each other at dinner a few hours earlier, and she was still wearing the same yellow skirt and white blouse.

"Good evening," said Gerlof with a gentle smile. "I just wanted to see if you were home."

"Gerlof."

Maja smiled and nodded, but Gerlof thought he could see a tense furrow among all the others in her forehead, beneath her white hair. His visit was unexpected.

"May I come in?" he asked.

She nodded a little hesitantly, and stepped back into the room.

"I haven't tidied up," she said.

"That doesn't matter at all," said Gerlof.

Leaning on his cane, he walked slowly into the room, which looked just as clean and tidy as the last time he'd been there. A dark red Persian rug covered most of the floor, and the walls were full of portraits and pictures.

Gerlof had been in Maja's room a number of times. They had had a relationship, which had begun a few months after Gerlof's arrival at the home and ended a year or so later, when the pain of his Sjögren's syndrome became too severe. After that they had continued a quiet friendship which was still strong. Both of them came from Stenvik; both had been left alone after a long marriage. They had plenty to talk about together.

"How are you feeling, Maja?"

"Fine. I'm keeping well."

Maja pulled out a chair at the small brown table by the window, and Gerlof sat down gratefully. Maja sat down as well, and a silence fell.

Gerlof had to say something.

"I was just wondering, Maja, if you could tell me about something we talked about once before . . ."

He reached into his pocket and took out the little white envelope Julia had given him the week before.

"My daughter found this letter in the churchyard, by Nils Kant's gravestone. I know you wrote it and put it there, that isn't what I wanted to ask you about. I'm just wondering . . ."

"I've got nothing to be ashamed of," said Maja quickly.

"Absolutely not," said Gerlof. "I didn't—"

"Nils never gets the best bunch of flowers," said Maja. "My husband always gets that . . . I always see to Helge's grave first, before I tidy Nils's."

"That's good," said Gerlof. "All graves should be looked after." He went on: "That wasn't what I wanted to ask about, it was something else . . . I remember you once told me you met Nils on the alvar, the same day he . . . dealt with the German soldiers."

Maja nodded seriously. "I could see it in his face," she said. "He didn't say anything, but I could see something had happened . . . but he didn't want to tell me what it was. I tried to talk to him, but Nils fled out onto the alvar again."

"I understand," said Gerlof, then paused before continuing cautiously:

"And you mentioned that you got something from him that day . . ."

Maja stared at him. Then she nodded.

"I'm just wondering if you could show me what he gave you," Gerlof went on. "And if you've told anybody else about this. Have you?"

Maja sat motionless, looking at him. "Nobody else knows anything," she said. "And it wasn't something I got from him, it was something I took."

"Sorry?"

"I didn't get anything from Nils," said Maja. "I took it. And I've regretted it so many times . . ."

"A package," said Gerlof. "You said it was a package."

"I followed Nils," said Maja. "I was young and curious. Far too curious . . . so I stayed hidden behind the bushes and I watched Nils. And he went to the memorial cairn outside Stenvik."

"The cairn? What did he do there?"

Maja said nothing. Her gaze was distant.

"He dug a hole," she said at last.

"Did he bury something?" asked Gerlof. "Was it the package?"

Maja looked at him and said:

"Nils is dead, Gerlof."

"It seems so," said Gerlof.

"It *is* so," said Maja. "Not everybody believes it, but I know. He would have been in touch otherwise."

Gerlof nodded. "Did you dig up the package when Nils had gone?"

Maja shook her head. "I ran home," she said. "It was later . . . after he came home."

It took a few seconds for Gerlof to understand.

"You mean . . . after he came home in a coffin?"

Maja nodded. "I went out onto the alvar and dug it up," she said.

She got up, smoothed down her skirt, and went over to the

television in the corner of the room. Gerlof stayed where he was, but turned his head so that he could watch her.

"It was one autumn day in the sixties, a couple of years after Nils's funeral," said Maja. "Helge was out in the fields and the children were at school in Marnäs. So I locked up the house and went out onto the alvar on my own, with a garden spade in a plastic bag."

Gerlof watched Maja struggle to lift a blue-painted wooden chest decorated with red roses from a shelf beneath the TV. He'd seen it before; it was her old sewing box. She carried it to the table and placed it in front of Gerlof.

"I crossed over the main road," she went on, "and after half an hour or so I got down to the alvar outside Stenvik. I found what was left of the cairn and tried to remember exactly where I'd seen Nils digging . . . and in the end I did."

She opened the lid of the chest. Gerlof saw scissors, yarn, and rows of cotton reels, and thought about when he used to mend torn sails. Then Maja lifted up the false bottom and placed it to one side, and Gerlof could see a flat case lying in the secret compartment underneath.

A metal box, discolored with old rusty patches.

At least, Gerlof hoped it was rust.

"Here it is."

Maja took out the case and handed it to him. He heard something rattling inside.

"Can I open it?" he asked.

"You can do whatever you like with it, Gerlof."

The case had no lock, and he opened it very carefully.

The contents sparkled and shone.

Perhaps it was just twenty or so bits of glass in a case, just trinkets—but it was difficult not to see something different, something more precious. And there was a cross lying alongside them. Gerlof was no expert, but it looked like a crucifix made of pure gold.

Gerlof closed the lid, before he was tempted to pick up the stones and roll them between his fingers.

"Have you told anyone else about this?" he asked evenly.

"I told my husband before he died," Maja replied.

"Do you think he might have told anyone else?"

"He didn't talk about things like that to other people," said Maja. "And if he had, he would definitely have told me. We didn't have any secrets."

Gerlof believed her. Helge hadn't been particularly talkative. But somehow the rumor that the soldiers Nils killed had had some kind of war spoils from the Baltic with them had begun to spread in the north of Öland. Gerlof had heard them too—so had John and Anders Hagman.

"So you've had them hidden here the whole time?" he said.

Maja nodded. "I've never done anything with them, I mean, they weren't mine." She added, "But I did try to give them to Nils's mother Vera once."

"Oh? When was that?"

Maja sat down carefully on the chair beside him, and Gerlof noticed that she drew the chair forward so that their knees were just touching between the ornate legs of the table.

"It was a few years later, at the end of the sixties. Helge had heard that Vera Kant had started to sell all her land along the coast, that she was getting short of money. So I thought maybe she should have the stones back . . ."

"Did you go and see her?" asked Gerlof.

Maja nodded. "I got the bus to Stenvik and went into Vera's garden . . . It was summer, so the outside door was ajar as I went up the steps. My legs were shaking. I was scared of Vera, like most people . . ." Maja stopped, then went on: "A gramophone or a radio was playing inside the house, I could hear music. And voices. She had visitors."

"She had a housekeeper for several years, so it might have been—"

"No. It was two men," Maja interrupted him. "I could hear two men's voices from the kitchen. One was mumbling, and the other one was speaking much more loudly and firmly, almost like a captain . . ."

"Did you see either of these men?" said Gerlof.

"No, no," said Maja quickly. "And I didn't stand there eavesdropping either . . . I knocked on the door as soon as I got to the top of the steps. The voices stopped, and Vera came hurtling out onto the veranda, slamming the kitchen door behind her. It was a shock, coming back to the village and seeing her after so many years. She'd got so thin and twisted . . . like a dried-out rope. But she was still suspicious, she looked at me as if I were a thief or something. 'What do you want?' she wanted to know. No hello, no politeness. I lost it completely. I had the case in my pocket, but I didn't even get it out. I started stammering something about Nils and the alvar . . . and that was probably stupid. It *was* stupid, because Vera screamed at me to go away. Then she went back into the kitchen. And I went back home . . . and she died a few years later, of course."

Gerlof nodded. Vera had died on the very same staircase Julia had fallen down. He asked:

"Did you hear what they were talking about? The two men?"

Maja shook her head. "I only heard a few words before I knocked," she said. "Something about longing. It was the one with the loud voice who said something about somebody longing: 'And of course you're both longing to see each other,' or something like that."

Gerlof thought about it.

"Perhaps they were relatives of Vera's," he suggested. "Relatives from Småland?"

"Perhaps," said Maja.

There was silence. Gerlof had no more questions; he needed to think this over.

"Well . . ." he said, reaching his hand up to pat Maja gently on the shoulder, but she leaned forward slightly so that his fingers ended up touching her cheek.

They stayed there, almost of their own accord, trembling in a movement which slowly became a caress.

Maja closed her eyes.

Gerlof released his breath softly, then leaned away.

"Well . . ." he said again. "I can't . . . not anymore."

"Are you sure?" asked Maja, opening her eyes.

Gerlof nodded sadly. "Too much pain," he said.

"Perhaps it'll disappear come the spring," said Maja. "That happens sometimes."

"Maybe," said Gerlof, getting to his feet as quickly as he could. "Thank you for talking to me, Maja. I won't spread this any further. You know that."

Maja stayed where she was, sitting at the table.

"It's fine, Gerlof," she said.

Gerlof realized he was still holding the case in his left hand, and put it back on the table. But Maja picked it up, took out the crucifix, and gave the case back to him.

"You take them," she said. "I don't want them any longer. It's better if you have them."

"If you're sure."

He nodded several times, like a clumsy farewell, and left Maja's room with the case in his pocket. It was heavy and cold, and rattled faintly as he walked along the empty corridor.

Gerlof closed the door behind him once he was back in his own room. He didn't usually lock it, but he did now.

The spoils of war, he thought. Soldiers are always looking for the spoils of war. From whom had the soldiers received or taken the precious stones? Had anyone else died for them, apart from the soldiers themselves?

And where should he put them? Gerlof looked around. He didn't have a sewing box with a false bottom.

In the end he went over to the bookcase. On one of the shelves was a ship in a bottle representing the final journey of the brig *Bluebird of Hull,* as he thought it would have looked that stormy night on the coast of Bohuslän. *Bluebird* was on her way to the Bohuslän rocks, where she would go aground, and six men would drown.

Gerlof picked up the bottle and took out the cork. Then he opened the case and slowly, carefully, tipped the stones into the bottle. He shook the bottle to get them in the right place. There, now, if you didn't look too closely it looked as if the stones were rocks the brig was about to run aground on.

That would have to do for the time being.

Gerlof put the ship back on the shelf and hid the empty case behind a row of books on a lower shelf.

For the rest of the evening, before he went to bed, he kept looking over at the bottle. After the twelfth or fifteenth time he began to understand why Maja had looked so relieved when she handed the old metal case over to him.

That night his only real nightmare from his time at sea came back to him.

He dreamed that he was standing by the gunwale of a ship sailing slowly across the Baltic, somewhere between the northern tip of Öland and the island of Oaxen. It was twilight, not a breath of wind, and Gerlof was standing gazing out across the shining water toward the horizon, with no land in sight anywhere . . .

. . . and then he looked down into the water and caught sight of an old mine from the Second World War.

It was floating just beneath the surface: a massive black ball of steel covered in algae and mussels, with its black spikes sticking out.

It was impossible to veer away. All Gerlof could do was to look on in horror as the hull of the ship and the mine slowly but remorselessly glided toward one another, closer and closer.

He woke up with a cry in the darkness of the home, just before the mine exploded.

23

Sunday morning: Julia was sitting by the window in Astrid's living room, her crutches leaning against the back of the chair, watching her older sister Lena and her husband Richard driving her car away out on the ridge.

She had managed to hold on to the car for a week longer than planned, but now it was over. Perhaps it was just as well; she couldn't drive anyway, with her broken bones.

Lena and Richard had arrived on Saturday for a short visit to Öland; they had called on Gerlof and had coffee in Marnäs before spending the night up in the summer cottage. In the morning they came down to Astrid Linder's to say hello, and it then became clear that they were also intending to take Julia back to Gothenburg with them.

Naturally they hadn't bothered to inform Julia of this plan. She didn't even know Lena and Richard were going to turn up, until she saw the dark green Volvo come up the road and park outside Astrid's house. And by that time it was too late to run away.

"Hi there!" called Lena breezily when Astrid let her in. She gave Julia a hug which made the pain of her cracked collarbone stab through her neck. "How are you?" Lena was looking at the crutches.

"Not too bad now," said Julia.

"Dad phoned and told us what had happened," said Lena. "Terrible . . . but it could have been worse . . . That's the way you have to think about it, it could have been worse." And that was all her sister had to say about Julia's broken bones. She added, "It's very kind of Astrid to let you stay here, isn't it?"

"Astrid's an angel," said Julia.

And it was true. Astrid was an angel who enjoyed living in the quiet emptiness of Stenvik, but she'd said that she also felt lonely sometimes. She was a widow after all, and her only child, a daughter, was a doctor in Saudi Arabia, and only came home at Christmas and midsummer.

Richard didn't actually have anything to say at all; he merely nodded impatiently at Julia, didn't take off his light brown autumn jacket, and started looking at his Rolex after just a few minutes. No doubt for him the only important thing was to get the car back to Torslanda, Julia thought, so that his daughter could use it.

Astrid offered them morning coffee and cookies, and Lena was full of enthusiasm for how quiet and peaceful it was in Stenvik at this time of year, when all the tourists were gone. Richard sat stiffly beside his wife and said nothing. Julia sat at the opposite side of the table looking out of the window, thinking about Vera Kant's house behind the tall trees.

"Right, well, we'd better be thinking about leaving soon," said Lena when they'd had coffee. "We've got a long journey home."

She quickly helped to clear away the coffee cups while Richard went out to help Astrid fix a gutter that was coming away at the back of the house.

Julia could do nothing but sit and watch. She had no legs, no job, no children. But life would still go on, somehow.

"Nice of you to come," she told her sister.

"We decided straightaway that we'd come over and help you get home," Lena said. "I mean, you can't drive now."

"Thank you," said Julia, "but there's no need. I'm going to stay."

Lena wasn't listening. "If I take you and drive the Ford, Richard can drive the Volvo home," she went on, rinsing out the coffeepot. "We usually stop for lunch in Rydaholm, there's a very nice restaurant there."

"I can't go home without Jens," Julia said. "I have to find him now."

Lena turned and looked at her.

"What did you say?" she said. "But there aren't any . . ."

Julia shook her head.

"I know Jens is dead, Lena," she interrupted, meeting her sister's gaze steadily. "My son is dead. I've realized that now, but this isn't about that. I just want us to find him, wherever he is."

"Okay, okay, that's fine. Dad enjoys having you here," said Lena, hastily. "So that's absolutely fine."

Yes, better than drinking wine and taking pills in front of the television in Gothenburg, thought Julia. For a second she felt all the wasted years like a heavy pressure against her breast—the years when the grief over her missing child had become much more important than all the happy memories of him that could have given her solace; a black hole of grief in which she nearly drowned, while avoiding life.

But now there was peace. Just a little peace.

In the end, when you were old enough, it all came down to being in a peaceful place where you felt at home, together with people you liked. Like Stenvik, with Astrid the angel. And Gerlof. And Lennart. Julia liked them all.

And Lena meant well. Julia knew that even her older sister somehow meant well.

"Good," she told Lena. "See you in Gothenburg."

Half an hour later, Richard was sitting in the big dark green Volvo outside Astrid's house and Lena was getting into the little Ford.

She leaned forward and waved to Julia through the windshield. And then they set off, first Richard and then her sister.

Julia breathed out.

A minute or so later the telephone out in the hallway began to ring.

"I'll get it," said Astrid. Julia heard her lift the receiver and listen, and then she called out, "It's the police, Julia, for you . . . It's Lennart."

Julia hobbled into the hallway on just one crutch and picked up the telephone. "Hi there."

"How are you feeling?" asked Lennart.

"Better," said Julia. "Time heals broken bones . . . and Astrid's looking after me."

"Good," he said. "I've got some news . . . but perhaps you've already heard it."

"Have you found Nils Kant?" said Julia.

It sounded as if Lennart were sighing quietly at the other end of the phone.

"It isn't a ghost who's been digging up that cellar," he replied. "Didn't Gerlof tell you?"

"We haven't had much chance to talk," said Julia.

"Your father helped me trace the owner of the snuff tins. You know, the tins that were down in Vera's cellar."

"Who was it?"

"Anders Hagman."

"Anders Hagman? You mean Anders . . . over at the camp-site? John's son?"

"The very man."

"Are you sure?"

"He hasn't admitted it himself, because we haven't managed to speak to him yet," said Lennart. "Anders is keeping out of the way. But all the indications are that it's him."

"So it wasn't Nils Kant who'd been sleeping at the house."

"No," said Lennart. "There's usually a simple explanation, Julia. Anders Hagman lives just a few hundred yards away. It was easy for him to sneak over to Vera Kant's house after dark."

"But why was he digging?"

"There are a few different theories about that. I have my own ideas, and I've discussed them with my colleagues in Borgholm. Do you know Anders? Did you see anything of him when you lived in Stenvik?"

"No. He's younger than me . . . four or five years younger." She had only a vague memory of a powerfully built, shy, silent boy. Anders Hagman had kept to himself, worked on his father's campsite, and never taken part in any of the midsummer dances or parties down by the jetty, or anything else in Stenvik—not that she could recall.

"He has a conviction for assault," said Lennart. "Did you know that?"

"Assault?"

"There was a drunken brawl at the campsite twelve years ago.

Anders knocked down a young lad from Stockholm. I went down there myself that night and arrested him. He got a suspended sentence and a fine."

"Is he suspected of anything now?" asked Julia. "Are you after him?"

"No, it's not a question of being after him," said Lennart. "We just want to find him, have a chat with him . . . find out what he's been doing at Vera Kant's. He's guilty of breaking and entering, at any rate."

So am I, thought Julia.

"Aren't you going to ask him about Jens?" she asked. "Where Anders was when Jens disappeared?"

"Perhaps," said Lennart. "Do you think we should?"

"I don't know," said Julia.

She couldn't remember if Anders Hagman had even met her son. But surely he would have? They'd swum over by the jetty in the summer, within sight of the campsite. Jens had run around on the shore all day long in his swimming trunks and a sun hat. Had Anders stood on the ridge watching him?

"Evidently Anders is in Borgholm. We'll track him down," said Lennart. "If we find out anything interesting, I'll be in touch."

Gerlof had also called Julia after her accident, but Julia hadn't let it turn into a long conversation. She was embarrassed. The more she thought about breaking into Vera Kant's house and her idea that Jens had hidden in there, the more embarrassed she felt.

On Monday morning Gerlof finally came to Stenvik in John Hagman's car and rang the doorbell. Julia struggled with her crutches to get to the door; she was alone in the house. Astrid was up in Marnäs, shopping.

John was the chauffeur, but he stayed out in the car. Julia could see him slumped behind the wheel, looking pensive.

"I just wanted to call in and see how you were," said Gerlof, leaning on his cane, out of breath after walking from the car to the house all by himself.

"I'm pretty good," said Julia, leaning on her crutches. "Are you and John off somewhere?"

"We're going to Småland," said Gerlof briefly.

"When will you be back?"

Gerlof laughed. "Boel asked exactly the same question at the home. She'd much rather I stayed in my room from morning till night. But it'll be this evening, or late this afternoon . . . We might call on Martin Malm too, if his mind is a bit clearer today than it was last time."

"Does this have anything to do with Nils Kant?"

"It might have," said Gerlof. "We'll see."

Julia nodded—if he didn't want to tell her any more, that was fine.

"I heard about Anders Hagman," she said. "That you told the police about him."

"I mentioned his name . . . I don't think John's too pleased about it. But they'd have worked out his name anyway, sooner or later."

"They want to talk to him," said Julia. "I'm not sure . . . but it seems as if the police in Borgholm might be on the way to reopening the investigation. Into Jens's disappearance, I mean."

"Mmm . . . but I think they're on the wrong track with Anders. And of course John thinks so too."

"Aren't you going to put them right, then?"

"The police don't listen to us pensioners, not when they think our ideas are too crazy," said Gerlof cheerfully. "We're not reliable."

"But you never give up. That's something to admire."

"Good," said Gerlof. "We do our best."

"You keep on looking," said Julia. "It can't do any harm."

That particular comment was ironic, although she didn't know it—the next time she saw Gerlof he would be dying.

CIUDAD DE PANAMÁ, APRIL 1963

Panama City in the canal country of Panama.

Tall apartment blocks and dilapidated shacks side by side. Cars, buses, motorbikes, and jeeps. Mestizos, military police, bankers, beggars, buzzing flies, and gangs of sweaty American soldiers along the avenues. The smell of burnt gas, rotten fruit, and grilled fish.

Nils Kant wanders through the narrow streets every day, the soles of his feet burning inside his shoes.

He's looking for Swedish sailors.

There aren't any in Costa Rica—at least, Nils has never met any. To be sure of finding Swedes, he has to come here, to Ciudad de Panamá.

The journey south by bus takes six hours. Nils has made five such journeys to the canal area in three years.

In the long canal between the oceans, ships line up to avoid the lengthy journey around Cape Horn. The sailors go ashore to enjoy themselves in the big port. Some stay behind: the bums.

He is looking for the right man among these forgotten sailors: those who gather at the docks when ships from Scandinavia arrive, at the Scandinavian church when they're handing out food, and who spend the rest of their time within reach of the bars and shops. Those who'll drink anything that contains alcohol, from cheap Colombian rum to pure spirit distilled from shoe polish.

On the second evening of his fifth visit, he is walking along the cracked cement sidewalks when he sees a shadowy figure clutching a bottle, crouching in a dark doorway a few blocks away from the entrance to the Scandinavian church. Sniveling, fits of coughing, and the stench of vomit.

Nils stops in front of him.

"How are you?" he asks.

He speaks Swedish. It isn't worth wasting time on anyone who doesn't understand what he says right away.

"What?" asks the bum.

"I said, How are you?"

"Are you from Sweden?"

The look in the Swede's eyes is more sorrowful and weary than dull, his beard is unkempt, but the lines around his mouth and eyes are not that deep. This man hasn't been drinking all that long, despite the fact that he looks as if he's just about thirty-five–around Nils's age.

Nils nods. "I come from Öland."

"Öland?" The bum raises his voice and coughs. "Öland, shit . . . I'm from Småland . . . shit. Born in Nybro."

"It's a small world," says Nils.

"But now . . . I missed the ship going through the lock."

"Really? That's a shame."

"Last year. I missed . . . the ship was supposed to go through the lock after two days. Up, down. Got arrested here . . . there was a fight in a bar, I was swigging beer straight from the jug." The man looks up with a new light in his eyes. "Have you got any money?"

"Maybe."

"Buy something, then, buy whisky . . . I know where."

The man tries to get up, but his legs are too stiff.

"I might be able to go and buy a bottle," Nils tells him. "One bottle of whisky, we can share it. But you'll have to wait here. Are you going to wait for me?"

The man nods, and squats down again.

"Buy something" is all he mutters.

"Good," says Nils, straightening up without looking the man in the eyes. "Perhaps we can be friends."

———

Five weeks later in Jamaicatown, which is the name of Puerto Limón's English quarter:

Tican Hotel it says on the sign, but it's hardly a hotel, and the lobby is just a cracked piece of wood balanced on a couple of table legs, and a register spotted with mold. A staircase on the outside of the building leads up to a few small guest rooms on the second floor. Nils can hear English being spoken loudly in a building on the opposite side of the street.

He goes silently up the steps, past a fat, shiny cockroach on its way down the wall. He reaches the narrow veranda on the second floor, and knocks on the second door in a row of four.

"Yes, sir!" calls a voice from inside, and Nils opens the door.

For the third time he sees the Swede who says he has come to help him get home.

The Swede is sitting on the only bed in the stifling hotel room, amid a heap of tangled sheets and brown-speckled pillows, his upper body bare and gleaming with sweat. He has a glass in his hand. A small fan is humming away on the bureau next to the bed.

The man whom Nils has begun to think of as the Ölander. He has never said where he's from, but Nils has listened carefully, and thinks he can detect a faint Öland accent when the man speaks. He has realized the man knows the island well. Did Nils meet him there?

"Come in, come in." The Swede smiles and leans back against the wall, nodding toward a bottle of West Indian rum on the bureau. "Drink, Nils?"

"No."

Nils closes the door behind him. He's given up drinking alcohol. Not completely, but almost.

"Limón is a wonderful town, Nils," says the man on the bed, and Nils can hear no hint of sarcasm in his voice. "I was out for a stroll today and I found a genuine brothel, purely by chance, hidden in some rooms behind a bar. Wonderful women. But of course I didn't indulge, to put it politely . . . I had a drink and left."

Nils nods briefly and leans against the closed door. "I've found somebody," he says. "A good candidate." He still feels uncomfortable speaking Swedish out loud after eighteen years abroad. He fumbles for the right words. "He's from Småland too."

"Good, that's good," says the Swede. "Where? In Panama City?"

Nils nods. "I brought him with me . . . The border controls have got stricter, I had to bribe my way through, but it went okay. He's in San José now, in a cheap hotel. He's lost his passport, but we applied for a new one at the Swedish Embassy."

"Good, good. What's his name?"

Nils shakes his head. "No names," he says. "You haven't told me yours."

"All you have to do is look it up downstairs," says the man on the bed. "I signed the register. You have to do that."

"I've read it," says Nils.

"And?"

"It said Fritiof Andersson," says Nils.

The man nods with satisfaction. "You can call me Fritiof, that'll be fine."

Nils shakes his head. "That's just a name from an old song about a sailor–I want to know your real name."

"My name isn't important," says the man, staring at him. "Fritiof will do very well. Don't you think?"

"Maybe." Nils nods slowly. "For the time being."

"Good." Fritiof wipes his chest and forehead with a sheet. "Now, we've got a few more things to talk about. I'm going to–"

"Did my mother really send you?"

"I've already told you that."

The man on the bed doesn't appear to appreciate being interrupted.

"She should have sent a letter with you," says Nils.

"That'll come later," says Fritiof. "You got money, didn't you? That was from your mother." He takes a swig of his drink. "But right now we have other things to discuss . . . I'm going back home in two days. You won't hear from me for a while. But I'll be back when everything's ready, and that'll be the last time. How long will it take, do you think?"

"Well . . . a couple of weeks, maybe. He has to get his passport and travel down here," says Nils.

"Fine," says Fritiof. "Keep an eye on him and do everything by the book. Then you'll be able to go home."

Nils nods.

"Fine," says Fritiof, wiping his face again.

Someone laughs down on the street, a motorbike roars past. All Nils wants to do is open the door and get out of this stinking room.

"How does it feel, by the way?" asks the man, leaning forward.

"How does what feel?" says Nils.

"I'm a little curious." The man who calls himself Fritiof Andersson is smiling among the filthy sheets. "I'm just wondering, Nils, purely out of curiosity . . . How does it feel to kill someone?"

24

Gerlof and John drove across the Öland Bridge, past Kalmar, then north along the coast of Småland. Neither of them said much during the journey.

Gerlof was mainly thinking about the fact that it had become much more difficult to leave the home in Marnäs—Boel had questioned him closely this morning about where he was going and how long he was going to be away. In the end she had hinted that perhaps he was too healthy to stay on at the home.

"There are many elderly people with severe mobility problems in the north of Öland who would like to get a room here, Gerlof," Boel had said. "We have to make sure we're prioritizing correctly. All the time."

"Quite right," Gerlof had said, and set off, leaning on his cane for support.

Didn't he have the right to care? When he could hardly move ten yards without help? Boel should be glad he got out into the fresh air sometimes, along with old friends like John. Shouldn't she?

"So Anders has gone off, then," said Gerlof eventually, when they were just a few kilometers from Ramneby.

"Yes," said John.

He always drove at the speed limit, and a long line of cars had built up behind them.

"I assume you told Anders the police were looking for him," said Gerlof.

John remained silent behind the wheel, but he nodded.

"I don't know if that was such a good idea," said Gerlof. "The police tend to get annoyed when you don't want to talk to them."

"He just wants to be left in peace," said John.

"I'm not sure that's such a good idea," said Gerlof again.

"Did you speak to Robert Blomberg when you were in Borgholm last week?" John asked. "The car salesman, I mean."

"I saw him," said Gerlof. "He was in the showroom. We didn't speak . . . I didn't really know what to say."

"Could he be Kant?" said John.

"If you're asking me straight out . . . I've thought about it, and I don't believe he could," said Gerlof. "It seems unlikely that somebody like Nils Kant would come back from South America with a new name, and manage to blend in in Borgholm with a new life."

"Maybe," said John.

A few minutes later they drove past the yellow sign telling them they were entering Ramneby. It was a quarter to eleven in the morning. A flatbed truck carrying a load of newly felled timber thundered past them.

Gerlof had never been to Ramneby before, either by car or boat. The village itself was no bigger than Marnäs, and they were soon on the other side of it, turning off for the sawmill.

There was a closed steel gate at the sawmill, and a parking lot outside it where John left the car.

Gerlof took his briefcase and they walked over to the wide gate and rang the bell. After a while there was a scraping noise from a small loudspeaker next to the bell.

"Hello?" said Gerlof, unsure whether he should be talking to the bell or the loudspeaker, or perhaps to the sky. "Hello . . . We wanted to visit the wood museum. Could you open the gate?"

The loudspeaker remained silent.

"Did they hear you?" whispered John.

"I don't know."

Gerlof heard a cawing noise behind him; turning his head, he saw two crows perched in a leafless birch tree beside the parking lot. They kept cawing, and Gerlof thought they sounded different from the crows on Öland. Did birds have different accents too?

Then he noticed someone approaching on the other side of the gate, an elderly man in a cap and a black padded jacket, moving almost as slowly as Gerlof himself. The man pressed a button on the other side, and the gate swung open.

"Heimersson," said the man, extending his hand.

Gerlof shook it. "Davidsson," he said.

"Hagman," said John.

"We wanted to visit the wood museum," said Gerlof again. "I called yesterday . . ."

"That's fine," said Heimersson, turning to show them the way. "It was a good thing you did. The museum is really only open in the summer. Including August. But if you call in advance, it's usually fine."

They had reached the factory area now. Gerlof had expected the smell of newly sawn wood in his nostrils and the sight of groups of men in caps carrying planks of wood around between heaps of sawdust—as usual he was stuck in the past. All he saw instead were roads and tarmac between huge gray buildings made of steel and aluminum. There were big signs on them with the name RAMNEBY TIMBER.

"I've worked here for forty-eight years," said Heimersson over his shoulder to them. "Started when I was fifteen, and stayed on. That's the way things turned out . . . Now I look after the museum."

"We come from the village where the owners used to live," said Gerlof. "In the north of Öland."

"The owners?" said Heimersson.

"The Kant family."

"The Kants don't own this place any longer," said Heimersson. "They sold it at the end of the seventies, when August Kant died. It's a forestry company in Canada that owns Ramneby nowadays."

"The previous owner . . . August Kant?" said Gerlof. "Did you meet him?"

"Did I meet him," said Heimersson, smiling as if the question were amusing. "I met him every day. He always drove his MG in . . . Anyway, here we are. This is the old office, it got too small in the end."

WOOD MUSEUM said a wooden sign above the door. Heimersson unlocked it, went in, and switched the light on.

"Right . . . you're both very welcome. That'll be thirty kronor each."

He had gone behind a counter with an ancient, enormous cash register on it.

Gerlof paid for both of them and received two receipts exactly like the one he'd found in Ernst Adolfsson's wallet, then they went into the museum.

It wasn't large, just two rooms with a short corridor between them. Some old saws and measuring equipment stood in the center of the room, and there were pictures on the walls. Lots of black-and-white photographs, framed and behind glass, all with labels explaining what was in each one. Gerlof went over to them in silence and stared at group photographs of sawmill workers, at forestry workers with saws in their hands, and at pictures of ships at anchor, their decks covered in piles of timber.

"There are some more recent photos in the other room," said Heimersson from behind him.

"Right," said Gerlof.

He would have preferred to look around alone, and noticed that John was carefully keeping out of the guide's way.

"Our first computer is in there too," said Heimersson. "That's progress for you . . . I mean, computers run all the sawing nowadays. I don't actually understand how it works myself, but it seems to be very effective."

"Right."

Gerlof kept searching among the black-and-white photographs.

"Ramneby exports refined wood all the way to Japan," said Heimersson. "I don't suppose you've ever done any business over there?"

"No," said Gerlof, and added quickly, "But there's limestone from Öland on the floor of Saint Paul's Cathedral in London."

Heimersson didn't reply, and Gerlof changed the subject:

"A friend of ours was here last month, actually, here in the museum. Ernst Adolfsson."

"From Öland?"

Gerlof nodded. "He used to be a stonemason. He was here in the middle of September."

"Yes, I remember him very well," said Heimersson. "I opened the museum especially for him, just like I have for you. I enjoyed meeting him. He said he lived on Öland, but that he came from this village originally."

"From Ramneby?" said Gerlof.

"Yes. He grew up down in the village, before he moved to Öland."

This was news to Gerlof, who had never heard Ernst talk about the village he came from.

He took a couple more steps, and then he saw it: the picture of Martin Malm and August Kant side by side at the sawmill harbor, standing stiffly in front of a row of younger workers.

A friendly business meeting on the quayside at the sawmill, 1959, said the typed strip of paper beneath the picture, despite the fact that only one solitary man in the group was wearing a friendly smile. The rest of them, Martin and Kant included, were staring at the camera with serious expressions.

1959. So that was several years before Martin bought his first big ship, thought Gerlof.

On this copy of the photograph, which was bigger than the picture in the book, the hand on Martin's left shoulder could be seen clearly, and that was at least a sign of friendliness. It had certainly never occurred to Gerlof to place an arm around Martin Malm's shoulder; he wasn't a person who invited any form of intimacy. But it had been fine for August Kant to do that.

"This is one of our friends," said Gerlof, pointing at Martin Malm's face. "A boat captain from Öland."

"Oh yes," said Heimersson. He didn't sound particularly interested. "There were cargo ships here all the time in the old days . . . They used to take wood to Öland. You haven't got much in the way of forests there, after all."

"We did have forests, but they were chopped down by people from the mainland," said Gerlof. He pointed at the picture again. "And that's August Kant, isn't it?"

"That's the boss, yes."

"He had quite a well-known nephew," said Gerlof. "Nils Kant."

"Oh yes, him," said Heimersson. "I've heard about him—he murdered a policeman. Read about him in the paper, too. But he died, didn't he? Ran off overseas and died?"

"Yes," said Gerlof. "But did he ever come here before that?"

"I don't think the boss was very keen on Nils," said Heimersson. "He never talked about his nephew. So nobody else talked about him either, not if the boss was around."

"Perhaps he didn't want to give away the fact that he knew where Nils was?" said Gerlof.

"Could be, I suppose," said Heimersson. "But Nils was here when he was running away from Öland, after he'd murdered that policeman."

"Was he? And did he meet his uncle?"

"I don't know. But he hung around here for a while . . . people saw him in the forest." Heimersson pointed toward the photographs. "Gunnar there was an errand boy like me at the time, and he boasted that he'd met him and got money from him. But then he boasted about a lot of things . . . I just remember that somebody tipped the police off in the end, told them Nils Kant was here. The cops came and watched the sawmill for several days, just in case he turned up. Everybody was a bit nervous . . . but we did our jobs, of course. And the murderer stayed well away from us."

Gerlof felt he could almost see young Nils creeping around the office building over on the far side, crouching low and trying to peep in through the windows to find his uncle August.

"Did our friend Ernst happen to mention this picture from the quayside?" asked Gerlof.

Heimersson thought it over.

"Yes, he did," he answered. "He stopped at that one. He wanted to know the names."

"The names?" said Gerlof. "Of the sawmill workers?"

"Yes. And I gave him the ones I remembered. You forget things like that as you get older; for example these days I can't—"

"Could you tell me the names too?" Gerlof cut in.

He'd got his notebook and a ballpoint pen out of his briefcase.

"No problem," said Heimersson. "Right, let's see, from the left . . ."

There were three men in the row whose names Heimersson couldn't remember, they were probably sailors, but Gerlof wrote down the rest: Per Bengtsson, Knut Lindkvist, Anders Åkergren, Claes Frisell, Gunnar Johansson, Jan Ekendahl, Mikael Larsson. Then he looked at the list he'd made, but didn't recognize a single name. He still didn't know what Ernst had been looking for.

Heimersson moved on cheerfully. He went ahead of them along the corridor to the other room.

"There's our first computer, over there . . . The size of a house. But that's the way they used to be."

Gerlof nodded absently and allowed Heimersson to show him around the room where the technological development of the sawmill and forestry in general was presented. Most of it dealt with statistics and big machines.

"It really is very interesting," said Gerlof after ten minutes. "Thank you so much."

"You're very welcome," said Heimersson. "It's always a pleasure to meet people who are interested in wood."

He went outside with them and pointed over to one of the steel buildings.

"We've just installed a new X-ray process to assess the quality of the wood. Perhaps you'd like to see that too?"

Gerlof caught a brief shake of the head from John, who had had enough of timber.

"Thank you," he replied, "but I should think that would be far too technical for us. But we would like to go down to the harbor and have a look around, if that's okay. On our own."

"The harbor?" said Heimersson. "I wouldn't call it that. It's too shallow here for the big ships to come in. All our wood is transported by truck."

"We'd still like to take a look," said Gerlof.

"Fine," said Heimersson. "I'll lock up the museum, then."

He was right—Gerlof could see it wasn't much of a harbor to speak of when they'd walked the hundred yards or so down to the water. There was hardly anything that could be called a quay, the asphalt was cracked, and the square granite slabs along what was left of the quay had become dislodged, with gaping spaces between them.

Beside the quay a wooden jetty extended a dozen or so yards out into the water. Even that needed repairing, in Gerlof's opinion. Was there really not enough timber from the sawmill to do that?

There was an old lone wooden skiff bobbing in the water by the jetty, silently waiting for its owner to lift it out before the winter storms came.

The wind was coming off the land, bitterly cold, and Öland could just be glimpsed as a dark strip along the horizon. Despite the fact that the coast of Småland was beautiful, with its islands and inlets, Gerlof was already longing to get back to the island.

"I assume it was here that Martin Malm's ships used to dock," he said.

"That's right," said John. "The picture was taken here."

There wasn't much more to see, and Gerlof was feeling the cold right through his overcoat. He had no desire to go out onto the jetty in this wind, and when John turned away he did the same.

On the way back Gerlof stopped and looked out over the open space between the sawmill buildings. It was still completely deserted.

At that same moment he was suddenly struck by absolute certainty. There was no logic to it; it came up from his subconscious like a dark fish, appearing and striking just beneath the surface of the water, and before he had even managed to think it through, he opened his mouth:

"It began here."

"What did?" said John.

"Everything began here. Nils Kant and Jens and . . . My grandchild died because of something that began here."

"Here in Ramneby?"

"Yes, here. Here at the sawmill."

"How do you know that?"

"I can feel it," said Gerlof, and he could hear how stupid it sounded. But still he had to go on: "There was some kind of meeting, I think it was a meeting. When Nils came here . . . He must have met his uncle August and reached some kind of agreement. Something like that must have happened."

But the feeling of certainty had already disappeared.

"Right. Shall we go home, then?" said John.

Gerlof nodded, and set off again.

Gerlof was sitting alone in John's car. It was parked next to the stone houses on a deserted Larmgatan in the middle of Kalmar. John had wanted to stop off in the town for a brief visit to his sister Ingrid before they went back to Öland.

Gerlof was thinking things over. Had they really got anything out of the visit to the museum? He wasn't sure.

On the other side of the street the door of Ingrid's apartment block opened and John came out. He walked straight over to the car and opened the driver's door.

"Was she all right?" asked Gerlof.

John settled himself behind the wheel without replying. Then he started the engine and pulled out.

They left Kalmar and drove out on the straight freeway toward Öland in silence, but it wasn't until they reached the bridge that Gerlof decided it had lasted long enough.

"Is something wrong?" he asked. "Did something happen at Ingrid's?"

"The police have got Anders," John said. "They picked him up there at lunchtime."

"Picked him up where?" said Gerlof. "At Ingrid's?"

John nodded. "Anders was at his aunt Ingrid's. He was hiding there. And now they've arrested him."

"Arrested him—are you sure about that?" said Gerlof. "The police only arrest someone if they think—"

"Ingrid said they walked in without knocking," John interrupted him. "They came in and told Anders he had to go with them to Borgholm. They refused to answer her questions."

"Did you know he was in Kalmar?"

John didn't say anything, he simply nodded again.

"As I said this morning," said Gerlof slowly, "it's never a good idea to take off if the police want to talk to you. It just makes them suspicious."

"Anders doesn't trust them," said John. "He was trying to prevent that brawl at the campsite. But he was the one who ended up in court, not those people from Stockholm."

"I know," said Gerlof. "And that wasn't right." He thought for a while, then asked as gently as he could, "But if . . . if the police think Anders might have anything to do with my grandchild's disappearance, and want to talk to him about it . . . Is there anything to suggest they might be right? I mean, you know Anders better than anyone else . . . Have you ever suspected anything?"

John shook his head. "Anders is a decent man."

"You don't even need to think about it?" said Gerlof.

"The only stupid thing I've ever seen him do," said John, "was one evening when he was creeping around in the juniper bushes by the jetty. He was spying on some girls who were getting changed at the swimming club. He was twelve or thirteen at the time. I told him never to do anything like that again. And he never did."

"That's not too serious," Gerlof said, nodding.

"He's a decent man," John repeated. "But they've arrested him anyway."

The car had crossed the bridge now, and they were back on the island.

Gerlof was thinking as he gazed out over the windswept alvar east of the main road. He nodded again.

"Okay, let's go to Borgholm," he said. "I'm going to talk to Martin Malm one last time. He's going to tell me what really happened."

25

"*I'm not the one* who's going to be talking to Anders Hagman," said Lennart to Julia as they were on their way to Borgholm in the police car. "An inspector from Kalmar is coming; he's trained in this sort of thing."

"Will it be a long interrogation?" said Julia, looking at Lennart behind the wheel.

He was wearing a new uniform jacket, a padded winter jacket with the police badge on the shoulder. Dressed for town.

"I don't think we'll call it an interrogation," said Lennart hastily. "It's just a chat, a conversation. He hasn't been arrested or held on suspicion or anything like that. There's no evidence for that. But if Anders admits that he's the one who broke into Vera Kant's house, and saved those old newspaper cuttings, then I'm sure they'll talk about your son too. And then we can see what Anders has to say about all that."

"I've tried to remember if he . . . if he showed an interest in Jens in any way," said Julia. "But I don't recall anything like that."

"That's good. You shouldn't start suspecting people of all kinds of stuff."

Lennart had called her as she was sitting drinking coffee with Astrid. He had passed on the news that Anders Hagman had been found in Kalmar and taken to Borgholm. Half an hour or so later he had come to pick her up in the police car. Julia was grateful that Lennart had allowed her to be involved in this investigation, or whatever it was, right from the start, but at the same time she was nervous about what was waiting for her.

"I won't have to sit in the same room, will I?" she said. "I don't think . . ."

"No, no," said Lennart. "It'll just be Anders and Niklas Bergman, the inspector from Kalmar."

"Do you have two-way mirrors . . . or anything?"

She regretted the question when Lennart began to smile.

"No, nothing like that," he answered. "They're mostly in American TV series, when you have witness confrontations and exciting stuff like that. Sometimes we use video, but that doesn't happen all that often either. I expect they have situations in Stockholm where they confront witnesses, but it doesn't happen here."

"Do you think it was him?" asked Julia when they were stopped at the first set of traffic lights in Borgholm.

Lennart shook his head. "I don't know. But we need to talk to him."

The police station in Borgholm was on one of the streets cutting across the main road into town. Lennart pulled up in the parking lot and opened the glove compartment. Julia watched him rummaging around among papers, business cards, and packets of gum.

"Mustn't forget this," he said. "Not that I'll need it, but I'm not allowed to leave it behind."

He took out his gun, which was in a black holster with the word GLOCK etched into the leather. Lennart quickly clipped it to his hip and waited until Julia had got out of the car and balanced on her crutches before he showed her into the Borgholm police station. She had to wait in the off-duty room. It looked just like any other room of its kind, but there was a television in one corner, and she found herself sitting in front of the same American TV shopping channel she usually watched at home in her apartment in Gothenburg in the daytime.

Now, this seemed completely incomprehensible. How could she ever have thought TV shopping was an interesting thing to watch?

Just before two o'clock, Lennart came back into the room.

"That's it, then," he said. "For now. Would you like to go for something to eat?"

Julia nodded, not wanting to reveal how curious she was. Lennart was sure to tell her at the appropriate moment. She followed him out of the station on her crutches.

"Is Anders still there?" she asked as they came out into the cold on Storgatan.

Lennart shook his head. "He's been allowed to go back to his apartment here in Borgholm."

He walked slowly along the sidewalk, adopting the same pace as Julia. The wind was icy cold and was making her fingers go numb on the crutches.

Lennart added, "Or it might be his mother's apartment, I'm not really sure. But he's promised not to disappear, in case we need to talk to him again. . . . How about Chinese? I've had enough of pizza."

"As long as it's not far," said Julia, and let Lennart lead her to a Chinese restaurant next to Borgholm church.

There were only a few customers left in the restaurant, and Lennart and Julia hung up their jackets before sitting down at a window table. Julia looked at the white church building outside and remembered the hot summer when she had been confirmed there; she'd been in love with a boy in the confirmation class called . . . What was he called? It had been so important then, but now she couldn't remember.

"But what was Anders doing in the house?" she asked quietly when they had ordered their food, five small dishes to share. "Did he say?"

"Yes . . . He says he was digging for diamonds," said Lennart.

"Diamonds?"

Lennart nodded and looked out of the window. "It's an old rumor . . . I've heard it too: the Germans Nils Kant killed are supposed to have had some kind of stolen treasure with them from the Baltic. Precious stones of some sort, so people say. Anders got it into his head that Nils had buried them in the cellar before he took off. So he dug and dug . . . but he never found them," said Lennart, then added, "So he says, anyway. He's a bit odd."

"And the newspaper articles?" asked Julia.

"They were hidden in a cupboard; he found them and put them up. Anders thinks it was Vera who saved them." Lennart looked at her. "Do you know what else he says? He says he's felt Vera Kant's presence in there. Ghosts . . ."

"I see" was all Julia said.

She didn't want to tell him she'd suspected the same thing. She didn't want to think about that night in Vera's house for one single moment.

Julia had one more question, but didn't know if she wanted to ask it. Just before their food arrived at the table, Lennart gave her the answer anyway:

"Anders swears he didn't see your son that autumn day. He said he didn't know anything about Jens. He stayed inside that day, it was too foggy and raw outside, and he heard what had happened when we asked for help with the search parties." He added, "Niklas Bergman got the feeling Anders was telling the truth. He was just as open about that as he was about breaking into Vera Kant's house."

Julia just nodded.

"So I don't think we're going to get much further with this," Lennart went on. "Not unless something new turns up."

Julia nodded again. She looked down at her hands and said:

"I've tried to move on . . . not to bury myself in the past. It hasn't gone too well before, but this autumn it's felt better. A bit better. I've been able to grieve . . . I couldn't do that before." She looked up at Lennart. "So I think it's been good for me to come to Öland . . . and to meet Dad again. And you."

"I'm really glad to hear that," said Lennart. "I was stuck in the past too, for a very long time . . . And I felt really bad sometimes, until I realized taking revenge on people doesn't make you happy. You have to move on. It's difficult to see the way forward, but I think you have to do it."

"Yes," said Julia quietly. "You have to let the dead rest in peace."

Nils leaves the beach known as Playa Bonita outside Limón when all the wine has been drunk and the party is almost over. He has emptied two bottles of Chilean wine all by himself during the course of the evening, and yet he still doesn't feel drunk enough for what is to come.

There have been few visitors to Playa Bonita today, and almost all of them went home long ago.

There are only two men left. They are sitting like shadows in the sand beside a small, glowing fire. They are singing quietly and laughing drunkenly with their arms around each other's shoulders. One of the shadows is the man Nils knows as Fritiof Andersson, the other is their victim. Nils sometimes thinks of the man as the guy from Småland, but usually he calls him Borrachon. *The alcoholic.*

Costa Rica is much better than Panama, Borrachon keeps saying; he can't understand why he didn't come here much sooner. And Limón is a fantastic town. In fact, he doesn't want to go home. Not ever.

Nils has told him he can stay as long as he wants.

It's Nils who has helped Borrachon get to Costa Rica. He made sure Borrachon dragged himself out of the fog of alcohol and got hold of a provisional passport from the embassy in Panama City, to replace the one he left behind on his last ship, then took the train north to San José. Nils has paid for a room in a cheap hotel by the central station, provided Borrachon with money for wine and a little food, then waited for Fritiof Andersson.

Borrachon has been so grateful, exhaustingly grateful. He has found a new friend, someone who understands him. Someone he would die for.

Nils has nodded and smiled at Borrachon, but inside he has been constantly wishing that Fritiof Andersson would return as quickly as possible and help out. *Here comes Fritiof Andersson* . . . Nils doesn't want to become friends with this defeated Swede who is so much like him; he just wants to go home to Öland. Fritiof has promised to organize it, and all he wants in return . . .

> *Hey, if you want, just say the word,*
> *and we'll go home . . .*

—all Fritiof wants are the hidden gemstones.

This is what Nils suspects. On the occasions when Fritiof has visited him, he's mentioned the stones several times. He knows what happened to Nils out on the alvar just after the war.

"Did they say where they came from, those Germans?" Fritiof has asked. "Is it true they'd brought something with them to Öland—some treasure? And if they did have something with them . . . what happened to it? What did you do with it, Nils?"

So many questions, but Nils suspects that this man who calls himself Fritiof already knows the answers to most of them.

Nils has answered the questions, briefly, but he isn't telling anyone where he hid the gemstones. That treasure is his, whatever it's worth. He's earned it, after living with no money for so many years now.

Very soon Borrachon became restless in the little room in San José, but Nils had to keep him there until Fritiof arrived. After three days they had run out of conversation, and after a week all that Nils and Borrachon had in common was drinking wine. They sat in the hotel room, surrounded by empty bottles, and outside the sun beat down on the street.

At last Fritiof's plane landed out at the airport, and he turned up at the hotel with a broad smile below his sunglasses. Borrachon woke from his drunken state without really grasping who this new Swede was and what he wanted, but Fritiof provided more bottles of wine and the party continued. Fritiof sang and laughed, but kept control all the time; he studied Borrachon with a steady gaze.

The day after Fritiof's arrival, Nils went on ahead to Limón by train. He returned to his little room, paid a final installment of rent to his landlady, Madame Mendoza, and had his hair cut just as short as Borrachon's. Then he went to the bar by the harbor and nodded to all the poor bastards who would never leave Limón. He drank wine and made sure he was seen on the muddy streets of the town for several evenings in a row, apparently very drunk indeed.

"*Echa*," he said. He thanked everyone.

And he told Madame Mendoza and several bartenders that he would soon be off on a little walking trip north along the coast, past Playa Bonita—but that he'd be back in a few days, when a Swedish friend was coming to visit.

"*Echa*," he says. "*Hasta pronto*."

At dawn on the final day in Limón he got up, left a little money in the kitchen drawers, and most of his possessions; he just took a few clothes and some food, his wallet, and the letters from Vera. Then he left Limón at long last. He went through the market in the square where the old fishmongers were already setting up, silent witnesses to the start of his journey home. He went on past the railway station and continued northward, out of the town, on the way to his meeting with Fritiof Andersson without looking back.

Not running away—going home.

For the first time in almost twenty years, Nils is on his way home to Öland.

26

It wasn't the young nurse who opened the heavy door of Martin Malm's house this time. It was an elderly woman with long gray hair, dressed in a blouse and pale-colored pants. Gerlof recognized her: Martin's wife, Ann-Britt Malm.

"Good afternoon," said Gerlof.

The woman was standing stiffly in the doorway. Her pale face remained serious; he could see that she didn't recognize him.

"Gerlof Davidsson," he said, moving his cane into his left hand and holding out his right hand. "From Stenvik."

"Oh yes," she said. "Gerlof, yes, of course. You were here last week, with a woman."

"That was my daughter," said Gerlof.

"I was at the window upstairs when you were leaving, but when I asked Ylva, she couldn't remember your names," said Ann-Britt Malm.

"Not to worry," said Gerlof. "I really wanted a chat with Martin about old times, but he wasn't too well. Perhaps he's feeling a bit better today?"

The ice-cold wind from the sound was on his back, and Gerlof was trying not to shiver. But he was desperate to get inside, into the warmth of the house.

"Martin isn't really much better today," said Ann-Britt Malm.

Gerlof nodded sympathetically. "But a little bit better,

maybe?" he said, feeling like a door-to-door salesman. "I won't stay long." He didn't move from the doorway.

In the end she relented.

"We can see how he's feeling," she said. "Come in."

Gerlof turned before he went in, and looked back toward the street.

John was still sitting in his car. Gerlof nodded to him. "Thirty minutes," he'd told him. "If they let me in, come back in thirty minutes."

Now John raised a hand and started the engine. He drove away.

Gerlof walked into the warmth, and his limbs gradually stopped shaking. He put his briefcase down on the stone floor of the large hallway, and took off his coat.

"It's almost like winter out there today," he said to Ann-Britt Malm.

She merely nodded, clearly uninterested in small talk.

The door on one side of the room was ajar, and she went over and pushed it open. Gerlof followed her.

It led into a larger room, a drawing room. The air was musty and stuffy, and there was the smell of stale cigarette smoke. Several windows looked out onto the back garden, but the dark curtains were closed. A chandelier hung from the ceiling, swathed in white fabric. There were tiled stoves in two of the room's corners, and in a third a television was showing cartoons, with the sound turned low.

The Flintstones, Gerlof noticed.

A wheelchair was positioned in front of the television; in it an old man was slumped, a blanket over his knees. His bald head was pitted with dark liver spots, and an old white scar ran across his forehead. His body shook constantly.

This was Martin Malm, the man who had sent Jens's sandal.

"You've got a visitor, Martin," said Ann-Britt.

The old shipowner jerked his head from the television. His gaze fastened on Gerlof and stayed there.

"Good afternoon, Martin," said Gerlof. "How are you?"

Malm's quivering chin dropped an inch or so in a brief nod.

"Are you feeling all right?"

Malm shook his head.

"No? Me neither," said Gerlof. "We get the health we deserve."

On the television screen Fred Flintstone jumped into his car and disappeared in a cloud of dust.

"Would you like some coffee, Gerlof?" asked Ann-Britt.

"No, thanks, I'm fine."

Gerlof sincerely hoped she wasn't intending to stay in the room.

Evidently she wasn't. Ann-Britt Malm turned with her hand on the doorknob and looked at Gerlof for one last time, as if they understood one another.

"I'll be back in a while," she said.

Then she went out and closed the door.

Everything went very silent in the drawing room.

Gerlof stood still for a few moments, then went over to a chair by the wall. It was several yards away from Martin, but Gerlof knew he hadn't the strength to drag it over to Martin, so he sat down on it where it was.

"There we are, then," he said. "We can have a little chat now."

Malm was still staring at him.

Gerlof noticed that the drawing room was free of maritime reminders, in contrast to the hallway and his own room at the home in Marnäs. There were no pictures of ships here, no framed charts, no old compasses.

"Don't you miss the sea, Martin?" he asked. "I do. Even on a windy day like this, when you shouldn't go out. But I've still got this . . ." He held up his briefcase. "I used to have all my papers in here when I was out at sea, and it's still more or less in one piece. And I wanted to show you something . . ."

He opened the briefcase and took out the memoir about Malm Freight, then went on:

"You'll recognize this, I'm sure. I've often looked at it and learned a lot about all your ships and your adventures at sea, Martin. But there's a photograph here which is particularly interesting."

He opened the book at the page with the photograph from Ramneby.

"This one," he went on. "It's from the end of the fifties, isn't it? Before you bought your first Atlantic ship."

He looked up at Martin Malm and saw that he had managed to capture the old shipowner's attention. Malm was staring at the picture, and Gerlof could see his right hand twitching, as if he wanted to raise it and point at the picture.

"Do you recognize yourself?" he asked. "I'm sure you do. And the ship? That's *Amelia,* isn't it? She used to lie beside my *Wavebreaker* at the quay here in Borgholm."

Martin Malm was staring at the picture without speaking. He was breathing heavily, as if there weren't enough air in the room.

"Do you remember where it was taken, this picture? I mostly took engine oil to Oskarshamn when I was sailing around Småland, but this is further south, isn't it?"

Martin didn't reply, but he still hadn't taken his eyes off the old photograph Gerlof was holding up. The row of men on the jetty stared back at him, and Gerlof noticed that Martin's chin had begun to tremble uncontrollably again.

"It's Ramneby sawmill, isn't it? There's no caption, but Ernst Adolfsson recognized the place. When this picture was taken, it was still possible to make a living sailing just one cargo ship. Just about, anyway . . ." Gerlof pointed at the picture again. "And this is the owner of the sawmill himself, August Kant. The brother of Vera Kant in Stenvik. You knew August pretty well, didn't you? You two did quite a bit of business together."

Martin tried to get out of the wheelchair to move closer to Gerlof. At least that's how it seemed; his shoulders were twitching and he was panting, his legs tensing against the footplates of the wheelchair. He was still staring at the photograph, and he opened his mouth.

"Frr-shoff," he said in a thick voice.

"Sorry?" said Gerlof. "What did you say, Martin?"

"Frr-shoff," said Martin again.

Gerlof looked at him in confusion, and lowered the book with the picture from the sawmill. What had Martin said? *Free something,* it sounded like.

Or had he perhaps said a name—*Fridolf*?

Or *Fritiof*?

Nils waits anxiously for over an hour in the darkness beneath the palm trees with his back to the beach. The mosquitoes are swarming around him. He waves them away and thinks of Öland, what it was like to wander over the alvar, free and without a care in the world. At the same time he is constantly listening, but nothing is to be heard from the beach down below.

Finally someone approaches in the sand behind him.

"That took a while, but he's sleeping now," says Fritiof.

"Good."

Nils goes back down to the beach with Fritiof. Borrachon the Swede is slumped by the glowing fire like a sack of coal, his head sagging, his hand on the last wine bottle.

"Good, you can get going now," says Fritiof.

"Me?"

"Yes, you." Fritiof stares at him. "It's been hard enough for me keeping this drunken lout awake for the whole journey. You can take over now."

Nils looks down at Borrachon, but doesn't move.

"He's worthless, Nils," says Fritiof. "He's valuable only to us."

Nils still doesn't move.

"Do you think you'll go to hell for this?" asks Fritiof.

Nils shakes his head.

"You won't," says Fritiof. "You'll be able to go home."

"It's here," says Nils.

"What is?"

"Hell," says Nils. "Hell is here."

"Good." Fritiof nods. "Then it's time for you to leave it."

Nils nods wearily, then he bends down and grabs hold of Borrachon's arms. The man mumbles in his sleep, but offers no resistance. Nils drags him off through the sand, away from the fire, and down toward the dark sea.

"Look out for sharks," warns Fritiof behind him.

The water is lukewarm and the waves broad but powerless. Nils backs right out into the Caribbean, dragging Borrachon's body with him.

Suddenly it moves. Borrachon coughs as the foam swirls over his face, and he begins to struggle. Nils grits his teeth, moves back a couple of yards more until the water is up to his thighs, then pushes Borrachon beneath the surface. He closes his eyes and begins to count: *One, two, three . . .*

The man flails wildly with his arms, desperately trying to get his head above water. Nils holds him firmly, thinks of Öland and keeps counting.

. . . forty-eight, forty-nine, fifty . . .

It feels as if it takes an hour before the body stops moving in the water. Nils remains where he is, rigid, holding it beneath the surface. All trace of life must be gone, nothing must remain. If he waits long enough, perhaps Borrachon won't turn up in his dreams, as the district superintendent has done.

"Is it over?" calls Fritiof from the beach.

"Yes."

"Well done, Nils." Fritiof wades out into the water, bends down to Borrachon, lifts one arm, and lets it drop. "Well done."

Nils says nothing. He stays where he is, feeling the pull of the waves, while Fritiof drags the body to the water's edge, and suddenly he thinks of his little brother, Axel.

It was an accident, Axel, I didn't mean it . . . Killing makes those who are already dead come back, stronger than ever.

Fritiof plows back up the beach, wiping his brow with his shirtsleeve. He breathes out.

"Good, that's done," he says, turning to Nils. "Okay, now you can tell me."

"Tell you what?"

Nils walks slowly out of the sea and stands in front of him.

"About the treasure you hid. Where is it, Nils?"

The body of the man from Småland is lying between them on the beach. Nils senses that Fritiof has the upper hand now, but he refuses to give in.

"In that case, what's your name, Fritiof Andersson? Your real name?"

The man in front of him doesn't reply.

"If you take me home," says Nils eventually, "I'll get you the goods."

"It'll take a while," says Fritiof, waving away a mosquito. "I'll take care of everything, but it'll take a while. One step at a time. The body has to be taken to Öland first . . . it has to be buried and forgotten, as far as possible. Then you can come home. You do understand that?"

Nils nods.

Fritiof pokes the body between them with his shoe.

"We'll drag it back out again now, just a few yards, cut the face up a bit and anchor it to the bottom . . . then we'll let the fish do their job. After that, nobody will be able to tell the difference between you." He nods toward Borrachon's little bag by the fire. "Don't forget to take his passport. You might not get into Mexico otherwise."

"And afterwards," says Nils, "you'll come back here?"

"Yes. You stay in Mexico City, and I'll come back here in a week or so. I'll haul the body onto the beach and get rid of any traces, then I'll drive back down to Limón and start asking people if anyone has seen my Swedish friend Nils. It's probably best if someone else comes and finds the corpse, but otherwise I'll have to do it."

Nils starts to get undressed. "We'll swap clothes, then."

Fritiof looks at him. "Anything else?" he says. "Have you forgotten anything?"

Nils pulls off his shirt in the darkness. "Like what?"

Fritiof points silently at Nils's left hand, at his two bent fingers. Then he bends down and grabs hold of Borrachon's arm, straightens it out so that the left hand is lying in the sand, and stamps down hard on the ring finger and the middle finger with the heel of his shoe. Harder and harder, until a quiet crack is heard in the darkness.

"There," says Fritiof, taking a handkerchief out of his pocket and tying the broken fingers to the palm at a crooked angle. "You'll soon be twins."

Nils just looks at him. This man, Fritiof, is ahead of him all the time when it comes to planning. How does he intend this to finish?

Nils pushes his unease to one side.

"Take off his trousers," he says. "I'll dry them over the fire. Then he can have mine instead, and my wallet."

All he wants to do now is go home. If he can just get back to Stenvik, all this will have a happy ending.

Then it won't matter that he's in hell.

27

"*We're old men after all, both of us,*" said Gerlof to Martin Malm. "And we've got time to think. And I've been thinking a great deal lately . . ."

He met Martin's gaze. They were still sitting opposite each other in the dark drawing room, where the TV was now showing pictures of Fred Flintstone hacking rocks out of the mountainside.

Gerlof still had the book with the photo from Ramneby in his hand.

"Your freight company wasn't that big when this picture was taken," he said. "I know that, because mine was just as small. You had a few sailing ships that carried cargo, stone, and timber and all kinds of goods across our own little Baltic Sea, just like the rest of us. But then three or four years later you bought your first steamship and started sailing to Europe and across the Atlantic. The rest of us limped along with our sailing ships for a little while longer, until the regulations about minimum crew numbers and maximum loads became too much for us. We couldn't get the banks to lend us any money for bigger ships; you were the only one who invested in modern tonnage at exactly the right time." He was still looking at Malm. "But where did you get the money from, Martin? You had just as little money of your own as any other skipper at that time, and the banks must have been just as miserly with you as they were with the rest of us."

Martin's jaw tensed, but he said nothing.

"Did it come from August Kant, Martin?" asked Gerlof. "From the owner of the sawmill at Ramneby?"

Martin stared at Gerlof, and his head jerked.

"No? But I think it did."

Gerlof reached into his briefcase again, then grabbed his cane and got up. He walked slowly around the television and over to Martin.

"I think you got paid for bringing home a murderer from South America, Martin. Nils Kant, who'd murdered a police-man . . . August's nephew."

Martin moved his head back and forth. He opened his mouth again.

"Ee-ra," he said. "Ee-ra A-ant."

"Vera Kant," said Gerlof. He was beginning to understand Martin a little now. "Nils's mother. No doubt she wanted her son home as well. But it was her brother August who paid, wasn't it? First he paid you to bring home a body in a coffin to Öland, which was buried up in Marnäs so that everybody would believe Nils Kant was dead. Then you brought Nils home several years later, more discreetly."

He stood in front of Martin, who had to twist his neck in order to look up at him.

"Nils came home, sometime toward the end of the sixties, and hid somewhere here on Öland. He didn't need to hide particularly carefully, because nobody would recognize him after twenty-five years. I'm sure he was able to visit his mother sometimes, and go walking out on the alvar."

Gerlof looked down at the man in the wheelchair.

"I think Nils was walking around out there one foggy September day, when he met a little boy who had got lost in the fog. My grand-son, Jens."

Martin Malm said nothing.

"And then something went wrong," Gerlof went on quietly. "Something happened and Nils got scared. I don't believe Nils Kant was as evil and as crazy as some people maintain. He was just scared and impulsive, and he could be violent sometimes. And that's why Jens died." Gerlof sighed. "And then . . . you probably know better than anyone. I think Nils came and asked you for help. Together you buried my grandson's body somewhere out on the alvar. But you kept one thing."

He brought out the object he had taken from his briefcase. It was the brown envelope with Malm Freight's logo torn off, the one Gerlof had received in the mail.

"You kept one of Jens's sandals. You sent it to me a couple of months ago, in this envelope. Why did you do that, Martin? Did you want to make your confession?"

Malm looked at the envelope, and his chin moved again.

"Unn-er's a-zee."

Gerlof nodded without understanding what the other man meant. He sat down slowly to get his breath back, and gave Martin one last long look.

"Did you kill Nils, Martin?"

Gerlof's final question received no answer, of course, so he answered it himself:

"I think you did . . . I think Nils had become too dangerous for you. And I think he was the one who gave you that scar on your forehead. But I can't prove that either, of course."

He leaned forward and wearily pushed the book and the envelope back in his old briefcase. It had been hard work, this performance, and he was exhausted.

On a bookshelf along one wall, framed family photographs were arranged, and Gerlof could see smiling youngsters on several of them.

"Our children, Martin . . ." he said. "We have to expect that they will forget about us. We want our children to remember all the good things we did in spite of everything, but that isn't always the way things turn out."

Gerlof was so tired now, just saying whatever came into his head. Martin Malm too seemed to have lost all his strength. Over in his wheelchair, he was neither moving nor attempting to say anything else.

The air in the drawing room seemed to have been completely used up, and the room felt darker than it had been. Gerlof got up slowly.

"It's time I was on the move, Martin," he said. "Look after yourself . . . I might be back."

He thought the last sentence sounded threatening, and that was his intention, to a certain extent.

The door to the hallway opened before he got there. Ann-Britt Malm's pale face appeared.

Gerlof smiled wearily at her.

"We've had our little chat," he told her.

It was actually only Gerlof who had done any chatting, and he hadn't received one single clear answer.

He walked past Martin Malm's wife, and she closed the drawing room door behind them.

"Right, well, thank you very much," said Gerlof, nodding to her.

"It was me who sent that," said Ann-Britt Malm.

Gerlof stopped. She was pointing at his briefcase, where the top edge of the brown envelope was sticking up.

"Martin has cancer of the liver," she said. "He hasn't got long left."

Gerlof remained rooted to the spot, not knowing what to say. He looked down at his briefcase.

"How did you know . . ." He cleared his throat. ". . . where to send it?"

"Martin gave me the envelope last summer. The sandal was already inside, and he'd written your name on it. All I had to do was send it."

"Did you call me too?" he asked. "Somebody called me after it had arrived . . . somebody who put the phone down."

"Yes. I wanted to ask . . . about the sandal," said Ann-Britt Malm. "Why Martin had it, what it might mean. But I was afraid of the answers . . . afraid Martin might have done something to your child."

"Not my child. Jens was my grandchild. But I don't know what the sandal means."

"I don't know either, and it's . . ." She fell silent. Then she said, "Martin didn't want to say anything when he got it out, but I . . . I had the feeling he'd taken the sandal as some kind of security. Could that have been the case?"

"Security?" said Gerlof.

"Against somebody else," said Ann-Britt. "But I don't know."

Gerlof looked at her. "Has Martin ever talked about the Kants? The Kant family?"

Ann-Britt hesitated, then she nodded. "Yes, but nothing more than to mention they were doing some business together . . . Vera invested money in Martin's ships, after all."

"Vera in Stenvik?" said Gerlof. "But it was August, surely?"

Ann-Britt shook her head. "Vera Kant in Stenvik put money into Martin's first steamship. And he really needed that money, I do know that."

Gerlof merely nodded. He had only one question left, then he wanted to get out of this big, gloomy house.

"When Martin gave you the envelope," he said, "had anyone been to visit him, just before that?"

"We don't get many visitors," said Ann-Britt.

"I think someone from Stenvik might have been here. An old stonemason . . . Ernst Adolfsson."

"Ernst, yes, that's right," said Ann-Britt. "We've bought a few things made of stone from him—he's dead now. He did call in to see Martin . . . but I think it was earlier in the summer."

Ernst had got there first again, thought Gerlof.

"Thank you" was all he said, picking up his overcoat. It felt much heavier now, like some kind of armor. "Will Martin be going into the hospital soon?" he asked.

"No, he won't," said Ann-Britt. "No hospitals. The doctors always come here."

Out on the steps the wind grabbed hold of him again, and this time it made him sway unsteadily. It had begun to drizzle. He screwed up his eyes to face the cold alone, but then he spotted John's car parked a dozen or so yards away.

John nodded as Gerlof opened the passenger door and got in.

"It's over," he said.

"Good," said John.

Only then did Gerlof notice there was someone sitting in the back seat: a broad-shouldered figure who had managed to sink right down and hide himself behind John. It was Anders, his son.

"I went over to the apartment," said John. "Anders is back home. They let him go."

"Excellent. Hi there, Anders."

John's son merely nodded.

"It's good that the police believed you, isn't it?" said Gerlof.

"Yes," said Anders.

"You won't go into Vera Kant's house anymore, will you?"

"No." Anders shook his head. "It's haunted."

"That's what I heard," said Gerlof. "But you weren't scared?"

"No," said Anders. "She stayed in her room."

"She? You mean Vera?"

Anders nodded. "She's bitter."

"Bitter?"

"She feels as if she's been deceived."

"Does she indeed," said Gerlof.

He was thinking about what Maja Nyman had told him, about the two male voices she'd heard in Vera's kitchen. Had one of them belonged to Martin Malm?

It kept on raining, and John switched on the windshield wipers as he pulled out into the street.

"I was thinking of staying here in Borgholm with Anders for a while," he said. "We're going to have a coffee with his mother. I'm sure you'd be welcome too."

"No, I'd better get back," said Gerlof quickly. "Otherwise Boel will have a fit."

"Right," said John.

"I can get the bus to Marnäs," said Gerlof. "Isn't there one at half past three?"

"We can have a look at the depot," said John.

Gerlof sat in silence as they drove through Borgholm, thinking things over. As usual he had the feeling he'd missed things at Martin Malm's, that he'd asked the wrong questions and hadn't interpreted correctly the few answers he'd been given. He should have made some notes.

"Martin can't talk anymore," he said with a sigh.

"Oh yes?" said John.

When the car turned right at the square, Gerlof turned his head and suddenly saw Julia through a window on the opposite side of the street.

She was sitting in a restaurant beside the church with Lennart Henriksson, the policeman. Gerlof felt no surprise at seeing them together.

Julia was looking at Lennart and she looked calm, Gerlof thought as the car moved away from the restaurant. Not happy, perhaps, but peaceful. And Lennart also looked better than he had for many years. Good.

"So you're okay catching the bus?" asked John.

Gerlof nodded. "I feel fine now," he said. This was partly true; he could walk, at any rate. "And we have to support public transport. Otherwise no doubt they'll get rid of the buses too."

John turned north toward Borgholm's bus station. It had been a railway station in times gone by, the terminus for the train Nils Kant had jumped off after he murdered the policeman—but now only buses and cabs stopped there.

The car pulled into the parking lot. John got out and went around to the passenger's side to open the door.

"Thanks," said Gerlof, wobbling to his feet. He nodded a farewell to Anders.

It had been a strenuous day, but he fought hard to walk steadily and with dignity toward the buses behind the station, with his briefcase in one hand and his cane in the other. The drizzle was coming down more heavily now. The bus going to Byxelkrok via Marnäs was already in; the driver was sitting behind the wheel reading the paper.

Gerlof stopped by the door of the bus.

"Anyway, it's finished now," he told John. "We've done as much as we could. Martin will have to live with what he's done. For however long he's got left."

"Yes. He will," said John.

"One thing . . ." said Gerlof. "Fridolf . . . have you ever heard of anyone Martin knew by that name?"

"Fridolf?" John said. "As in Little Fridolf? In the comic strip?"

"Yes. Or maybe Fritiof," said Gerlof. "Fridolf or Fritiof."

"Not that I know of," said John. "Is it important?"

"No. I don't think so."

Gerlof stood in silence in front of John for a few moments as two teenage boys in black padded jackets and with spiky hair pushed quickly past them and leapt onto the bus without so much as glancing at the two old men.

Gerlof suddenly realized it wouldn't matter at all if he'd just unmasked a murderer or not. It wouldn't change a thing. Life was carrying on as normal around him, and Öland was still a sparsely populated island.

He felt depressed. Perhaps he was having an eighty-year-old's crisis.

"Thanks for today," he said to John. "I'll call you when I get back."

"You do that."

John nodded and held his cane as Gerlof struggled up the high steps onto the bus. He took his cane, paid the driver for his journey, including his senior citizen's discount, and went to sit on the right by a window. He watched John walk back to his car and get inside.

Gerlof leaned back, closed his eyes, and heard the bus rumble into life. As slowly as an old cargo boat, it began to pull away from the station.

Fridolf or Fritiof, he thought. *And a meeting in Ramneby, where Ernst grew up.*

Fridolf? Fritiof?

Gerlof didn't know anyone on Öland with either of those names.

28

"*No, I'm not married,*" said Lennart. "Never have been, either."

"No children?" said Julia.

Lennart shook his head. "No children, either." He looked down into his half-empty glass of water. "I've had precisely one serious relationship in my life, but on the other hand, it lasted almost ten years. It ended five years ago . . . she's living in Kalmar now, and we're still friends." He smiled at Julia. "Since then I've devoted most of my energy to the house and the garden."

"Perhaps northern Öland isn't the best place," said Julia. "If you want to meet somebody, I mean."

"You mean there's not much choice," said Lennart, still smiling. "That's very true. I suppose it's much better in Gothenburg?"

"I don't know . . ." said Julia. "I've almost stopped looking." She drank some of her water and went on: "I've really only had one serious relationship as well. And it was even longer ago than yours . . . It was with Jens's father, Michael; he was always restless, and it ended . . . well, afterward. You know."

Lennart nodded. "You have to be very determined to maintain a relationship."

Julia nodded.

"But what are your plans now?" said Lennart. "Are you going to stay on Öland?"

"I don't know . . . maybe," said Julia. "There isn't much to keep me in Gothenburg. And Gerlof isn't all that well. He probably doesn't want anybody keeping tabs on him, but I think he might need it."

"Northern Öland needs nurses, I know that," said Lennart, looking at her. "And I'd like you to–"

He was interrupted by a persistent bleeping, and Julia jumped. Lennart looked down at the pager on his belt.

"They're after me again," he muttered.

"Is it something important?"

"No. It looks as if I just need to call in at the station for a little while." He got to his feet. "I'll go and pay our bill."

"We can split it."

"No, no." Lennart waved the suggestion away. "I was the one who dragged you over here."

"Thanks," said Julia.

As usual she was short of money.

"Shall we say we'll meet up at . . ." Lennart looked at his watch. ". . . a quarter to four over at the station? I should be done by then, and we can get out of the big city and head home."

"Fine."

"Perhaps you'd like to come and see where I live? It isn't a big house, but it's right by the sea north of Marnäs. The sun rises out of the sea with each new day, if you want to put it poetically."

"I'd like that," Julia told him.

They parted outside the restaurant. Lennart walked off quickly toward the station, and Julia hopped much more slowly toward Kungsgatan on her crutches to have a look at the shops. There didn't seem to be any clothes sales on this week, but at least she could study what was in the windows.

She went past a newsagent's and automatically read some of the headlines on the placards outside—SERIOUS ACCIDENT ON E22—DEAD NOT YET IDENTIFIED; CAROLA HAPPY AGAIN; ALL YOU NEED TO KNOW ABOUT THIS WEEKEND; HAVE *YOU* WON THE LOTTERY?—without them affecting her in any way.

She felt fine now, despite her broken bones. She even felt . . . happy. Happy that she and Gerlof had grown closer to each other than ever before, happy that she and her sister Lena had parted more or less as friends, and happy too that Lennart Henriksson seemed to enjoy her company.

She was even happy that the police had let Anders Hagman

go. It would have been terrible if anyone in Stenvik had been involved in her son's disappearance. Despite everything, it would be better if Jens had gone down to the shore in the fog that day without anyone seeing him. He had conquered his fear of the sea and started jumping around on the rocks out in the water, just like any little boy would, and he'd slipped.

Julia believed that now.

"*It's not large,* but it does have a view over Lake Vättern," says the owner of the property, pointing out of one of the windows. "And the kitchen equipment and the bed are included in the rent."

The owner is puffing and blowing in the narrow room. The elevator in the building is broken, and his forehead is shiny with sweat after plodding up four flights of stairs. He's a man in a suit, with a very big belly beneath his shirt.

"Fine," says his potential tenant.

"There's good parking too."

"Thanks, but I don't have a car."

It takes no more than five minutes to inspect the whole apartment, less than five minutes actually. One room and a kitchen, right at the top of Gröna gatan in the south of Jönköping.

"I'll take it. For six months. Maybe longer."

"A traveling salesman? With no car?"

"I use the train and the bus," says his tenant. "I move around quite a bit . . . and I'm waiting for my bosses back home to send for me."

Nils is still trying out his new name and his new life. He is slowly growing into it, and can feel his old life fading away. But it never disappears completely. It's like having another life preserved beneath a cheese-dish cover. His new life is freer—it has an ID number and a passport that is accepted at borders—but despite that, it never feels completely real. Not in Costa Rica, not during the years in Mexico or the year outside Amsterdam or the last six months in an almost completely empty apartment out in Bergsjön outside Gothenburg, when he sometimes woke up in a cold sweat, believing he was back in the steaming heat of Costa Rica.

"Do you mind if I ask how old you are?" says the landlord.

"Forty-four."

"Best time of life."

"Maybe."

When Nils asks when he's actually going to be able to go home to Öland, all he's had so far from Fritiof are evasive answers.

"An impatient person makes mistakes," Fritiof had said to him over a crackling telephone connection three weeks earlier. "Just be patient, Nils. The coffin is buried in Marnäs; the grave is starting to get overgrown with grass and your old mother puts flowers there from time to time. She's waiting for you."

"Is she all right?" he wanted to know.

"She's fine."

Fritiof pauses, then goes on: "But she's had postcards. Lots of postcards. First of all from Costa Rica, then from Mexico and Holland. Did you know that?"

Nils did know that. He has sent letters and postcards to his mother throughout all those years, but he's always been careful.

"I didn't put my name on them," says Nils.

"Good. I'm sure they made her happy," says Fritiof, "but now there's a rumor that Nils Kant is alive. The police aren't listening, of course, they're not interested in village gossip, but that's what people are saying down in Stenvik. That's why you mustn't be impatient. You do understand that?"

"Yes. But what happens when I get home to Öland?"

"What happens . . ." says Fritiof, as if the answer weren't interesting at all. "What happens is that you come home, to your mother. But first of all we're going on a treasure hunt, right?"

"That's what we said. If I get home, I'll show you where the treasure is."

"Good. We just have to wait for the right opportunity," says Fritiof.

"And when will that be?"

But Fritiof had already hung up.

This man, whose name is definitely something else, simply put the phone down. Nils has a feeling that he's already a completed project for Fritiof Andersson, a dead man. Dead and buried in Marnäs churchyard.

"The rent is payable in advance," says the owner.

"That's fine," says Nils. "I can pay now."

"And it's a month's notice."

"Fine. I don't need any longer."

Nils is not dead, he's on his way home.

And the man who calls himself Fritiof shouldn't make the mistake of thinking anything different.

29

Gerlof was sitting on the bus to Marnäs thinking things over. He'd nodded off for a while on the road between Borgholm and Köpingsvik, but he woke up when they got out onto the alvar. Now he was thinking.

He'd come out with far more than he'd intended during the meeting with Martin Malm, a whole lot of baseless hypotheses that it would presumably be impossible to prove. He hadn't got a confession out of Martin, but at least he'd managed to say everything.

Now he could try to move on. Make more ships in bottles. Ask John over for coffee. Read the obituaries in the newspaper and watch the winter approaching outside the home.

But it was difficult to forget. There was so much to think about.

He picked up the book about Malm Freight again, the anniversary book that was starting to look rather dog-eared from constantly being taken out and put away. Gerlof opened it at the page with the picture on the quayside at Ramneby, and once again he saw Martin Malm and August Kant standing side by side in front of the stern-faced sawmill workers.

He thought about what Ann-Britt Malm had told him—that it was Vera Kant who had lent the money for Malm's first big ship, and not August. In other words, that Vera had paid Martin to bring Nils home.

But if August Kant hadn't wanted anything to do with his nephew—and perhaps would have preferred him to stay out of the way in South America forever—then what did this picture mean, this close business link with Martin Malm? August's hand on Martin's shoulder . . .

Because it *was* August's hand, wasn't it? Gerlof took a closer look. The thumb appeared to be on the wrong side of the fingers.

He stared at the picture until his eyes ached, until the black and white contours began to blur and merge. Then he took his reading glasses out of his briefcase, put them on, and kept looking. When that didn't help, he took them off and held them above the picture like a magnifying glass. This made the white, staring faces of the sawmill workers come nearer to him, but at the same time they dissolved into black and white dots.

Gerlof moved the lens over the picture and peered more closely at the hand on Malm's shoulder. There it lay, resting in a friendly way close to the back of the shipowner's neck, but now Gerlof could clearly see that what should have been August's right hand was in fact a left hand. And just behind the hand . . .

Gerlof looked at the smiling faces in the picture.

Suddenly he saw for the first time what Ernst must have seen.

"Christ," he said.

To invoke the name of Jesus was a very old curse—over seventy years ago Gerlof's mother had forbidden him to utter it. He hadn't sworn like that once since then.

In order to be really certain, he took out his notebook, flicked through until he found the list of names he'd written down at the museum in Ramneby, and read it.

"Christ . . ." said Gerlof again.

For a few seconds he was completely stunned and absorbed in his discovery—then he looked up and remembered he was on a bus traveling northward toward Marnäs. But they weren't there yet, they were still south of Stenvik, and just as he looked out of the window the bus was passing the first signpost that said CAMPSITE 2 KM.

Stenvik, the bus was nearly in Stenvik. He had to talk to John about his discovery.

Gerlof reached up quickly to press the red stop button.

As the bus began to slow down at the stop a hundred yards

north of the turnoff for Stenvik, he pushed the book and his glasses into his briefcase and stood up, his legs trembling.

The central doors of the bus opened with a hiss, and Gerlof climbed down the steps and out into the cold and wind. Sjögren was muttering in his arms and legs, but the pain wasn't making too much noise so far.

The doors closed behind him and the bus pulled away. He was alone at the bus stop, and it was still drizzling. There used to be a little wooden shelter where you could sit if it was raining, waiting for the bus or waiting to set off home, but of course that had been taken away. Everything that was good and free was quickly taken away.

When the dull roar of the engine had died, Gerlof looked around him at the desolate landscape, buttoned his coat right up to the top, then looked over at the yellow signpost pointing down toward Stenvik. That was where he was going.

He looked around several times to make sure he wasn't going to be run over as he crossed the road, but there wasn't a car in sight. The main road was completely deserted. He covered the fifty yards over to the turning for Stenvik quite quickly, but when he set off down the road the wet wind was blowing directly into his face, and he had to slow down.

He must have gone two hundred yards along the side of the road toward the village when he suddenly remembered that John Hagman wasn't down in Stenvik.

John was in Borgholm.

Gerlof stopped dead on the road, blinking into the lashing wind.

How the hell had he managed to forget that? He'd only left John at the bus station less than half an hour earlier, but he'd been so elated by what he'd discovered from the picture that he'd completely forgotten about that.

But somebody would be at home in Stenvik, surely? Julia might not be back yet either, but Astrid should be there. She was almost always at home. Anyway, there was nothing else for it but to keep on going–Marnäs was even further away.

His footsteps felt heavier now, and the cold was beginning to penetrate right through his coat. The wind was pulling and dragging at him, and he bent his head.

One step at a time on the cracked tarmac. He counted them: *one, two, three*—and at the twenty-fifth step he looked up again, but the trees on the horizon marking the end of the alvar and the beginning of the village didn't appear to be any closer.

For the first time Gerlof began to feel a little anxious, like a swimmer who has boldly decided to set off across an icy lake, but suddenly loses all his strength when he gets halfway. Going back to the main road was impossible, but it was almost as difficult to keep on going.

He suddenly stumbled on the tarmac, almost falling into the ditch. He only about managed to keep his balance with the help of his cane, and that was when he heard the dull roar of an engine once again.

It was a car, and it was coming from Stenvik.

The car was big and shiny and dark green, Gerlof could see as it came closer: a Jaguar, its windshield wipers swishing rhythmically to and fro.

It didn't drive past, it pulled up and the tinted side window slid down, revealing a face with a gray beard.

"Hi there!" called a cheerful voice.

Gerlof recognized Gunnar Ljunger from Långvik.

The hotel owner who was always talking about more ships in bottles every time they met was the last person Gerlof wanted to meet right now, but he felt obliged to raise his hand in a tired greeting.

"Good afternoon, Gunnar," he said in a weak voice which the wind almost drowned out, and took one step further along the road.

"Hi, Gerlof," called Ljunger from inside the car. "Where are you going?"

It was a very stupid question that might have merited a very stupid answer, but Gerlof simply nodded toward the village and said:

"Down to Stenvik."

"Are you going to visit someone?"

"Yes, maybe." Gerlof swayed in the wind. "Astrid, perhaps."

"Astrid Linder?" said Ljunger. "It didn't look as if she was home when I drove past . . . I couldn't see any lights in her windows."

"Oh?"

If Astrid wasn't home either, then nobody was home in Stenvik—and Gerlof would freeze to death down there in the wind from the sea. The police would find his cold, stiff body the next day, behind some juniper bush.

He thought about it and looked at Ljunger.

"Might you be going to Marnäs, Gunnar? Past the home?"

"Sure . . . I was going to do a bit of shopping at the ironmonger's. I'll give you a lift."

"Would you?"

"Of course." Ljunger leaned across and opened the passenger door. "Hop in."

"That's very kind of you."

Gerlof clambered laboriously into the warmth of the car with his cane and his briefcase.

It was quiet and very warm in the car; the heating was turned up high. Ljunger was sitting there with his yellow padded jacket unbuttoned, and despite the fact that Gerlof was still frozen, he too unbuttoned his coat.

"Okay, let's go," said Ljunger. "Marnäs, here we come."

He floored the accelerator and the car shot away with such power that Gerlof was pressed back into his seat.

"Any particular time you have to be back, Gerlof?" asked Ljunger.

Gerlof shook his head. "No, but I'd like—"

"Good, then we've got time to take a look at something."

They had already reached the main road, and it was just as empty as it had been earlier. Ljunger pulled out onto it. But heading south, not north.

"I don't think I can—" Gerlof began, but Ljunger interrupted him:

"How's it going with the ships in bottles, then?"

"Fine," replied Gerlof, although he hadn't touched them for the last week—he hadn't even thought about them. "You can come over and see me at the home sometime before Christmas, and we can have a look at them . . ."

Ljunger nodded. He drove along the main road for just a few hundred yards before he turned off again along a narrow, stony track with no signposts, running between a plowed field and an old stone wall. It led eastward, toward the sea.

"I was just thinking . . . Is it too late to have all the hulls completely in red?" asked Ljunger. "If it's possible, that would look really nice."

"That shouldn't be a problem." Gerlof nodded and took a deep breath. "Gunnar, where are we actually going?"

"Not far," said Ljunger. "We'll soon be there."

He didn't speak again after that, but merely slowed the car along the narrow track. All Gerlof could do was go along for the ride, staring at the windshield wipers monotonously swishing back and forth.

He looked down into the storage space between the seats. Gunnar's cell phone was there; it was black with silver edges, and was much smaller than any Gerlof had seen before—it was only half the size of Julia's.

"Where are we going, Gunnar?" he asked quietly.

Ljunger didn't reply—it was as if he were no longer listening to Gerlof. He was looking only at the sodden gravel track ahead of the car, avoiding the potholes and bumps with a light touch on the wheel. He was smiling.

Gerlof's forehead was greasy with sweat.

He ought to say something, make some casual, everyday remark. A polite question about how things were going in the hotel industry, perhaps. But he was tired and his head was completely empty of small talk at this moment.

In the end Gerlof could come up with only one question:

"Have you ever been to South America, Gunnar?"

Ljunger shook his head, still smiling.

"I haven't, unfortunately," he replied, then added, "The closest I've been is Costa Rica."

ÖLAND, SEPTEMBER 1972

From the passenger seat of a blue Volvo, high up on the new bridge, Nils Kant leans forward toward the windshield and looks out across Kalmar Sound. It's afternoon, and a mist hangs over the water; a thick bank of fog has been created in the sound, and is on its way in over the island.

"It'll be a foggy night," he says.

"Just what we were hoping for," says Fritiof beside him.

"We?" says Nils. "Are there more of you?"

Fritiof nods. "You'll get to meet them soon."

Nils tries to relax and look out over the railings. He can almost see himself as a young man down there in the sound, swimming for his life toward the mainland, barely twenty years old.

How could he get so far in the cold water? He's forty-six now, and couldn't even swim a hundred yards.

The Öland Bridge is enormous, tons of steel and concrete erected above the water to form a structure that is almost as wide as a freeway and several kilometers long. Nils could never have imagined that his island would have such a link to the mainland.

"How old is the bridge?" he asks.

"Pretty new," says Fritiof at the wheel.

He hasn't said very much since he came to Nils in Jönköping the previous evening. He gave Nils dark clothes for the journey and a black knitted hat to pull down over his forehead, but he's hardly said a word.

The cheerful, charming Fritiof Andersson who sought him out in Costa Rica more than ten years ago is gone; actually, he's been gone since the man from Småland drowned in the sea north of Limón. Since that night Fritiof has mostly treated Nils like a parcel, moving him around from place to place and from country to country, renting small, cheap apartments or rooms in hostels in seedy parts of town for him, and only getting in touch by telephone once or twice a year.

The night before they left for Öland, Fritiof started on about the treasure again. Where was it? Where had Nils hidden it? In the house?

Nils shook his head. And in the end he told Fritiof:

"It's buried on the alvar, just to the east of Stenvik. By the old memorial cairn. We'll go and get it together."

Fritiof nodded. "Good, that's what we'll do."

Nils has waited a long time to make this final journey. Now he's here.

"I'm going to stay at home from now on," he says to Fritiof.

He closes his eyes as they drive across the new bridge. Back on Öland, at last.

"I'm going to stay at home," he says again. "I'm going to stay with my mother and make sure nobody sees me." He pauses, then asks, "She's still well . . . Vera?"

"Yes indeed."

Fritiof Andersson nods briefly, then the car speeds up as they drive out onto the great alvar, heading toward Borgholm.

A great deal has changed on Öland since he was young, Nils realizes. There are more shrubs and trees on the island, and the narrow gravel track to Borgholm has become a broad, asphalt highway, just as even and straight as the bridge. The railway which ran from north to south must have been shut down, because Nils can't see any tracks out on the alvar any longer. The rows of windmills that towered above the shoreline to catch the wind from the sound are gone too; only a few remain.

It seems as if there are fewer people on the island—but yet there are plenty of new cottages down by the water. Nils nods toward them.

"Who lives in all those houses?" he asks.

"Summer residents," replies Fritiof tersely. "They earn their money in Stockholm and buy cottages here on Öland. They drive across the bridge and lie in the sun on vacation, then they drive back fast to earn some more money. They don't want to be here in the winter . . . it's too cold and miserable."

It sounds as if he sympathizes with them.

Nils says nothing. Fritiof seems to be quite right about these summer residents, because virtually every car he sees is driving in the opposite direction, traveling away from the island. The summer is over, it's autumn.

The ruined castle is still there, at least, and it looks just as it always has, with its empty eye sockets on the hill above Borgholm.

Once they've driven past the castle, they're almost down in the town, and the fog is beginning to fill the air. Fritiof slows down and pulls into a small parking lot just on the edge of the town, within sight of the ruined castle. He stops the car with no explanation.

"Okay" is all he says. "I told you we'd be having company."

He opens the car door and waves.

Nils looks around. Someone is walking slowly along the road: a man who looks as if he were in his fifties. He's wearing a gray woolen sweater, gabardine trousers, and shiny leather shoes that look expensive, and he nods to Fritiof.

"You're late."

The man is wearing a hat, pulled down low over his forehead. He isn't carrying anything except a half-smoked cigarette. He takes one last drag and looks warily around before coming over to the car.

"Nils, I think you should get in the back now," says Fritiof quietly. "It'll be safer when we get to Stenvik."

Then he gets out of the car. There's a telephone kiosk at the far end of the parking lot, and Nils watches Fritiof walk quickly over to it. He pushes in some coins, dials a number, and speaks very briefly into the receiver.

Nils also gets out of the car, and the expensively dressed man tosses his cigarette aside, grinds it out with his right foot, and merely looks at him without saying hello. He gets into the front seat.

Nils doesn't get into the back seat right away. He walks along the road, enjoying being back and being able to move about freely on the island once again.

His island.

Suddenly a couple of cars drive past on the main road. Nils sees pale faces staring back at him from behind the windshields. He follows them with his eyes, until they disappear in the fog.

"Come on!" shouts Fritiof behind him in an irritated voice.

He's back at the car.

Nils walks back reluctantly, opens the back door, and hears the man in the front seat asking quietly: "Did it go okay, Gunnar?"

Then he looks quickly around at Nils, nervous and guilty, as if he's let the cat out of the bag.

The man who has called himself Fritiof all this time also turns around and smiles.

"It doesn't matter, we might as well all introduce ourselves properly now," he says. "I'm Gunnar, and this is Martin. And Nils Kant is with us in the back seat. But we all trust each other here, don't we?"

Nils nods briefly and closes the door. "Of course."

So Fritiof is called Gunnar. And Nils knows he's met him somewhere, but he still can't remember where.

"Let's head for Stenvik, then," says Gunnar, firmly.

The car pulls out onto the road again, past Borgholm and northward. The landscape is becoming more and more familiar to Nils, but the fog from the sound is growing thicker, smearing and then erasing the horizon.

The air is becoming grayer and grayer. Gunnar knew it was going to be foggy, he was counting on it, and that's why Nils was allowed to come home on this particular day. What else has he worked out so carefully? Nils wonders.

North of Köpingsvik, Gunnar switches on the fog lights and increases his speed. Nils can see the yellow signs rushing by. The familiar names of Öland villages. But it's the landscape that he can't tear his eyes away from: the fields, the grass growing wild, the stone walls that start by the road and disappear off into the fog.

And the alvar, his very own alvar. The alvar extends in all directions; with its heavy, muted colors and its endless sky, it's just as big and beautiful as he remembered.

Nils is home again.

No one in the car speaks, and after a quarter of an hour Nils sees the sign he's been waiting for. STENVIK. Beneath it is a big arrow with the word CAMPSITE on it.

The road down to the village is tarmac now, and Stenvik has acquired a campsite. When did that happen?

The car drives past the turning for Stenvik before slowing down.

"We'll take the northern entry road," says Gunnar. "There's less traffic there, and we won't have to drive through the village."

A few minutes later he turns the car onto the northern route into the village, beside a milk stand, empty and abandoned by the roadside. Last time Nils saw the milk stand, it was full of milk churns from the farms along the road; now it's spotted with white lichen, and looks as if it's about to fall to pieces.

The whole of Öland has changed in twenty-five years, but this northern road down into Stenvik is almost exactly as he remembers it: narrow and twisting, and still graveled. It's completely deserted, with grass-filled ditches on both sides and the alvar beyond them.

Gunnar allows the Volvo to move slowly forward, and after a few hundred yards he stops completely. He turns to look at Nils, and beside him Martin turns around, too.

Gunnar is looking steadily at him, Nils notices. Martin's gaze wavers.

"Okay," says Gunnar seriously, "we've brought you to Stenvik. And now you're going to dig up your treasure by the cairn. Right?"

"I want to see my mother first," says Nils, gazing steadily at Gunnar.

"Vera isn't going anywhere, Nils," he says. "She can wait awhile longer. It's best that way, because it's better if it's really dark before we go down to the village. Don't you think so?"

"We'll split the stones between us," says Nils quickly.

"Of course. But we've got to get them up first."

Nils looks at him for a few seconds longer, and then he looks out of the side window. The fog is dense now, and soon it will be twilight.

He nods. He'll give Gunnar and Martin half of the gemstones, then they'll be quits.

"We'll need something to dig with," he says quietly.

"Sure. There are shovels and a pick in the trunk," says Gunnar. "We've thought of everything. Don't worry."

But Nils doesn't relax. He's on his own against two strange men now, just as the man from Småland was on his own on the Caribbean beach in the darkness. The difference is that the man from Småland trusted his new friends—Nils doesn't.

Gunnar doesn't park by the road; he brakes by a narrow opening in the stone wall and turns the wheel. The car leaves the village road.

Slowly they move out onto the flat, grassy plain of the alvar.

Nils turns his head, but all he can see through the back window is fog. The road leading down to his home village has completely disappeared.

30

Gerlof sat in silence in the passenger seat beside Gunnar Ljunger, his back rigid as they headed out into the wilderness south of Marnäs. The conversation he had tried to start had foundered, because Ljunger didn't answer him. All Gerlof could do was to go along with him, trying to unbutton his overcoat and struggle out of it, because the heat inside the car was positively tropical. Perhaps there was some way to regulate the air vents on the passenger side himself, but he didn't know how. Everything seemed to be controlled electronically, and if Gunnar knew he was increasingly uncomfortable, he made no attempt to help him.

They were near the east coast of the island now. The car was driving slowly along a two-foot-high embankment, several yards wide, running through the flat landscape. Gerlof recognized where he was. This was where the railway had crossed the alvar, before the national rail company closed it down.

He looked at his watch. It was almost five o'clock.

"I think I'll have to get back now, Gunnar," he said quietly. "They'll soon be starting to wonder where I am at the home in Marnäs."

"Maybe," Ljunger said, nodding, "but they're hardly likely to start looking for you out here, are they?"

The threat was so blatant that Gerlof turned away from him and started tugging at the door handle.

The Jaguar wasn't moving at a great speed and he would have

been able to throw himself out, he might even have managed to avoid breaking any bones and made his way back to the main road before dark—but it was impossible to open the passenger door. Ljunger had locked it using some kind of remote control device.

"Gunnar, I want to get out," he said, trying to sound decisive, like the sea captain he had once been.

"Soon," said Ljunger, driving on.

They crossed an old rusty cattle grid between two stone walls, and beyond it the Baltic finally appeared. The sea looked gray and cold.

"Why are you doing this, Gunnar?" asked Gerlof.

"Actually, it was quite unplanned," said Ljunger. "I was following the bus from Borgholm, and I saw you get off at the southern turning for Stenvik. All I had to do was head straight to the northern turning, drive through the village, then pick you up." Ljunger slowed down even more, and turned to face him. "What were you doing at Martin Malm's today, Gerlof?"

Gerlof felt as if he'd been found out. He took his time before answering.

"At Martin's?" he said. "What do you mean?"

"You and John Hagman," said Ljunger. "You went in and John waited outside."

"Yes. Martin and I had a bit of a chat . . . We're both old sailors, after all," said Gerlof, and added: "How do you know about that?"

"Ann-Britt Malm called me on my cell phone while you were sitting there talking over old times with Martin," said Ljunger. "She was worried about all these visits Martin keeps getting from old sea captains . . . first Ernst Adolfsson, and now you. Twice in the last few weeks, apparently. It's been pretty busy at Martin's house."

"So you and Ann-Britt are good friends," said Gerlof wearily.

Ljunger nodded. "Martin and I are former business associates, but you don't get much of a conversation with him these days," he said. "Ann-Britt looks after his affairs, and she usually asks me for advice."

Gerlof leaned back in his seat. Might as well stop pretending the sun was shining now. He couldn't see anything out the window but darkness and blowing rain.

"Associates," he said. "You worked together for quite some time, didn't you? Ever since the fifties?"

He reached into his briefcase and took out the book about Malm Freight again.

"I showed Martin this picture," he said, "and I've looked at it many times . . . but it took a long time before I saw what was really there."

"Oh yes?" said Gunnar, swerving around a clump of low-growing trees. They must be near the sea, Gerlof thought. "But now you have? Seen what's really there?"

Gerlof nodded. "There are two powerful men on the quayside in Ramneby: August Kant, the factory owner, and Martin Malm, the captain of a cargo ship, standing in a group of young sawmill workers. And August's hand appears to be resting on Martin's shoulder in a friendly gesture. But it isn't August Kant's hand. It belongs to the man standing *behind* Martin Malm on the quayside. I only noticed it a little while ago, on the bus."

"A picture speaks more than a thousand words," said Ljunger, braking. "Isn't that what they say?"

The eastern shore of the island was now in front of them, on the far side of a grassy meadow that had turned yellow. The rain was falling over both land and water, a cold rain that really wanted to be snow.

"And the man standing behind Martin Malm is a sawmill worker called Gunnar Johansson. Who later changed his name," said Gerlof. "Isn't that right?"

"Not quite, I was a foreman at the mill at the time," said Ljunger. "But it's true, I did change my name to Ljunger when I came to Öland."

He switched off the engine and everything went very quiet. The only sound was the wind and the rain.

"That picture should never have been included in the book," said Ljunger. "It was Ann-Britt who put it in, I didn't even know about it until after the book had been printed. But only you and Ernst Adolfsson recognized me. Ernst remembered me from school . . ."

"He grew up in Ramneby," said Gerlof. "For me it wasn't that easy to recognize you. But one thing I am wondering . . ."

He knew he was close to the end now; Ljunger would kill him, just as he had murdered Ernst.

". . . I'm wondering, you were a foreman at the sawmill and you must have heard the stories about August Kant's terrible nephew Nils. Was that when you got the idea to . . ."

"I actually met him," Ljunger broke in.

"Who?" said Gerlof. "Nils Kant?"

"Nils, yes." Ljunger nodded. "I'd started as an errand boy at the sawmill after the war, and Nils came there, he'd escaped from Öland on the run from the police. He was creeping around in the bushes when he spotted me on the road. He told me to go and speak to August Kant. And I did, but the boss didn't want to know a thing about his killer nephew. He shoved five one-hundred-krona notes at me to give to Nils, to get rid of him. I pocketed two of them and gave Nils three." Ljunger was smiling at the memory. "Then I lived like a king on the money for the rest of the summer."

"So you realized early on that there was money to be made out of Nils Kant," said Gerlof, looking out through the windshield at the rain.

"Yes," said Ljunger, "but not exactly how *much* there was to be made. I had no idea. I thought I might get a few thousand and a free trip across the Atlantic to fetch Nils, maybe, when all the fuss had died down. That was what I suggested to August, once he'd made me foreman at the mill, but the old man turned me down flat. He wasn't in the least interested in bringing the black sheep of the family home to Sweden."

He lifted his hand and pressed a button next to the steering wheel, and there was a click in the door beside Gerlof.

"It's open now," he said. "Get out."

Gerlof stayed where he was.

"But you didn't give up," he said, looking at Ljunger. "When August said no, you contacted Nils's mother, Vera Kant, in Stenvik. You made her the same offer. And she said yes, didn't she?"

Gunnar Ljunger sighed, as if he had a particularly stubborn child sitting next to him. He gazed out through the windshield at the coastal landscape.

"It was Vera who made me discover this beautiful island," he said. "I came here for the first time in the summer of '58. I took the ferry across to Stora Rör, then the train north. They were in the process of closing down the railway at that time, and seafaring on Öland was coming to an end too. I suppose many people thought Öland was dying . . . but I heard people on the train talking about a bridge that might be built. A long bridge, so that people could get off the island when they wanted to. And so that people from the mainland could come here."

"The rich people from the mainland," said Gerlof.

"Exactly." Ljunger took a deep breath. "And then I came up here to northern Öland and discovered the sunshine and all the beaches where you could swim. Plenty of sunshine and water, but hardly any tourists. So I'd been doing some thinking, even before I knocked on the door of Vera Kant's house in Stenvik." He sighed. "Vera was sitting there in her big house, all alone and longing for her son. I started talking to her."

"Lonely and unhappy," said Gerlof. "But extremely rich."

"Not as rich as you might think," said Ljunger. "The quarry was well on the way to closing, and her brother had claimed the family sawmill in Småland."

"She was rich in land," said Gerlof wearily. "Land along the coast . . . beach land."

He wondered how he was going to die. Did Ljunger have some kind of weapon with him? Or was he going to pick up one of the millions of stones on Öland and simply smash Gerlof's skull, more or less as he had done with Ernst?

"Vera had a great deal of land, yes," said Ljunger. "I don't think anybody in Stenvik actually realized how much land that old woman owned, both north and south of Stenvik. Of course it was worthless as long as she didn't do anything with it, but the right person would be able to take it over and sell it to people from the mainland . . . In the fifties there were only a few summer cottages up here, but I knew there'd be a demand for plenty more—and hotels and restaurants too. And when the bridge was built, the prices would skyrocket."

"So you got Långvik from Vera," said Gerlof.

"I got nothing." Ljunger shook his head. "I bought all her land, perfectly legally. At a very low price, of course, and with money I'd borrowed from Vera, but it's all documented and perfectly legal."

"And Martin Malm borrowed money from her for bigger ships."

"Exactly. We'd met when Martin was transporting timber to Ramneby," said Ljunger, nodding. "I needed reliable people to work with . . . somebody who would bring Nils's coffin home from overseas, and later Nils himself. Of course it was going to have to be some time before Nils could come home, because the minute he did, Vera would stop giving me land. I realized that, naturally."

He smiled at Gerlof with satisfaction. "Let's go."

Ljunger opened the driver's door.

Gerlof looked out through the windshield. He saw a desolate meadow leading to the shore, with the wind and rain pressing the grass down to the darkened ground.

"What's here?" he asked.

"Not much," said Ljunger, getting out of the car. "You'll see."

31

"Get out, Gerlof."

Gunnar Ljunger had closed his own door, quickly walked around the car, and opened the passenger door. He was waiting impatiently for Gerlof to get out.

"I need to put on—" Gerlof began.

But Ljunger reached in with a gloved hand.

"You don't need a coat, Gerlof." Ljunger wore his yellow padded jacket, with LÅNGVIK CONFERENCE CENTER in black on the back. "You're warm now, aren't you?"

Ljunger was at least fifteen years younger than Gerlof, tall and broad and with plenty of strength in his arms. He gripped Gerlof firmly under the arm and lifted him easily out of the car.

"Come on."

He slammed the car door, pointed his key ring at it, and pressed a little button. The car doors locked with a quiet click.

For Gerlof this sort of thing was almost like magic. He had his cane with him, but his briefcase was still on the floor inside the car. He took a few uncertain steps, out onto the rain-soaked meadow by the sea, beginning to get an idea of Ljunger's intentions.

For the first minute it was actually quite pleasant for his body to get out of the sauna-like heat of the car; the wind was oddly refreshing, and it felt as though he didn't need any outdoor clothes.

But Gerlof wouldn't survive without his overcoat, he knew

that. The cold was crippling out here, only a few degrees above zero. The wind was gusting in off the Baltic, and the drops of rain were like little nails on his face.

"Look at this, Gerlof." Ljunger had gone a short distance along the gravel track beside the meadow and was pointing to a stone wall in front of a small clump of trees. A solitary, stunted tree was growing next to the wall. "Can you see what this is?" he asked.

Gerlof took a few stumbling steps toward him.

"An apple tree," he answered quietly.

"Exactly, an old apple tree." Ljunger gripped his arm and pulled him carefully but firmly toward the shore. Once again he pointed. "And over there," he said, "you can hardly see it, but it's actually an old gooseberry bush." He looked at Gerlof. "And what does that mean?"

"An abandoned garden," said Gerlof.

"Exactly. There are stones from the foundations of the house beneath the grass." Ljunger looked around. "I found this beach a few years ago. It's usually peaceful here, even in the summer. You can sit and think and sometimes . . ." Ljunger looked at the apple tree again. "Sometimes I just sit here and think about this old tree and about the people who used to live here. Why aren't they still here, when it's such a lovely spot?"

"Poverty," said Gerlof, shivering for the first time.

He was trying to hold himself erect in the wind, not to shake or sway. But all he had on his upper body was a thin shirt and an almost equally thin undershirt, and he was beginning to feel the autumn chill penetrating through the fabric.

"Yes, they would definitely have been poor," agreed Ljunger. "Maybe they sailed away across the Atlantic, like Nils Kant and thousands of others from Öland. But the point is . . ." He paused again. "The point is that they never saw all the great opportunities here on this island. People from Öland never have."

Gerlof merely nodded; Ljunger could say whatever he liked.

"I want to get back in the car," he said.

"It's locked," said Ljunger.

"I'll freeze to death soon."

"Go home to Marnäs, then." Ljunger pointed at the wall beside the stunted tree. "There's a gap in the wall over there. Behind it a path leads north along the shore, past an old open-air dance floor . . . It's actually only a couple of kilometers up to the village, as the crow flies."

Gerlof wobbled in the wind. He didn't care what happened now; he had something important to say.

"I know, Gunnar."

Ljunger looked at him without replying.

"Like I said before . . . I worked it all out on the bus, when I saw that it was you standing behind Martin Malm."

Ljunger shrugged. "Ernst Adolfsson waved that picture at me too," he said, "but he started gabbling about a whole lot of other stuff too, old land registrations and so on. I'm not that easily scared."

"He got there ahead of me," said Gerlof tiredly. "I thought Ernst told me everything, but he didn't. What did he want from you?"

"The quarry. He wanted to buy the quarry from me for a pittance, and in return he wouldn't tell the whole world what he knew about my dealings with Vera."

"That wasn't too much to ask, surely?" said Gerlof.

"Don't say that," Ljunger snapped. "The land is worthless now, but it could be extremely valuable in the future. A casino set into the hillside on Öland . . . who knows? So I turned down his offer." Ljunger looked at Gerlof. "But you old sea captains overestimate your own importance, I think, if you imagine anyone else is interested in things that happened decades ago."

"*You're* interested, Gunnar," Gerlof had to remind him. "Otherwise we wouldn't be here, you and I."

"I can't have a load of old farts running around mouthing off about things," said Ljunger wearily. "You do understand that, don't you? It's not just current projects . . . We've got important plans for Långvik that are with the building authorities at the moment. We're talking about major investments here. Sixty new plots to the east of the village are going to be sold within the next six months—how much do you think that's going to be worth?"

Gerlof understood.

"But I'm the only one who knows," he said. "Nobody else. Not John, or my daughter."

Ljunger smiled at him, amused. "It's very noble of you to take all the credit, Gerlof," he said. "And I believe you."

"Did you kill Vera Kant too, Gunnar?"

"No, no. She fell and broke her neck on the stairs, so I've heard. I've never killed anyone."

"You killed Ernst Adolfsson."

"No," said Ljunger. "We had a discussion, Ernst and I. It turned into a minor quarrel."

"He threw one of his sculptures down into the quarry during the quarrel, didn't he?"

"He did, yes. And then I gave him a little push and he fell and pulled one of the big stone sculptures down with him. It was an accident, just as the police assumed."

"You killed Nils Kant," said Gerlof.

"No."

"Then Martin did," said Gerlof. "And Jens? Which of you killed my poor Jens?"

Ljunger wasn't smiling any longer. He looked at his watch.

"Did Jens bump into you out on the alvar?" Gerlof went on in a louder voice. "Why didn't you let my grandson live? He was five years old . . . he was no threat to you."

"Let's leave this depressing topic, Gerlof. I have to go now, anyway."

And it was no doubt true—Gunnar Ljunger had a packed schedule. Killing Gerlof was just one item on his agenda for the day.

Gerlof closed his eyes against the cold and the rain. He wouldn't be able to stay on his feet much longer. But he had no intention of falling to his knees in front of Gunnar Ljunger, that was beneath his dignity.

"I know where the gemstones are," he said.

He took one step back toward the car, leaning on his cane. If he got close enough, he might be able to whack it with his cane and put a serious dent in the shiny bodywork.

"The gemstones?"

Ljunger was staring sharply at him, his hand resting on the door handle.

"The soldiers' spoils of war. I've got them and I've hidden them. Help me into the car and we'll go and get them."

Ljunger merely shook his head, smiling once more.

"Thanks for the offer," he said. "I asked Nils about them

several times, but actually it was mainly Martin who wanted the stones, not me. There isn't even any guarantee they're worth anything. For me, Vera's land was enough . . . One mustn't be too greedy."

And with that he quickly opened the door and got in.

The car engine didn't even roar, it simply hummed into life, expensive and perfectly tuned.

Ljunger put the Jaguar into reverse and the car glided slowly backward along the gravel track, just as Gerlof managed to take the final step forward and raise his cane.

Too late. Christ!

Gerlof stood there alone on the meadow, helpless. He slowly lowered his cane and watched the car, and with it his overcoat, disappear out of reach.

Ljunger was sitting comfortably at the wheel, not even looking at Gerlof; he'd twisted his head so that he could reverse rapidly along the track. Up by the ridge where the railway line had been, he swung the car around and headed off.

Still further away, almost at the main road, the Jaguar stopped briefly. Gerlof narrowed his eyes against the icy rain and saw Ljunger open the door and hurl out his briefcase, then his overcoat. Then he closed the door and drove off. The sound of the engine died away.

Gerlof remained where he was, with his back to the rain. The bitter wind whistled in his ears.

He was thoroughly soaked and frozen, and would never be able to make it back up to the main road, or to Marnäs. And Ljunger knew that perfectly well.

He lifted one foot and moved his unsteady body in a semicircle, turning himself around with small, wobbly steps. The shoreline was gray and desolate.

The old garden Ljunger had pointed out was perhaps fifty yards away. He might just be able to make it that far, and then the stone wall would give him at least some protection from the wind.

"Go on, then, do it," he muttered to himself.

Gerlof began to move. One step at a time, with the cane as a trusty support each time his own legs betrayed him. He held his free arm across his wet shirtfront, as a feeble shield against the wind.

The gravel track beneath his feet was hard and firm, built from crushed limestone many years ago. Gunnar Ljunger's car had left no trace on it, and if there were tire tracks further back in the muddy puddles on the road, the rain would soon obliterate them. It was as if Ljunger had never been there, as if Gerlof had come here under his own steam.

"The police do not suspect any crime." That's what it would no doubt say at the end of the item in *Ölands-Posten* when they found him frozen to death out here.

The sky above him darkened.

One step at a time. Gerlof raised a trembling hand and wiped cold drops of rain from his forehead.

As he slowly got closer to the shore, he could hear the waves more and more clearly, splashing rhythmically onto a narrow strip of sand below the meadow. Further out, above the open water, a solitary seagull hovered in the wind. It wasn't the only sign of life, because several nautical miles out to sea Gerlof could make out the blurred gray silhouette of a big cargo ship on its way north. But he could have waved and yelled at the ship for all he was worth—nobody would have seen or heard him.

He'd never been to this little meadow by the shore before, at least not that he remembered. Gerlof longed suddenly for Stenvik's steep coastline, barren and beautiful. Here on the east coast of Öland, the landscape was too flat and overgrown for him.

The gravel track suddenly came to an end, and a narrow path continued through the grass. Nobody had walked there for quite some time, because the grass was tall and difficult to move through, at least for Gerlof, who could hardly lift his feet. From time to time a particularly strong gust of wind slammed in off the sea, making him stagger and almost fall. But he kept on going, one step at a time, and at long last he reached the apple tree. That distance of just a few yards had taken almost all his strength.

It was a miserable tree, spindly and twisted by the harsh winds from the sea. The branches didn't have a single leaf left on them, and offered no protection, but Gerlof could at least lean back against the rough trunk and catch his breath for a while.

He felt in his right trouser pocket. There was something hard in there, and he took it out.

It was Gunnar Ljunger's black cell phone.

Gerlof remembered. He'd picked up the little phone from the space between the seats when Ljunger had got out and was walking around the car. Just before Ljunger dragged him out of the car, he'd managed to slip it into his pocket.

But stealing the phone was no help, because Gerlof had absolutely no idea of how to make a call. He tried keying in some numbers—John Hagman's number—but nothing happened. The cell phone was dead.

Slowly he put it back in his pocket.

Should he be grateful for the fact that Gunnar Ljunger had allowed him to keep his shoes? Without them he wouldn't have been able to move at all.

No, he wasn't grateful. He hated Ljunger.

Land and money—that was what this whole thing was about. Martin Malm had got money for new ships. And Gunnar Ljunger had got lots of land around Långvik to rape and exploit.

Vera Kant had been lied to for years and years, just like Nils.

And so had Gerlof, of course.

Gerlof now knew more or less everything about what had happened; that had been his goal all along, but it was no longer enough. He wanted to tell other people, to tell John and the police. Most of all, he wanted to tell Julia.

All this time he had wanted to stand in front of all those involved in the drama, to explain exactly what had happened, then point out who had done it, who had killed Nils Kant and little Jens. Great excitement, murmuring voices throughout the room. The murderer would break down and confess; everyone else would be amazed at the truth. Applause.

"You just want to feel important," Julia had once said to him. And she was probably right. That's probably what all this was about, feeling important. Not old and forgotten and half dead.

But he was almost dead now. Life was light and warmth, and now that the sun had gone down, the warmth was dwindling away. Gerlof's feet were like blocks of ice in his shoes; his fingers had lost all feeling. The cold was crippling, but also strangely relaxing—almost pleasant.

He closed his eyes for a few seconds. In his mind's eye he could see Gunnar Ljunger driving off in his big car. He had thrown out Gerlof's coat and briefcase to lay a false trail, Gerlof presumed. For those who eventually found them, everything would be perfectly clear: a senile old man had got off the bus and lost his way, wandered off in the wrong direction, and in his confused state had taken his outdoor clothes off. In the end he'd frozen to death by the shore when darkness came.

It wasn't enough for Ljunger to take Gerlof's life; he had to make him look like an old idiot too.

He inhaled the cold air in short, panting breaths. When did the body give up and stop working? Wasn't it when the temperature of the blood dropped below eighty degrees?

He ought to do something, perhaps go down to the shore and try to scratch a message in the sand before he died: GUNNAR LJUNGER—MURDERER, in big letters that the rain wouldn't be able to obliterate. But he didn't have the strength.

This was like falling overboard from a ship out at sea, just as cold and wet and lonely. Gerlof had never really learned to swim, and falling into the water far out at sea had always been one of his fears.

He thought about Ella. He'd always believed that he would somehow sense her presence when he was close to death, but he felt nothing.

Then he thought about Julia. Had she left Borgholm yet? Perhaps she was driving past at this very moment in Lennart's police car, up on the main road. He hoped Ljunger would leave her in peace.

I never stand when I can sit, and never sit when I can lie down. That was a quotation Gerlof had read somewhere, but right now he couldn't remember where.

His legs gave way. Gerlof began to slip slowly downward, his back scraping painfully against the bark of the tree.

Beneath the leafless crown of the apple tree, he slid down, his legs buckling, and he knew he would never be able to get up again.

It would be a big mistake to sit down and close his eyes under the apple tree, Gerlof knew that. Once he'd sat down, sooner or later he would want to lie down on the ground and close his eyes and drift into the darkness.

Going to sleep would be an even bigger mistake.

But in the end Gerlof gave up, and slid slowly down onto the grass.

He'd just sit down and close his eyes, just for a little while.

Gunnar has an iron pick and two shovels in the trunk of the Volvo. He lifts out the tools, gives one shovel to Martin, then looks at Nils.

"Okay," he says. "Where are we going?"

Nils stands there in the cold, looking around him in the fog on the alvar. He picks up the familiar scent of grass and herbs and poor soil, and he sees juniper bushes and rocks and faintly marked pathways, just as it was in his youth—but he doesn't know where he is. All his landmarks have disappeared in the fog.

"We're going to the memorial cairn," he says quietly.

"I know that, you said that last night," says Gunnar irritably. "But where exactly is it?"

"Here . . . somewhere near here."

Nils looks around again, and begins to walk away from the Volvo.

Martin, who has hardly said a word all the way here, quickly catches up with him. He had lit a fresh cigarette as soon as he got out of the car, and he's sucking on it now, his lips thin and tense. Gunnar joins them and walks alongside him.

Nils slows down, as if he were in no hurry. He wants both men in front of him, so he can keep an eye on them.

The fog is thicker than Nils can ever remember; actually, all he can recall is constant sunshine on the alvar when he used to go walking out here as a teenager. Now it feels as if he's walking along the seabed in a pocket of air. He stops. Ten yards away the land-scape has already been obliterated, the only color is grayish white, and every sound is muted. He is wearing only a thin sweater, a dark leather jacket, and jeans, and he's freezing in the chilly air.

"Are you coming, Nils?"

Gunnar has stopped, too, and turned round. He's just a big gray shape ahead of Nils, the outlines blurred like a charcoal draw-ing. His expression is difficult to read and impossible to interpret.

"We don't want to lose you," Gunnar says, but before Nils has caught up with him, he turns and sets off again, without waiting, striding out across the cowering grass.

Twilight is slowly falling across the alvar. It will be late before Nils gets home to his mother. Does she know he's coming today?

Nils walks past a flat stone with uneven edges in the grass; it's almost like a triangle, and all at once he recognizes it. Now he knows where he is.

"It's more to the left," he says.

Gunnar changes direction without saying a word.

Nils thinks he can hear a faint sound in the fog; he stops again and listens. A car on the village road? He listens hard, but hears nothing more.

They're close now, but when Gunnar and Martin finally stop at a fairly big mound of grass, Nils still doesn't think they've ar-rived. He can't see the stones of the cairn anywhere.

"Here it is," says Gunnar tersely.

"No," says Nils.

"Yes."

Gunnar kicks at the grass a few times, revealing the edge of a stone.

Only then does Nils realize that the memorial cairn doesn't exist anymore. It's been forgotten. No traveler has placed a stone on it to honor the dead for decades, and the yellow grass of the alvar has swallowed it.

Nils thinks about the last time he was here, when he hid the treasure. He was so young then, young and almost proud of hav-ing shot the soldiers out on the alvar.

Nothing has been right since then. Everything has gone wrong.

Nils points. "Here . . . somewhere here," he says. "Dig here."

He looks at Martin, standing there with the shovel in his hand, fumbling as he tries to get yet another cigarette into his mouth. Why is he so nervous?

"Get digging," says Nils. "If you want the treasure."

He steps aside and walks round to the other side of the cairn. Behind him he can hear a shovel being driven into the ground. The digging begins.

Nils gazes out into the fog, but nothing is moving. Everything is silent.

Behind him Martin has begun to dig a deep trench in the ground. His shovel has already struck several rocks, which Gunnar has had to remove with the pick, and he is red in the face. He is breathing heavily and looking nastily at Nils.

"There's nothing down here," he snarls. "Just rocks."

"There must be," says Nils, looking down into the hole. "This is where I hid it."

But the hole is empty, he can see that—just as Martin says.

"Give me that," says Nils crossly, reaching for the other shovel.

Then he begins to dig himself, with rapid, deep thrusts.

After a minute or so he sees the flat slabs of limestone he took off the cairn so long ago—the slabs he placed around the metal box to protect it.

They're still there, blackened by the earth now, but the treasure is gone.

Nils looks up at Martin.

"You've taken the treasure," he says quietly, taking a step closer to him. "Where is it?"

32

"*Here we are,*" said Lennart, switching off the engine of the police car. "What do you think of my little hideaway?"

"It's lovely," said Julia.

He'd turned onto a private drive a few kilometers north of Marnäs, driven slowly along between the trees, then stopped in a glade. The blue-gray sea lay ahead, and in front of it Lennart's red-brick house and his little garden.

It wasn't big, just as he'd said, but the location was wonderful. The only thing visible beyond the house was the sweeping expanse of the horizon. The neatly cut lawn sloped down toward the sea, almost imperceptibly blurring into a broad, sandy beach.

The bare trunks of the pine trees framed the garden like the walls of a church, providing shade and subduing any sound.

Once Lennart had switched off the engine, the silence had an air of solemnity about it; the only sound was the wind soughing in the treetops.

"The pine trees were brought in and planted, of course," said Lennart, "but that was long before my time."

They got out of the car, and with her eyes closed, Julia inhaled the scent of the forest.

"How long have you lived here?"

"A long time . . . almost twenty years. But I'm still very happy here." He glanced around, as if he were looking around for the first time, then asked, "Are you allergic to cats? I've got a Persian called Missy, but I think she must be out somewhere."

"No problem, I'm fine with cats," said Julia, following him into the house on her crutches.

Its brick walls looked sturdy, as if no winter storm from the Baltic would ever be able to move them. Lennart unlocked the door and held it open for her.

"You're not very hungry yet, are you?" he asked.

"No, I'm fine," said Julia, walking into a small entrance hall that led into the kitchen.

Lennart wasn't a fussy housekeeper, just tidy. The whole house was much neater than Julia's little apartment in Gothenburg, with copies of *Ölands-Posten* tidily arranged in a wooden newspaper rack on the wall. The only clue to his profession was a few copies of the magazine *Swedish Police* in the same rack. There were several fishing rods in the hall, two or three plants in each window, and a well-stocked shelf of cookbooks above the stove in the kitchen.

Julia couldn't see any beer cans or bottles of alcohol anywhere. She was pleased about that.

Lennart moved around switching on lamps in the windows of the big room beyond the kitchen.

"Do you want to go down to the shore," he called out, "before it gets too dark? If we take an umbrella?"

"Love to, as long as I can manage on my crutches."

Lennart laughed. "We'll take it carefully. If you go out onto the point, you can see Böda on a clear day," he said, adding, "You know, the bay with the big sandy beach."

Julia smiled. "Yes, I know where Böda is," she said.

"Of course you do. I forgot you were brought up here. Shall we go?"

She nodded, and glanced at the clock. A quarter past five.

"Do you mind if I use the phone first?" she asked.

"Of course not."

"I'll just give Astrid a quick ring and tell her where I am."

"It's on the countertop," said Lennart.

Astrid always gave her number when she answered the phone, so Julia had learned it off by heart. She keyed it in quickly and heard the phone begin to ring. On the fifth ring Astrid picked up, with Willy barking furiously in the background.

"Julia," she said when she realized who it was. "I was out at the back raking leaves. Where are you?"

"I'm in Marnäs, or rather north of Marnäs, at Lennart Henriksson's. We've–"

"Is Gerlof there with you?"

"No," said Julia. "I assume he's at the home."

"No, he isn't," said Astrid firmly. "The lady who's in charge there, Boel, rang me a little while ago, wondering where he was. He went off this morning with John Hagman, and he hasn't come back."

"I expect he's with John, then," said Julia.

"No," said Astrid, again firm. "It was John who called Boel. He'd left Gerlof at the bus station, and Gerlof was supposed to phone him when he got home."

Julia thought for a moment. Gerlof ought to be allowed to do whatever he wanted, and he was sure to be fine, but . . .

"I'd better ring the home, then," she said, despite the fact that all she really wanted to do at the moment was to go down to the shore with Lennart.

"Good idea," said Astrid, and they said goodbye.

Julia hung up.

"Everything okay?" asked Lennart behind her. He was standing in the doorway and had already put his jacket back on. "Shall we go? We can have a cup of coffee when we get back."

Julia nodded, but she had a thoughtful furrow in her forehead.

The sky had darkened now; it was almost evening, and even colder than before. The soughing of the wind in the tops of the pine trees surrounding the house sounded even more desolate now.

None of the dead has been identified, thought Julia.

It was a headline about a car accident she had read on a placard down in Borgholm, she remembered. It was going round and round in her brain: *None of the dead identified, no dead identified . . .*

She turned.

"Lennart," she said, "I know I'm being a pain and I know I'm worrying for no reason . . . but can we go down to the shore a bit later on this evening, and drive down to the home in Marnäs now? I need to check that Gerlof has got there."

"Treasure? I haven't taken any fucking treasure," says the man whose name is Martin.

"You hid the metal box," says Nils, taking a step forward. "When I turned my back on you."

"What box?" says Martin, taking his cigarette packet out again.

"Let's just all calm down," says Gunnar behind him. "We're all on the same side."

He's standing too close, right behind Nils's back.

Nils doesn't want him there. He glances quickly behind him, then looks at Martin again.

"You're lying," he says, taking another step forward.

"*Me?* I was the one that got you home!" snarls Martin angrily. "Gunnar and I organized everything. We brought you home, on my ship. As far as I'm concerned, you could have stayed where you were."

"I still don't know you," says Nils, thinking: *My treasure. My Stenvik.*

"Really?" Martin lights a cigarette. "I couldn't give a fuck whether you know me or not."

"Put the shovel down, Nils," says Gunnar.

He's still behind Nils, and way too close.

Martin is too close too. Suddenly he raises the shovel.

Nils senses that Martin is planning to strike him with the shaft, but it's too late. Nils has a shovel too, and he's already lifted it.

He's holding the shaft with both hands, and he swings it just as hard as he swung the oar at Lass-Jan thirty years ago. The old rage wells up; all patience is swept away. He has waited and waited.

"It's mine!" he screams, and the man in front of him suddenly blurs.

Martin moves, but he doesn't have time to duck. The shovel strikes Martin on the left shoulder, keeps moving and slices into the skin beneath his ear.

Martin staggers, howling, and Nils strikes again, this time at Martin's forehead.

"No!"

Martin roars, spins around, and falls, right onto the cairn.

Nils lifts the shovel again, and this time he is aiming for Martin's unprotected face.

"Stop it!" roars Gunnar.

At Nils's feet, Martin raises his arms. Blood is pouring down his face; he is waiting for the killing blow.

But Nils can't strike him.

"Stop, Nils!"

A hand has gripped the shovel's shaft. Gunnar is holding the spade, and he pulls it so hard that Nils lets go.

"That's enough!" Gunnar says loudly. "There was absolutely no need for this at all! What happened, Martin?"

"Fucking . . . hell," whispers Martin, his voice thick and his arms still raised protectively above his head. "Do it, Gunnar! Don't wait until . . . Just *do it!*"

"It's too soon," says Gunnar.

"I'm going now," says Nils. He takes a step backward.

"Fuck the plan . . . We need to do it," says Martin. "He's fucking crazy, that one . . ."

He tries to get up, but the blood is pouring from his nose and from the gash in his forehead.

"Someone has taken the treasure . . . you or someone else," says Nils, staring unblinkingly at Gunnar. "So the deal's off." He takes a deep breath. "I'm going home now. Home to Stenvik."

"Okay . . ." Gunnar sighs wearily. "No more deals, then. We might as well finish it here."

"I want to go," says Nils.

"No."

"Yes. I'm going now."

"You're not leaving," says Gunnar. "It was never the plan that you should leave this place. Don't you realize that? You're staying here."

"No. I'm going," says Nils. "It doesn't end here."

"It does, actually . . . after all, you're already dead."

Gunnar slowly lifts the heavy pick, looking around in the fog as if he wants to make sure nobody can see what's happening.

"You can't go home," he tells Nils. "You're dead. You're buried up in Marnäs churchyard."

33

Gerlof was dying, and dead people were showing themselves to him.

They were making noises too. The bones of a warrior who fell in some long-forgotten Bronze Age battle were rattling down on the shore—he closed his eyes to avoid seeing the ghost dancing down there, but he could clearly hear the rattling.

When he opened his eyes he saw his friend Ernst Adolfsson walking around in circles in the meadow looking for stones in the grass, his body spattered with blood.

And when Gerlof looked out to sea, Death himself was sailing by in the twilight, straight into the wind, aboard an old wooden ship with black sails.

The worst thing of all was when his wife, Ella, sitting beneath the apple tree in her nightgown, looked at him with a sad and serious expression and asked him to give up the struggle. And Gerlof closed his eyes and really wanted to give up and go with her aboard the black ship; he wanted to fall asleep and escape the rain and the cold, to stop worrying and just pretend he was in bed in his room at the home in Marnäs. He didn't know why he was trying to stay awake. Dying was taking a long time, and that bothered him.

The rattling continued down on the shore, and Gerlof slowly turned his head and opened his eyes.

The horizon, the line between sea and sky, had completely disappeared in the darkness.

But was it really old bones rattling down there? Or something else? Was there a living human being somewhere nearby?

Somewhere within his numb body a faint spark still flickered, a faint echo of the will to live. It was like hoisting a mainsail in a strong wind, Gerloff thought—difficult, but not impossible. He counted: *One, two, three,* then he pulled himself up to his knees, using the old apple tree for support.

Heave-ho, heave-ho, he thought, placing his right foot on the ground.

Then he had to rest for a few minutes. He stayed completely still, apart from the trembling in his knees, before he made the final lurch into a standing position, like a weight lifter.

Heave-ho, heave-ho.

It worked. He managed to get up, with one hand clutching the tree and the other gripping his cane.

The mainsail was hoisted, now the ship could begin moving toward the sea. He could use the engine if necessary. Gerlof had always taken good care of his machinery. His cargo ships had been equipped with compression-ignition engines. They needed greasing every hour when they were running, but he'd never once forgotten to do it.

"Heave-ho," he said to himself.

He let go of the tree and took a shaky step toward the sea. It felt pretty good; his joints had gone numb, and were no longer aching.

He kept close to the stone wall, where the grass was shorter than out in the meadow, and slowly drew closer to the shore. The wind was blowing in off the sea—it felt as if it were cutting straight through Gerlof's wet shirt and into his upper body. But the rattling noise was growing louder and louder, and the sound drew him on. He was beginning to grow more and more certain that he knew what it was.

He was right—it was an empty plastic bag.

Or a garbage bag, to be more accurate, big and black and half-buried in the sand. Presumably thrown overboard from some ship out in the Baltic. There was more garbage further down the shore: an old milk carton, a green glass bottle, a rusty tin. It was shameful, the way people threw garbage overboard–but if Gerlof wanted to survive, he was going to need that plastic bag. If he pulled it up out of the sand, made holes in the bottom, and put it on, it would protect him from the rain and retain his body heat during the night.

Good.

Not bad thinking, for a frozen brain.

The problem was getting down onto the shore, because where the meadow ended, the waves had created a sharp ledge. It dropped straight down, like a step.

Twenty years earlier, perhaps even ten, Gerlof would have stepped down onto the shore quickly and easily, without even thinking about it–but now he no longer trusted his balance.

He screwed up his courage, took a deep breath in the ice-cold air, and stepped out into the wind, his right foot raised and his cane outstretched.

It didn't go well. The cane hit the shore first and sank deep into the wet sand.

Gerlof toppled forward, let go of the cane too late, and heard it snap with a sharp crack.

He fell and fell toward the shore, trying to break the fall with his right hand. When he landed, the surface of the sand was as hard as a stone floor, and all the air was knocked out of him.

Gerlof lay there, a few yards from the plastic bag.

He couldn't move–something was broken. Trying to reach the bag had been a good plan, but this time he wasn't going to be able to get up.

Once again he closed his eyes. He didn't even open them when the purr of a car engine reached his ears.

The sound was nothing to do with him.

34

The police radio beside the steering wheel in Lennart's car had been silent until he started making calls to an emergency center in Kalmar—after that it started broadcasting crackling responses Julia couldn't understand.

But Lennart was listening with great concentration.

"The dog patrols will be a little while," he said, looking out into the darkness through the windshield, "but a helicopter will be here soon."

"When?" said Julia.

"They're taking off from Kalmar in a few minutes," said Lennart, and added, "And they've got a thermal imaging camera."

"A what?"

"A camera," repeated Lennart. "It registers body heat. Very useful in the dark."

"Very," said Julia, but it didn't make her feel any better.

She kept on looking out of the windows, but it was so dark out there. It was half past six and it was almost pitch-black.

Earlier, back at the home, Boel had been annoyed at first because Gerlof hadn't been in touch.

"Are we going to have to lock him in?" she said with a heavy sigh. "Are we?"

But all too soon she had become almost as worried as Julia. She'd pulled together a search party made up of staff on the evening shift, who set off on foot from the home to see if Gerlof was sitting at some bus stop.

Lennart had been calmer, but he too knew the situation was serious. He had used his radio to alert the duty officer down in Borgholm.

After a few brief telephone calls he had also managed to locate the bus driver, who had turned around in Byxelkrok and was back in Borgholm with his bus. The man hardly even remembered that Gerlof had been on board, but he did know that he had made at least a couple of stops on the main road before Marnäs, and at least three more between Marnäs and Byxelkrok.

It was just after six when Julia and Lennart got back in the car and joined the search. Two other cars with staff from the home set off at the same time. Boel stayed behind in her office to man the phone.

It was raining hard. Julia and Lennart drove south from the home—even if it wasn't definite that Gerlof had got off the bus there. He could have fallen asleep and got off after Marnäs. But they had to start looking somewhere.

Lennart kept his speed down, driving not much faster than a moped, and pulled in at every bus stop and parking lot so that he wouldn't miss anything.

"You can't see a thing . . ." Julia muttered impatiently.

Not that there was much to see; nobody was out wandering along the main road on this frigid, rainy evening. All she could see was black ditches, bushes, and pale trees twisting in the wind.

The police radio started crackling again.

"The helicopter's taken off," Lennart said. "They're heading for Marnäs now."

Julia nodded. It was probably their only hope, she realized with a sinking heart.

"Is this like Gerlof?" said Lennart after a while.

"What do you mean?"

"I mean . . . has he been . . . unreliable before?"

"No." Julia shook her head fiercely, feeling a spurt of anger at Lennart. Then she thought about it and added, "But I'm not totally surprised . . . I mean, if he has got off the bus and just wandered off, or whatever it is that's happened. I think he thinks too much."

"We'll find him," said Lennart quietly.

"He had his winter overcoat on when he set off this morning. He'll be all right in that, won't he?"

"He'll be perfectly all right if he's outside all night, as long as he's got his overcoat," said Lennart. "Particularly if he can find some shelter from the wind."

But there was no shelter from the wind out on the alvar, thought Julia.

"Gerlof! Where is it, Gerlof?"

Gerlof opened his eyes reluctantly, awakened from yet another warm dream about sailing. He blinked into the slashing
rain.

"What?" he said hoarsely—or maybe he just thought he said it.

He was still lying on his back down on the shore. There was a
throbbing pain in his right leg.

Up above him on the grass, like a great shadow against the
evening sky, stood Gunnar Ljunger. The hotel owner wore his
ugly yellow jacket with the advertising slogan.

Was he really standing there? Yes, it wasn't a dream. But
Ljunger wasn't smiling his chummy smile now, Gerlof noticed.
Instead there was an angry furrow between his eyes.

"Where's my phone?" he wanted to know.

Gerlof swallowed; his mouth was dry and he could barely
speak.

"Hid it," he whispered.

"Have you called anyone?" demanded Ljunger.

Gerlof shook his head wearily. He hadn't been able to call,
had he? All those little buttons. It was impossible to know which
one to press.

"Where is it? Have you shoved it up your ass?"

"Come down here and look for it, Gunnar," hissed Gerlof
quietly.

But Ljunger didn't move. And Gerlof knew why; if Ljunger came down onto the shore, his shoes would leave deep prints behind. Not even the rain would get rid of them.

The cell phone was in Gerlof's trouser pocket, not particularly well hidden, but Ljunger had to figure out how he was going to get hold of it.

"You're tough, Gerlof" was all the hotel owner said, straightening up. "But I see you've fallen and hurt yourself."

Gerlof didn't seem to have a voice anymore, because when he opened his mouth, no sound emerged. His lips felt frozen stiff.

" 'Most peaceable are the dead,' " said Ljunger calmly, looming above him. " 'Death is harsh but honorable, so sing hey and ho . . .' That's Dan Andersson, in case you didn't know. I love his songs, and Evert Taube's old songs about the sea and sailors, too. It was actually Vera Kant who got me listening to them. She had lots of old records."

"She had land and money," whispered Gerlof into the sand.

"What?"

"Vera's land. Her money . . . That's all this is about."

Ljunger shook his head. "It's about a lot of things," he said. "Land and money and revenge and big dreams . . . and love for Öland too, as I said. I love this island."

Gerlof watched him reach into his jacket pocket and take out a pair of leather gloves.

"I think it's time for you to go to sleep now, Gerlof," Ljunger said. "And when you've done that, I'll find my phone. You shouldn't have taken it."

Gerlof was tired of listening to Ljunger. Talking and talking. The hotel owner stood up there on the grassy ledge talking and talking, refusing to leave him in peace, just as a faint rushing noise had begun to make itself heard in the darkness.

"Time to say thank you and good night," said Ljunger. "I think we'll–"

He suddenly fell silent and turned his head.

The rushing sound could be heard higher and higher above the shore, like roaring water; it was as if the wind out over the sea was increasing to storm force.

The noise was swiftly becoming a roaring gale that ripped at Gerlof's thin clothes.

He could also see that the figure up above who was Ljunger had turned his face up to the sky in silent amazement.

Gerlof looked up. A shadow swept over him.

An enormous body with blinking eyes was hovering above the shore. Its upper half was dark and its lower half was pale; it was making a constant clattering noise.

Ljunger was no longer standing there watching over him. He was gone, he'd run away—like a troll who has been discovered and unmasked, he was running away along the gravel track with long, desperate strides.

Gerlof stared. The roar increased. Huge blades clattered round, round. The fat, ungainly body dipped forward, slipped in over the meadow, and began to descend.

The helicopter landed carefully, and Gerlof closed his eyes.

He felt neither joy nor relief; he felt nothing. His brain was still waiting for the ship of death to come and take him out to sea. But it didn't come. He opened his eyes again.

The clattering of the rotor blades died away, and the door opened. Two men wearing helmets clambered out, stooping. They were wearing uniforms like gray overalls; they were pilots or flying policemen, and they were moving quickly across the grass toward Gerlof.

One of them had a thermal blanket under his arm, and the other was carrying a white bag. Gerlof began to understand why they had come, and breathed out.

The helicopter was there for him. He was going to live.

36

"*There he is!*"

Julia had shouted loudly, and Lennart braked so quickly that the car skidded. But it stopped almost immediately, slewed across the road. They were just south of the turning down to Stenvik.

"Where?" said Lennart.

Julia pointed through the windshield. "I can see him. Out there . . . on the field. He's lying there!"

Lennart leaned forward. Then he put his foot down and swung the wheel around. "There's a track here . . . I'll drive down." The car spun around sharply on the wet road.

But when they pulled onto the little gravel track, Julia could see she was wrong. It wasn't a body. It was . . .

Lennart slammed the car to a stop and Julia scrabbled for the door. But her crutches made her slow, and he got there first.

He bent down and picked up the object from the little ditch by the track.

"It's just a coat," he said, holding it up so she could see it. "A coat someone's thrown away."

Julia came forward and looked at it. "It's Dad's," she said.

"Are you sure?" asked Lennart. "It looks like a–"

"Look in the inside pocket."

Lennart opened the coat and burrowed in the pocket. He took out a wallet and opened it.

"Should have brought a flashlight . . ." he muttered, trying to hold up the wallet in the car's headlights.

"It's Gerlof's," said Julia. "I recognize it."

Lennart pulled out a worn-looking driver's license and nodded. "Yes. It's his."

Then he looked around.

"Gerlof!" he shouted. "Gerlof!"

But the wind and the sound of the car engine drowned out his cry.

"I don't recognize this track," he said. "I think it goes down to the shore. We'd better take the car and have a look."

At the police car, he spoke briefly into the radio mike.

Julia followed him.

"The helicopter knows where we are now," Lennart told her.

He put the car into first gear and began to crawl forward, peering out through the smeared windshield.

"I'll turn the lights off," he said, "then we'll be able to see better."

The track in front of them was abruptly, impenetrably dark, but when Julia's eyes had become accustomed to it, she could see the alvar on both sides. Every new shadow that appeared out there looked like an old man swaying upright in the grass, but each shadow turned out to be only a juniper bush.

Suddenly Lennart pointed up at the sky.

"There it is!" he exclaimed. "Thank God."

Julia stared up at a pair of rapidly flashing red-and-white lights moving across the sky. She realized it was the helicopter, just as the police radio crackled into life again.

"I think they've found something," Lennart said. "Down by the water."

He increased his speed, swung around a bend—and a second later the entire car was suddenly illuminated by a dazzling white light. It was another car.

"Shit!" yelled Lennart beside Julia.

He stamped on the brakes, but it was too late. The car racing toward them around the bend did not slow.

"Hang on!"

Julia gritted her teeth and grabbed hold of the dashboard, bracing for the inevitable crash.

The impact flung her forward, but the seat belt held her as she watched the car hood crumple like paper.

The seat belt held, but the blow to her ribs was agonizingly painful.

Silence. A few seconds of silent immobility followed the crash.

Julia could hear Lennart breathing out behind the wheel, and swearing quietly.

Then he switched on the lights again. Only one of them appeared to be working now; it illuminated the shiny car that had slammed into them.

Lennart reached over to the glove compartment. It had flown open, and now he took out his gun holster.

"Are you okay, Julia?"

She blinked. "Yes . . . yes. I think so."

"You stay here. I'll be back soon."

Lennart opened the driver's door, letting in the cold. Julia hesitated. Then she opened her own door. But she stayed in the car. Pain raced through her body, bringing tears to her eyes.

Almost simultaneously the door of the other car opened. A tall, broad-shouldered man stumbled out.

"Who are you?" she heard Lennart shout.

"Where the fuck did you come from?" The new voice was even louder than Lennart's and furious. "Put the fucking headlights on! Why are you driving with no fucking lights on?"

"Calm down," said Lennart. "Police."

"Who's that . . . is it Henriksson?" demanded the other voice.

Julia swung her legs out and fumbled for her crutches. She managed to get to her feet, although the ground was uneven and she nearly stumbled and fell.

"Have you come from the shore?" Lennart asked the stranger.

In the lights from the tangled cars she suddenly recognized the other driver. He came from Långvik, and he was a hotel owner.

Then she remembered his name too: Gunnar Ljunger.

"Who are you?" he shouted, voice thick with rage.

"Calm down, Gunnar," Lennart said. He obviously recognized him as well. "Where have you been?"

"Down . . . down by the shore. I've been out for a drive."

"Have you seen Gerlof Davidsson?"

"No."

"We're looking for him." Lennart pointed. "The helicopter over there is looking for him too."

"Really?"

Ljunger seemed remarkably uninterested, Julia thought. She took a step forward and called to Lennart:

"Is it far to the shore?"

"I don't think so," he replied. "A few hundred yards."

"I have to get down there," Julia insisted.

Gripping her crutches firmly, she started hopping along, past Gunnar Ljunger's car and down the gravel track.

"Gunnar, you'll have to reverse out of the way," she heard Lennart say behind her. "I'm driving down to the shore."

"Henriksson, you can't possibly . . ."

"Move the car," repeated Lennart, more crisply. "Then stay in it, we need to figure out . . ."

His voice was swiftly lost in the wind. Beyond both cars, Julia could see the lights of the helicopter again; it had landed a couple of hundred yards away.

She hurried along, slipping in muddy puddles on the track, but she kept going.

Getting closer, she could see two men in light gray overalls trapped in the beam of the helicopter's searchlight; they were bending over something on the shore. A body. They lifted it up out of the sand.

"Dad!"

The men glanced over at her.

The body on the beach was lying in a blanket, unmoving. *Not again,* Julia thought. *I can't lose you, too. Please . . . Not again.*

The body coughed. A dry, frail sound.

"Dad!" Julia called out.

"Julia . . ." He slowly turned his head toward her.

He coughed again.

"Careful, now," warned one of the men. "We're going to pick you up."

They lifted Gerlof in the blanket and carried him quickly away.

"Can I come with him?" implored Julia, following clumsily. "I'm his daughter. And I'm a nurse."

"Not possible," said the man closest to her, without looking up. "We haven't got room."

"Where are you flying?"

"To the emergency department in Kalmar."

She went with them as far as the helicopter anyway, despite the fact that her crutches kept getting stuck in the grass. She fought to stay close to the body in the blanket.

"I'll follow you to the hospital, Dad."

Just before they lifted him into the helicopter, Gerlof raised his head and for the first time she could see his face. It was chalk white. But his eyes were open and feverishly bright, and suddenly they focused on her. He said something, quietly and inaudibly.

"What?" She leaned forward, listening hard.

"Ljunger did it," whispered Gerlof.

Julia whispered back: "Did what, Dad?"

"Took . . . our Jens."

Then he was gone, lifted like a parcel into the helicopter. The door closed behind him.

"You need to get out of the way," said one of the pilots before slamming his own door.

Julia shuffled back reluctantly, head spinning.

When the blades began to rotate again, she was fifty yards away; she watched them spinning faster and faster. The wonders of technology. A loud clatter in the darkness—and the helicopter carrying her elderly father lifted toward the black sky, climbing higher and higher before speeding off to the southwest.

Implacably the softer sounds of the wind and the waves returned. Julia heard a distant cry, and turned her head.

It was Lennart. Both cars were still tangled on the bend in the road, and although Julia's arms were aching by now, she gripped her crutches firmly once again and made her way back along the gravel track to the scene of the accident.

"Was it Gerlof?" said Lennart.

Julia nodded. "Yes. They've taken him to Kalmar."

"Good."

Gunnar Ljunger now sat in his car with the door open, but apparently hadn't been able to reverse out of the way to let the police car through.

He'd switched the engine off after the crash, and couldn't get it going again. The only sound was a feeble click when he turned the key.

Ljunger struck the leather-covered steering wheel in a temper.

"Lock the car and leave it here," said Lennart. "You can come to Marnäs with us."

Ljunger sighed, but he had no choice. He took a briefcase out of the Jaguar, then got into the passenger seat of the police car next to Lennart. Julia had to sit in the back behind Lennart.

During the drive to Marnäs she leaned forward, watching Ljunger.

What had he done down on the shore? What had he said to Gerlof?

Ljunger sat there with his back straight, apparently unaware of her scrutiny, but the atmosphere in the car was tense.

"Are you going to tell me now?" Lennart asked the hotel owner after a few minutes.

"Tell you what?"

"What you were doing here on the coast road?"

"Enjoying the weather," said Ljunger tersely. "Is that a crime?"

"Why were you driving so fast?"

"I've got a Jag."

"Did you know Gerlof was lying down on the beach?"

"No."

Julia sighed. "He's lying," she told Lennart.

Ljunger ignored her.

"The helicopter picked up your body heat, Gunnar," said Lennart. "Gerlof's body temperature was too low. Lucky for us you were there."

Ljunger didn't comment. He was looking out of the windshield with his eyes half closed, either uninterested or just bone tired.

There was a space in front of the Marnäs police station, and Lennart parked the car. He unlocked the door of the station and all three of them went in.

He switched on the light, went over to the desk, and turned on his computer. Ljunger positioned himself in the middle of the floor, like a soldier facing his troops.

"I shall make a short statement, nothing more," he said, eyes locked on Lennart. "I have no intention of staying here any longer than necessary this evening. I want to get home."

"We all want to get home, Gunnar," remarked Lennart. He logged on to his computer. "Coffee?"

"No." Ljunger looked at Julia and asked: "Is she staying?"

Lennart seemed to stiffen when Julia was referred to as *she*—but Julia herself merely shook her head. She had other things to worry about.

"*She's* going to the hospital to see her father," she told the men, "to see if he's going to survive." She stared at Ljunger. "And to ask him what happened down there on the shore."

"Good. You do that."

Ljunger wasn't even looking at her, but there was a clearly perceptible smile at the corners of his mouth. It was as if he found the whole encounter most amusing.

"Sit down, Gunnar," said Lennart, pointing to the chair next to his desk.

Then he took a couple of steps over to Julia by the door and lowered his voice. "Will you be okay now?"

She nodded and picked up her crutches. "I'll see if there's a bus," she said. "Otherwise I'll get a cab."

"Will you call me?" said Lennart. "I'll be home as soon as I'm done here."

Julia smiled and nodded, as if everything were fine this evening. "Of course I'll call. See you soon."

She wanted to give Lennart a hug, but not in front of Gunnar Ljunger.

She went down the steps, back out onto the cold, deserted street, and looked over at the bus depot on the far side of the square. There was a bus standing there—but was it heading south?

A cab to Kalmar would cost several hundred kronor, but if worst came to worst, that's what she would have to do. Even if she had to empty her account, and even if she just ended up sitting around in the emergency room all night, she had to get to the hospital. She wanted to be there when Gerlof came around. Lennart would understand that she had to be with her father right now; besides, he had plenty to do himself this evening.

She set off across the street toward the square.

She suddenly thought about that smile—Gunnar Ljunger's curious little smile.

He'd smashed up his car and more or less been called a murderer by Gerlof, but as he stood there next to Lennart's desk in the police station he still had that little smile at the corners of his mouth, as if an escape route was waiting for him in there.

As if he thought . . .

Julia stopped dead on the sidewalk on the other side of the street, heart thudding. She was halfway to the bus depot, but without even thinking about it she turned back. She began to hop along on her crutches, back to the police station.

It was only a hundred yards or so, but Julia still didn't get there in time.

She was still out on the sidewalk when she heard the shot. It was just a short, sharp crack with no echo, but it came from inside the station.

She heard a dull thud through the window.

Another shot was fired seconds later.

Julia took three more steps on her crutches, but it was too slow. She threw them down and ran.

She took the steps up to the door of the station in two strides, sending pain stabbing through her foot.

She could smell the gunpowder as she pushed through the door, and only then did she stop.

Everything was quiet. There wasn't a sound in the police station.

Julia peeped in tentatively, and first of all she could only see Lennart's legs sticking out beside his desk. Her heart faltered—then she realized he was moving.

He was on his knees by the desk, one hand on the floor and the other firmly pressed against his bleeding forehead.

Lennart's holster was undone, and he slowly rolled around and looked up at Julia with a hazy, confused expression.

"Where is he?" he asked. "Ljunger?"

Julia saw what had happened.

It wasn't Lennart who'd been shot—it was Gunnar Ljunger.

Julia could see him now, and she realized the hotel owner had indeed found an escape route.

Ljunger wasn't smiling any longer. His body was lying on the floor on the other side of the desk, and his shiny leather shoes were twitching. A rivulet of blood had begun to trickle from his head, and the yellow padded jacket was spattered with pink stains. The blood was shining as it caught the light.

Ljunger was staring up at the ceiling, his mouth half open. He looked astonished, as if he didn't really understand that it was all over.

In his right hand he still gripped Lennart's service revolver.

37

"How are you feeling?" asked Gerlof quietly from his hospital bed.

Lennart shrugged his shoulders wearily. "Not so bad. I should have been more alert." He sighed heavily. "I should have realized what he intended to do."

"Don't think about it anymore, Lennart," said Julia from the other side of Gerlof's bed.

"He fooled me. He'd sat down, and I thought he'd given up ... but then he hurled himself forward and threw me against the desk and ripped open the holster. I wasn't prepared." He sighed and touched the thick bandage on his forehead. "I'm too old, my reactions are too slow. I should have–"

"Don't think about it, Lennart," said Julia again, this time more firmly. "It was Ljunger who hurt *you*, not vice versa."

Lennart nodded, but seemed unconvinced.

Gunnar Ljunger's first shot had only hit the wall of the police station, but Lennart had banged his head on the edge of the desk during the desperate struggle for his service revolver. He had several stitches in his forehead now, binding up the gash underneath the bandage.

Lennart and Julia were now sitting on either side of Gerlof's bed in the hospital at Borgholm. It was late afternoon, and a deep-yellow autumn sun was splashing its final light over the town outside the window.

Gerlof hoped the visit wouldn't last too long; all he really wanted to do was to be alone. To sleep. He had no strength to talk or to get out of bed.

He still didn't remember much about the last few days. Presumably he wouldn't have survived without the rapid response of the emergency medical crew. He had been in critical condition for two days. Then he had finally improved and become more stable, and on the fourth day he had been taken by ambulance to the hospital in Borgholm.

There was more privacy there than in Kalmar, and Gerlof had his own room on the second floor with a view of Slottskogen and the houses of Borgholm. Julia and Lennart had come to visit him; it was the fifth day since Ljunger's attempt to kill him on the shore outside Marnäs.

"This is the fifth time in five days I've been to see you, Dad," Julia told him. "But it's the first time you've been awake."

Gerlof merely nodded tiredly.

His left arm was in a splint and bandaged after his fall onto the sand. One foot was in a cast. A tube leading from a bag of some kind of nutrient solution was attached to a needle in his arm; another tube was attached to a catheter; and he was lying under a double layer of blankets—but he still felt better than the previous day. His temperature had slowly but surely gone down.

Gerlof tried to sit up so that he could see Julia and Lennart, and his daughter quickly got up and slipped an extra pillow behind his back.

"Thank you."

His voice was very weak, but he could talk.

"How are you feeling today, Dad?" she asked.

Gerlof slowly raised his right thumb toward the ceiling. He coughed and inhaled laboriously.

"At first they thought I had . . . pneumonia." He took a ragged breath, then said, "But this morning . . . they said I've only got bronchitis. And they're pretty sure I'll . . . be able to keep both feet." He coughed, then added, "I'd like to do that."

"You're tough, Gerlof," said Lennart.

Gerlof nodded at the big policeman. "Gunnar Ljunger . . . said the same thing."

Lennart's pager suddenly bleeped from his belt. "Not again . . ."

The policeman sighed wearily. He glanced down at the display.

"Looks as if my boss wants to talk to me again, the questions are never-ending . . . I'd better go and call him. Back soon."

Lennart smiled at Julia, who smiled back and nodded toward the bed.

"Don't run away, Gerlof," he added.

Gerlof nodded slowly back at him, and Lennart closed the door.

There was silence in the sickroom, but for once it wasn't an uncomfortable or menacing silence. There was nothing that really needed to be said. Julia placed her hand on Gerlof's coverlet and leaned forward.

"Everybody sends their love," she said. "Lena called from Gothenburg last night; she's coming soon. And Astrid sends her love, too. John and Gösta came to see you yesterday, but they said you were asleep. So everybody you know is thinking about you."

"Thank you." Gerlof coughed again. "And how . . . are you feeling?"

"Fine," said Julia quickly. "I've been spending some time with Lennart over the past few days, up at his house in the pine forest—it's lovely there. Although of course he's had to spend most of his time sitting writing a load of reports, or he's had to be down in Borgholm . . . so I haven't been able to do a great deal for him. I've spent most of my time sitting in the next room, worrying about you."

"I'll . . . be fine," whispered Gerlof.

"Yes. I know that now," his daughter said. "And so will I."

Gerloff coughed and went on: "You're feeling strong, then?"

"Sure." Julia smiled, as if she didn't really understand what he meant. "I'm much stronger, anyway."

"I've been thinking . . ." Gerlof said. "I'm not sure . . . but I think I know how it all happened now."

Julia started to shiver.

"All of it?" she asked.

"All of it," whispered Gerlof. "Do you want to know . . . what happened to Jens?"

"Did Ljunger tell you exactly what happened, Dad?"

"He said . . . a few things. Not everything, I suspect. So part of what happened . . . I've only guessed. But it's . . . not a happy ending, Julia. The ending is just the way it is. Do you want to know?"

Julia found she was holding her breath. Did she really want to know?

"Tell me," she said.

"Do you remember, when you came to Öland I said . . . that the murderer might be tempted to turn up . . . to look at Jens's sandal?"

Julia nodded. "But he didn't come."

Gerlof looked over at the sun setting above the trees outside the window. He wished he were a little boy listening to the spine-chilling stories in the twilight hour, instead of being old and having to tell them himself.

"I think he did," he said. "The murderer came to us . . . even if you and I didn't see him."

Gunnar stands directly in front of Nils and slowly raises the heavy iron pick. He looks around at the fog, as if he wants to make sure nobody can see what is happening out on the alvar. Or what is going to happen.

"You can't go home, Nils," he says. "You're already dead. You're already buried."

Nils shakes his head. "Let go of the pick," he says.

It seems as if a deathly silence has suddenly descended on the whole of the alvar, as if all the air beneath the sky had disappeared.

"Let go of the shovel first, Nils."

Nils shakes his head again. He steals a quick glance at the other treasure hunter, Martin, who is breathing heavily as he lies sprawled on the ground a few yards away, clutching his forehead. He's no threat.

But Gunnar is dangerous. He's standing there with his legs braced, gripping the pick and listening; suddenly his head cocks slightly, as if he hears something in the distance.

"Okay," he says. "I'm dropping the pick now."

And he does. It lands beside the cairn with a heavy thud.

"Good." And Nils drops the shovel too, but he doesn't relax. "And now I want to go down to . . ."

Suddenly he can hear a noise as well. It's getting louder. A faint hum from the village road, which rapidly swells to a dull roar.

A car engine.

"I think we've got company," says Gunnar.

He doesn't seem surprised.

Seconds pass. Then a broad shadow takes shape in the fog behind them. A shadow moving across the grass on four wheels.

It's another Volvo, a gleaming brown Volvo creeping slowly toward them out of the fog. It stops next to Gunnar's car, and the engine is switched off.

The driver's door opens.

Nils doesn't recognize the car, or the man who gets out. But he can see that the man is much younger than him, and is dressed in a neatly pressed uniform. He's wearing a gun in his holster. The man closes the car door, straightens and adjusts his jacket.

The man who has just arrived stops in front of Nils. His eyes are fixed on Nils.

"We've never met," says the man. "But I've thought about you a great deal."

Nils is staring, openmouthed.

"You murdered my father," says the man.

For several seconds Nils understands nothing.

"Nils, this is Lennart," says Gunnar. "Lennart Henriksson. His father was the district superintendent. You remember, when you were young, many years ago . . . You met on the train to Borgholm."

The district superintendent's son.

Finally, Nils understands. He understands what's going to happen, and he finally reacts. Nils sees Henriksson fumbling with his holster. He steps backward into the fog and begins to run.

"Stop!"

Nils doesn't stop, of course; he keeps on running. The trap which has been set is starting to close, but he hurls himself out of it.

He is no longer young, and his progress across the grass is far too slow, but this is the alvar, his ground. He flees through the smoky fog with his head down, breathing hard, aiming for the nearest big clump of bushes and expecting at any moment to hear a shot behind him—but he manages to reach the juniper bushes before it comes.

Nils hears several shouts in the fog.

He doesn't stop. Straight ahead, with long strides.

Is this the way down to the village?

Nils thinks it is. He's on his way home now, he's going home to his mother at last, and nobody can stop him.

Nils suddenly sees a figure taking shape in the fog ahead of him, and he stops, bewildered.

This is no pursuer. This is a little boy, maybe no more than five or six years old. The boy comes forward out of the gray fog and stops just a few short steps away.

The boy is small and skinny, dressed in shorts and a thin red shirt, with a pair of little sandals on his feet. He looks up curiously at Nils in silence, hesitating, as if he isn't really afraid, but knows he should be.

But Nils isn't dangerous, not to a child. He has never done anything but defend himself, and he really did try to save his brother from drowning that summer's day, even if it was too late—and he's never harmed a child in his entire life. Never.

"Hello there," rasps Nils.

He tries to calm his heavy breathing so that he won't frighten the child.

The boy doesn't reply.

Nils quickly turns his head and looks around, but it doesn't seem as if anyone's chasing him. The fog is protecting him. He can't stay here long, but just for the moment he is safe from his pursuers.

Then he looks at the boy again, without smiling, and asks quietly:

"Are you on your own?"

The boy nods silently.

"Are you lost?"

"I think so," says the boy quietly.

"It's all right . . . I can find my way anywhere out here on the alvar." Nils takes a step closer. "What's your name?"

"Jens," says the boy.

"Jens what?"

"Jens Davidsson."

"Good. My name's . . ."

He hesitates—which of his names should he use?

"My name's Nils," he says in the end.

"Nils what?" says Jens. It's a bit like a game.

Nils gives a short laugh.

"My name is Nils Kant," he says, taking another step forward.

The boy stands still, in a world made only of grass and gray stone and juniper bushes. In the fog, there is nothing but grass and stones and bushes. Nils tries to smile at him, to show that everything is okay.

The fog closes in around them, not a sound is to be heard.

"It's all right," says Nils.

He's intending to take the boy down to the village and find out where he lives, and then he himself will go home to his mother.

They are standing very close to each other by now, Nils and Jens.

Then the rumble of an engine comes echoing out of the fog behind them, and Nils tries to turn and run, but he hasn't time to take one single step.

The noise swells and swells, and it seems to be coming from every direction.

It's the car, the brown Volvo, and it comes hurtling between the rocks and the bushes, slithering across the grass before straightening up and aiming at him, aiming directly at Nils. It doesn't slow down.

Right or left?

The car is growing, it's so wide. Nils has only seconds to decide, one second—and then it's too late. He can only watch, with his arm around the boy. There is no protection.

Everything disappears for a while.

Everything falls silent. Cold darkness.

The sounds return like dull echoes. The fog, the cold, and a car engine ticking over.

"Did you get him?" asks a voice.

"Yes . . . I can see him."

Nils is lying on his back, stretched out on the grass. His right leg is twisted beneath him at an odd angle, but he feels no pain.

The car is just a few yards away from him, with its engine running. The driver's door opens. The policeman slowly gets out, his revolver in his hand.

The passenger door on the other side opens too. Gunnar steps out too, but stays by the car, looking out across the alvar.

The policeman steps over to Nils, then stops.

He says nothing, he merely stares.

Nils suddenly remembers the boy in the fog, Jens—where did he go?

He's gone.

Nils hopes that Jens Davidsson has disappeared, that he got away in the fog and ran back down to Stenvik in his little sandals. A successful flight. Nils wants to follow him, to go back home, but he can't move. His leg must be broken.

"It's over" is all he says.

It's over, Mother. It ends here on the alvar.

Nils is very tired. He could crawl down to Stenvik, but he hasn't the strength.

The dead are gathering around him, mute gray shadows crowding in.

His father and his little brother, Axel. The two German soldiers. The district superintendent on the train and the Swedish sailor from Nybro.

All dead.

Standing over him, the young policeman nods.

"Yes," he agrees. "It's over now."

The policeman releases the safety catch on his gun with the barrel pointing downward, then he raises it, aims at Nils's head, and pulls the trigger.

38

Gerlof had told the story of Nils Kant's death in a series of slow whispers.

Julia had been forced to lean closer to him in order to hear. But she heard everything, right to the very end.

Now she sat there by his bed, stiff and mute. She does not look at Gerlof.

"This . . . happened?" she said after a long silence. "What you've just told me? It happened . . . Are you sure about that?"

Gerlof nodded slowly. "Pretty sure," he whispered.

"Why?" said Julia. "How can you be sure?"

"Well . . . things Ljunger said to me . . . when he was waiting for me to freeze to death," said Gerlof. "He said . . . this wasn't just about getting Vera Kant's money and land. He said it was about revenge too. But . . . revenge on whom? And who wanted revenge? I've been lying here thinking about it . . . and I could only come up with one person."

Julia shook her head. "No," she said.

"Why should Nils Kant be brought home . . . at all?" persisted Gerlof. "Not for Gunnar Ljunger's sake. For Ljunger, Nils was more valuable over in South America . . . He was no danger to Ljunger there, and with each year that passed, Gunnar could get more land out of Vera . . . The Germans' treasure was of no significance in comparison to all the land Gunnar could get his hands on." He took a breath. "But somebody else wanted Nils home . . . and to let him almost get home to his mother before he was executed. It was to be a fitting punishment."

Julia shook her head again, but there was no strength in the movement.

"Someone who helped out," Gerlof went on. "Who helped Gunnar Ljunger and Martin Malm get the coffin to Öland, and who was there when it was opened and examined . . . Someone who could convince everyone that Nils's body had come home. A reliable young policeman."

Gerlof turned his head and looked toward the door.

Julia turned.

Lennart was back. He'd opened the door of Gerlof's room without her noticing. He came in as if everything were perfectly normal.

"That was my boss on the phone again," he told them. "They've finished their investigations up in Marnäs now, so I can get back to work when I . . ."

Lennart stopped, seeing their grim expressions.

"Has something happened?" he asked.

"We were talking . . . about the sandal, Lennart," said Gerlof. "Jens's sandal."

"The sandal?"

"The one you borrowed from me," said Gerlof. "Did you ever get a reply from your forensic technicians over on the mainland? Did they find anything on it?"

Lennart shook his head. "No," he said. "No traces . . . They didn't find anything."

"You said you'd sent it," said Julia, looking at him.

"You did send it, didn't you?" said Gerlof. "I'm sure we can check . . . that they got it?"

"I don't know . . . maybe," said Lennart.

He was looking at Gerlof the whole time, but there was no anger in his eyes. No emotions at all. His face was pale, and he slowly lifted his hands and placed them on the back of the chair.

"One thing I was wondering about, Lennart . . ." said Gerlof. "When did you actually meet Gunnar Ljunger for the first time?"

Lennart looked down at his hands. "I don't remember," he said.

"Don't you?"

"It must have been . . . '61 or '62." His spoke in a monotone. "In the summer, when I'd just joined the police in Marnäs. He'd had a break-in at his restaurant in Långvik . . . and I went to take a statement. We started talking."

"About Nils Kant?"

Lennart nodded. He wouldn't look at Julia.

"Among other things," he said. "Ljunger knew . . . He'd found out I was the son of the district superintendent who'd been shot. A few weeks later he called me. He asked me to come and see him again. He wanted to know if I was interested in trying to find Kant, to entice him back home, so we could bring him to justice for what he'd done to my father . . ."

Lennart stopped speaking.

"What did you say to him?"

"I said I was interested," replied Lennart. "I would help him, and he would help me. It was a business arrangement."

Gerlof nodded slowly. "Did it come to an end a few days ago?" he said quietly. "At Marnäs police station? Were you afraid he'd start telling your colleagues things about you? Who was actually holding the gun, Lennart . . . the one Gunnar Ljunger was shot with?"

"It doesn't matter," he said.

"A business arrangement," said Julia quietly.

She looked out of the window. She could see the twilight out there, but this time, she wasn't thinking of the twilight.

She was thinking about the fact that Martin Malm had got money for new ships.

And that Gunnar Ljunger had acquired lots of cheap land to sell at a high price.

And that Lennart Henriksson, the man she had come to believe she was in love with, had finally got his revenge on Nils Kant.

All at the price of her son's life.

"It was just an arrangement," Lennart told them. "I would help Ljunger and Martin Malm with certain things . . . And they would help me."

"So you met in the fog on the alvar . . . that day," said Gerlof.

"Ljunger called me that morning and said they were going to

the memorial cairn," said Lennart. "We were to meet there. But I was delayed, and by the time I got there everything had gone terribly wrong . . . Martin Malm was lying on the ground, covered in blood. Kant had hit him with a shovel. Malm never really recovered . . . He had his first brain hemorrhage just a few days later."

"And my Jens?" said Julia in a low voice.

"It was an accident, Julia. I didn't see him . . ." said Lennart, his voice thick; he still wouldn't look at her. "When Kant was dead, we found . . . we found the little body underneath the car. He didn't . . . have time to get away when I ran over Kant . . ."

He fell silent.

"Where did you bury him?" asked Gerlof.

"He's down in the churchyard, in Kant's grave." Lennart was speaking like someone forced to recall a terrible dream. "We took the boy's body and Kant's up there in the darkness. We put a bell on the church gate so we'd hear if anybody came along, and lifted the turf. We put the earth on a tarpaulin. Then we dug half the night. Martin Malm, Ljunger, and me. All three of us . . . we dug and dug. It was dreadful."

Julia squeezed her eyes shut.

By a stone wall, she thought. *My Jens is buried by the stone wall surrounding Marnäs churchyard, murdered by a man filled with hatred—just as Lambert had said.*

She took a deep breath.

"But before you buried Jens," she said, her eyes closed and her voice faint, "you came down to Stenvik that evening and helped look for him. You led the search for the boy you'd killed . . . my son . . . And then you drove around pretending to search on the alvar, so you could get rid of any traces you'd left behind."

"But it hasn't been easy," he said quietly, still not looking at her. "I just want to say that, Julia, it hasn't been easy keeping quiet. This autumn, when you came back . . . I really wanted to help you. I tried . . . I wanted to forget everything that happened twenty years ago. I wanted *you* to forget too." He stopped, then added, "I really thought it was going to work."

"So Nils Kant is really lying in his coffin," said Gerlof.

Lennart nodded. "I haven't spoken to Gunnar Ljunger for many years. Not about this . . . I had no idea what he was intending to do to you, Gerlof."

He let go of the back of the chair and turned slowly around; once again he looked just as exhausted as the first time she'd seen him, at the quarry, the day she found the body of Ernst Adolfsson. Perhaps even more exhausted.

"One thing I can say . . . shooting Ljunger felt better than taking revenge on Nils Kant," he said.

Lennart opened the door and left the room.

Gerlof breathed out in the silence of his hospital room.

He looked at his daughter. "I'm . . . sorry, Julia," he whispered. "So terribly sorry."

She nodded and met his gaze, tears pouring down her face.

At that moment Julia felt she could see what Jens would have looked like as an adult. She could see it in Gerlof's face.

They would have been very much alike, grandfather and grandson. Jens would have had big, slightly sad eyes, thoughtful furrows in his broad forehead, and a wise, understanding gaze that could see both darkness and light in the world.

"I love you, Dad."

She took Gerlof's hand and held it tightly.

It was the first real spring day, a day of sunshine and warmth and flowers and birds, when the sky above Öland seemed to rise like a pale blue sheet in the wind. A day when life seemed to be full of possibilities again, however old you were.

For Bengt Nyberg, the local reporter, spring had always felt like the real start of the new year on Öland—when it condescended to turn up. He was happy to spend as much time outdoors as possible on days like this.

Bengt had a lot of vacation time due him. He could have taken days off to go walking in the spring warmth, listening to the nightingale's carefree song out on the alvar, where the last pools of water formed by the melting snow were just drying up in the sun—but he wanted on this particular day to work.

Bengt closed his eyes for a few seconds in the sunshine, then opened them and looked across toward Marnäs church on the other side of the stone wall.

When the grave had been opened up last winter, there had been plenty of curious, uninvited spectators by the churchyard, a veritable sea of people kept at a distance by the police barriers. At the funeral this Thursday there were only a few, and they had been asked by the priest to remain on the other side of the wall.

So Bengt was standing there with his notepad as the only reporter, and beside him a young photographer was stomping around, sent from the head office in Borgholm, despite the fact that Bengt had said he could take the pictures himself. But this was a big story, something they might be able to sell to the nationals, and in that case of course Bengt's simple camera and quick shots wouldn't do.

The photographer they'd sent hadn't been working there long; he was a young lad from Småland, called Jens just like the little boy, and presumably he regarded *Ölands-Posten* as the first stepping-stone in his career—a career that was bound to lead to one of the evening papers in Stockholm in a few years. He was ambitious, but boring. When he wasn't taking pictures, he talked constantly about celebrities he wanted to take sneaky shots of, or horses he wanted to win money on, and Bengt wasn't remotely interested in either topic.

Jens was restless. As soon as the journalists had been directed to a spot outside the wall by the churchwarden, the young photographer started to look for a better vantage point, his camera poised.

"I think I can get into the churchyard," he said to Bengt, looking eagerly over the stone wall. "If I just creep along . . ."

Bengt shook his head and didn't move.

"Stay where you are," he said quietly. "It'll be fine here."

So the two men stood outside the wall waiting in the sunshine, and after a while the funeral cortege came out of the church. Jens's automatic camera began to whir.

Julia Davidsson, the mother, walked along the path behind the priest, her face calm and her body very still. Beside her was Gerlof, the grandfather. Both were dressed in black. Behind them came a tall man about the same age as Julia, wearing a black coat.

"Who's that?" whispered Jens when he had lowered the camera.

"The boy's father," answered Bengt.

Julia Davidsson was holding on to her father's arm, and the old man leaned on her all the way over to the grave, which lay south of the church tower. They stood side by side as the coffin was lowered into the ground. Gerlof bent his head; Julia threw a white rose on top of the coffin.

This felt pretty good, in Bengt's opinion. So many terrible things had happened around here in just six months: Ernst Adolfsson's terrible death in the quarry at Stenvik last autumn,

Gunnar Ljunger's violent end at the police station just two weeks later, and the discovery of the second sandal belonging to the boy, found by the police in Ljunger's office safe at the hotel in Långvik—a little shoe that matched the one Martin Malm, the late shipowner, had sent to Gerlof.

It had seemed as if the case was closed, but suddenly Lennart Henriksson had demanded a new police investigation of how Ljunger's death had occurred, which had led to the policeman being charged with the murder of Gunnar Ljunger and with the manslaughter of Jens Davidsson.

Finally, Nils Kant's grave had been opened up one cold, gray winter's day.

The police technicians had erected a scene-of-crime tent over the grave, like a little church made of white fabric beside the big church, and had worked there quietly for several days, occasionally seeking warmth inside the heated porch. During the exhumation they had found not only Nils's body in the coffin but also the remains of another man, still unidentified, who was presumably a Swedish national who had lived in South America for many years. The rumor was that he had been killed there.

Hidden in a hollow beneath Nils Kant's coffin, the police had also found a third body, much smaller than the other two. And with that the case had finally been solved.

The evening papers and national radio and TV reporters had swarmed to Marnäs to follow the whole thing. It had been a hectic time for a local reporter at the center of events—but Bengt had found it difficult to maintain a journalistic distance from what was going on, and had often felt a piercing sadness while he was filing his reports. He had known Lennart Henriksson for several decades: there was nothing to rejoice over in this drama.

But now the sun was shining; it was a kind of Öland New Year. After more than twenty years in the ground, a little boy could finally be buried properly.

When the short ceremony at the graveside was over, Julia and Gerlof Davidsson began to move slowly back toward the church, followed by Jens's father, Michael.

Julia and Gerlof weren't talking to each other, as far as Bengt could see from the other side of the wall. He hadn't seen them speak at all during the whole ceremony. But he still had a strong feeling that they were as close as two family members can possibly be—and he even felt a slight pang of envy.

"That's that, then," said the photographer, lowering his camera. "Are we done?"

Bengt took one last look at the faces of Julia and Gerlof—accepting now—and realized the fog he'd glimpsed in them once had at long last lifted.

"We are," said Bengt. "We can go home now."

He hadn't written a single word on his notepad, and would probably just write a brief piece to go with the picture in the paper.

That would have to do. But if anyone were to ask him later what the little boy's funeral had been like, Bengt Nyberg would be able to reply that it had felt bright and dignified and peaceful, like—well, like a kind of conclusion.

Acknowledgments

Echoes from the Dead is set mainly at some point in the mid-1990s on the beautiful island of Öland—but an Öland which to some extent exists only in the author's imagination. Neither the characters nor the businesses in the story are based on real-life individuals or companies, and many places are also invented.

For all the stories and memories they shared with me from their eventful lives, I am grateful to my grandfather, sea captain Ellert Gerlofsson, and his brother, the hairdresser and diver Egon Gerlofsson. For historical facts I would like to thank Stellan Johansson, a sea captain in Bohuslän; Kristian Wedel, a journalist in Gothenburg; and Lars Oscarsson, an attorney in Jönköping.

Many friends have helped me in a variety of ways while I have been writing *Echoes from the Dead*: thanks to Kajsa Asklöf, Monica Bengtsson, Victoria Hammar, and Peter Nilsson in the writers' group Litter; Jacob Beck-Friis, Niclas Ekström, Rikard Hedlund, Caroline Karlsson, Mats Larsson, Carlos Olguin, Catarina Oscarsson, Michael Sevholt, Kalle Ulvstig, and Anders Weidemann; as well as to my relatives Lasse and Eva Björk in Kalmar, Hans and Birgitta Gerlofsson in Färjestaden, and Gunilla and Per-Olof Rylander in Borgholm.

I would also like to thank all my excellent, hardworking editors, above all Rickard Berghorn of the journal *Minotaur* and Kent Björnsson of the publishing firm Schakt, who have taken good care of many of my short stories, as well as Lotta Aquilonius at

Wahlström & Widstrand, who took equally good care of *Echoes from the Dead*.

My mother, Margot Theorin, deserves a considerable eulogy for all the old and new books and newspaper articles about life on Öland with which she has so generously supplied me.

And finally, thank you and a big hug to Helena and Klara for putting up with my daydreaming.

Johan Theorin

About the Author

JOHAN THEORIN was born in 1963 in Gothenburg, Sweden, and has spent every summer of his life on northern Öland. He is a journalist and scriptwriter. His second novel, *Night Blizzard*, will be published by Delacorte Press.

About the Author

JOE [...] was born in 1964 in Columbus, Sweden, and [...]